<u>*Acknowledgements*</u>

To the late, great Dr. Randy Clark…one of the finest, smartest, most earnest, most giving men I've ever had the pleasure of knowing. Thank you so much for everything you taught me and all of your students over the years…you brilliant, beautiful, angry, pop-culture knowin', Batman-lovin', Pepsi-sippin'…surrogate father to us all.

Fox Fire Publications would like to thank <u>www.SelfPubBookCovers.com/FrinaArt</u> for this gorgeous cover.

MIDNIGHT PRINCESS

THE ALPHA BLOODLINE

BY:

TJ BERRY

FOX FIRE PUBLICATIONS, LLC 2021
EIGHTH BOOK OF THE CLAIMED SAGA

The Alpha Bloodline Chapters

Chapter 1: Eve

"Get back here, you son of a bitch!" I yell. I try my best to run at a nice human pace after the two coven-less vampires. Seven months into the life of a vampire and not only am I the Chief Magistrate for all vamps' personal assistant, not to mention being her sire-daughter, but I'm also head of her investigation squad. Raven put the twins in charge of the Blutschutz, and Richard still oversees the training of New Bloods…ugh…like me, technically. I'm just lucky enough to be in control of the impulses that control most New Bloods, or else, I'd probably act just like one of the bastards I'm chasing.

They're fast though. They're a lot faster than I thought. I could catch them if I really wanted to…but there are too many people around. I wipe away more of the coffee. I can't believe he threw that girl's latte in my face. Well, at least, the burns have already healed, and she won't turn into a midnight snack for these two rogues. They cut down an alley on the right.

"Get back here!" I yell again like they're actually going to do it. The good thing about New York, you see someone chasing someone else, and you ignore it. You've gotta love this city! They reach the fire escape, and one helps the other up to it. The ladder falls, and the first one takes hold. They climb up quickly. As soon as they reach the second floor, they pull the ladder up. I look back down the alley and then steal a glance in the other direction. No one's watching. I jump up to the third floor just as they make it to the fifth.

"Crap, she's right behind us!" the one closest to the top spits.

"No kidding," the other one replies.

They've been killing random girls that they meet in bars, attracting them with all the advantages that come with being a vampire; the looks…the natural calmness, easily mistaken for confidence…even our scents. They string the girl along until it's time to feed. Why does that sound familiar? Anyway, I just wish I had found them sooner, and I can't let them get away now. The other one crosses over to the top of the building, as I make it to the sixth floor… the next stop is the roof.

I reach the top, and the first one swings a pipe at my head. I lean back and watch the pipe sail over my face. He comes back around to swing again. Screw this! I'm done playing. I take out my knife and stab him in the forearm. He yells. I kick him in the chest so hard that I crack a rib or two. He hits the rooftop and scatters some gravel. His 'bat' tumbles away. He recovers. Great, they're tougher than I thought, too.

"Stay down," I growl at the bastard. He gets up anyway. He jumps at me, and I kick him on the side of his head…hard. He spins, does a barrel roll, and lands face down on the rooftop with a thud. I'm on him again so quick that he probably doesn't even know what's happening. I grab his knife-holed arm and wrench it. He groans but doesn't move. I slap the cuffs on him that Raven had specially made for this type of stuff. They're made of vanadium steel, but they have silver woven in and out of the cuff…restraint without burning through someone's wrists…unless, of course, they try to break them.

After I secure the second cuff, I stand, getting ready to track down his partner. His partner who I can hear screaming. He sounds like he's getting closer. I was right. He falls at my feet. "What the hell?" I shout as soon as I see who caught him.

Natavius walks over to us. "I thought he was gonna get away." I shake my head. "What? You were taking too long with that one."

"I had 'em," I whine.

"I know. I was just bored. Oh, besides…Raven sent me to find you. She said you haven't been answering your cell, and she's worried about you."

I look at him like he just said something to me in German. "Why would she tell you th…? How did she tell you that?"

"Okay, please," he says, putting his hands up between us. "Do we really have to keep pretending that we don't know that they're married?"

I swallow deeply. "I really have no idea what you're talking about," I practically choke on. "And yours is getting away." I point at the fleeing vampire.

He half-turns just enough to see his rogue, scampering across the rooftop. "Eh." He yawns. "So, you REALLY don't know?" I shake my head. "Wow, I thought for sure she would've told you by now. I mean, he told Nate, and she told Lana." I point at the rogue again, who jumps down to the opposite fire escape. He shrugs. "I figure I should give him a fighting chance."

I tweak one eyebrow. "…a fighting chance…? …someone in a foot race…? …against you…?" He points one shocked finger at himself. "Uh-huh."

Natavius thinks for a moment with one eye closed. "Hmm, I am me, ain't I?" I nod once, and he vanishes.

I chuckle. The other rogue struggles in his restraints; he grunts and growls while thrashing around. I kick him on the leg. "Shut up!" I snap. "Three, two, on…" Before I even finish, Natavius reappears with the first one over his shoulder…hogtied. He throws him down and snickers. "I actually made it to one."

Natavius continues laughing. "I would've been back sooner, but he actually tried to hide. If I hadn't taken a second to laugh, you wouldn't have even made it to three." Natavius giggles. I laugh, too.

Rogue number one looks up at me with very pissed off eyes. I tap the tip of my nose. "You're not the only ones with a great sense of smell, you know." He bangs his head against the roof.

"Okay, guys," I start again, squatting between them. "Now, you have a choice to make." I draw my lips into my mouth before exhaling loudly. "You can either join us…and by us, I mean the coven of vampires that I'm a part of or I can kill you both right here, right now."

"You can't kill us," the one I caught spews like vomit. "You're like us. You wouldn't." I snicker. "What?"

"Oh, nothing," I sigh, covering my eyes with one hand and waving my knife in the other. "I've killed vampires before," I lie.

"When?" Natavius jokes.

"Shhh," I fire off quickly. The rogues laugh this time. I kick the one closest to me. "Shut it," I bark while flashing my knife again. "Make up your minds, join our coven or die." When I think back on it, I'm just really glad Richard never gave me a choice. Although, considering the fact that he's my sire-brother, and that he's a complete and total softy, I don't think he would've had the heart to do it, even if I'd refused. "Come on, guys. Time's a wasting. I got better things to do than wait on you guys all night." I turn to Natavius. "Right?" He nods. "See. Now, what's it gonna be?"

"Bite me," Natavius's captured vampire yells.

"Oh, that's just the wrong answer, and a bad way to respond to a vampire all rolled into one," Natavius scoffs.

"Don't you get it, guys," I say like a complaint. "If every vampire in the world went around acting the way you do, you'd draw attention to us…and then the humans wouldn't stop until we're all dead."

"You were human once, right?" mine says back. "They're weak! They could never…"

"What…? …use high-powered UV lamps against us…? …figure out that silver burns us…? …create all new and efficient ways to detect and kill us…? Yeah, they would if they ever found out about us." I frown. "And if guys like you are left out there on your own to act like knuckleheads…it won't be long before we all burn or end up being guinea pigs in a lab somewhere." I sigh, and my eyes close lazily. "Come on, guys, make the right call."

"Pfft," the angry one spits. "You were right. She can't do it…she's too much of…"

I kick gravel in his direction as I walk toward him. I hate this part…Raven showed me what to do on my tutorial patrol. My teeth grind together just before I bare my fangs, and my eyes faze blue. "Yeah…that was the wrong thing to say," I growl. I kneel next to his chest. "Last words…?"

He sneers at me. I inhale deeply and nod. I exhale an exasperated breath and then… "Hah!" …I drive my knife into the side of his skull.

His eyes look shocked for a couple of seconds before glazing over…like Devon's did. I hear his flesh burn against the blade. He trembles, and a spat of blood erupts from his nose, mouth, and his right eye. His partner sits up and looks at his quivering, twitching carcass. Fear…this guy wears it like it's a fresh coat of face paint from the carnival.

The smell of burning flesh starts to turn my stomach…nope, it's already at barrel roll levels. I swallow deeply and snatch the knife out of the corpse. That's it. I have to keep doing exactly what Raven told me to do. Think of it clinically or use my sire-sister's logic. 'They're not people if they won't be a part of our coven. They kill people…and people don't kill people. Monsters kill people.' I take another deep breath and walk over to the other one. I hold my knife up to his face, vampire blood still sizzling and smoldering against the blade. 'And I kill monsters.' "Your turn."

"I'll join, I'll join…just show me were to sign!" he shouts.

Natavius erupts with laughter. I turn and look at him. He passes me a handkerchief, and I pass him my handcuff keys. He walks over to my vampire and picks him up by the arm. He sniffs Natavius and almost jumps out of his skin. Natavius shows him the key, and he settles down…a little. I use Natavius's handkerchief to wipe the burned blood off my knife and put it back in its sheath.

I turn around and start walking toward the fire escape. "What's your name?" I ask the new member of Raven's coven.

"Mike," he responds quickly. "It's short for Michael…Michael Bos…"

"I don't need to know your last name," I cut him off. "Just come with us."

"He smells funny," Mike says looking back over his shoulder at Natavius.

"Speak for yourself," Natavius retorts, shoving Mike in the back.

"He's a wolf," I nip. "Let's go."

"He's a what?" Mike almost chokes on.

Natavius growls in a very human way. "Wolf," he repeats.

"Come on. You're a vampire, and you don't believe in big bad wolves," I exclaim. He shrugs and glances at Natavius again. I take a hold of the fire escape.

"What about Ryan?" Mike poses.

"Who?" Natavius and I reply with matching furrowed brows. Mike points at the body of his partner.

"Oh, him…," I reply rubbing the back of my hand against my forehead. "Leave him. The sun will be up in a few hours." I hear Mike gasp. "Or would you prefer to carry a body down the fire escape and out onto the streets." I look back at his shocked face. He shakes his head and takes a few steps closer. "Alright, then get your ass down this fire escape."

As we reach street level, Natavius's cell phone rings. "Yeah," he answers. "No way…okay, where? Yeah, we're like two seconds from there by Johnny's Pizza." Man, I miss Johnny's Hawaiian special. I wonder if there's a blood equivalent. "Yeah, we'll wait on you." He ends the call and shoves it into his pocket quickly.

"Raven?" I ask looking back at him. He shakes his head. Mike takes a step past me, closer to the street. "Don't even think about running…because when we catch you this time, you're dead on the spot." He holds up his hands and shakes his head.

Natavius chuckles. "Listen to you sounding like the big bad ass." I raise one eyebrow as my hands snap to my hips. A cab stops behind me. "Oh, and that was my sister on the phone. She's here." The car door swings open as he points to it.

"Great," a familiar girl's voice exaggerates, stepping out of the cab. "My brother is hanging out with vampires…still," she adds dryly.

I turn and see… "KYRA!" I shriek. She looks at me like I'm an alien with green skin, three eyes, and four arms.

Natavius takes me by the shoulders. "Glad you remember my baby sister," he whispers, way too close to my ear. How did he know that I knew his sister?

I shake my head for a moment as I examine her wearing her knee-high pink boots, her customary too short black mini-skirt, and pink top with the plunging neckline. Her hair is still dyed deep red and hangs straight along the contours of her head. Her skin still has a tan so amazing that it makes most other girls look sickly and pale…even if they aren't a vampire. Her platinum cross is still ever present…leading right down between her awe-inspiring, at least according to the guys from our high school, boobs.

"How do you know me, vampire?" Kyra asks, crossing her arms and stepping up to me. I forgot how short she is. She hikes herself up on her toes and gets closer. Her eyebrow tweaks and then she leans in so close to me that I almost stagger backward. "Ange?" she asks. I nod. "No way…you're a damn, dirty, stinking vamp?"

"I wouldn't say it exactly like that, but yeah," I respond, rolling my eyes. "What about you…you're a wolf?"

"Yeah," she responds, tossing her blood red hair off her shoulder. I always wondered why she dyed it that color, but never asked. "But I've been a wolf my whole life. What's your excuse?" She growls a bit at the end. "I can't believe you let yourself get bitten by a disgusting parasite. What the hell's the matter with you?"

"Same problem as him," I brag while pointing my thumb at Mike. "Now," I finish with a big smile and bare my fangs slightly. Kyra crouches. My fingers wrap around my knife before I remember telling them to.

"Whoa," Natavius shouts, appearing between us. "Put the claws…and fangs away ladies…seriously." He turns to me. "You have a meeting with the Chief Magistrate," he reminds me. "And you," he rumbles to his sister. "I don't know why you're even here. Why are you here?"

She crosses her arms. "I came so that you could meet your nephew."

"YOU HAVE A SON?" I squeal. She frowns and looks away. Wow, the cold shoulder I'm getting from Kyra actually makes me wistful for the train wreck that my reunion with Tiff ended up being. "K…you are…were…like my best friend…and you never told me that you were a wolf. You chose to keep that from me. I didn't choose to be a vampire, but I'm making the best of…"

"Are you done with the speech, vampire?" Kyra snaps. I frown. "Aw, did I hurt the vampire's feelings? Wait, no…vampires don't have feelings or emotions or souls…" Natavius growls over her shoulder. "What?"

"I didn't raise you to act like this toward anyone, vampire or anyone else," Natavius says seriously…for the first time ever. I frown and stare into his eyes. His eyes meet mine then dart away instantly.

"Maybe, I should go," I say, looking at Kyra. "We," I amend, motioning to Mike. "Maybe, we should go." I nod and walk past Kyra and Natavius, heading for the sidewalk. "Come on, Mike." He follows. I put my hand up over the edge of the street. I put my index finger and thumb in my mouth and cut loose with a sharp whistle. "TAXI!" I half-turn back to Kyra and Natavius. "Thanks for the assist, Natty." He smirks. "Kyra, it's been…" My mood sinks even more. "…something." Mike pulls the cab's door open for me. "Thanks," I breathe and climb inside. He glances at Natavius and Kyra as I give the driver the manor's address, and he then moves in beside me.

I sigh. "Was that guy…that wolf guy…?" I look at Mike as if I'm about to punch him in the face. "…never mind."

"Go ahead, ask," I breathe, shaking my head.

"Was he your boyfriend?"

I shake my head again. "No, he's just a friend."

"He's fast."

"So am I, thanks to him." Mike nods.

"So, what's going to happen to me?"

My eyes cut to the driver and then back to Mike. "Can you hear me?" I whisper softly.

"Yeah," Mike returns.

"Quiet," I snap. "At this volume, the driver shouldn't be able to hear me, but you still have to be quiet when you reply." Mike nods. "Once we get back to the manor, you'll be taken upstate for New Blood training."

"New Blood?"

"How long have you been a vampire?"

"Only a couple of weeks."

I nod. "New Blood," I return. "It's short for 'New to the Blood.' It's a way of identifying vampires who are less than a year old." I look at him. "Older vampires will look at you like you're a baby deer, standing up for the first time…" Mike smiles. "…and then they'll try their very best to knock you off your feet again and then put their boot on your neck." He swallows deeply. I look away.

"So, listen…um, Ange," Mike continues. I frown. "Did I say something wrong?"

"Only my friends call me, Ange. It's Angela to you, or Ms. Price-Gregory…" My face scrunches up. "…you know what, stick with Angela, or I may stab you." Mike nods. He stares at me. "You wanted to ask me something."

"Yeah," Mike sighs. "Do you have a boyfriend?" I punch him in the nose without even thinking about it. "Ow," he whines, holding his nose. The cab slows.

"I didn't tell you to stop," I complain.

"And I didn't say you could assault my passenger."

"Well, I'm paying," I hum and slip a hundred-dollar bill through the little window slot. "So, who's more important me or the guy soft enough to get beaten up by a girl in the back of your cab?" The cab driver begrudgingly claims the bill. "You okay?" I pose, loud enough for the driver to hear.

"You're so violent," Mike whines and wipes his nose again.

"Sorry about that," I whisper. "That's kind of a sensitive subject with me." He looks at me and checks his nose one more time. "See, there's a guy…I kind of love him…don't know if I'm still IN love with him, but I definitely feel something for him."

"You should tell him," Mike spits.

"Not done talking, Mike." He nods while getting his guard up, just in case. "See, he's marrying my sire-aunt tomorrow night…well, tonight…this is literally the eve of his wedding day." I look at Mike, and the last twinges of purple drain away from his nose. Ryan and he must have waited a week or so between feedings. Not as bad as we thought, but that means whoever turned the two of them is making other vampires. I sigh. I won't be able to keep up if this continues. I converted five other rogues that I found…Ryan was my first kill…first vampire kill.

"Sorry about that," Mike says.

"Huh?"

"The guy," he replies. "I'm sorry that the guy you like is marrying your…aunt?"

"Thanks," I sigh.

"I guess you really like her too, huh?" I frown. "I mean, otherwise you'd just go for it with the guy, right?"

"Mike, this is the part of the cab ride where we stop talking to each other, 'kay?" He nods. I sigh, cross my arms over my stomach and slump down on the seat.

"Whoa," Mike hums as the cab slows to a stop. I sit up, and we're at the iron gate outside the manor.

I toss another bill over the seat. "Keep it and forget where you dropped us off." The cab driver nods. "Follow me," I snap at Mike. I move out of the car, and he follows.

We approach the gate, and it opens slowly. We make it halfway up the long driveway…and I sense something. It makes me uneasy. It's like…when I fought Devon…only stronger, more intense…makes me want to run more.

"Hey." I don't know what it is, but it's close… "Hey." …feels like it's close enough to reach out and… "Hey." …I feel a hand on my shoulder. I grab the thumb, wrenching the elbow the wrong way, and draw my knife…ready to stab…

"Mike?" I sigh. His eyes move down to the knife hovering just an inch away from his diaphragm, and he looks like he's about to drop a brick. I let go of him.

"I-I-I called you," he says. "You didn't answer."

I sigh and look around. I don't sense it anymore. Whatever it was is gone now. Suddenly, I sense something that would stop my heart…if it were still beating anyway.

"Nate," I breathe a second before he appears in front of me. He looks over my head and then to my right and left. Mike stumbles and falls on his butt. He crabwalks away from Nate as best he can. Nate eyes him like a bug and then motions to him. "New Blood," I hum, trying not to look at Nate. He nods and keeps looking around. "Whatever it was is gone now."

"Looks like," Nate agrees. "You okay? You look spooked."

"Nobody says 'spooked' anymore, Nate," I return and walk over to Mike. I move my knife to my left hand, offer him my right, and help him to his feet. "I thought it was bad luck to see the bride before the wedding." Mike gasps and looks at Nate. He points at him, then me, then him again, and opens his mouth to say something. "Quiet," I bark and punch him in the stomach with the butt of my knife.

"Oomph!" He coughs…a lot.

"Being a little rough with the newbie, aren't you?"

I grab Mike and shove him in the direction of the house. He marches that way, and I follow. "Why do you care?" I snarl, putting my knife away. Nate follows us. "Haven't seen your mangy butt in days, and you just…"

"You see me all the time in school."

I glare at him. "I skipped the last two weeks of school…" He frowns. "Plus, school's been out since May…it's already almost the end of July, Nate… nice to know you noticed."

"How old are you guys?" Mike poses. I smack him on the back of the head. "Ouch. Mean."

"You're gonna get a lot worse from my brother."

"I'm sorry," Nate says.

"Yeah, well…'stuff your sorries in a sack…'"

Nate laughs. "So, you've been watching Seinfeld reruns?"

"I blame you," I complain as we reach the porch. "You're such a Jerry, and you don't even know it." He smirks. His eyes do that humble apology thing. "Go," I sigh. "It is bad luck to see the bride before the wedding…and since it's almost four in the morning…technically, it is your wedding day." He nods. "I'm happy for you, Nate." He opens his arms, and I step into him. I put my arms around him and inhale his scent…crap, he smells so good. Why does he have to smell so good?

"I'll see you tomorrow."

"Cool, I'll be the one in the Maid of Honor dress."

Nate backs away. "I'm glad you told me. It would've been really embarrassing if we showed up wearing the same thing." I laugh. He does too. He nods, lifts his hand… "Adieu." …and vanishes.

I sigh. "Adieu, mon ami," I whisper and push the front door open.

#####

Chapter 2: Rain

I step up to the jewelry counter and stare at the baubles enclosed there. "May I help you, miss?" The woman with large golden curls says, but I detect a hint of hostility. Admittedly, I'm standing here, staring at jewelry that costs tens of thousands of dollars, and I'm wearing a jean jacket and sundress of all things. Honestly, I know what will happen next.

I'll say something like… "No, thank you, ma'am. I was merely looking over your baubles…debating what might look nice with my skin tone." …and instantly my accent sweeps away her hostility.

"Well, I think diamond earrings would suit you perfectly," she hums with a happy chirp. Yes, just like every other person from the States I encounter. I have no idea why they find my accent so appealing. I sigh. I hate to admit it, but I probably would find it charming if I were from the States as well.

"I suppose," I hum as she retrieves a pair and holds them up to my ear. I examine myself in the tiny mirror atop the display case. I shake my head. "No, they don't suit me." She takes the earrings away, and I spot a watch…it's a platinum and gold pocket watch. "How much is this watch?"

She looks it over. "Three thousand?"

"Three thousand pounds? No, wait…the States…so, it's three thousand dollars. Would you gift wrap it for me?" I place the black credit card that Raven gave me on the counter with my left hand. "I think it will be the perfect wedding gift for my Nathan." She examines the card, and the admittedly, impressive ring on my finger. She smiles warmly. I have been so absent-minded lately. I suppose the old wives' tales are true.

I tap the glass with my right pointer finger. I have to wonder if I am getting Nathan this gift for the wedding or if I'm doing it simply to lessen the blow from what I have to tell him. I should tell him. I should've told him last night. I almost did, but something stopped me. He has every right to know. I must. I have to. "I have to."

"Ma'am?" the woman says as she places the silver box on the counter in front of me. Next to the box, I find two sales receipts and a pen. I scribble my name across the top receipt quickly…not fighting the urge at all to sign my name: Alana I. Gregory-Dumont. I smile and draw a little heart behind it. "When's the date?"

I smile. "Today," I breathe simply and claim the box.

"T-today…? But don't you have to…?"

"Tonight, to be more accurate…late ceremony…later dinner…and then he and I depart for our honeymoon."

"Going someplace nice?"

"I honestly don't know…he told me it was a surprise, and I trust him. He knows me very well."

"Best of luck to you, ma'am and congratulations," she sings as I walk away.

"Thank you," I return moving toward the egress.

I step out of the shop. I inhale the water-saturated air and peer up at gray skies just starting to release their bounty. I pull mother's ribbon free and slip it into my jacket pocket. I tuck Nathan's gift neatly away in the jacket's interior…that Raven promised would keep dry regardless of how much I stand in the rain. I inhale deeply. It is time to test that belief, I suppose. I step out into the downpour. I throw my head back, staring up at the sky. "Oh," I moan aloud as I get a familiar sensation at the back of my mind. My Nathan, you knew me before I really knew me…I love this sensation.

"Young lady," calls a young man in a suit. I look at him and arch my eyebrows. He offers me his umbrella.

I shake my head. "No, thank you," I breathe. "I prefer walking in the rain." He insists and renews the offer. I decline again with mother's eyes. I tell him to ignore the silly rain-dwelling girl. He walks away without another word. I smile and toss my soaking wet strands from left to right.

I smile and look down, letting my long dark hair hang around my face. My clothes are soaked through already and cling to body. I turn to the right and walk in the opposite direction of the umbrella man.

I sense my Nathan, drawing closer. My smile becomes more wistful. An automobile pulls up next to me. It moves into an empty space just ahead and waits with the engine idling. I reach the rear tire, and the passenger window comes down. "Excuse me, miss," Nathan begins. I catch him leaning over to get a better look at me from the corner of my eye. "Do you need a lift?" I stop and remain facing forward. I renew my smile and tilt my head back.

"I…," I pretend to ponder. "…do not think my fiancé would like that very much." I turn and look at him.

"Well, he doesn't have to know."

"Oh, I could not bring myself to lie to him. I love him far too much for that." I take a step closer to the auto.

Throwing the door open, he returns, "Normally, I probably wouldn't act like this, but the thing is…you're such a beautiful woman that I find…I just can't help myself."

"Probably?" I repeat with a nod. I put one hand on the door as a clap of thunder sounds in the distance. I tuck a few errant strands of hair behind my ear. "Well, I…normally, would not do this but…you are such a devastatingly handsome man," I flirt and then climb in. "That I find I cannot help myself,"

I moan while tilting back against the headrest. My eyes never leave my Nathan's handsome face.

He puts his arm around the back of my seat. I nibble my lower lip and tremble with anticipation of our impending kiss. Turning to face him, I put both of my hands on either side of his face. I kiss him, tugging his lower lip between mine gently. "Mmm, and just as I thought," I purr and kiss him again. "Your lips are so delicious," I breathe as we part. I pull the door closed as the rain picks up again.

He pulls away from the curb. I reach over and caress the back of his head. His scent fills the air. His scent seems sadly muted…I wonder if he notices the same about me. I should tell him…he needs to know…it has made me so monumentally happy. I wonder if it will do the same for him. I run one wet finger across his lower lip. He peers at me, and I smile warmly. I swipe that same finger across my lip. That did it. The emotion I'm getting from him…he's been pushed over the edge.

The automobile turns to the right and moves down an alleyway behind a small store. The rain falls harder against the roof as he shifts into park. I look at him, grin and lean over to him. "It would seem that you had an ulterior motive in picking me up, sir," I whisper into his ear.

I press the button on his seatbelt and guide it across his lap. I adjust admittedly, a bit awkwardly in my seat, preparing to and managing to cast my right leg over both of his thighs. I hike my dress up over my thighs and take a new seat…in the lap of my mate with my back against the steering wheel. I put my left hand on his chest and reach down to the seat controls with the other. With a mechanical whir, his chair glides back and reclines toward the backseat. "Luckily for you," I begin as the seat comes to a rest. "I had the same idea the moment I saw you."

My fingers move up his firm chest and then around the outside of his neck. I move my hands along until I'm able to stroke his earlobes with my thumbs…because I know how much he loves that. He inhales gentle. His jaw clenches. He's struggling with himself. I have to admit that I am struggling not to rip his clothes off right here and now. I stare into his eyes. I should tell him now. "I love you," I whisper against his lips. *Not that, you goofy Brit. He already knows that.*

"I love you, too."

I sigh. "Marry me."

"What about your fiancé?" he asks with that roguish smile that stole my heart almost a year ago. My smile matches his. "The poor bastard, but that sounds good to me. How about we get married tonight?" he poses, indulging in what he perceives as a game.

"No." My fingertips trace the line of his jaw. "Right now."

'Now?' he mouths as I press my lips against his cheek. I nod. "But...we're getting married in six hours..." I sit upright. "...just...six hours, Love."

"Not...good enough. I want to be Mrs. Alana Gregory-Dumont...right now. I do not want to wait another moment."

"You know, up here..." He taps his left temple. "...you've been Mrs. Dumont since our very first date. Here too," he adds, tapping the center of his chest.

I rub my lips against his. "Scent-bonded." I close my eyes. "I know, and that is wonderful, but..." I undo the top two buttons of his shirt. "...I think that it is time we let everyone else in on the secret." I tremble...secret...I should tell him...I have to tell him. He runs his tongue from my exposed collarbone up to my left earlobe mind-numbingly slowly. I moan involuntarily. "Yes," I say as question and admission of pleasure into his ear.

"Yes." My Nathan sits back. He takes his mobile out so quickly that it startles me. He puts the phone up to his ear. "Call Christopher." The phone complies. I nibble my bottom lip as the phone attempts to connect. Christopher answers with more of a growl than usual. "Cousin, how hard would it be to move the wedding up?"

"Your wedding's today," Christopher groans. "How much more can we move it up?"

"How about...now?" my Nathan replies with his lips puckered as I undo another button.

"NOW?" Christopher snaps. "Are you kidding me? One, it's the middle of the day. Two, you...we would have to round up all your guests...all 500 hundred of them. And three, we already moved your wedding up a month at your fiancée's request...it's in...five hours and forty minutes, you can't wait?"

I slip one hand inside of his shirt and rub my palm against his rippled stomach. My other hand rests on his left cheek with my thumb sweeping across his bottom lip...my eyes flash silver, telling him, "No...I really can't. Today is overcast all day so the vampires will be fine. We only need the pack, Quinton, Raven, and a few select members of the coven there. Remember...rule number one, is one that you taught me yourself." He stares into my eyes as my tongue streams along my upper lip. "Always give the woman what she wants."

Christopher sighs. "I would argue with you, but I can hear Alana breathing right in front of you. I'll see what I can do. You two, just get over to the church." He ends the call abruptly.

"'Always give the woman what she wants?'" I ask as he tosses his phone onto the passenger seat. I smile. "I like the sound of that. Can you guess what 'the woman' wants right now?"

"No, but I can hope, wish, and pray she wants what I want." He places his hands on my hips.

"This would have been a REALLY good guess," I utter before kissing him.

When we part, horrible reason sets in. "We have to get to the church, Love," he sighs. "We don't want to have everybody waiting on us."

"Well," I begin, tucking more hair behind my ear. I place both of my hands on his chest before continuing. "We could rush off right now or we could do all of the wonderfully naughty things that I want to do to you right now." He smiles as I start in on his last two buttons.

"…but," he continues fighting a battle that he doesn't want to win.

"You also have to consider three things. One, you drive insanely fast, so we would get there in no time. Two, it will take Christopher some time to gather everyone up." I open his shirt and pull it down past his shoulders. "And three, I feel that I should mention that when I left the house this morning..." I pause as my eyes trace up from his Photoshop worthy stomach to meet his eyes. I undo his belt before he even realizes. "…I neglected to put on my knickers."

"You…are very good," he whispers as his nose nuzzles my neck just below my chin. I smile remembering the last time that he told me that.

#####

One month ago...

"You're very good," Nathan says offering me his gloved hand. Sweat covers the front of his tiny form fitting tank top. I almost laugh thinking about the padded gloves that he's wearing for my protection. Strength like his, he could still knock down a brick wall with one punch…even through padded gloves. His black workout pants fit him just well enough to hug his hips and show off his firm buns. "What are you staring at?" he asks, looking deeply into my eyes. No, it feels more like he's delving into my soul. It only makes sense; he has taken up permanent residence there.

"You, lover," I breathe and wipe my chin. His smile flips and becomes roguish. I love it when he stares at me like that…possessive…honest…desire-filled…lustful…he wants me. He spies my pink sports bra…and leaves himself wide open. "Heh," I laugh…and then focus on my speed the way that he and Natavius have been teaching me. I am behind him in an instant. His back is wide open, his hand…still extended, there is no way he can defend himself. "HA," I bark as I drive all my strength into this one punch, praying that he was not simply bragging when he said he can take anything I can dish out.

In the time between drawing my arm back and propelling my fist forward, he spins on his heel and catches my fist. "No," I whine. He wrenches my arm and hurls me to the ground. "Oof," I spit as my bum hits the floor. He laughs…again.

A hand descends over my shoulder. "That's what I'm talking about," he exclaims. "That would've worked on anyone else."

"Except you," I complain as I take his hand. He pulls me to my feet. A ballerina's twirl later, and I am in his arms. "How did you predict that?"

His eyes lazily half-close. "Easy, I trained with Natavius." I giggle. "After having someone's fist come at you from six different directions at the same time, you kind of get used to being attacked from behind."

"Yes, I can see how that would prepare you," I say, stepping away.

I reach the weapons case on the far wall before he is behind me again. He wraps one arm around my waist while pulling the pink ribbon out of my hair.

"What are you doing?" I ask while reaching for my practice sword. He pulls my tangled mess of hair to the left and kisses my neck. "I," I begin but cut off with a swipe of his tongue just below my ear. "Oh," I exclaim as familiar desirous emotions rip through my body. My eyes shut, and I lean back into his waiting lips.

"No," I bark…from across the room. "We have plenty of time to play later. Now is training time." He nods once as he removes his twin swords from the wall. "By the way, once we are done here." I point my practice sword at him. "I am going to rip every stitch of clothing off you and then I will proceed to do wonderfully devilish things to that amazing body of yours." He tweaks one eyebrow…Oh, how I wish it were later already.

I sigh and then bound at him full speed with my sword pointed at his heart. He crosses his blades and deflects the hit upward. My free hand fists and then settles into his diaphragm. He slams into the wall a second later. The concrete wall crumbles a bit, and his swords fall to the floor. Immediately after, he joins them, clutching his stomach, doubled over in pain, and gasping for air.

"NATHAN," I scream and dart over to him. Before I can check on him, he already has his swords at my throat in a scissor fashion. I gasp as the dull steel edges close in on my throat.

"Gotcha," he huffs while staring up at me.

I knock the swords away, bruising my forearms in the process. "You ass," I growl, snapping back at him. "I thought I really hurt you." He takes hold of my face and kisses me before I even realize. It is not an apology, but his kiss could make me forget the rest of the world. Our lips part. "What was I saying?" I moan as he stares lovingly into my eyes. "Were you supposed to apologize for something?"

"I don't know," he feigns. He collects his swords and rises to his feet. "Are we done here? Can we make with the clothes ripping now?" he asks, tugging at his top. I shake my head. "More?"

"An exhibition," I return. "Christopher told me that you were an amazing swordsman." He spins the sword in his right hand. "When you were on the ship…with Rosalind," I finish feeling a choking sensation that has surprisingly stayed around even to this day whenever her name comes up. "He said that by the time he reached the deck, Quinton had already fell six vampires by himself…and you had taken four. How did you…?"

He looks despondent for a second. "I don't think so," he growls and hurries past me back to the weapons case.

"Why not?" He turns back to me…and my heart sinks. The look on his face would tear me up inside if his emotions weren't doing the same.

"It's something that my brother taught me," he mumbles. "He calls it 'The Dance of Death' or at least, that's what the translation meant." He looks down at the swords still in his hands. I try not to laugh at the ridiculous title considering the mood that uttering it has put my Nathan in. "Pay attention," he exclaims, while renewing his grip on the weapons. "I'm only going to do this once." His eyes meet mine. "This is only to be used when fighting multiple opponents…with no allies near you." I nod once.

What happens next…defies proper explanation…or logic. He leaps about two feet off the ground, spins, and swings the swords around his body. At several times, the blades seem to move independent of his hands. They seem to attach themselves to various places on his body when necessary. This twirling unrelenting attack continues for what feels like several seconds, and I merely try my best to keep up with the number of cuts levied. …twenty-two, twenty-three, twenty-four… However, combined with the assault, he seems to be moving to defend himself as well. After three seconds, his swords would have delivered fifty-two cuts and would have defended against at least that many attacks. With his strength pushing the swords, those weapons would have dismembered anything…vampire, daemon, or otherwise.

For all of the schooling that I have endured, all of the tutors that have disciplined me, and all of the languages that I know, "Wow" is all that I manage to emit. He swings the swords around until they run the length of his forearms. "That was…amazing," I breathe. "It was a perfect defense coupled with an indefensible offense."

He nods twice then walks over and returns the swords to the weapons case. "Quinton is the best fighter we wolves have ever had." I look on still bewildered by the feat that I just witnessed. "Probably the best Alpha, too," he adds as he looks at a long silver claymore hanging horizontally above my *Isis* sword. The sword that Alexander gave me still shines as new as the day that I unwrapped it. I sigh.

"Nathan," I call as his ungloved hand wanders dangerously close to the claymore. "What are you doing?"

"Lupus et daemonium quod unum," he reads from the massive blade.

"The wolf and the demon as one," I translate. He nods.

"My brother asked our best weapons smith to make this sword for me when I was six. When he saw it, he yelled so loud at the old wolf, that I came running." He turns to me and swallows deeply with tears in his eyes. "I saw the sword and asked if it was for me. The smith…of course…grinned and said that it was. I grabbed it and began swinging it like a toy." He chuckles. "It made me happy." A tear falls away. "My brother growled and knocked it out of my hands. 'Never touch this again!' he demanded.

"I was scared. I had never seen him so angry." I cross the room in what felt like a step and put my arms around him. "I began to cry…I was only six years old." He peers at me. "He gave in after all of a minute of my tears. He told me I could have it as long as I never learned Latin."

"Oh," I sigh into his chest and squeeze him tighter. "I am…guessing that when I translated that…it was not the first time you heard it." He shakes his head slowly.

"They always called my mother 'the demon,'" he sobbed. "Said her scent was wrong…that she was insane and tried to kill me." His eyes flash honey and emerald. The whites of his eyes slowly give way to intruding darkness. "It turns out that father lied to cover up the fact that she didn't love him."

"She…fell out of love with him?" I ask incredulously.

"She NEVER WAS in love with him," he explains. "She…always loved someone else. My father stole her from him. HE STOLE HER AND THEN HE MURDERED HER," he practically roars. He drops to his knees and cries.

"Shhhhhh, I am…so, so sorry, my love," I say, kneeling and embracing him. He rests his head on my chest and puts his hands on the small of my back. "I am so sorry that that brought such a painful memory to the surface, Love."

He releases me and wipes his eyes. "It's okay. I'm okay." He looks at me with his normal, heartwarmingly russet eyes. He huffs a chuckle. "You're…probably wondering why that came up."

I shake my head. Looking over at the claymore, "You saw the inscription on the sword and…"

Another breathy snicker escapes him. "No. 'The Dance of Death,'" he begins again. "My brother taught it to me. My mother taught it to him." He stands up. "I'm gonna go take a shower."

I turn back to the sword then stare after the wolf that I love…I can still feel the pain slipping through him like mercury. A tear slides away from my eye. I rise and follow him quickly.

"Ungh," I groan as my stomach rumbles. "Na-," I try to call him…but before I can…a repugnantly familiar feeling moves over me. He starts the shower. I try to run after him…but the feeling strikes again, only harsher. I hurry over to the nearest waste bin, falling to my knees…I empty the contents of my stomach. I stare at the pool of blood in the bottom of the waste bin, a grim reminder of Nathan and my failed marriage attempt.

This time it is different though. I do not feel ill, weak, or wobbly. Just…profoundly…queasy, I believe the best word for it is…or perhaps, nauseated. My stomach rumbles again…suddenly, my eyes move over to silver on their own…and I see the angelic brown eyes of a beautiful child.

#####

Present Day

"What?" my Nathan asks looking at my blank expression. "What are you thinking about?"

"Training," I admit. His hands caress the tops of my thighs. His thumbs threaten the tender inner part. I touch the side of his face and give him a gentle peck.

"Training?" he repeats after our kiss.

"Yes," I respond. "We have not trained in so long. I miss it."

He laughs. "It's only been a month since the last time we trained together."

I roll my eyes. "I know, but still…I miss it." My hands rest on his shoulders. "I will miss it," I complain while moving in and planting a kiss on his neck. I inhale deeply. His scent is still like aerosol-based sex to me. It's electric and intoxicating. I love it. I kiss his neck again.

"Wait," he stops me. "What do you mean, 'you will miss it?'"

"I said, 'I miss it.'" I try to kiss him again.

"No. You said that 'I miss it' and then you said, 'I will miss it,'" he repeats imitating my accent at the appropriate points. "What'd you mean by that?'"

"No. Nothing," I lie. "I…meant that once we are married. We probably will not be training as much." His lips part and allow his tongue to slip through them. It caresses his upper then lower lip before returning to his mouth. I want a taste. He looks deeply into my eyes.

"You know that if you lie to me…I can tell," he states plainly. I close my eyes and nod. "So please, tell me the truth." I open my eyes slowly and see the silver reflected in his eyes. "No," he breathes as his eyes shift to honey and emerald. *Love, please…what's going on?* Ah, the benefit of our mutual eye phasing reaction…our wordless communication.

I meant that I would miss it, once we get married, I reply.

Okay, I can tell that that's true. But there's more to it than that. What aren't you telling me? No response. *Please, love…you know that you're my world.*

As you are mine.

Then please, be honest with me. I know I'm not the one who should be preaching honesty in our relationship, but we both agreed. And ever since, I've been completely honest with you on everything from family history to Rosalind. I swallow deeply, remembering the pain that washed over me as he told me about his brief first marriage and his wife's sudden death. *Are you having visions…?* He must have gleaned something of my errant thought. *…like your mother had before…you were born?*

No, I lie.

You're lying.

Yes.

Why? If you're dreaming of your own death, then…

Then it is what will come to pass my love, my Nathan. I rub my lips against his. He kisses me and holds me tight…and I feel the love emanating from him. It is warm and enveloping, and I find that I just want more and more of it. Our foreheads touch, and our eyes meet.

I can't lose you.

You will always have me.

Promise?

With all my heart. He nods against my forehead as my eyes drift closed. I have to tell him. "I have something to tell you," I whisper.

"Is it about your dream?"

"Yes," I sigh. "I have not dreamt of my death…" I lift my eyes to meet his again. He gives me his full attention. "I dreamt of an angelic little girl with honey-toned skin, black hair, and large brown eyes…" He frowns. "…those eyes changed from brown…to deep blue…and then from deep blue to the color of silver with honey and emerald entreating on the outskirts…"

"What?"

I nod with a smile stretching my face. He smiles as well. "Yes, Nathan…I am pregnant."

#####

Chapter 3: MOH

"Yeah, I have absolutely nothing to do in the middle of the day, so of course, let's move up the wedding to accommodate Alana's whim," I complain, glad she's not here so that she can't tell anyone the real reason I'm upset. I sigh. I thought I had a whole day to get ready to watch the guy I'm in love with marrying my sire-aunt.

"Aaaaaaawwwwww," Natavius purrs.

"Shut up, fake boyfriend," and the only other person who knows the real reason I'm upset. I walk over to him and straighten his black bow tie. "You do look pretty hot in a tux though." I move down to brush his lapels, before pushing his shirt into his vest a little more.

"Babe," he returns. "I look hot…" He moves his left hand out to the side with his middle and index finger pinched together with his thumb. "…period. The tux is just icing on a very delicious cake." I laugh. It'd be less funny if he were lying.

"You two seem comfortable toget'er," Raven breathes.

"Yeah, well…" I motion to Natavius. "…Best Man…" And then to myself. "…and Maid of Honor. Plus, we're used to it, pretending to be boyfriend and girlfriend at school." Raven frowns. "Don't ask, long story from my first day. Just know that high school girls are crazy."

"Guys aren't any better," Natavius adds with a chuckle.

"Right?" Raven's frown intensifies. She steps closer to Natavius and stares into his eyes. Her eyes dart to me and back to him.

"No, freakin' way," she breathes.

"What?"

"See? Even your sire-mom agrees, I'm hot in a tux," he says, turning to face me. I hold my hand out and wag it in a so-so fashion. He laughs again, which causes me to laugh. "Well, I'll tell you what," he continues. "I'll concede that you make even this bridesmaid's dress look hot if you'll say just once that I'm hot sans tux."

"Okay." I wave my hand in his face. "First of all, this…" I motion to the simple pink, strapless dress that goes all the way down, hugging my hips and thighs, to meet matching pink shoes. "…I'm pulling this off." He opens his mouth immediately after a sly, flirty grin. I wave my finger in his face. "I mean, I'm working it…not getting naked for you or anybody else. And while we're on the subject, I do not want to think about you 'sans' tux." He laughs again. I shove him in the chest and laugh again, too. "So," I start, trying to change the awkward subject. "…we're still going to Meredith's party tomorrow night, right?"

He arches his eyebrows and lets them fall. "Back to school jam. Woo-hoo." He tried to suck all the sarcasm out of that statement and failed miserably.

"Hey," I point at him. "The golden couple is going on their honeymoon, so we have to keep the lie alive."

"Keep the lie alive!" he bellows in a 'deeper than his voice' voice. I giggle. He does too. That's why I like Natavius so much. He totally gets my sense of humor.

"Crap," I complain as soon as I catch the scent that really makes me feel the exact opposite of that. Natavius frowns. "They're here."

"Who? Them?" Natavius asks, tipping his head back toward the handful of wolves and… even fewer vampires. If not for our coven we wouldn't even have reached double digits. He takes a deep breath. "Oh! Them!" He frowns. "How did you…?"

"Shut up!"

"Places everyone!" Raven says. "T'ey're here. Everyone, get to yer seats." The vampires quickly move into the chapel. The wolves practically snarl at her.

"Angela," a sexy baritone says behind me. I turn to the massive Alpha Quinton. "Good to see you again." I smile and nod as he takes my hand. "Natavius." Natavius smirks and nods. "Everyone," he growls with the Bark, building in the back of his throat. "MOVE INSIDE." The wolves hustle inside without another peep.

"Don't have to tell me twice," the woman with the scowly wolf says. What's his name again?

"Christopher," Alpha Quinton says and wraps one arm around him. That's right. Christopher…his name's Christopher Dumont. He's Nate's cousin. "…Rachel," he hums, hugging the human. Ugh, I hate that I think like that already. Quinton lets her go with a wave of his arms. "Go on. Go inside. Take your places. I'll be in in a second." They nod and head inside. Quinton turns to us. He smiles. "You two, too." I frown. He tips his head to me. I turn to…

"HOLY CRAP," I exclaim. Alana and Richard step up behind us…and her dress…her dress is just… "Wow."

She smiles. "How does it look?" she asks, sliding her hands down her heart-shaped, strapless bodice that looks diamond encrusted. The dress comes in tight around her waist, moves down in ruffles, before moving outward like mermaid's fin below her knees.

"It looks amazing," Natavius says, causing a new smile to move across her face. "You're gorgeous, Alana."

"Yeah," I murmur, stepping closer to her. "You look so freakin' good." She nods and mouths a 'thank you.' Her hair looks amazing. It's in an up do with two dangly curls hanging off the front left side. I continue checking the rest of her appearance…ignoring the black ribbon wrapped around her left wrist in a bow…next to her belly…that seems…off somehow. "But…" She frowns. "…I don't know…it seems kind of tight…" I pinch at her waist. "…around…"

She smacks my hand. I glare at her, and she does it right back. Her eyes flash silver. "Don't."

I nod and take a few steps back. My head tweaks, and I glance at her sideways. My power kicks in. Her aura seems off, different. Her normal aura is sort of a pale, metallic blue…but now…there are swirls of deeper grays but somehow it feels warmer. Her aura's more inviting. I take a deep breath. Her scent is off, too. It doesn't just feel like Nate's here with her, it smells like it, too. I gasp, and my eyes swell. I stare at her perfect little body again…and realize it's perfectly not perfect. There's a tiny little bump around her belly button.

My eyes come up to meet silver staring back at me. She holds one finger over her mouth and shakes her head subtly. I nod, but my eyes remain bulged.

"What's wrong?" Natavius asks.

#####

Chapter 4: Bliss

"N-nothing," Angela lies. "I'm… just surprised by how good my big bro looks in his tux." I move my finger back to my mouth and shake my head subtly again. "What?" she asks in a confused tone. "What? Natavius? As if Nate didn't already tell him."

"Tell me what?" Natavius asks. Her jaw drops. Natavius's brilliantly bright eyes move from Angela to me. "Tell me what?"

"He didn't tell him?" she asks.

"No, because when my Nathan makes a promise, he keeps it." I frown. "Most of the time."

"All the time," she says. "Don't do that to yourself. It's your wedding day, and the man…wolf you love is at the end of that aisle. Get pumped."

"Yes. I must pump myself," I misspeak on purpose. Natavius, Angela, and Richard snicker. I smile. Good, that did lift her spirit, even if only a little. I know this entire day is breaking her heart. Perhaps, if she knew how he felt about her. My eyes move to Natavius as the music starts.

"Okay, you two," Richard says. "You're on."

Angela hooks Natavius's arm. "Let's go, fake boyfriend." They move closer to the double doors. "Keep the lie alive," she whispers to Natavius… and wipes a tear away.

He pats her hand. "Keep the lie alive," he returns with a soothing tone. They wait for the right moment in the song, the place designated for them to march into the cathedral.

"You're forgetting this," Richard says, passing me the bouquet, consisting of wildflowers that hint at my Nathan's natural scent.

"Thank you." I nod and hold them closer to gather their fragrance. Richard extends his arm to me. "You're really going to walk me down the aisle, again?" He nods. The opening between his arm and side is so inviting. I slip my hand inside. "Perfect," I breathe into his ear, before taking another whiff of the flowers.

"I never got to walk my own daughter down the aisle," Richard returns with a warm smile. "It's nice that I'll get the chance to walk one of the two women that I think of as my little girls down the aisle." He peers over at Angela.

She appears next to us, on Richard's side. She startles him a bit. She exhales causing her lips to flutter briefly, while looking away from him. Her arms disappear behind her back, and she hefts herself on to her toes. "That's really sweet, big bro," she murmurs before kissing him on the cheek. Her eyes meet mine, and I force a smile.

"Well, I guess I should get going," she says, as the music reaches the place that Raven dictated is the entry point of the Best Man and Maid of Honor. Natavius steps forward. Two attendants pull the doors open, and she meets him just before they march through the open doors.

I sigh, feeling bad for her. I made her my Maid of Honor when she's clearly still in love with the groom. She accepted, but she really didn't have to. Did she feel pressured from me? And what about me. Am I truly that cruel? I mean, she did help us get back together…even helped us work through some of our issues and…

"Ready?" Richard asks. I sigh. I nod, and we move toward the doors. My mind won't seem to move away from Angela and her shattered heart though. She could've refused. I gave her that option and told her that I would understand if…

"Are you alright?"

"I'm fine, Richard. Why do you ask?"

"Well, miss…you're breathing extraordinarily loud." I sigh again and nod again.

"I suppose so. Nerves most likely," I lie. "…the last time we did this…" I bob my head unevenly and peer up at him. "…it did not go so well."

He nods. "I can't seem to stop thinking about my daughter," he whispers. I gasp and stare at him. "I died…became a vampire when she was still very young. I've dreamt of walking her down the aisle every day. I broke into the church the night before her wedding. I stayed out of sight until it started, stood in the back as she and her husband exchanged their vows." He shakes his head. "I didn't even get to see her first dance." He sighs. I do too, my emotion going down with his.

He pats my hand resting on his forearm. "I consider it an honor…to walk you down the aisle…both times…" I smile. "…this time will go better, I promise."

"I know," I whisper as 'Here comes the bride' starts.

"Here we go."

The doors open again, and we march forward. We enter…and I feel it all…only multiplied…the baby is feeling it as well…she moves unevenly. My breathing accelerates again. I catch ever pair of eyes watching me…feeling their disdain for our union…empty as it may be…the pressure of this room feels so heavy, it feels oppressive, it feels… I gasp. …like the purest thing, I have ever felt. My eyes move to the front of the room…to what I am marching toward…to what WE are marching toward. My Nathan stares at me…the look upon his face tells me that he believes I am the most perfect thing in the world at this moment…a tear falls from my left eye at the same time one falls from his right. He is so amazingly…blissfully happy.

"Alana," Richard whispers through gritted teeth.

"Yes," I return absently.

"You're getting ahead of me…you're walking too fast…"

I stop. He does as well. I look at him. I shake my head as the overwhelming joy I feel tugs at my heart, pulling me toward the altar.

"I am sorry, Richard…but I cannot wait one moment longer." He frowns. I slip my arm out of his, lift the front of my dress with my bouquet filled hand and…move as Natavius and my Nathan taught me. I am in his arms before I even realize it. The smell of the mountain air in summertime…of wild flowers and fresh earth washes over me. "Hello," I whisper to his smiling face.

"Hey," he returns and pulls me in for a kiss. I inhale deeply just before our lips come together. I drop my bouquet and wrap my arms around his neck.

"Nathan…Alana…," Vance whispers. "…we are still a ways off from that part."

We part. Nathan cups my face in both of his hands. He presses his forehead against mine. I shake my head. "I love you."

"I love you," he moans back before pressing his lips against mine again. He wraps his arms around me and holds me close to him and his warmth moves over my entire body. Our lips part. He breathes heavily and so do I, staring into his brilliant eyes. Vance clears his throat.

We separate but continue holding each other's hands. I peer over my shoulder. Angela shows me my bouquet, having claimed it from the floor. She smiles…despite the pain streaming off her. "Thank you." She nods as her eyes glisten with a fresh wave of tears…and a subtle glance beyond me…at what she's giving up.

"Go get 'em," she whispers with a nod. I return to my Nathan.

"Dearly beloved," Vance begins. "We are gathered here to witness the joining of this man, Nathan Jerome Dumont, and this woman, Alana Isis Gregory, in the bonds of holy matrimony. Before we begin a prayer…

"May God bless you with Hope enough to keep sunshine in your love, and Fear enough to keep you holding hands in the dark.

"May God bless you with Unity enough to keep your roots entwined, and Separation enough to keep you reaching for each other.

"May God bless you with Harmony enough to keep romance in your song, and Discord enough to keep you tuning your love so it becomes sweet music to all who may hear it."

Nathan and I both laugh at that one.

"May you both create, with God, a piece of Heaven on Earth. Amen." The room remains quiet, save Raven, Richard, Quinton, and Rachel whispering 'Amen.'

"Nathan and Alana have written their own vows to one another…" He looks to me and nods.

"Right, vows," I murmur. "Um…" I nibble my lower lip. I laugh absently. "…believe it or not, I had vows written…prepared for weeks and weeks…and they were bloody brilliant, Nathan." He nods. "But here I am, staring at you, and my mind's a blank." He nods again. "…staring into your eyes…feeling your love…something does come to mind.

"Nathan, if I had known then only a fraction of what I know now…the moment I met you, I would have told you…" I nod, mustering my confidence for what comes next. "…Nathan, I will make your life better." I tremble as fresh, happy tears fill my eyes.

"I will make all the loneliness…all the solitude…mean something. I will make it mean something because I will take it all away. I will take all of that grief and replace it with a bright and shining future…a truly glorious future, because that…that is what you have done for me." I nod as a tear escapes. "I will make you happy…I will make you so very happy, I swear it…and I will spend the rest of my life trying to keep you that way…it's only fair because it is what you have done for me…and I will love you forever for that."

Nathan's smiles that earth-shattering smile that stole my heart. I feel giddy and laugh with a happy bounce and more tears. He leans in close to me, as if we're the only two in this hall. I love it when he does this. He makes me feel that way…as if we are the only two beings on the planet.

"Those were my vows," he claims, peering deeper into my eyes. I nod, feeling the truth of his words. "So, I guess I'll just have to go from the heart."

"You never disappoint when you do."

He nods. "I never thought," he whispers breathlessly with tears swimming in his eyes. "…that I could EVER be as happy as you make me. I would've never believed…this degree of…" He shakes his head as tears begin to trickle away. "…this…bliss was possible without experiencing it firsthand. I lost myself in the pains of my past…I was an ocean of turmoil…a swirling tempest of rage…then I met you, at the tip of a sword of all things…"

I stifle a laugh and feel flush. He smiles before drawing both of my hands up to his mouth and kissing them.

"…the beautiful Midnight Princess…and everything in me…became calm, you stilled those troubled waters…no, not stilled. You drew them toward you…made me move with you, and I have continued to every day since then…and I will continue to for the rest of my life. You are the shore that I will always return to, my angel…" He winks at Vance. "…you are my little piece of Heaven on Earth." I spring forward and kiss him. He inhales deeply as I tug on his lower lip.

Vance clears his throat again. "Still not there yet," he whispers.

We part, and he glimpses at Vance. My Nathan smirks. "You can skip…ALL…of the middle stuff…" He comes back to me. "…and get to our, I dos. My wife and I have to begin our life together." I smile and draw my lips into my mouth. I nod and put my forehead to his.

"Does anyone here object to this union? Speak now or forever hold your peace," Vance poses. I glance to the first row on Nathan's side. Quinton stands and glares at our attendees with his arms crossed over his chest. My eyes come back to Nathan, and he is smiling devilishly, staring at my first row…and Raven, who is doing the same thing as Quinton. I laugh.

"Fine, fine," Vance continues with a bit of a laugh.

"Nathan, do you take this woman as your wife before God and his company, to have and to hold, in sickness and in health, for richer or for poorer, keeping thee only unto her, until death parts you?"

"Forever and ever and even beyond all that, I do."

"Alana, do you…"

"I'm holding you to that," I interrupt while pointing at Nathan's heart.

He smiles. "Good."

I turn to Vance. "I absolutely do," I pant.

"The rings?" Natavius passes my Nathan my ring. Angela gives me Nathan's ring. Nathan holds my ring close to my finger. "Nathan, repeat after me." Nathan nods. "With this ring…"

"With this ring…"

"…I thee wed."

"…I thee wed." My Nathan places the ring on my finger.

"Alana," Vance says. "Repeat after me. With this ring…"

"With this ring…" I hold the ring near Nathan's extended finger.

"…I thee wed."

"…I thee wed," I finish, slipping the ring onto his ring finger. He takes my corresponding hand and gives my fingers a gentle squeeze.

"Now," Vance says like a complaint. "…by the power vested in me, I now pronounce you…" Before he can finish, my Nathan pulls me in for another kiss. "…yeah, that," Vance complains. The room falls silent…but it doesn't matter. In this moment, the room could fall into oblivion, and I wouldn't notice. I'm busy kissing my husband…my Nathan…mon petit loupe.

#####

Chapter 5: Reception

"…and so," Natavius continues after the laughter dies down. "Nathan was sitting there in the mud, and Quinton asked him what he was doing there…" He motions to Nathan and me. "…and…he didn't say anything back…he just started squealing…" He giggles as the wolves laugh along. So, do I. "…and so I joined in and said, 'nobody here, but us pigs.'" Nathan erupts with laughter. I lean into him, laughing as well.

"…but as you can see, Nate cleaned up and got it right…just like he always does eventually." Nathan nods to his pack brother. "And he couldn't've gotten it righter than with Alana." I smile. "You make him shine as bright as I always thought he could and for that…I thank you." He raises his glass. "Salut."

"Salut." I repeat and smile as Nathan nuzzles against my neck. "See? That was not nearly as bad as you feared it would be."

"Yeah," he murmurs. "But I fully planned on NEVER telling you the pig pen story." I laugh.

"Excuse me," Quinton calls. I lift my eyes to him…and Raven, standing next to him, across the table from us. "We…" He peers at my sister. "…agreed that in lieu of dancing with the parents…"

"…the two of ya could dance wit' us," Raven suggests. "We hope."

Nathan rises, still holding my hand. He places my hand in Quinton's. The Alpha guides me around the intimate, little table never releasing my hand. We move to the dance floor as a light jazz tune begins to play. Quinton puts his arm around me as best he can as I barely come up to his chest. He is surprisingly light on his feet though.

"You smell like my…" He pauses. "…brother."

"I should hope so," I whisper back. "We are…"

"No," he groans, keeping his voice low. "I mean, YOU smell like my…"

"I know," I interrupt and try to choke down the knot in my throat. I could not do anything about the shiver moving up my spine.

"You remember what I told you when I first agreed to let you two marry, right?" I tremble and peer into his stern expression and cold eyes. My breathing accelerates, and there's nothing I can do about that either. What will he do to our daughter…? Will he…? He leans in close and kisses me on the cheek. "Keep it a secret for as long as you can," he murmurs into my ear.

"You mean, you're not going to…"

He shakes his head slowly. "I could never hurt my own flesh and blood…and that includes you now." I nod. His tone is so possessive, like Nathan's when he talks about me. He means that we are HIS flesh and blood, but does he mean...

We separate a bit, and I stare into his eyes…eyes filled with pride and love. "Thank you." He smiles as the music comes to an end. He bends and kisses me on my forehead. My eyes drift closed.

"Now, I'd like to have a word with your husband." I nod as he steps away. Raven and Nathan part as Vance asks for the next dance. Raven smiles at him…flirtatiously, and it makes me smile, seeing the two of them together. I turn back toward our table and catch the eye of Nathan's great-great-uncle…what was his name again?

The old wolf waves his hand toward himself as if calling me over. My interest tweaks just like the tilting of my head. I glance around reflexively and then return to him. I motion to myself. He nods and waves me over again. I lift the front of my dress slightly and walk over to him. The other wolves scatter with every step that I take closer to him. I try to sigh as quietly as possible, but their lingering hatred still hurts.

"Ignore them, angel," the old wolf says in a gruff voice as I reach his cane. He reaches out to me, and I offer him my hand not sensing any malice. He smiles and nods as he takes it. He then motions for me to sit next to him. "They don't…recognize what you represent…" He nods. "…in fact, what this very marriage represents."

"And what does it represent, elder?" I ask him coyly taking my seat. "This blessed day for my husband and me."

"I wish I could've given up on being an elder over three centuries ago, girl," he explains. "I'm just a humble wolf who's probably seen too much come and go."

"Or one who has attained wisdom…" I lean in closer to him. "…even beyond his many years," I compliment.

"Well met, girl," he says, leaning back slightly. "I see why the pup loves you so much." I smile and look around the room hoping to steal a glance at my husband, my Nathan.

I spy him having a word with his brother Quinton, his oldest nephew, Quinn, and his cousin, Christopher. Odd, my Nathan seems worried about something. His demeanor, his stance even the way he surveys the room have all changed slightly. The difference would probably be lost on someone who had not spent so much time staring at him. I wonder what troubles him.

His brother on the other hand, seems more relaxed than I have ever seen him. The way he looks at my Nathan…strangely, it makes me very happy. I smile reflexively. I do not think he told my Nathan that he knows, but…

I sigh, and I lean over to the old wolf while catching my Nathan's eye. Nathan waves and smiles warmly. I return his grin as that familiar warmth washes over me all over again. "You never said what our marriage represents," I remind the old wolf.

"I didn't, did I?" he asks, sounding surprised by his lapse in memory. "Your marriage marks the end of the old races' dominion over us all," he answers, lowering himself a bit. "Forgive me...where are my manners? We've been talking all this time, and I never introduced myself." He turns to me. "My name is Malcolm," he says plainly. "But a very long time ago, I was known simply as Mosif...brother of Mosi." He pauses as if seeing another world completely separate from this one.

"Mosi?" he begins again as if I should recognize the name and I do, but I decide to humor him. I shake my head to pretend that I did not. "Mosi was the first Alpha of the A'kani. Yep," Mosif continues. "I am your husband's great-great-great uncle."

"I believe you said one too many greats," I giggle.

Mosif thinks for a moment while scratching his chin.

He continues to tickle the whiskers under his mouth, and his eyes wander back to that other world. He releases a rustling chortle. "Yeah," he starts again adjusting his cane. "Yeah, I guess you're right," he lies. He tilts his head back away from me to get a better look at me. His russet eyes have so much wisdom in them that it is almost overwhelming. His caramel complexioned skin seems as soft as silk to the touch. His deep brown hair with gray encroaching at his temples adds to his adorableness. He smells of warmth and arid air.

"You know that I'm lying, don't cha?" I nod once vacantly. "Wish I could tell you why...but I know that if your husband doesn't know, then it ain't my place to say."

"True," I respond with a confident bob of my head. He smiles warmly. "I will not press the issue then." He frowns for a fraction of a second and renews his grip on his cane. "The old races?" I ask him while peering around the room again. "You mean, the angels and the daemons," I inquire.

"Very good," Mosif says through an eye crinkling grin. "Did you know that vampires and wolves were created...?"

"...by the daemons and angels, respectively, to continue the war after both races had passed from the Earth," I conclude.

"That's not quite right," Mosif says staring down at the floor in front of him. "That's what they said the reason was...but only a few of the original vampires and a couple of the original clans know the truth of things."

I reach over and place one hand on top of the two of his on the cane's handle. He does not react in the slightest to my touch. "But there are no original vampires left...my father was the last and even he was a child compared to the others...and apart from the Mosi'sons and the Mosif'sons...there are no old clans with unbroken bloodlines either..."

"No," Mosif whispers. "You're right about that." He looks down and leaves this plain of reality again. "I keep forgetting that," he whispers. A deep sadness rolls off the old wolf. "We've lost so many," he weeps. A single tear streams away from his left eye, rolls down to his jaw, and then falls onto my arm.

"I am so sorry," I breathe leaning in near his cheek.

"Well," he states with a bit of irritation in his voice. "What are you waiting for?" I lean away from him and shrug. "Go ahead and do the emotion thing," he adds after a second. "Make your happiness mine." At that moment, Nathan walks over to us. I glance at his concerned face and feel flush. "There it is," Mosif says with a smirk on his face.

"You seem to know an awful lot about me, Mosif," I exclaim while standing to greet my husband.

"He should," my Nathan says as he collects me in his arms. "When Uncle Malcolm was a pup, Aldiens were still one of the dominate species."

"Show some respect, boy," Mosif snaps at my Nathan. "Don't have to talk so clinical about your wife's people." My Nathan smiles then nods once in agreement. "Besides," Mosif continues. "If not for her mother, we'd probably all still be slaves of the Aldien's."

I glance at my Nathan and note that his confusion equals, if not surpasses mine. Mosif pats the chair that I left vacant. I return to my seat and Nathan pulls up a chair next to me. I take Mosif's hand and watch his facial expression closely.

"Slaves of the Aldiens?" I begin. "That doesn't sound right. I thought that the Aldiens were essentially good?" Despite the nightmare that I had the first night Nathan and I spent together. "Weren't they and the daemons the first races?"

"Not by a long shot, child," Mosif returns. "Fae, Elves, Dwarves…they all came and almost went before angels and daemons even started fighting each other. And Aldiens…" He smiles. "…somehow, the word got mangled over the centuries and became synonymous with angel. Probably because of their looks," he supposes. "They were all as beautiful as you and your mom…at least, the ones I met were."

He stares at me. "What?" I say as a laugh.

"You look exactly like her." I nod and smile. "My brother loved her so much…he would've done anything for her." His expression becomes serious. "I guess it runs in both families, eh?" Nathan puts his arms around me. "Anara," he murmurs.

I look to Nathan. "Anara?" I exclaim with excitement.

"Later, my love. We'll discuss it later." I smile and kiss him on the cheek. He was firmly against naming our daughter, Kya, after his mother…but I was hoping that he would not protest naming her after mine. I suppose we'll just have to discuss it later as he said… I look to Mosif and his curious smile. …when we're alone.

#####

Chapter 6: Specter

Alana stands there...in the middle of the room looking even more radiant than she normally looks. She appears to be glowing. An amazing tranquility seems to be streaming off her. She's happy, really and truly happy. Wait...who's that standing behind her. Whoever he is he feels wrong. He feels...empty...cold... He just feels...

"Malevolent," Nathan says taking a step past me. My eyes dart automatically between the two of them. "She's surrounded by it. It's some kind of malevolent force." Nathan looks at me. "You see something."

He isn't asking. "Someone," I confirm not able to take my eyes off the guy. Knowing Nathan, I just start in on the description. "He's tall...at least, six-two, vampire-pale, but he's definitely not a vampire. His jet-black hair is all messy chic, like he's a rock star or something. Whatever energy he's releasing...making him invisible...is covering his suit too." Nathan stares at me. "I can see it too. The pinstripes of his dark blue suit might as well be painted onto his narrow frame it's so well-tailored. He feels like a daemon..." I nod. "...but off, you know?"

"Then maybe we should step in," Nathan says, staring at his wife with intensity so strong that it's almost visible. I nod as he takes his first step toward her. The stranger takes a step closer to her. He appears to have tears streaming down his face...but they look like tears of blood. He's bleeding from his ears too. A little is drizzling out of his nose even.

"This is too weird," I breathe, as Nate sifts through the crowd. I stare at Alana and the phantom guest. "Wait," I call to Nathan. He doesn't even pause; he just keeps making his way through the guests. "He's saying something to her." Nate looks at me. "'Anara...why do you play at these games?'" I repeat the ghost's words. Nate looks at Alana. She seems to be able to hear him too.

The ghost raises his hands and places them on Alana's shoulders. She tenses all at once. "He's touching her," I snap. Nathan vanishes and reappears next to his wife. The ghost lets go and steps back.

"'You are not Anara,'" the ghost breathes taking a step back. "'You are some...pale imitation of her...her offspring.'" Alana's face crumples. She looks crushed. Nate takes her hand and puts his other hand on her back. He peers at the general area that the ghost is standing without being able to pinpoint him. The ghost glowers back at him. "'Sleep now, child,'" the ghost utters. "'Rest until I am able to determine what our next move will be.'"

With that, Alana falls backward. Nathan catches her. "ALANA," he practically screams. The crowd surrounds them. The ghost walks out of the room slowly, calmly. He's walking as though nothing happened. And everyone is walking past him like they really can't see him. I was right. Nathan couldn't see him. He could just detect the malevolence around him…the evil in his intentions, moving around his body. I peer at Nathan. He looks down at Alana…tears streaming down his face. His eyes flash gold and green. He looks at me and then looks after the ghost. I nod and run after the ghost.

He makes his way to the elevator. The doors shut just as I round the corner. I debate climbing into the other elevator. I head for the stairs, instead. It's weird. I can sense him. He is standing in the elevator, remaining perfectly still. I run at normal speed because I sense several humans coming up. I reach the bottom floor just in time to see him cross the lobby and head out the front door. He glances back at me and smiles. I guess the rain stopped. The clouds have even cleared away. The last rays of the sun shine through the large front windows of the building. I dash across the emptying lobby after him.

I hit the doors so hard that I swear the glass is going to crack. It holds thankfully. He wipes the tears away from his eyes, and the cloak that he was wearing vanishes along with the blood.

"Hey," I bark at him. He turns to face me. "What the hell did you do to Alana?" His brow furrows, and he leans in closer to me. "What's your damage? Back up or I stab you through the heart, and I don't care who's watching."

"You're…vampire," the ghost states like a question. I nod as my fingers curl around my knife. "But…the sun…"

"Is my problem, not yours," I growl. "Start talking before I start pounding on you like a brand-new set of bongos."

He takes a step back and smiles. His lips curl up over his perfectly white teeth. His long slender nose wrinkles slightly between his perfect emerald eyes. If I didn't want to stab him so bad, I might tell him how hot he is. "So," he begins taking my hand so quickly that I didn't realize until it was pressed against his lips. "The vampires have discovered the secret of daywalking again." I want to snatch my hand away from him, but I can't. It's not that I'm unable to…I just can't seem to make my arm transfer the thought into action.

"I'm one of a kind," I lie. My fingers tighten around my knife. "I'm the only one that can go out in the daytime." His tongue streams along the back of my hand. That does it. I take my knife out and swing at his mid-section. He vanishes. "How the hell…?"

"You are special," he calls from over my shoulder. "I am Balthazar. May I have your name…?"

He moves the hair away from my neck. I tremble. I can't believe how fast he is. The people walking around us didn't even realize he wasn't always standing behind me. I try my best to hide the knife from them. "An-Angela," I reply finally.

"Angela," he sighs. "That is a beautiful name for a beautiful woman." I swallow a massive lump. "You saw me, didn't you? Upstairs when I invoked my glamour, you could still see me clearly," he asks. I nod. "Well, well…isn't that surprising." He steps around me. "I want you to deliver a message for me. I came here seeking evidence about what happened to the Vampire King, Adamar and the Aldien, Anara…my brother and sister as it were."

"Brother and sister?" I squeak in confusion. "B-but, you're a daemon." He breathes a laugh against the exposed skin on my shoulder. His breath is warm, not nearly as warm as a wolf's breath is though. Soft strands of his hair tickle my ear. I have to fight the urge to smile by grinding my teeth together. "Anara…and I guess you mean, Alexi…they're both dead…her, for a little over a hundred years and him, about 7 months now."

"I felt as much, but I thought they were merely hiding from us again."

"Us?" I glance at him over my shoulder. "Again?"

His massive hands close around my shoulders. "As I said, I want you to deliver a message for me. Tell the happy couple, that I am one of the original eight members of En Quosque, which has apparently fallen to four once again. Two of my remaining brothers, one current and one who seems to have lost his way, were also in attendance at this celebration."

I gasp. "Who…?"

"Ah, ah," Balthazar laughs. "Trust me, knowing him, he'll tell you all when the time is right. You should let the happy couple know that we are merely the harbingers of His return. That is all." He steps around to face me again then peers up at the building. "If my suspicions hold true, that being that I encountered upstairs…she is the offspring of Anara and Adamar." I try to take a step back, but my legs won't move. "It's fine. I don't need you to confirm it. Besides, we have company. I'll be seeing you, gorgeous. Good day."

Between two ticks of a watch, Balthazar vanishes and Natavius appears in his place. "Where'd he go?" Natavius demands. I shake my head. "Damn it!" he barks. A few twitches of his nose, and he practically twirls in a circle. "His scent," he growls. "I can't pick up his scent." He turns to me. "Can you…?"

I shake my head frantically. Natavius leans into me. "What is that?" he grumbles moving down my arm. I shake my head again. Why can't I talk? My hand lifts quickly but without a violent jerk. Natavius's nose barely grazes the back of my hand. "What the hell is this smell?" he demands peering up at me.

A tremble makes its way up my back, remembering Balthazar holding my hand similarly. Natavius seems skittish now though. He's way jumpier than I've ever seen him. Why is Natavius acting like this though? Did something happen to…? "Is Alana okay?" I squeak out in one word. He takes one last look around and then nods.

"What happened?" Vance asks, stepping from behind the door at Natavius's back. Natavius looks at him for half a second. "Oh," Vance returns looking down. "We should regroup," he says waving the two of us over. Natavius bops on his heels twice and vanishes. I look around expecting him, or Balthazar to reappear…why would I expect Balthazar to come back?

#####

Chapter 7: Plan

"I'm fine," I tell my Nathan for the fifth time. He kneels in front of me, taking in my every breath. "I was overcome with emotions and…" I inhale deeply. "I suppose, I felt lightheaded…"

"Lana," he murmurs with that throaty, sexy bass. That voice makes me want to bite him, in the good way. "I sensed someone behind you before it happened…Angela's ability allowed her to see someone standing behind you."

"Ability?" Alpha Quinton says in a stern voice. I frown and look to my Nathan. His brow creases as well. "Don't worry," he renews. "No one's here except both of your inner circles and a few vampire magistrates and their entourages and wolf elders and theirs." He looks to Raven. "I'm sure everyone here knows how to keep a secret, right?"

"Aye," she returns in a purr. "So, tell us what really happened to ya."

"I heard a voice," I admit. "It was strange…I couldn't actually hear it with my ears. It was more like this person was speaking to my mind." I hold my hand in a claw over my heart…probably because that's how it felt before I fainted. "He said something about my mother…he thought I was her. I tried to sync with his emotions, feel him out more, but that was a ruse. He lured me in and then he hit me with an overwhelming desire to sleep." I shake my head and bow it until it collides with my Nathan's shoulder. "And so, I did."

"I warned ya about the dangers of ya empat'ic abilities."

"I know, I know." I nod, still resting my head against Nathan's shoulder, drinking in the intoxication of his scent. I lift my head and stare into his eyes. "I'm sorry that I frightened you."

He caresses my cheek. "As long as you're alright."

"Is she?" Angela asks, returning with Natavius and Vance.

"I'll be a lot better if you caught him." Her head sinks, and Natavius's does along with hers. "Oh," I purr.

"Are you though?" Angela continues. "Are you…?" She pauses, and her eyes flick downward for a moment as if to gauge my belly. "…alright?"

I swallow a lump, look to Quinton, and then settle on my Nathan. "Yes. Everything is fine. Everything."

"Good," Quinton says.

Nathan does not reply. He simply nuzzles his nose against my cheek. "What did you find out about him?" he asks without removing his face from mine. My eyes instantly return to Angela.

"Well, he's a daemon," she starts. "He has the ability to cloak himself by bleeding out of his orifices apparently."

"How could ya possibly know that?" Raven asks.

"It seems logical," she returns. "He wiped the blood away from his eyes, ears, and nose and then I could see, hear, and smell him as clearly as I'm doing with you guys. But he waited until he got outside to…"

"Outside?" the woman elder growls. Angela nods with a frown. "How could you go outside?" She points at the window. "The sun broke the cloud bank!"

Angela looks to Raven. She nods, but steps closer to her sire-daughter in a protective way. Angela follows by looking to Nathan, one of the two people, whose opinion matters to her as much as Raven's. He nods. Her eyes move to me. I choose to be different. I smile.

Angela sighs. "Okay, Elder Amelia…um…cards on the table and for the sake of catching this guy…um…I can walk in the sun without being burned." The wolves gasp except for Nathan's pack, Alpha Quinton, and Mosif…and oddly the older man speaking to him that I can't seem to read as vampire or wolf.

"Blasphemy," the woman elder snarls, drawing all focus back to her. Her eyes phase to a bright blue. Her canines and incisors descend from the top and rise from the bottom of her mouth. She's changing into the wolf.

Several of the other wolves nearby take similar positions including a younger woman, who bears a striking resemblance to the elder. "It's enough that we've had to put up with this farce of a marriage," the younger wolf says. Nathan growls. "…but this…this is too far vampire."

Natavius and Vance move between Angela and the approaching wolves. "Relax," Natavius says calmly. "We knew that she was a daywalker. We kept it a secret because she's harmless. She'd never hurt a human, and she's never even had a single drop of human blood."

Angela stares at Natavius, confused by his adamant defense of her. She wonders if he's the same lovable goof she's used to seeing. Her heart moves with him to a degree…that's good.

Vance steps forward with a calmer demeanor. "I can attest to that. This vampire has not drunk any blood that came from a human."

"And who told you that? Her magistrate?" the older wolf continues with a rumbling in the back of her throat.

I caress Nathan's temples. I lower myself a bit and whisper, "Perhaps, you should…"

"You two knew?" the younger wolf asks, pointing an accusing claw. Natavius and Vance nod. "That just makes the two of you as culpable…" She motions to Angela. "…as this freak is."

"She's nae a freak," Raven complains.

"Don't call her that," Natavius growls at the same time it rumbles from my Nathan's throat. "Don't EVER call her that," Natavius continues, sounding on edge.

"Boy," the elder continues.

"Boy?" Natavius snarls. "I'm older than you by almost two thousand years…"

The elder retreats a moment but stands firm. "You address an elder; my word comes second to the Alpha and only the Alpha. Step aside."

"Over my dead body," Natavius growls. Angela puts her hand on his shoulder causing him to extend his hand out to her protectively.

"Stand down!" Alpha Quinton barks. Every wolf, save my Nathan, winces and lowers their head. He turns to the elder wolf. "I knew about Angela's ability to walk in the sun as well," he lies. He glares at the elder wolf, towering over her. "Are you going to hold me culpable as well, Amelia?" He glares at the younger wolf. "Cassandra?" She swallows a lump and takes a step back.

Every wolf remaining seems to relax a bit more and move away from Angela. She steps around Natavius and looks him in the eye. "Thanks, man." He swallows a knot and nods. I can feel his emotions swirl intensely, then again so are Angela's… but hers are all over the place. She turns to the wolves. "Look, I didn't tell you guys this to start a fight. Truth be told, I didn't have to tell you at all."

I think her upfront and honest nature unsettles the wolves. She motions to herself. "I'm no threat to you wolves or humans…" She points toward the windows. "…but this daemon, Balthazar is."

Natavius winces at the sound of the daemon's name. Guilt swells in him, and he peers at the floor. I clear my throat. His eyes meet mine briefly. "Are you alright?" I mouth quickly. He nods and steps away.

"Think about it," Angela continues with her arms extended to her sides. "A daemon…strolled through a party filled with vampires and wolves…and only three people in the whole room even knew he was here…because I could see his aura…" She motions to Nathan. "…Nate could feel his malevolence…" She adds me. "…and Alana could feel his mind."

Angela shakes her head. "All of that and we barely got a glimpse of him…add to that, he's almost as fast as Natavius…and this guy is trouble." She sighs. "We have a common enemy to track down…and if you still feel like my daywalking will be a problem after that…" She nods. "…then we'll deal with that later, but only after this daemon is found."

"Well said," Alpha Quinton compliments. Angela nods. "Since Angela Price's conversion to a vampire, she has used all of her abilities to aid my…my brother and his wife…wolf and vampire. She has proven a friend to us wolves, and she speaks the truth now about our shared threat. So, let it be known…any wolf who does harm to her, does harm to your Alpha…is that clear?"

"Yes, Lord Alpha," the wolves bark in a chorus.

He nods firmly. "Any other information that you can share about him, Angela?"

She sighs. "Not really. I caught him near the entrance…he moved too fast for me to get a hand on him…told me his name…" She frowns and looks to me. "…and asked me to deliver a message."

"What message?" Nathan growls.

"He told me to tell the 'happy couple' that he and his brothers…are 'the harbingers of His return…and that he'll return once they've determined what to do with the offspring of Adamar and Anara.'" I shiver.

"En Quosque," my Nathan snarls.

"It would seem so," Raven says.

"The Claimed? That ancient organization?" Quinton says. "They're a legend. Nothing more."

"Well," Angela says. "One of those legends just waltzed through this reception as if it was nothing." Quinton yields a concession nod. "We have to find the others."

"We will," Nathan says, rising to his feet.

"No," Quinton returns. "You have your honeymoon to go on…we'll start the search."

"But…" I tug on my Nathan's hand. He turns to me. "…if they…"

"We have time," I say in what I hope is a soothing voice. "This…Balthazar…?" Angela nods. "…he said that he would return after he has discussed their next move with his brothers. I say we take this opportunity to NOT be here when he returns."

"I like t'e sound of t'at," Raven says.

"Me too," Richard adds.

"Other than Angela," Alpha Quinton says. "You two have the best chance of detecting him if he gets close."

"Then isn't that more of a reason that we should stay," Nathan protests.

Christopher takes Nathan by the shoulder. "Rule one," he says simply. Nathan sighs. "Besides…isn't it ANOTHER anniversary."

"Right," Nathan returns. "Arlington."

"What is in Arlington?" I ask.

"Trust me?"

"With my life." I stand and wrap my arms around him. His head bows, and his ear comes closer to my mouth. "With our lives," I whisper.

#####

Chapter 8: Party

"I can't believe we're still doing this," I complain, staring at my reflection in the gold tinted elevator doors.

"Alpha and Chief Magistrate's orders," Natavius says. "We act normal and continue with whatever we had planned until more information about…Balthazar and the evil cabal," he says with a sinister tone to his voice. "…emerges…" He straightens up and shoves his hands into his back pockets with a sigh. "…or at least, until Lana and Nate come back from parts unknown."

"Arlington's hardly unknown…"

"Ritual," Natavius says. "Nate goes to Arlington cemetery every five years on…" He points down for emphasis. "…this night since World War II… to visit a grave."

"Of course, he does," I complain. Oddly enough, even taking your new wife to a cemetery seems fitting with Nate.

"After Arlington, they'll be going on their actual honeymoon." I ignore the pit in my stomach on the word 'honeymoon.' He's her husband now…they're having a child together…you lost, Ange.

"You okay?"

"Yeah." The elevator dings, and the doors slide open. "Holy crap," I complain stepping out into the foyer at Meredith's house. I look around at the eggshell-colored walls with gold and rose-colored accents. The sick gold chandelier hanging from the ceiling looks like it costs more than mom's apartment in Brooklyn, paid in full thanks to my new sire-mom.

A heavy, hip-hop beat thrums from farther inside the penthouse apartment. Natavius and I walk forward slowly…cautiously. "Your invitation please," a guy… A quick sniff confirms human. …in a dark suit says. Natavius slips it out of his back pocket and passes it to the guy. He looks it over and scans it with a little wand reader.

"May I take your purse, ma'am?" another guy in a black suit says.

"Um, sure," I say and pass my clutch…with my knife inside…to him. He swaps it out for a ticket with the number 34 printed on it.

"Very good," the first guy says after the beep and motions toward the interior of the apartment. "Enjoy the party." Natavius nods and steps past him. I follow.

"I can't believe I let you talk me into wearing a skirt," I growl. He looks down at the little black number that Raven…more than likely she'll just tell me to keep, but for right now…loaned me. It stops just short of showing butt cheeks. As if he didn't get an eye full back at bio-mom's place. I wore black stockings underneath though and paired it with black ankle-high, heeled boots and a white sleeveless blouse.

"What?" Natavius purrs. "You look hot."

"I'll say," Matt Stensmore says, giving me the once over, with all the swagger of a high school quarterback, destined to fall from grace after graduation... I contain a snicker. ...complete with letterman jacket at a party. I mean, seriously, how cliché can one guy be?

"My aunt told me to stay away from you," I complain, pointing at his chest.

"You only have to stay away if you think I'm dangerous," he returns. This time, I work to contain vomit...well, blood.

"Wow, the ego on you. You're seriously flirting with me with my boyfriend standing..." I tug on Natavius's arm for emphasis. "...right here." If we're gonna keep up the charade, might as well play it to the bone as my dad used to say.

Matt leans in closer. "Yeah," he whispers, so close that I can smell his vodka laced breath as it bounces off my neck. "...but I don't really see you staying with some...what...? ...Indian...Arab guy?"

Natavius, having heard every word out of the little racist's mouth, shoves Matt away with one hand to the chest. "Watch yourself," he warns with a possessive sexy vibe. If I were any other 'high school girl,' we'd be looking for a closet for a major make out session right about now. "Come on," he grumbles with a hand on the small of my back.

"Bye, Todd," I say.

"Who's Todd?"

"It's Matt," Matt claims.

"I thought it was Todd," I tell Natavius.

"You know, he kinda looks like a 'Todd,'" Natavius returns.

"My name is MATT!" Matt snarls.

"So, sad about Jeremiah," I hear two girls whispering in a distant corner. The heavy smell of vodka cranberries wafting over from that direction.

"Yeah," another starts. "I heard they found him at the city dump. It looked like someone mugged him and cut his throat."

"Well, what'd you expect," one of the vapid blondes from Meredith's entourage complains. "...you know he lived in Queens or the eastside of Brooklyn or something. I mean, who from Queens can afford to go to Middleton, seriously?"

I start to storm over there to tell the little priss off, but Natavius catches my wrist. "Let's get a drink in you," he whispers. I pull against him. "Uh-uh, drink first, and if you still feel like biting the head off the blond squad, I won't stop you."

I sigh, and my head bows. I try not to let tears fill my eyes, but I can't help it. Every time I think about using my fangs or even someone mentions biting someone…Devon pops into my head. Well, Devon and the last thought I had before I passed out. "Fire."

"What?"

"I said, fine, but you know it has to be straight liquor…none of this vodka cranberry crap."

He nods and let's go of my wrist. "I know what to get you." He takes a step and pauses.

"I'll behave until you get back. Promise."

He points at me. "Do you have your knife with you?"

"In my clutch…" He arches his eyebrows. "…with the doorman, remember?" He nods and steps away to get my drink like a good fake boyfriend.

"So, he's your boyfriend now?" whispers an eerily familiar voice. I turn and…see nothing. I focus, and my ability kicks in…and the outline of a solid-colored, dark suit comes into view. He steps closer.

"You," I snarl.

"Balthazar."

"I know who you are. What are you doing here?" I look at Middleton Prep's students, spread out in this huge space, thankful that none of them are paying any attention to the blonde girl in the embarrassingly short skirt, talking to herself.

"Would you believe I came to see you?"

"Stalk me, you mean."

"Hmm, perhaps." He leans in closer. "But you seemed a bit more receptive yesterday."

"I was in a good mood yesterday. I just came from a wedding…I was the Maid of Honor," I say, trying to stall so that…

"Are you expecting Natavius to come back and save you?" I gasp. My eyes must have given me away. "How can he? He can't see or hear me." He points at my heart, just above the plunging neckline on my blouse. "Only you can." I swallow a lump. "I like that about you."

"Yeah," I return nervously. "Well, find someone else to stalk, I'm busy."

"Yes, I see." He checks the room. "Pretending to be…a high school girl."

"I AM a high school girl."

"No, you're not," he says in a laugh. "…not knowing anything else about you Angela, I know that."

"You remembered my name?"

"It's only fair. You remembered mine." He frowns. "Ah, but your 'date' is coming back. I'll leave you to your 'fun.' I just wanted to confirm that you could see and hear me at any time." I swallow another lump of dry nothingness. "I'll be in touch…Angela." He steps past me…his hand glancing off my hip and then across my stomach. His warm breath tickles my cheek with the scent of peppermint. I turn, and he's already gone.

"Hey," Natavius says, drawing my attention back to the right. "I got you a…" He offers me a glass of some clear liquor. I take it and down it before he finishes talking. "…shot of gin."

I pass him back the glass, as the alcohol burn subsides. "Another," I pant, throat still a little raw. He frowns but takes the glass and makes his way back through the mob. I sigh. Is this for real? Is some over 2000-year-old daemon stalking me now? It can't be. He has to have another reason for being here, right?

"Angela," Meredith says. I turn to her. She gives my outfit a once over. "Wow, you look hot!"

"Thank you," I say as dry as my gin tickled throat feels.

"Hey, is Anna…" She really gets a good look at me. "…are you okay?" I nod. "Tell that to your face."

I take a deep breath and try to collect myself. "I'm fine. Really. What's up?"

"I was gonna ask if Anna…"

"Alana," I correct her.

"…A-LAH-NAH," she stretches out. "…and Nate were really gonna skip out on my party."

"Can't be helped," I reply. "Family vacation…" Meredith frowns. "…his family…and they wanted her to come…something about a big announcement and they wanted her to share in it," I add, hoping that I'm laying down a foundation, in case Nate and Alana want to make it public knowledge that they're married and having a kid together.

Meredith nods, accepting this explanation. A Goth girl with pigtails walks up to Meredith. I don't recognize her. I don't think she even goes to Middleton.

"Meredith," the girl shouts over the music.

Meredith turns to her. "BETHANY! What are you doing here? Mom didn't tell me you were coming into town!"

"She doesn't know. I needed to get away from that hick town for a while." Meredith nods. "Can we go somewhere and talk?"

Meredith nods then turns to me. "Oh, right. Angela, this is my cousin from North Carolina, Bethany Sloane."

"I'm NOT from North Carolina, I'm just stuck in that stupid little town with all of its stupid little people," Bethany grumbles.

"Fine, fine," Meredith says. "This is my cousin who *lives* in Edenton, North Carolina, Bethany. Beth, this is Angela Price."

"Nice to meet you," I say, offering a handshake.

"Hmph," Bethany replies, proving that she really is Meredith's cousin. "Can we go?" Bethany says, tugging on Meredith's arm. She nods in response and the pair walk away...but as they do...my power kicks in...kicks in...? No, I think I forgot to switch it off from when Balthazar was here. Bethany's aura...matches Meredith's only it's bigger...more intense.

"Here you go," Natavius says. "One refill." He offers the glass. I take it from him without looking, still staring after Meredith and her creepy cousin. I down this one in one gulp too. "Geez," he complains, taking the glass from me. "This would be so much easier if I could move fast." He steps away.

I catch his arm. He pauses and comes back to me. "What?"

"Something's up," I say and follow Bethany and Meredith. Natavius follows me, giving the empty glass and his full one to James...can't believe his parents did this to him...Brown.

"Now, when you say something's up..."

"Balthazar was here!"

Natavius catches my arm and pulls me back around to face him. "What? Why didn't you tell me?"

"Bigger issues," I grumble between clenched teeth. "He's still playing it harmless...but the girl with Meredith..." I nod absently. I point to my eyes. "...she reads witch." He nods, begrudgingly and let's go.

We hurry and wade through the area clearly meant to be the dance floor, since a collection of sophomores and juniors have made it into a grind pit. "Ugh." Someone just grabbed my butt. Don't even look just keep walking, a life may be at stake.

"Wait," Natavius pants, catching my wrist again.

"What?" He scowls. No worse than that, his nose scrunched up. "What is it?"

"Vampires." He sniffs. "New Bloods at that." I point to myself. "No, I'm talking brand new."

I grit my teeth. "How'd they get in here? Wouldn't they need to be invited?"

"Maybe, they were." That does not help with the clenched jaw. "Divide and conquer. You go after Merrie and the witch; I'll handle the vampires."

"Handle?"

"If they're here to party, no problem. If they're here to *party*, problem." I nod, and he vanishes. I make my way through the rest of the crowd and kick my ability into high gear. I follow the trail that Bethany, if that's even her real name, left. It leads upstairs...weird. Crap, she has another security guy posted at the bottom of the stairs. I shove one of the Ambers as she walks by and her vodka cranberry spills all over the guy. She apologizes and flirts with him a little. He flirts back. Good for you, Amber E. I dart behind him and hurry upstairs.

I reach the second floor and follow the witch's trail…and Meredith's scent to…a cracked door at the end of a long, dark hallway. A faint yellow glow makes a line across the plush carpet. "Merrie," I whisper. A whimper comes from the lit room. I run down and peak in.

"MERRIE," I shout, busting in…to Bethany with her mouth inches from Meredith's. A deep purple mist moving from Meredith's open mouth to Bethany's. "WHAT ARE YOU DOING TO HER?" Bethany doesn't answer, but glares at me. Tears pour from Meredith's panicked eyes. I move over to them in a blur and punch Bethany in the face.

Bethany stumbles and releases Meredith, who I catch just before she hits the floor. "She…" Her voice sounds weak and creaks with dryness. "…nearly…drained me…dry." Her head slumps, and she blacks out. Her skin looks pale and feels rough to the touch. I tilt her head back, and her lips are pale blue. It's hard to believe this is the same girl I saw downstairs only a few minutes ago. I open her bloodshot eye, and her pupil doesn't dilate with the light.

"Merrie?" She doesn't respond. I listen…air rustles in her lungs, and her heartbeat thrums steadily. It's weak, but steady. I lay her down and stand when Bethany does. "What did you do to her?"

"What I've done to all my descendants, vampire," she replies.

"Oh, good…we know each other's secret." I nod. "That'll save some time, witch." Although, I really wanted to start that last word with a B. I reach for the small of my back…for my knife…that isn't there…because it's in my clutch…with the doorman.

Bethany smirks. "You don't stand a chance here, vampire."

"Can't blame a girl for trying."

"Flamma," Bethany snarls, and a palm-sized flame hovers above her open right hand. Weird. I feel the flame…not its heat, so much as it. It's like a living, breathing thing. I stare at it. "No need to be paralyzed with fear, vampire. I'll burn you to ash quickly. Save you the pain."

I nod absently, and she throws it at me. I open my right hand and whisper, "Flamma." The fire stops directly in front of my hand.

Bethany gasps. "That…that's impossible."

I turn my hand over, and the fireball holds above my hand just like it did with hers. "Says the witch to the vampire." She sneers at me. "Sorry, I'll have to give this back…since I didn't get you anything." I push my hand outward like she did, and the fireball flies at her only faster.

"Ugh," she ducks out of the way, and the fireball collides with Meredith's bed. It catches instantly. Bethany stares at it and then glares at me. "Extermino," she growls with her hand pointed toward Meredith. A stream of fire crawls along the carpet toward her.

"Damn it," I run over and scoop Meredith up, just before the fire reaches her. I turn and Bethany ducks out of the orange tinted room as the fire alarm sounds. Sprinklers spray the room, but that doesn't do much against the blaze.

This fire is calling to me, too…screaming at me. I move closer, extending my fingers slowly and Meredith groans in my arms. "Party pooper," I complain and dart out of the room with her, carrying her to safety…I hope.

"Natavius," I say at normal speaking volume, hoping he can hear me over the sound of our classmate's panicked screams. I hope that's because of the fire alarm and not because near-rabid vampires are biting their heads off.

"Yeah," he says back.

"I got Meredith, but that witch was doing something to her…draining her, I think."

"The newbie vamps were definitely here to party…the bad kind. I dealt with them. I was coming to help you when the fire alarm sounded. I smell smoke."

"Yeah, about that…" I look over the railing at the empty party. Natavius meets me at the second step from the top. "Here." I put Meredith in his arms. "It'll look less crazy if you're carrying her." He nods and hurries downstairs. I look back up the stairs. What just happened? Did I really catch and throw a fireball? Did I hear fire?

#####

Chapter 9: Responders

"How is she?" Natavius asks over his phone. The blue and red flashing lights throw their alternating hues across his face sequentially. I hug myself and look around before stepping closer. "No, not you," he says into the phone before I can get a word out. He tips his head toward me and then leans into the phone on his left ear.

"She's...um...gonna be okay." I keep walking, and he moves with me toward the end of the block, trying to get away from prying eyes and ears. We make our way past the last in a series of police cruisers, ambulances, and fire trucks... I guess, when your family's name is on a building or two in New York, they pull out all the stops.

I turn to Natavius. "The paramedic says it looked like she's suffering from severe malnutrition and dehydration...which we wrote off as a crash diet...add to that the smoke inhalation and..." I bob my head unevenly. I shiver. "Her pulse was so weak, Natavius."

He frowns. "Wha..."

"If I was just a couple of seconds later..." I don't even like Meredith, but I can't stop the tears. "...she would've been..." I cover my mouth as one slips away and then another.

"Come 'ere," he purrs, motioning for me to come closer. I do, and he wraps me up, the fingers of his free hand winding through my wavy, wet hair. "You're okay," he whispers and kisses me on the temple. I nod, before nuzzling in just under his chin. The tears disagree with both of us because they just keep coming. "What's going on with you lately? You've been kinda..." I look up at him. "...well, kinda weepy since you and Nate got back from Paris. Did something happen between...?"

I sigh and shake my head.

"Come on, you can talk to me about anything. You know that, right?"

"I killed someone," I blurt out. His frown intensifies. Is he angry? Does he think...? "That's how the ritual works. I had to kill a higher order daemon...and drink him dry..."

"You HAD to...?"

I nod, and his hand slips back into my damp hair, until his palm holds the back of my head. He pulls me into him until my forehead rests on his collarbone...in terms of hot guy consoling moves...this was THE move. I can honestly say I've never felt so...supported by a guy before who wasn't my dad. I wrap my arms around his waist...but another shiver rips up my spine. Devon's face...his human face flashes through my mind...just before I sank my fangs into his throat.

"...he just looked like a regular guy though," I weep. "I'm no better than that witch who tried to drain Mer-"

He steps back, hand moving away from my head. I stumble forward, thrown by the sudden separation. Feeling a little abandoned honestly. I look into his eyes, and he looks pissed all over again.

"Don't EVER say that!" he growls, his eyes phasing a brighter shade of brown. I sniff, just before he wipes a tear away with the side of his hand. I shudder from the warmth of his touch. "Do you think that witch is crying over what she did to Meredith?" I shrug. "Do you think she even cares if Meredith survived?"

I shake my head. He's right...she didn't seem to care at all...and Meredith said that that girl was her cousin.

Natavius steps closer again...like...close enough to kiss me. Is he going to? Why did my mind go there? His head tilts and mine tilts in response. "You're a vampire," he whispers, his warm breath dancing off my lower lip. "That witch was a monster!"

"You sound like my sire-sister," I pant in a laugh.

He smiles, and his focus moves back to his phone. "Natavius?" a voice grumbles on the other end.

"Yeah?"

"You said the girl's name was Bethany Sloane, right?"

He looks at me. I nod. "Yeah, Bethany Sloane is what her 'cousin' said her name was." I unconsciously nibble the tip of my thumb.

"Well, according to my guy," the voice continues. "...a high school student named Bethany Sloane has been exchanging emails with Meredith Sloane." The voice pauses, and the line goes silent. He exhales and then continues, "...most of their correspondences have talked about Meredith's summer plans...if she was traveling and the like..."

"Keeping tabs on her?" Natavius suggests. I nod.

"That's what I was thinking too," the voice continues. "The IP address that this Bethany was emailing from...originated in...Edenton, North Carolina..."

"Edenton, North Carolina," Natavius says. "Never heard of it."

"I have," I admit in a sigh. "My cousin Meghan lives there with her mom." I shake my head. "Wait...and that witch...that witch...and that guy that Nate and I ran into in New Orleans, they're from there, too."

"Ask her the witch's name," the voice says.

"Christopher, she's a vampire. She can hear you just as well as I can."

I focus on the memory of that ebony haired bombshell as best I can. "...um...Baggett...yeah, Daphne Baggett, is what she told Nate her name was 'now.'"

"Doesn't ring any bells," Christopher returns. "I know a Daphne McCabe…who is a very power Witch of Light…but…"

"Maybe, she got married," Natavius says. I purse my lips.

"Probably," Christopher adds.

"Daphne Baggett," I start again. "She was with a guy…a super-hot guy…"

"Super-hot guy?" Natavius asks dragging it out with his eyebrows arched. I shrug, feeling a little guilty for some reason. I don't know when Natavius looks at me sometimes, like he's looking at me right now, I feel different…I feel… I don't know. …like if things were different…maybe…

I shake my head trying to get rid of the random thoughtness. "…yeah, the guy…Nate knew the guy too…but he seemed surprised that he was there…maybe, he thought the guy was dead or something. I didn't think to ask. Maybe, the guy was her husband…" I frown. "…no, that can't be right. He looked like he might be twenty at best, and she had to be every bit of thirty-two or thirty-three." I nod. "What was that guy's name? Um…um…Qu…Quincy?"

Christopher gasps. "His name was Quincy? Was he tall? Dark hair? Lots of muscles?"

"I'll say," I breathe unconsciously. Natavius huffs. I ignore him and push through. "Yeah. Who is this guy?"

"Well, that proves our suspicions were right," Christopher says. "Whatever we're going to find out about this witch…apparently, it's in Edenton. That's where we'll find Daphne and Quincy…" Christopher groans. "…hopefully, not Tony though."

"Who's Tony?"

"Oh, that Quincy," Natavius says. "Quincy and Tony…pair of daemon brothers…"

"He's a daemon?" Natavius nods. "I didn't get that impression from his aura…in fact…" I think back. I remember his aura, almost as red as the woman who was with him. In fact, his aura was warmer than hers was. "…he read witch to me…"

"They're transubstantiated fae," Christopher says. "Their mother was a shaman in the 1800s, and their father was a daemon that was trying to become fae."

"What?"

"Their father was a daemon who fell in love with a human witch. He made a deal with a powerful being to guard a town. In exchange, he'd become fae. Their father bound them to that town in his stead…shortly before he died. Tony manages to get out every few decades with the aid of a witch."

"How do you know so much about these guys?"

"Once upon a time," Natavius jumps in. "Tony and Nate were best friends."

Christopher continues, "On one of Tony's escapes, he and Nathan created a group of daemon and vampire hunters together." I groan. "Don't worry. They investigated before killing."

I nod. "Sounds like Nate."

"Well, he and Nathan had a falling out over a young fae, who wanted to join them. Nathan read her aura or whatever and said that malevolence followed her..." I swallow a lump...that's why he left Alana because malevolence surrounded her. "...Tony insisted on keeping the child-fae with them, and Nate left the group...actually, splitting the entire group."

"It was pretty rough," Natavius says, scratching his head. "He came back to New York for a few days...didn't even tell us he was here until he was leaving again." He shakes his head and looks at me. "I only barely got the whole story."

"Either of you ever meet these brothers?"

"No," Christopher says as Natavius shakes his head.

"Okay. So, what's our next move?"

"I don't know," Christopher admits. "We should get this information to the Alpha and Chief Magistrate ASAP. No matter what, we should probably wait until Nate comes back to move on it."

"Really? Why?"

"He lived in Edenton for a while," Natavius says. "He said something always seemed off about that town, but he couldn't figure out what it was..."

"I think we're gonna have to figure it out..." I turn to the ambulance, pulling away slowly, carrying Meredith to the hospital. "...and sooner rather than later."

#####

Chapter 10: Foraging

"Is this going to work?"

"Not if you keep talking, love," Nathan whispers.

"Alright, but I don't see the point."

"Shhh." He peers through the shrubbery again. We have been nestled in these woods for nearly two hours and…

"…we did not fly to the Canadian wilderness to hunt; we came here to enjoy our honeymoon."

"You're welcome to leave if you want to, Princess."

I huff. "You know that I have no idea where we are."

"Exactly," he whispers. "Raven told me that you've been 'given' blood every time you've fed."

"Not EVERY time." I think back on the two dogs that I fed on in New York…and of course, Jeremiah, the vampire hunter who befriended and fell in love with me. I sigh.

My Nathan nods. "I want you to learn to hunt with a clear conscience." I frown. "Think of it like this, there are mountain lions all over this area." He motions toward the bush with the four fingers on his right hand. I gaze through the hedge and find a doe, sipping from a small stream. "If not us, more than likely one of them will eat this little guy."

I return to my Nathan. "Girl."

He smirks. "Or a hunter, who won't even eat her most likely."

"That is horrible."

"It's actually helpful." He stares at the doe again. He pulls his shirt off over his head. "If not for hunters, they may overpopulate. Some would starve to death, and others would migrate to areas populated by humans in search of food." He shakes his head while unfastening his trousers.

My eyes swell. He blushes and holds on is disrobing efforts. "We are married now," I whisper. "You can undress in front of me."

"Where's the fun in that?" His eyes phase to honey and emerald. His flesh ripples and erupts with reddish-brown fur. He goes down on all fours, stepping out of his trousers along the way. He shakes himself out, and his tail sways from side to side.

"Spoil-sport."

He looks at me and huffs a wolf-laugh. His eyes narrow as the sound of a heartbeat picks up. He returns to me. I nod, and he does as well. He darts through the hedge…catching the doe completely unaware. He catches her by the neck and slams her down to the ground. The birds clear the area, their songs becoming panicked flights. Several other, smaller animals scamper away quickly. He could have had any of them given his stealth, speed, and power.

He growls. I look at him standing over the creature. He motions for me to come closer. Admittedly, he didn't have to…the moment I caught the smell of blood in the air, our daughter forced me to go to it instantly. I sink my fangs into the wound he created. The warm blood tastes sweeter than any other animal blood I've had, but not as good as human sadly. Our daughter seems happy all the same, and that's all that matters to me.

"Ah," I hum standing and wiping my mouth. I settle into the rush of blood restoring me…restoring us. I throw my head back and lick my lips. I remember when I used to be embarrassed by the thought of Nathan seeing me feed. I lower deep blue eyes to the wolf I love. Not anymore…never again. I take a deep breath as the blood flows through me…our daughter moves about happily. "I have had my…our fill, my Nathan."

He bows his head and whines. "You watched me eat, why can I not watch you?" He whines again, and this time, my only response is an arch of my brow. He sighs and raises up. He bares his fangs and bites into the deer's side. He snaps off a large chunk of fur, flesh, and blood…and…oh no…now, I know why he did not want me to see…he…

He stops eating as I turn away. I cover my mouth. "No…" I manage. "…finish…I'm feeling…" I run back to our original hiding place and lose a good portion of the blood I just drank. Nathan's head parts the brush. "I'm fine," I breathe and wipe my mouth again. "Queasy." He nods with a huff. "And by the way, calling it 'morning' sickness is a gross misrepresentation." He wolf-laughs again. "They should call it, 'any time that it feels like descending upon you and wreaking havoc on your bloody day' sickness." I rub my forehead. "Have you eaten enough?" He nods. I return the gesture.

His fur ripples and quickly recedes back into his skin as he stands. He picks up his pants and his trousers. "Not so fast," I moan, pushing him against a tree. I undo the buttons on my blouse. He smiles and kisses me. He still has some of the deer's blood on his lips. Despite my queasiness from just a moment ago, it tastes…

"Ugh," I grumble, stepping back.

"Still queasy?" he whispers. I shake my head. My eyes phase silver, causing his to move to honey and emerald again instantly. *What is it, Love?*

I am picking up emotions…

I don't hear anything. He sniffs. *Or smell anything.*

I know. I think our daughter has better empathic abilities than I do.

He nods and dresses quickly. *What type emotions are you picking up?*

Why do you think we're communicating like this, my love? He nods again.

Click. A twig snaps. My Nathan grabs my hand and runs in the opposite direction. I keep up as best I can…even though we're not running at full speed…not the way Natavius taught us. Even like this…I pant. Nathan ducks behind a tree.

"Are you alright?"

I nod. "She takes a lot of energy. I can't imagine what my mother went through with me." He sighs and presses his forehead against mine. "No," I grumble, before he can even say it.

"You have to," he replies to the start of a conversation we no longer need to have out loud anymore.

"I am NOT abandoning you, you silly wolf."

"Listen, Princess," he growls. "You're not allowed to make that call anymore." I scowl. "You are carrying our daughter with you." I touch my stomach. "Which means that her safety and consequently yours come before mine."

"I am carrying the baby, aren't I?" He nods. "Promise you won't kill any of them, if you don't have to."

He steals a quick peck. "I promise…nothing." He vanishes. I sigh and hurry back the way we came, thankful that I caught his scent from when we originally made this trek. I pant and puff. If our daughter takes this much out of me and we're only now approaching the three-month mark…how much sustenance will she need at six? Nine?

"No," I lament, catching more emotions ahead of me and with the benefit of being downwind, I catch scents as well. They are human, but they all smell like Jeremiah. Six of them in all. "Hunters," I whisper. I peer back the way Nathan left. I duck behind a tree, trying to catch sight of them.

"Careful," a young woman's voice says. "She was headed this way."

"Then shouldn't you be quiet?" a man's voice grumbles.

"She's downwind of us," the girl growls back. "If anything, she smelled all of us coming and that's why she stopped. Now, fan out…and if you encounter her, do not engage alone."

I feel queasy again. "Not now, my beautiful girl," I whisper and caress my stomach. "Not now…"

An assault rifle's muzzle passes by…and the vampire hunter carrying it soon after. I grab the barrel and kick him in the diaphragm, knocking the air out of him. I then punch him in the face, before using the gun…with its strap wrapped around him…to pull him around and ram him into the tree. He falls unconscious.

I pant wildly. That took far too much energy.

"Report in," the girl says.

"Avery, here," a woman says.

"Martinez, check," a man says.

"Gooding, here," another man says.

"Fuller, good," the man who argued with their leader says.

There is a breath of silence. "Williams?" the girl calls.

"I think, Williams is down," Martinez says.

"Martinez, Gooding, you were closest to his position. Check it out." I swallow a lump and move away from Williams. I hurry down the slope, moving back toward my Nathan and the other vampire hunters no doubt.

"Harper," Gooding says. "We found Williams."

"Is he dead?" their leader asks.

"No," Martinez says. "Just unconscious…" Martinez pauses. "…he's not even bitten. Ma'am, what kind of vampire doesn't bite."

"The smart kind," Fuller grumbles. "If she'd bitten him, we could follow the scent of his blood back to her. She's been out here long enough that her scent's blending with the woods." I sigh in relief. "But not the sound of her breathing," Fuller follows from right next to me. He swings a blade at me, and I duck. I stumble and slide down the hill covered in decaying, muddy leaves.

I swallow a lump as I come to a stop. "Martinez, Gooding," Harper yells. "Move to Fuller's position. I'll join ASAP. Avery, check on Williams."

"Ma'am," Martinez, Gooding, and Avery bark.

Fuller moves toward me, pulling a semi-automatic pistol from his holster. "Neat little trick I learned," he brags. "Throw your voice effectively and you can make even the best vamp think you're somewhere you're not."

Like Williams and Jeremiah, he's completely covered in black riot gear and goggles, which means my compulsion is useless. My stomach rolls. Our daughter feels my fear and multiplies it. I hyperventilate, while crawling away.

"Awwww…don't run, you dirty stinking vamp. I'll make it quick. I promise." I shiver. He means it…there is no emotion coming from him. He regards me with as much compassion as he would a target on a practice range.

"Fuller?"

"Over here," he says.

Two others, Martinez and Gooding, join him. They have their assault rifles trained on me. I pant. Ordinarily, I would try to be brave…I would try to face them with dignity…but it is not my safety, I'm concerned with.

"Please," I beg. "I have done nothing wrong…I fed on a deer only moments ago. I have never harmed a human, nor would I."

"Nothing wrong, it says," Fuller says to his fellows. They chuckle. "Sweetie, being a vampire is all the wrong you needed to do." He stares down the barely of his gun at me.

"And being an idiot is all the wrong you had to do," my Nathan says. He appears in a blur and shoves the one on the left so hard that he knocks the other two down.

They scramble to recover. Nathan kicks the nearest one in the side, sending him crashing into a tree several feet away. Martinez or possibly Gooding, readies his rifle. Nathan catches it, twists it outward, and grabs the man. He slams him to the ground and punches him in the face. He tosses his rifle aside. I move over to it.

Fuller rises and draws his knife again, having lost his gun. "I'm gonna enjoy this," he brags. "Two vamps for the price of one."

He swings at Nathan and rather than avoiding, my Nathan punches him in the face. Fuller staggers back.

"I'm not a vampire," my Nathan growls with honey and emerald eyes.

"What?" Fuller barks, never noticing me sneaking up behind him. I hit him with the butt of the rifle, knocking him unconscious. I toss the weapon away.

"Did you kill any of them?" I whisper.

"No," he moans, wrapping his arms around me. He kisses my cheek before kissing my lips. I inhale deeply. I almost lost this…my family. "I had already knocked out four of them, when I got your telepathic S.O.S."

"Mine?" He nods. "Nathan, I didn't call for help." We part.

He stares at my belly then kneels and kisses our daughter. "Thank you for saving your mother and yourself."

I sigh. "What were these hunters doing here? Were they looking for me?"

"Let's find out," my Nathan says, waving a radio at me. I frown. "I copped it from him." He tilts his head toward Fuller. "Hold this." He gives it to me. He scoops me up and carries me further down the hill.

"Fuller?" Harper whispers behind us. Nathan ducks behind a tree and lowers me to my feet. "Martinez? Good…" She breaks off. She groans a sigh. "Amateurs," she barks. She must have found them.

"Harper, come in," comes from the radio in my hand and Harper's location. Nathan grits his teeth and instantly, turns a knob on top of the radio. "Harper, come in," the voice repeats, but only from Harper's location. "Team Two, come in," the voice demands.

"Harper, here, sir. Over," she replies begrudgingly. I think she heard our radio and hoped to pinpoint our location.

"Sit rep. Over."

Harper sighs. "Fuller, Martinez, Gooding, and Williams are down, sir. Over."

"Dead?"

"No, sir. Unconscious. Over."

"Same on our end."

"Sir, what kind of vampire knocks people out? Is that why our orders were to bring her in alive?"

Nathan scowls and bears his fangs, canines and outer incisors. I put my hand on his chest, and my eyes flash over in silver. I shake my head subtly, and he nods.

"That's not our concern, Harper. For now, hunker down and get your people on their feet."

"But sir…the target…"

"…is NOT more important than your men, Harper! Is that understood?"

"Yes, sir, Commander Baggett, sir."

"Over and out."

Harper sighs. "I know you're out there, and you can hear me. You've been given a pass…I recommend you take it."

Nathan plucks the radio out of my hand and tosses it far away. He sweeps me up again, and his eyes phase honey and emerald…only this time, the whites of his eyes slowly give way to black. They've only done that when he fought Jeremiah after he kidnapped me. We move…not at all at a human pace. We move the way Natavius taught us.

We reach the cabin in no time, the woods a blur behind us. My Nathan pants wildly. Moving that fast while carrying someone still takes far too much out of him. I caress his cheek as he lowers me to the ground. "Are you alright?"

He nods, still breathing heavily. "Pack. We…have to…" Pant. "…get out of here."

"Do you think they'll track us here?"

"I know they will," he breathes wearily. "I recognized that voice over the radio. James Baggett…he was a part of my group of demon and vampire hunters a few years back." I nod. "Never knew he was a hunter-hunter."

"Rest," I breathe, pulling him toward the cabin. "I'll pack." I drag him inside and lay him down on the sofa. I hurry about our temporary bedroom gathering our belongings, including his wedding ring that he left behind. I carry our bags to the auto… "No," I whine realizing how close to dawn it is.

I hurry back into the cabin. "Nathan…Nathan…wake up!" He snores. "Nathan…please! I don't know if I'm strong enough to carry you, and the sun will rise soon!" He groans and rolls over. I take his face in my hands and hold my forehead to his. "Nathan, please…we will be trapped here if we don't move…now!"

"Ugh," he groans…his eyes flutter open. "Alright," he sighs. He stands, wobbly on his legs, but lumbers over to the door. He pulls it open…and sunlight breaks the tree line.

"NO," I wail, and he wraps me up with his back to the invading light. Strange, I still feel sunlight against my forehead…but it doesn't burn. "Nathan." I tap his hips. "Nathan?" He releases me. I look past him at the sun…shining on my face. I gasp. I hold my hand up to the light to be certain.

He glances between the sunlight and me with a frown. "How?"

I shake my head. "Our daughter," I gasp. "Her blood…is seventy-five percent non-vampire…which means…"

"Which means we should get you to the car, quickly." I nod as he walks with me to our Range Rover. He helps me inside and quickly moves to the driver side. He starts the automobile and peels away quickly, kicking up dust and rocks. He peers at me…still staring at my hand, hanging from my open window…not burning in the sun.

"Alana." I look at him as happy tears move away from my eyes. "I know, but…there's the possibility that you're feeding on our daughter to maintain this immunity to the sun." I swallow deeply and nod. I raise the window.

"We'll…" He looks at me, as we pull onto the main road. "…we'll have Vance examine you when we get back to New York." I frown. "If that's okay?"

I take his hand, still resting on the plotter. "Of course. I trust Vance."

He nods and pulls my hand up to his mouth. He kisses it. "We will protect our family."

"No matter what," I join. He nods once firmly and pushes harder on the accelerator.

#####

Chapter 11: Departure

"How have I never realized just how comfortable Raven's couch is until now?"

Nathan caresses the side of my head lovingly. "That's because you've never just come back from your honeymoon cut short because you had to flee for your life from a group of vampire hunters only to rest your head in your adoring husband's lap."

I stare into his warm brown eyes. "Yes," I breathe. "I suppose that would do it." He smiles. "Aside from wanting, but understanding my reluctance, to run several dozen additional examinations…Vance said that *everything* is fine."

Nathan nods. "I figured it would be, but…"

"You wanted to be sure." He nods again. "Good. So, did I." He holds the tips of his ring and middle fingers to his lips and then presses those same fingers to mine. I purr as he strokes my hair again. I am exhausted, so I can only imagine how he feels. He hasn't slept since I woke him…and… I sigh.

"What is it, Love?"

I shake my head. He frowns. "I was wondering if it is permanent or simply a result of…everything."

"If it is only temporary…you could always go through with the ritual."

I shake my head. "I don't think I could bring myself to kill anyone…unless forced to."

He groans. "Forced to…that pretty much describes what Duchess did to Angela."

I subdue a groan of my own. He says her name so delicately. He knows how she feels about him…and possibly, worse…she knows exactly how he feels about her. She has a place in his heart…I don't think he'd every risk what we have for her, but… I sigh. …he has a connection to her. It's deep and profound. Worst of all…

Raven's office door swings in. "Well, you were the one who wanted dessert, so we had to wait," Angela says to Natavius directly behind her.

…I can't even hold it against her and not because she's so ridiculously sweet…but because despite how she feels about him…

"Oh," she whispers, seeing the two of us. "You guys are back. No wonder we got the emergency texts." She nods and shoves her hands into her jumper pockets. "So, how was the…honeymoon?"

I smile. …she is the reason this happened. I am certain Nathan, and I would have resolved our issues eventually, but she helped speed things along tremendously.

"Great," Nathan says. "Until we were attacked by a group of vampire hunters."

"The Eye of Ezekiel Order?" Natavius asks. My Nathan nods and glares at Natavius. They exchange something in this look. I feel anger swelling in my Nathan and guilt emanating from Natavius.

"What's that?" Angela says.

"The Order is…," I begin.

"No, Natavius told me all about the vampire hunters. I was…" She motions between Nathan and Natavius. "…asking, what was that?"

"Nothing," they lie, looking away from each other. Angela's eyes meet mine with a matching frown.

The door swings in again. Raven marches in, followed by Christopher and Vance. Raven goes to her desk and sits. Vance stands next to her. Christopher reclines on the near side of her desk and straightens his cuffs.

"We apprised Raven of our findings," Christopher says.

"So, everyone's up ta speed, ya?" Raven asks. I nod and so does Nathan. Angela crosses her arms and glares at Natavius, who has his back to us.

"Yes," Quinton's voice comes in clearly. Christopher places a tablet on Raven's desk. I smile, taking in Quinton's warm smile. "Nathan…Alana…" He leans closer. "…how is…everything?"

"Fine," I say. "We're…" I gently caress my stomach. "…fine."

"Good." He leans back. "Chief Magistrate, I leave Nathan and his pack under your vigilance. I have a lead on the vampire and the fae of En Quosque. My son, Quinn, and I are in Japan…attending a wedding celebration. Thanks for the tip, Raven."

"Yer welcome."

"Take care of yourselves…and each other." Quinton reaches for the screen. "Alpha Quinton out." The screen goes dark. Christopher lies the tablet flat.

"Very well," Raven starts, clasping her hands together. "Wit' t'at…I t'ink it's probably the best strategy to have Nat'an follow up on t'is witch."

"Makes sense," he growls. He looks down at me. "James Baggett is from the same town as Quincy and Tony, the daemon brothers. I wonder if he even knows what's going on there since we saw Quincy and Daphne…James's wife…in New Orleans."

"Wait," Angela says. "I don't think we put that one together. So," she pauses to count off one finger. "…Daphne and Captain Gorgeousness were in New Orleans for what reason we still don't know."

"Captain Gorgeousness?" I ask.

"Yes," Natavius grumbles. "Apparently, she thinks Quincy is attractive."

Angela shrugs, ignoring the venom in Natavius's voice and continues. "The witch I fought, Bethany is living there…stealing my shtick of playing a high school senior, and we just happened to see both in the span of five months."

"Coincidences like this can't be ignored," Vance says.

Christopher and Raven exchange a look, and she nods. "Christopher has arranged a meetin' between me and the local leader of the Order." Natavius half-turns to them before glancing at Nathan. "We want ta understand t'e reason so many a' t'eir hunters have taken a 'shoot first, questions later' stance on vampires."

"And if they want war," Christopher says, crossing his arms. "We're more than happy to give them one. No one attacks my family." My eyes meet his. I mouth a 'thank you.' He smirks and nods.

"Hopefully, it won't come to that," Vance says. "But as a sign of good faith, Christopher and I will accompany Raven and the twins to this meeting."

"Nathan," Christopher picks up. "We figured you'd be the best person to go to Edenton and find out what's going on there."

My Nathan moves uncomfortably and bows his head. "What's wrong, my love?" He shakes his head. My eyes flash silver causing his to reciprocate in honey and emerald. *Love?*

That town has a persistent presence. I can't put my finger on it. It's not exactly malevolent, but it's definitely not benevolent either. It's always there, and it's always watching…waiting.

"I still think that Natavius should go with him," Christopher continues a conversation that Nathan and I missed.

"Well, we could send Angela," Raven says. Angela looks at us. A wave of pain washes over me. Why would Raven wish to torture her own sire-daughter like that?

"If we're going that route," Christopher starts. "Then we might as well send…"

"Alana can't go," my Nathan grumbles as if reading my mind.

"What?" Christopher asks. "Why not?"

"Because she's under my observation," Vance says with a quick wink for me. "They used some sort of chemical agent on her out in the woods, and it has left her vampiric abilities impaired. I need to study her blood work and see if I can create an antigen or possibly a vaccine."

"Fine," Christopher submits. "I'm still not in agreement that two of the people who can detect this invisible daemon are going…but…"

"It makes t'e most sense," Raven admits. "Nat'an knows t'e brothers and t'is witch, Daphne…and perhaps, he can use t'at connection to gain some insight on her husband's activities."

Angela nods. "And I know the town…I visited my cousin, Meghan, and her mom a couple of times a few years back."

"Natavius," Raven starts. "I want ya to stay here…stick close to Alana. Ya may not be able ta see t'is daemon, but wit' her senses and yer speed, it could bridge the gap." Natavius looks at me and nods.

"Is this okay with you, love?" my Nathan asks. "I mean, we only just got married and…" His eyes move to Angela and return.

I sigh. "It is not ideal…considering we are still on our honeymoon." I nod. "But it is the most logical move."

"Then you can leave immediately," Christopher says. "I've booked you a flight leaving JFK in two hours. It won't take much work to change the ticket from Alana to Angela."

"I have to pack," my Nathan says. "We have to pack." I frown. "I don't want you staying at the apartment alone. You should stay here with your sister and her coven until I get back."

"There's no room for me anymore, Nathan. With the addition of Mona and the new blood that Angela captured a few weeks ago…" I shake my head.

"You can stay in Angela's room until she returns," Raven offers, much to Angela's shock.

"Yeah, you can take my room," Angela says. "Not like I'll be using it…and it was your room so…" She nods.

"Then we all have our marching orders," Christopher says. "Let's get to it." The door slams, and Natavius is already gone. Vance walks over to Christopher, and they start a conversation. Angela talks to Raven quietly as well.

"Walk with me," Nathan requests. I nod and lift my head. He stands and helps me to my feet. We step out into the foyer and quickly make our way outside. We head toward the marker where Alexander once lay. I reach out and take his hand then intertwine our fingers. He pulls my hand up to his mouth and kisses it, but he's trembling…uneasy.

"Nathan? Are you alright?"

"No."

"What is it…?"

"If I go…then…" He steps in front of me. "I feel like I'll be abandoning you…again." His fingers seem to vibrate against mine. I can see the internal struggle tearing him up despite his attempts to block his feelings. I place my index finger on the back of his hand. I trace the lines of his knuckles. His skin doesn't feel warm to me anymore. It feels almost the same temperature as mine. My eyes drift lazily from his hand to his face. He's staring at me with screaming honey and emerald eyes.

I smile. "No, you won't, because this time I know what is going on. I understand that you have to go and…" I put one hand on the bottom and the other on the top of my swollen stomach. "…I can't go with you this time." He places his hands on the sides of my stomach. "Besides…," I look down at our hands embracing our unborn child. "…I have you here with me still."

"Always," he says with a smile wrinkling the corners of his eyes. "I love you, Lana…I love you both so much."

"I know," I exclaim as my arms wind their way around his waist. His hands move seamlessly up to my face. "I love you too, Nathan…my Nathan." I smile again sheepishly. "Our Nathan," I breathe onto his kissably close lips. We kiss. I purr as we part.

"You know," I resume. "We should start thinking of names for her soon. I've been thinking of her simply as 'our daughter' for weeks now." He nods. "I was thinking…are you certain you don't want to name her after your mother…Kya?" He frowns. "What's wrong with your mother's name? You can pay homage to her memory…as a proud skinwalker and chief's daughter."

He shakes his head. "Nothing, but I was thinking that…your mother's name would be more appropriate…Anara." He nods. "She'd have quite a legacy to live up to…she's seen as a bit of deity to my people."

I inhale deeply. "That is a rather large legacy to have our daughter live with. Why don't we compromise? We'll give her both names…Kya Anara Dumont."

He shakes his head again. "What about Anara Kya Dumont?"

"Well, I'm carrying her so…I choose the order of the names."

He laughs. "You are carrying her, aren't you?" I nod and mouth a 'yes.' "Very well, Princess, but…I'm still calling her Anara."

"…and I will call her Kya, and we will see which she prefers."

"Deal." Suddenly, emotions rush over me, and tears cascade down my face. "Love, are you…?"

"I'm fine. It's just…" I huff a laugh with more tears accompanying it. "…we just named our daughter…Princess Kya Anara Dumont." He nods and kisses me. I wrap my arms around him and enjoy the kiss…before he goes away…again…

#####

Chapter 12: Intruder

Now, where did Natavius go? I wanted to talk to him, and he said he'd hang out for…I sniff. That's weird. I smell food…human food. Alana's outside with Nate, so I know it's not a pregnancy craving. Vance and Christopher…and apparently, Natavius…have already left, so nobody else would be…I follow the scent toward the dining room.

I throw the black lacquer-covered double doors open and walk into the dining room, looking around…Demetri, Kyle, and Liz are playing cards at the far end of the long, black dining room table. They look at me. I frown and keep checking the room.

"Is something wrong?" Demetri asks. I shake my head subtly, but I try to convey with my eyes anything but that. He nods and puts his cards face down. Kyle does the same. They both slip their hands inside their jackets and take out their guns. Liz reaches into her purse and does the same. Hers is bigger than theirs are.

I take a deep breath. "Ugh," I gripe.

"What?" Kyle asks, looking around.

"I smell…potatoes?" I frown. "That can't be right, can it?"

"Ya know," a young voice says from the opposite end of the table. All three guns aim at the blonde with the pixie cut, sitting at the other end with her head bowed over a Styrofoam bowl. She takes a deep breath before lifting bright green eyes. She points at us with a spoon, before putting it in the cup. She takes a spoonful of what looks like potato soup and puts it in her mouth. She can't be vampire, right? She hums and then leans her chin on her spoon-filled hand over the cup, causing steam to move around her face on either side. That spoon is friggin' huge.

"Muh taste buds may be tellin' me I'm eatin' dirt," she continues in an Irish accent that rivals Raven's for charm. She swallows. She swallowed it? "…but muh nose tells me I just downed a little spoonful'a Heaven." She stands, pushing her chair back at the same time, resting both hands on top of the table. "It's almost wort' t'e indigestion I'll suffer later."

"WHO ARE YOU?" Demetri snarls.

"Me? Um t'e person t'at's gonna slaughter t'e lot o' ya." I frown. "You're all traitors to vampire kind, so you gotta go."

"Look, chick," I start. She glowers at me. "I don't know who you are or what makes you come in here talking crazy and eating your potato soup or whatever, but this is the Chief Magistrate's home…and we're her coven. You don't get much more official than us."

Blondie shrugs. "T'at still does nae change t'e fact t'at I'm 'bout to kill everyone o' ya."

"I've heard enough," Demetri snaps. He squeezes his trigger. The bullet flies and metal strikes metal. The blond girl holds the spoon in front of her heart. She smirks and tugs on her pale gray, silk scarf with her free hand. "What the…?"

"Don't ask," Kyle snaps. "Kill her." The three of them unload on her and with every bang, metal strikes metal. I focus, the way Natavius taught me. Everything slows down. The bullets still move pretty fast, but I can track them at least. The girl deflects ever shot with the bowl part of her spoon. This continues until all three guns click empty.

"That's not possible," Liz whines, staring down the barrel of her empty weapon.

"Not only is it possible," the blonde girl says. "…makes it easier ta kill t'e four of ya." She licks the dented and dinged spoon.

"Who are you?" I ask.

She glares at me. "I thought I covered t'at…with t'e spoon, lass." I frown. "I'm t'e person who's gonna kill ya."

"Y-you're gonna kill us with a spoon?" Kyle asks.

"It's not even silver," Demetri adds.

"Well, d'uh. It's stainless steel. T'at's how I was able ta deflect yer silver bullets wit' it."

"It's not sharp," Liz says with a tremble to her voice.

"I know. Makes it hurt worse when I dig out yer hearts." She nods. "Ya know? T'e killin' ya part?"

"Doubt it," I snarl, glaring at her, hand on my knife.

"Who's first?" She points the spoon at Liz, then Kyle, and finally lands on Demetri.

"ME," I bark.

She slams her free hand on the table and pushes up. She springs forward…spoon first. I push off too. My knife collides with her spoon pushing it up. I twist and throw my left leg at her. She puts her free hand on my knee stopping me. Our deep blue eyes meet…she smiles and winks. I catch her scent. I push off, and she does, too. She lands back where she started, and I do too.

"You smell like…" I rub under my nose to be sure.

"MARY MARGARET GREGORY!" Raven snaps from the doorway between the foyer and dining room. The blonde girl looks at her. "What on God's green Eart' do ya t'ink yer doin'?"

"MA," Mary Margaret says throwing her arms around Raven.

"Mom?" Kyle, Demetri, and Liz say at the same time, confirming what I smelled. She smells almost exactly like Renee. She's my sire sister, Maggie.

"Answer tha question," Raven insists, pushing her off.

"Just puttin' t'e newbies through t'e ringer."

"New?" Demetri says. He points his thumb at himself. "I've been with Raven for over twenty years now."

Maggie looks at Demetri over her shoulder. "Yeah, well when ya hit t'e fifty-year mark, lemme know." She looks around. "Speakin' of which, where's muh baby brot'er? I haven't seen him in at least twenty years."

"Haven't you people ever heard of video messaging services?" I ask.

Maggie glares at me again. "Who's t'e New Blood?" she asks, pointing her thumb.

"I'm your new sister, Maggie," I say with a smile.

"No," Maggie says in a gasp, while glaring at Raven. Raven nods in return. "I t'ought ya said Richard was yer last!"

"She was a special case."

Maggie nods and walks over to me. "Yer good, baby sis."

"You're not so bad yourself. That spoon thing was REALLY scary."

"I'll say," Liz groans.

"Well, ya know. I was trained by t'e best." She tips her head toward Raven. "Speaking of trainin'…" She steps back and extends her hand to me. "I'm Mary Margaret Gregory. You can call me, Maggie."

I tip my head back. "The other three people you scared the bejesus out of are…" I motion to… "Demitri…Kyle…and Liz…"

"Hey," Kyle and Liz groan. Demetri huffs.

I shake her hand. "And I'm Angela Nicole Price-Gregory."

"Oh, holdin' on to a part of yer old life?"

"My mom's a witch so…"

She purses her lips and nods. Raven takes her by the arm. "Well, I hafta go…mum business." Raven walks out tugging Maggie behind her. I follow them.

"Angela," Raven says. I freeze in the doorway. "Don't you hafta pack for yer trip?"

"Yeah," I say, awkwardly. "Yeah, pfft…packing. Right." I clap my hands like an idiot.

"So," Raven starts, moving toward her office. "T'e twins finally tracked ya down, huh?"

"Yeah, outside of Budapest."

"Why were ya t'ere?" Raven closes her office door and switches on the little noise canceling gadgets…effectively, punching a hole in my ego. I sigh. With Renee pulling that ritual crap on me and being MIA for the last hundred years, I thought I was a lock for favorite sire-daughter.

I march toward my room. I don't know why it bugs me so much. I mean, I have an actual mom…and I'm not even willing to discuss which one of those is my favorite…birth mom, of course, but if I ever told either of them that they were the fav, the other would kill me.

I reach my bedroom door…that apparently, will be Alana's bedroom door again, while I'm in North Carolina with her husband… I sigh. …who I'm still in love with. I have to ask Natavius how he got over Alana so fast. I close my door behind me and…something feels off.

I feel uneasy. I look around. There's no one here, but it feels like there is. I focus on my ability…and I still get nothing. This damn feeling just won't go away though. Okay, I need to calm down. Going on another mission with Nate…meeting Maggie the way I did, just probably has me on edge or something. I mean, I'm in my bedroom with the door locked. My bedroom in the Chief Magistrate's home no less.

"Hello, gorgeous," Balthazar whispers. I turn quickly, barely registering how fast I moved, and put my knife so close to his throat that I'm surprised I didn't cut him. "You're not very good at taking compliments, are you?" A slight trickle of blood slips from under the blade. I guess I was closer than I thought. I check that and steel my resolve as Raven likes to say.

"What the hell are you doing here?" I spit between clenched teeth. "Are you still stalking me?" He smiles. "Answer me, damn it!"

He moves back to the bedroom door so quickly that I stumble forward. A snarl makes my top lip curl up. I feel on edge, but not 'I'm about to throw down with someone' on edge. I almost feel happy to see him again because he's a harmless distraction. At least, he has been. That actually pisses me off more than if he were just some random jag off trying to kill me.

Balthazar wipes his nose, then the blood from under his eyes, and finally clears it away from his ears. He returns his handkerchief to his inside jacket pocket…I can't help but notice that the blood vanishes even before he puts it away. "I should've known you'd be able to hear me despite my glamour." I hiss and bare my fangs. "Okay, okay," he spurts holding his hands up in surrender. He half closes those beautiful green eyes of his.

"Would you believe me, if I told you that I came here to see you?" he breathes, while moving a strand of my hair out of my face. I'd be impressed with the fact that I didn't flinch if I wasn't paralyzed from standing this close to him. Why does he have to be so damn hot?

"I've heard that before…" He purrs, staring into my eyes. "…and I'd say you were lying, but that's what you do right?"

His jaw clenches. "Well, I can understand that you don't believe me. I mean, I'm the 'bad guy.'" He makes ridiculous air quotes at 'bad guy.' He does it again. "'Bad guys' lie. Part of the job." He takes my free hand in his. I almost gasp as he puts it up to his mouth. "But how about this…I vow that I will never…EVER…lie to you." He kisses the back of my hand.

"How can I believe the promises of a liar? I'm a New Blood…but I'm not a new person, and if I've learned anything from my dating life, it's that you can't trust a liar. "

"Come with me."

"What? Come with… No! I'm not going anywhere with you!"

His eyes become steel. They are sharp and menacing…and I don't want them to leave me. What kind of power does this guy have over me? His jaw clenches again, and he sighs quietly. My hand drops, and I feel him ruffle the back of my hair. This time I actually gasp. What is this the 1950's? Why am I nervous about a boy…a daemon boy, but a boy all the same?

"Then you leave me no choice," he says, moving my hair to the left. I swallow a hard lump as he bends down, putting his mouth right next to my ear. He IS going to kill me, and apparently, I'm going to let him. My arms feel like loose noodles, and my legs could buckle at any minute. "Please," he whispers. I drop my knife. A chuckle comes from across the room. He lounges on my bed as if nothing's happened.

"Did you just say, 'please'?" He hops off the bed. "Stop screwing around with me!" I snatch my knife from the floor and rush him. Guess my legs and arms really aren't useless. I aim for his heart. He disappears. I freeze in place after the tip of the knife passes the point where his heart would have been. His hand creeps slowly over the two of mine on my knife's handle. "Let go," I squeak without pulling against him.

"I can't seem to," he murmurs. "Love at first sight and all that." I peer up at his serious stare with its tiny hints of playfulness. I tremble. Why is he toying with me? Why doesn't he just ki- "Think about it, gorgeous. If I wanted to hurt you, I could've kept my glamour going, done the deed and been gone before your body even hit the floor."

Was that supposed to convince me that he wasn't going to kill me, let alone convince me to go with him? Sadly, I think it did on both counts, at least, a little.

"Stop calling me 'gorgeous,'" I whine and let my knife fall again. I feel a tear roll down my cheek opposite him. "My name is…"

"Angela. I remember. In fact, I did some homework, Angela Nicole Powers-Price…sire daughter of Raven Gregory, current Chief Magistrate of all vampires." I mouth the word 'how.' "I know, people," he returns succinctly. He releases my hands and wraps his arms around me…pinning my arms to my sides. I hate this…because this is the feeling that I imagine whenever Alana talks about how Nathan feels like home to her. How he makes her feel comfortable and off balance at the same time.

"I shouldn't even be here," Balthazar starts again. Ugh, even his stupid name is starting to sound good to me. "I was told to keep an eye on a wayward wolf. But here I am, being VERY stupid." His head bows, and I feel his breath on my neck. "Because of you." I feel his eyelashes come down against my temple. "You make me do very, very stupid things. Did you know that?"

"I'm feeling kind of dumb right about now," I admit. I try to muster a little strength and pull away from him, but how can you pull away from someone that you want to hold close? "Why are you doing this to me?"

"I was going to ask you the same thing," he replies. "From the moment I met you, I haven't been able to stop thinking about you." I close my eyes. That voice of his is what I imagine an honest to God angel's sounds like. "I have walked this Earth for almost three thousand years. In all that time, no one has ever been able to see me when I don't want them to." He moves around and pulls my face up to his. My eyes flutter open. "But you see me…" He hits me with the full shimmer of those emerald pools. "…don't you?"

I nod absently. "Yes, I do, but I can't. I can't go with you."

"No?" I shake my head slowly. "Then…a kiss as we part ways?" My mind goes completely blank as I stare at his perfect mouth. He pulls me closer. "Just one?" I think I nod as our lips meet. I tremble…again. His kiss is amazing. His lips are soft but forceful and demanding. And when the kiss ends…I feel like I want to beg for more.

He takes a step back letting me slide from between his arms. Don't let go, don't let go, don't let go. I open my eyes, and he's already gone. I sigh and put my hand over my heart. It would be pounding if it was beating. I pick up my knife and there's a note attached.

I open it and take out the card inside:

> If you find that, you can't stop thinking about me either. I'll be at the address on the back of this card later tonight.
>
> With all my love,
> Your Bal

I turn it over and check the address. Uptown. I sigh and fan myself with the card, suddenly feeling really warm. Is he serious? What if this is a trap? Why would it be a trap? Like he said, he could've killed me anytime. I slip my knife back into its sheath and shake my head. "I have got to be the dumbest vampire ever."

#####

Chapter 13: Standoff

"Why are we sitting here?" I complain, leaning back in this uncomfortable wooden chair, that's making my ass numb. The smell of coffee, cinnamon, and hazelnut is suffocating me. These brown stone poo-colored walls irritating my eyes, and the locals staring at us as if we're a sideshow…and they don't even know that we're a wolf and a vampire.

"Because," Nate starts, sipping his caramel latte with an extra flavor shot. "…if you want to find out anything about Edenton, you go to the square and you pay attention to the people." He looks around. "And Jelly Bean Coffee is just as good a place as any to pay attention to the people."

I lean forward. "And what does paying attention to this pack of hicks tell you?"

He sighs. "First, they're not hicks…collectively they're surprisingly nice."

"Yeah, well last time I was here, they heard my accent and treated me like I was a pit bull about to bite their kids."

"Are you sure that wasn't just your personality?"

I hiss back. He laughs and sips his drink again. I pretend to drink mine.

"You know you can drink coffee…black coffee…" I glare at him. "…that's what I ordered for you."

"Yeah, because…I definitely want to sit around drinking black coffee like a sociopath." The corners of his mouth turn down, and he nods. "Look, I know it helps vampires not be so cold to the touch…but I hated the taste…even before. Thanks for getting it for me anyway."

"Oh, that reminds me…I got you something else…" I frown. He places a platinum lighter on the table. It has a skull carved out on the side. I arch one eyebrow. "I got it at the general store across the square. My friend wasn't there, but his wife was…I felt obligated to buy something."

I shrug and swipe it. It reminds me of the kind my dad used to carry. I flick the top against my leg and bring it back forward, lighting it against the same leg. I smirk. Just like dad used to do. He didn't smoke, so he probably just did it to look cool. I close it and slip it into my pocket.

"Thanks," I breathe. He nods and sips his drink again. I can't blame Nate for my sour mood. Balthazar threw me for a loop the other night. He kissed me…I let him kiss me. He's En Quosque…the guys we're supposed to be fighting against…and I'm making out with him instead. My eyes drift across the table…and then there's Nate. I still feel like a ton of bricks sits on my chest every time he looks at me…or when I look at him.

His phone rings. He stands and steps away from the table. Yep, four hours on the dot…I don't know if Alana's just being overly cautious checking up on him constantly, if she just misses him that much... I cross my arms and rest them on the table. ...or if she still doesn't trust me around her husband. I can't blame her for that either. If I could sense emotions, and I knew how a girl felt about my man...I'd be super sensitive about them taking a trip together.

"Do you need a refill?" our waitress, Emily, asks. I shake my head. She smiles turning up her caramel-colored cheeks and bows her cinnamon-colored hair that hangs around her face in little ringlets. Man, with descriptors like that, she definitely picked the right place to work. "Do you want anything else? Scone? Muffin, maybe?"

"No thanks."

"How about your boyfriend?"

I laugh. "He's NOT my boyfriend. Just a friend." Subtle, Emily. If you want to ask him out, then go right ahead and get shot d-

"Because I was wonder if you weren't doing anything later, then maybe..."

"Oh," I hum. "I'm...um...not..."

"Oh my God, you're not..." I shake my head. "I mean, I didn't know...and you're with that guy...but you're not *with* him...and even I can see how hot he is...so...I was hoping..." She turns away with her cheeks changing from caramel to apple red. "...I'm such an idiot."

"No, Emily..." I stand. "...Emily, listen, it's cool...I mean, that's the first time that's happened to me...and I can concede you are a hottie..." She laughs into a flirty smile. "...but I like guys. I am flattered though."

"Sorry," she repeats. "It's just...my head's been all messed up because my last girlfriend..." She opens her mouth, and nothing comes of it, but a head shake. "...I don't even know what to say about Stefana...or even what I can say."

"What is she like a spy or something?"

"She's...something..." I frown. I get her meaning, but she doesn't know that I get her meaning. Stefana is a supernatural being.

"You sound like you're hung up on her still."

Emily groans. "Maybe, a little." I nod. "Okay, so a lot. She was so hot and so brave and strong, and I could just listen to her talk about her family for hours..."

"Call her."

"I can't..."

"What are you afraid of?"

She looks into my eyes. "Nothing." She nods. "I'm not afraid of anything...but not seeing her anymore. Thanks...um..."

I offer her my hand. "Angela."

She shakes my hand. "Thanks, Angela. Excuse me."

Emily walks away as Nate comes back over. "What was that all about?"

"Definitely something supernatural about this town, Nate." He frowns and looks at Emily, huddled over her phone…ringing on the other end with no answer. "Not her. Her ex-girlfriend."

"Did she tell you that?"

"No, but I could tell." He nods. "Guess you were right…as always." He smirks. "Don't let it go to your head, dude." I huff a laugh, punch him on the shoulder, and something catches the corner of my eye. I turn to the door to get a better look.

"What is it?" He turns and stares at the two guys walking down the street, across the square. One…a little cutie with brown hair and green eyes…the other, almost as cute, with spikey blond hair and blue eyes…but that's not what got my attention.

"They read like you," I comment on my ability.

"Wolf?" I look at him and shake my head. "We'll follow them." He nods. "But if they really are skinwalkers, then they probably have enhanced senses too."

I move toward the door. "So, we won't yell 'We're following you' while we're following them. Come on."

Nate catches my arm and turns me back to face him. "Are you alright? You've been extra snarky lately."

"All of my snark is based on impending battle with the forces of evil." He nods. "And a lack of bran in my diet. You can never underestimate the importance of bran."

He laughs. "You're such an Elaine."

"Shut…up…!" I shove him in the chest with both hands, causing him to laugh harder. I think that this is why Nate considers me his best friend. Even though we're here to hunt a witch…and we had to leave his pregnant wife, the target of an evil organization, in New York…somehow, I made him laugh.

"They're on the move," he says and slips out the door.

"Because I miss you," Emily says into her phone. I half turn, and she waves with a big smile. She points at the phone and mouths, 'her.' I give her a big, over exaggerated thumbs up and step out after Nate.

He waves me over to our little tan colored rental. At least, it's not a mini-Cooper. "They're heading west," he says, while holding my door.

"Then get in and get this thing moving. Go. Go. Go." He nods and hurries around the car. I climb in, and he's already in his seat. He starts the engine and roars out of the space. We dart around the town square with me pressed up against the door the entire time and follow the old school convertible out of town. It speeds down a country road causing the tall grass to sway in the breeze. Grass doesn't get this tall in New York...you know if there is grass.

"I know where they're going."

I lean forward and stare out the weird, rounded windshield. "How?"

"Because I've been this way before...and there's only one thing out this far." He growled that entire sentence and if I were anyone else...except maybe Alana...he would've just scared the hell out of me. "It's Tony's mansion on the outskirts of town."

"Those daemon brothers?" He nods. "Was your fall out with him REALLY that bad?"

"Worse."

"You guys fell out over a girl, right?"

"Not exactly." He grips the wheel tighter. "Shay...she's a half siren-half human...beautiful little girl...stood three and half feet, skinny almost nothing..." He inhales deeply. "This sadistic vampire cult, operating out of Chicago, murdered her family in front of her...saved her for last because she 'smelled' the most appealing." My stomach turns. "We finally tracked them down just as she was about to be the main course. Tony, James, and I made short work of the cult...until all that was left was a woman...and Shay. Even though Shay was her hostage and human shield...Tony threw a spike throw her eye after the woman sank her fangs in."

I groan with the image of Devon's pale face moving through my mind.

He inhales deeply and turns to me outright. "Shay was infatuated with him from that point on...of course, she was too young for him...she was only nine years old."

"Well, if he's almost 200 years old, no matter what, she's too young for him." He arches his eyebrows. "Sorry. Go on."

"We argued literally for days about what to do with her. James wanted to track down other fae and leave her in their care. I wanted to put her in a foster home...hoping that she'd get the care that she'd need to lead a normal life there. Tony...wanted to know what she wanted." He peers at the wall of vaguely rectangular stones behind him...that's not moving. In fact, the car isn't moving.

I look around and we're parked on the opposite side of the street next to a gray stone wall. "What...?"

"I'll tell you in a second." I nod. "Shay having seen what we could do...wanted to join us...James and I said absolute not...him because he has a daughter close to her age...and me..." His eyes flash green and gold and return to normal brown. "I saw the malevolence that followed her. She was so angry and hurt by what happened to her parents that I knew it would lead her headlong into danger." He takes a deep breath. "That anger's going to get her killed one day." He throws his door open. I do too.

I round the car quickly and move to his side. "Got your knife?" I nod. He takes out his staff. "We're here for a reason."

"So, they really turned in at Tony's house." He nods. He tips his head to the wall. I frown and focus on the wall. It's weird…I feel a buzz coming from it. It's like an electric hum. I look just above the wall and there's a dome. It's orange with white shapes all along it…different Latin words inscribed in circles with triangles in them. "Weird."

"See the barrier?" I nod. "That's why we're here…" He twists his staff twice, and a blade emerges from the tip. It's not the same blade he used against Ephraim. This one seems…duller…less lustrous. He heaves the staff behind him and drives it into the wall. The bricks splinter and crack. He does it again two bricks down…and repeats the action until he has carved out a dotted circle. "Hold this." He tosses the staff. I catch it and twist it twice the other direction. The blade retracts.

Nate lowers his shoulder and pushes through…the bricks fall to the inside of the wall. He smirks and extends his hand. I give him the staff. "Ready to run?" I nod, despite the fact that he doesn't even look back. "Follow me…and…GO!"

He vanishes in a blur. I follow in a blur. We run through waist high grass tossing its seeds in every direction. We dart through a small forest, dank and a little brown, especially considering that it's August. Finally, we break into a field of low-lying grass that smells sweet and as if it were just cut, before coming up on a huge two…no, three-story brick mansion.

Nate comes to a dead stop and extends his hand to me. I slide, and he catches me, wrapping his arms around my waist. All the air rushes out me at once. I take a deep breath and hold it. He pulls me down…and places his finger over his mouth. He points that same finger in the direction that we were running. The two boys climb out of the convertible and walk toward the black double doors at the front of the house. I check the old school mustang and the other old school convertible parked on either side of the skinwalkers' GTO.

Nate waves his hand in my face. He points at the door. I nod. We watch as the boys walk into the house. Nate holds up three fingers. The door drifts close. Two fingers. Only the slightest sliver remains. One finger. Nate's on his feet and moving. I follow. He catches the door, just before it closes. A huge red seal appears over both doors…another circle with a triangle inside and lots of Latin words.

Nate holds his finger up to his mouth again. He taps that finger against his ear and makes a circle in the air. He repeats the action with his nose. I nod.

He pushes the door in and steps into the house. I step into the woodgrain foyer with stairs leading to the next floor in the shape of a Y. I push the door almost closed.

"That's far enough," growls a forceful, but young voice. An orange and brown, clawed hand extends in front of my throat. "You huff and puff too much when you use swift paw," the clawed boy growls. I steal a glance at him, and he looks like a tiger, but judging from his clothing, he's the blond-haired boy.

"Who are you guys?" another voice growls across from Nate.

This one… I gasp. …he looks like a fox…or a wolf…or both…but his eyes…they're amber colored and black where the whites should be.

"Nate," I whine.

"Be cool, Ange." I nod as much as the claws at my throat allow. "You're out of your depth here, boys," Nate warns with that sexy, dangerous timber to his voice. "Think this through before we have to hurt you."

"Hurt us?" the tiger growls in a mocking voice. "Please…I have your little vampire here…"

"VAMPIRE?" the fox boy says. "She can't be…it's still daylight out."

"NOW," Nate barks. I grab the tiger by the wrist and twist his arm outward. He carps in pain.

Nate catches the fox boy by one arm and his throat and slams him to floor. He should consider himself lucky…I've seen what Nate can do.

I sweep the tiger's legs out from under him and put him down on his stomach. I twist his arm up behind his back…until it feels like his shoulder's going to come out of the socket. He roars with pain again.

"WHAT'S GOING ON OUT THERE?" a voice yells from a pair of double doors to my left. I look at Nate. He puts his left wrist to his right and taps it. I nod then take out a pair Raven's special made handcuffs and toss them to him. I take another set and slap them on the tiger.

"Seriously, who are you guys?" the tiger growls.

The double doors swing open and out marches a young-looking guy with short cut brown hair…and a slim, but muscly physique. He scowls. "VAMPIRE!"

My ability kicks in. He reads just like that guy in New Orleans. He must be Tony. He draws a knife from behind his back. I pull mine. He rushes over to me in a blur with his aimed at my heart. I prepare a block when my legs come out from under me. Nate sweeps my legs, puts his left arm behind my back to catch me, while catching Tony's wrist with his right hand.

"NATHAN!" Tony growls.

"Tony," Nate replies with a low rumble. Nate pulls on the left side of my belt; causing me to twirl like a top…I spin and land on my feet. He and Tony get into a…well, I'd say tussle, but I can't tell what's happening…they're moving so fast that I only barely catch glimpses when one maneuvers out of the other's grip.

"TONY?" the tall sexy one, Quincy, calls from the stairs. "NATE?" They continue fighting as if he hasn't said anything. Quincy continues scanning the foyer until his eyes land on me. "Vampire?"

"Will everyone stop calling me that? I have a name, you know?" I complain.

"Yeah," Quincy says, extending his right hand. "Is it 'charcoal'? FLAMMA!"

"ANGE!" Nate roars, just before Tony punches him in the face.

"Flamma," I spit, throwing my hand forward like I did with Bethany. I catch this fireball too. I also breathe a sigh of relief and count my lucky stars that I didn't pee my pants.

"That's not possible," Quincy says, marching down the stairs.

"Oh, yeah? Then how am I doing it?" Instead of throwing this one back and setting fire to another home, I snuff it out, by crushing it.

"Don't know. Don't care," a mature male voice says behind me. I half-turn to a guy in his thirties with medium brown hair and…

"UGH!" I'm on my back…he did something that took my legs out from under me. Another person dressed in all black riot gear steps into view…with a silver spike raised above her head. "CRAP!" I spin, throwing my legs out. I manage to kick her in the side. She recovers as soon as I jump to my feet. She's on me again…and she's good.

"Nate," I yell. "We're outnumbered here." Nate steps between the girl and me. He catches her spike-wielding arm, twists it up and behind her head. I put my knife to her throat. The new guy puts a gun to my temple. Nate extends his staff to him with the sharp, shiny blade out. Tony appears behind Nate with his knife to Nate's throat.

"Great," I complain.

"Good ole fashioned Mexican standoff," Quincy says, leaning against the banister at the base of the stairs. "No matter what, Nate…you lose this round."

"WHAT THE HELL IS YOU GUYS' PROBLEM?" a peanut-skinned redhead snarls from the landing between floors. "Alex, are you…?" She stops at about the third step from the bottom when she realizes the guy with the gun is staring at her… Her big brown eyes swell and fill with tears instantly behind her horn-rimmed glasses. "Daddy?"

#####

Chapter 14: Cravings

I toss another copy of my uniform out of my closet…Angela's closet. She was kind enough to give up her room while she and my Nathan are…away. I traded my husband for my old room. I exhale a haughty breath, staring at my wedding and engagement rings. He is my Nathan…mine. "Ours," I amend with a gentle caress of my stomach to calm our daughter, who already registers my emotions.

I sigh. It doesn't matter if she's still in love with him. He loves me…us. "Ugh," I groan and toss another uniform…it's skirt pinches my hips. Now, ridiculously, the thought of hips took my mind to my widening bum, which made me instantly jump to rump and now, I would literally kill for a bite of roast. Thank you for yet another random, ass-widening craving daughter of mine.

"What's wrong?" Raven asks, pushing the bedroom door closed. She quickly surveys the collection of pleated, plaid skirts at my feet.

"I um…" I hedge. "I believe that my and Nathan's cleaning efforts towards my school uniforms have caused them to shrink. Yes. So, now none of my uniforms fit me any longer."

"Yer uniforms are dry clean only and Nat'an knows t'at. He's been volunteerin' to take yers to t'e cleaners since t'e two of ya got back toget'er in t'e spring." She walks over as I swallow a lump. I move away from the closet and return to the bed…covered in slightly larger outfits Nathan bought for me. "Alana, what's goin' on?"

"Nothing," I return, trying to find something that would work as a passable bottom for my return to Middleton Prep. "I don't know how to explain the smaller clothing…" I continue going over the new clothing. "…I mean, I suppose…"

"…it could be t'e child growing inside yer womb."

I gasp and turn to her, my eyes as large as saucers. My mouth agape and as dry as a desert. I swallow down that dryness. "I-I…" I shake my head…more of a fidgeting spasm really. "…that is ridiculous…"

"Lana." I swallow another knot as she glares at me, her lecture on the other Magistrate's edict fresh in mind. No child was to come of the union between Nathan and me. The Wolf Elders requested similarly of the Alpha…and I accepted both terms so that I could marry my Nathan, but that was before I even realized that we could have children together.

Alpha Quinton knows about the child…he seemed happy, proud even…in a strange way. I am getting no emotional read on my sister though. That may be the baby reacting to my panic and throwing that panic back at me like a mirror.

I return her stare and take a deep breath. "What if...it were true?"

"T'is true," she returns. "Yer cheeks are a little chubbier t'an normal an' so's yer waist, sister. Also, yer skin has t'e same glow as yer mot'er's when she carried ya. It's as if yer skin's generatin' its own light."

She takes a step closer. I take a step back, closer to the sword that our brother had specially made for me at the bedside. This time my Nathan's words echo in my mind. We sat in his car just before our wedding...and I asked him what we'd do about our child, considering the warnings that I...and apparently, only I...received from my sister and his brother.

"We will protect her," he said confidently. "We will protect our daughter with everything we are...with everything we have...to our last..." I nodded along joyfully. "...like any good parents would."

"We will protect our family no matter what," I mutter to myself softly. "Even if it is from our family."

I take a deep breath, and my eyes meet my sister's emerald pools. She steps closer again, and I retreat that much more...my left hand behind my back, skimming the hilt of my sword. Raven stops and tilts so that she can see behind me. I tremble at the thought of what may transpire next.

"You'd fight yer own sister to protect t'is child?"

I tremble as tears fill my eyes. I place my hand on my stomach. "I would fight ANY and EVERYONE for OUR daughter."

"Good," she replies. I frown. "Remember t'at as we let out yer uniforms and anytime you have to go out in public. We have to keep yer pregnancy a secret fer as long as we can, understood?"

I nod absently. "You'll help me...help...?" I look down...my hand never left my daughter. "...us, despite what the other magistrates ordered?"

"Yer muh sister...t'at's muh niece. You'd never hafta fight t'e world alone...because I'd be right beside ye...well, me an' Nat'an, of course."

I huff a laugh. "I love you, sister."

"I love you, too." She approaches, still hesitant. I motion for her to come closer. She does and gives me a quick hug before she goes to the bed. "Now, I love yer husband...but his taste in women's clot'ing...awful..." She nods. "...we'll take some of yer uniforms wit' us. I know a tailor t'at could let t'em out in a matter of minutes and hopefully...we kin get ya ta school on time." She looks at me. I wrap my arms around her again and tears pour from my eyes. "Mood swing?"

"Yes, but I am also so relieved to be able to tell you about this. It has been killing me to keep it a secret from you for this long."

"How far along are ya, dear?" she asks as we part.

"Ugh."

"What? Is it the baby?"

"No. You said 'dear,' and then my mind went to 'deer' the animal... Which is amazing, we should get some. ...and from that brought me to venison. So that now, I could catch a deer with my bare hands and eat it whole." She laughs. "And I just got my mind away from roast...and pork chops and streaky bacon..." I groan while rubbing my stomach. "...this girl is more wolf than anything. And should I be having cravings after only three and a half months?"

"Yer mother was drinkin' sheep's blood after ya were in her womb two weeks."

I nod. "Was it hard for her?" Raven's expression goes even. "Carrying me? Was it hard for her?"

"No."

"Raven?"

She sighs. "Yes. She nearly died several times over..." I gasp. "...but every time..." She stares at me with deeply soulful eyes. "Now, mind ya...we cared very much fer yer mot'er." I nod. "...every time that we almost lost her...Alexander and I would volunteer ta...relieve her of her burden."

I shiver. "You would've..."

"...fer yer mot'er? Fer our mot'er...? Yes." I nod. "But every time we'd say t'at...and mind ya, we were vampires t'e entire time she knew us, she'd look at us as if we were monsters. She could not process how we'd be willin' ta sacrifice ya fer her." I touch our daughter. "An' ya look so much like her...holdin' yer stomach t'at way."

"Anara," I breathe. Raven frowns. "That's...what Nathan wants to call her. He wants to call her Anara Kya Dumont after our mothers. I want to call her, Kya Anara."

"I like yer husband's way better." I laugh. All humor drains from her face. "So, you know t'at t'e child is a girl?" I nod. "Have you been havin' dreams about her?" I frown but nod again. How could she...? "Yer mot'er saw yer whole life play out...up ta marryin' Nat'an..." She steps closer and moves my hair away from my shoulder. She moves behind me and secures mother's ribbon. "...tell me trut'fully sister...did ya see yersefl dyin' in yer dreams?"

"No...but..." My heart sinks. "...one thing has constantly bothered me about all of the visions of Kya's future." I turn to my sister. "Out of all of the dozens and dozens of visions I've had..." A tear escapes. "...I have yet to see my Nathan with our daughter."

#####

Chapter 15: Explanations

I move through Middleton Preparatory's mint green tinted vestibule with cautious optimism. Yes, that's it. I have cautious optimism. Perhaps, no one will notice my swollen belly or that my clothing has been let out to accommodate an expanding waistline or that I'm wearing my engagement and wedding rings on a necklace because my fingers have swollen to the size of proper bangers, and I can't even get the stupid bloody thinks on my fat fingers anymore!

I sigh. I must get these mood swings under control. They wouldn't notice the latter because as far as they're concerned, I'm returning to school after an extended vacation spent with my boyfriend and his family. I touch my stomach absently. Our family.

"OMG, ALANA!" Oh no. Has someone noticed already? I turn to little Lucy Stillwater…or should I say big Lucy Stillwater. She grew several inches over the summer and has…ahem…blossomed almost as much as Raven says that I should expect to in the next few months. "Did you hear?"

"Is there another new student this year?"

She shakes her head with a solemn expression on her face. She straightens her stylish frames and steps closer. She hooks my arm and walks with me down the hall. She looks around suspiciously and bows her head to whisper. "They found Amber T behind the school."

"They found her?"

She nods with her eyes as large as saucers and as empty as the halls for the most part. "I managed to sneak back and get a look at her…you know, for the paper."

"Lucy?"

"Okay, so I can tell the truth if the school tries to spin negatively against her." I nod. "I mean, I've never been a fan of Amber T, but I wouldn't say that she was an enemy either…"

"Lucy!"

"…right…well, I tried to make it look like an accident, but when I got back there, these guys were standing around her, and they did NOT look like cops."

"How do you mean?" We reach my locker. She takes out her phone and shows me an image of one. I stifle a gasp and only barely. The man on her phone. He wears black riot gear, covering him from head to toe exactly like Jeremiah…

"Alana?"

…and the men who attacked us during our honeymoon…

"Alana?"

…they are vampire hunters.

"Alana?"

What are they doing here? Unless…

"Alana?"

"Lucy, what happened to Amber T?"

"That was the weird thing," she says in a sort of gasping whisper. "If I didn't know any better, I would swear her throat had been torn out by a wild animal or something." That clenches it. They are here to investigate Amber T's murder. Have these rogue vampires become so bold as to attack from the shadows near daybreak.

"There some of them are now." Two of the men stand near the end of the hall, talking to the vice principal, Mr. Buchman. Of course, they have lowered their masks and have removed their goggles.

I try to listen as Mr. Buchman extends a hand to the one on the right. "Thank you so much, officers, for keeping this incident under wraps. To think that something like this could happen on our campus."

"Don't worry," the hunter on the left says as Buchman shakes his hand. "We'll find whoever did this and take them down." Buchman nods, and the two men walk away. "So, we're looking for a girl vampire…probably 5'1" or 5'2", right?"

"According to the examiner, given the jaw radius and angle of the bite, that seems to be the case. Pretty bold of a vampire, killing someone this close to sunrise."

The other hunter nods. "Maybe it was one of the students here…turned vampire."

"We need Baggett on this one. He's good with weird."

"When's he getting back from visiting his kid?"

"Which one?" the other says with a laugh that carries over to the first as they go around the corner.

"ALANA!" Lucy practically screams.

"Yes?"

"Sorry. You did it again. I was calling you and calling you and…" I sigh. "I don't know what to do. I'm freaking out a little because I barely snapped that pic of the guy with my phone before they shooed me away…I tried to go around another way but there were like eight more of them there to stop me."

I take Lucy by the shoulders and push her back against the lockers. "Ow," she objects.

"Listen to me very carefully, Lucy." She nods. My eyes move over to silver. "Delete that photo immediately. Forget what you saw this morning. All you know is that there was a disturbance behind the school and nothing more. Is that clear?"

She nods absently.

My eyes return to normal. "Trust me. It's for your own good."

"What's for my own good?"

"Leaving," Meredith snarls.

Lucy nods and walks away without argument. Meredith follows Lucy with her eyes, exploring every inch of her changed height and more mature physique.

I glower at Meredith. "You did not have to-" She looks around as distractedly as Lucy did when she first approached me. "Are you alright?" She nods. "Did you hear what happened to Amber T?"

"No. What?"

"I-" I shake my head, deciding that whatever she feels right now is clearly already upsetting her enough…and that's without my ability.

"No…I…" She runs her fingers through her hair and messes it, well, messes it more. I also notice that her clothing is less revealing than it ordinarily is. She wears a cardigan, and it is closed…her blouse is buttoned fully, and her tie is in place. She wraps her arms around her waist. "…have you seen Angela?"

I frown. "No. From what I understand, Raven sent her on a campus tour…to a university in the south." She emits a stuttering sigh and huddles away from a group of girls walking by. She must be reeling from her ordeal with this witch, Bethany. "Merrie, are you sure you're alright?"

She shudders and nibbles her thumb. She shakes her head. "I know what I saw…I know what happened…my mom…" She extends her hand in a claw, gripping upward. "…sent me to three shrinks over the last week…but I know what I saw…"

I extend a hand…slowly. "Merrie," I whisper.

"No," she snaps, moving her hands away. "I am NOT lying…" She points an accusing finger…at her mother, her three therapists, and me. "…and I'm NOT crazy. My cousin Bethany tried to kill me…I could feel it. It felt like she was draining the life out of me." She shudders again. "Angela saved my life, and Bethany tried to set her on fire…with fire from her hand…" She extends her hand in a halting fashioned. "…and Angela…caught the fire…"

"Merrie," I murmur, catching both of her wrists.

"NO!" she shrieks. "Let me go!"

I look around and notice the few students in the area, staring at us. I bow my head a bit. I feel wave after wave of anxiety from her…and my daughter…Kya sends an emotion back through me. My daughter has not steered me wrong thus far.

"Meredith," I say with a calm voice. My eyes move to deep blue… Meredith gasps. …and then silver. She weeps and tries to pull away again. "I need you to calm down," I compel. She nods. Her breathing and heartrate slow. "Listen to me very carefully. You are not mental. Everything that you saw was real."

"Why are you telling me this?" she breathes. "Are you going to kill me?"

"Of course not, Meredith. You are my friend. I would never do anything to hurt you." She frowns. "I'm telling you this because I want you to know that you are safe now."

"I'm telling you…" I tilt my head to the right. "…I smell vampire somewhere around here," I hear from the corner behind me.

"No," I gasp.

"What's wrong?" Meredith asks, her voice trembling with fear.

"You can trust me," I compel. She nods blankly. "Follow me and keep your voice low." I take her by the hand and guide her to the library, away from the vampire hunters. I pull her towards the back and find the bomb shelter that Nathan helped build. I move the cart filled with random books including a copy of *Satanic Verses* and the Bible ironically. I wrap my free hand around the door handle and drive my shoulder into it. Even with my strength, it only barely yields. The door opens, and I shove Meredith inside.

"What just happened?" She shakes her head and takes in the narrow mint green room with its rows of stacked bedding. "How did we get here? And where is here?"

I sigh. "It is a bomb shelter that my Nathan showed me on my first day of college…I mean, school." She nods absently. "He knew about this shelter because he helped build it, back in the nineteen-forties."

"What?"

"What if I told you that every movie, every television program, and every book about supernatural beings…was true to a degree?"

"No." She scoffs and turns away to come back. "No, that's impossible."

"Not only is it possible, Meredith, it's true…and you know it."

"And my mom sent me to a shrink?" she asks, showing hints of her old self.

"Meredith, I am proof that it is all real. I am a vampire." She shakes her head. I lower my fangs as my eyes move over to deep blue. She backs away quickly. "I will not hurt you…" I hide my vampire side away. "…I promise. I am your friend, Meredith."

"Alana, you're…you're…"

"And now you get my name right."

She shudders into a tear-filled laugh. I laugh as well. I sigh and lean against the nearest bunk bed. Kya takes so much out of me. My mother went through this without the benefit of my accelerated healing. She must have loved me as much as I love my daughter.

"Alana…" I look at her. "…are you alright?"

"That is…a long story…will you hear it?"

"I didn't feel like sitting through my first day of school anyway…to have everyone looking at the poor little rich girl, who got so delirious, because of a stupid crash diet…" She scoffs. "…that she tried to burn down her own house."

I nod. I tell her the story of my birth…I recite what I know of my Nathan's life…which surprises even me that I know so much. I tell her about my years of Rapunzel-like lifestyle. I tell her about coming to school here after meeting Nathan…and the ordeal with Jeremiah…

"So, Jeremiah was a vampire hunter?"

I nod. "We…backtracked to his lair after, we…" I shudder this time. "…dumped his body…" I weep…though I cannot honestly say if it is caused by mood swing or memory. "…we couldn't even give him a proper burial." She places a comforting hand on my shoulder. "He was my friend…he gave his life to save mine."

She nods.

I sigh and muster the strength to continue. I tell her the real reason behind my and Nathan's break-up, which also surprises me with how much anger I still feel from that time. I tell her the truth about Nathan and Angela's trip to New Orleans and Paris. I tell her…still with giddy joy about my and Nathan's reconciliation and…how we celebrated our reunion.

"OMG," she carps. "How did I not notice before?" I frown. "You're pregnant."

"I…"

"I can tell…your cheeks are rounder, and your nose is broader…"

"Hey!" I warn, covering the tip of my nose.

She laughs. "…and your waist…it's bigger…not to mention…" She stares at my chest. I scoff and close my cardigan around me. "…how far along are you?"

"Well, it did not happen the first time…but…I'm over three months along."

"YEEEEE," she practically squeals. "I'm going to be a Godmother…wait, am I?"

"Sorry. Nathan wants Angela to be her godmother since she helped with our reconciliation."

"Wow, so she took all that crap I gave her about you two, and she's a part of the reason you're together again."

"She is a good person." Meredith nods. I continue and tell her about Nathan and my wedding.

"YOU'RE MARRIED?" I draw my necklace up, pulling my rings from my apparently increasing bosom. "THAT IS ONE HUGE ROCK!" She cups both rings in her hands. "Why aren't you wearing them?"

"We've decided to keep the marriage a secret in favor of maintaining our new identities here." She nods. I sigh. "Also…my fingers are already swollen to the point that I can no longer wear them comfortably." I weep again.

"Mood swing?" I nod while covering my mouth. "My cousin used to get them." She gives me a hug. "She was so much worse than you."

I nod. I dry my eyes before continuing through our honeymoon and Angela's report of the party.

"So, my cousin Bethany is a witch…?" I nod. "…and Angela saw that…in me too…and she thinks that Bethany was trying to drain whatever magic I had away." I nod again. "Why?"

"That…is the REAL reason that Angela and Nathan aren't here today."

"Why didn't you go?" I touch my stomach. "Right."

"And…because I thought that I would be the best person…to be here for you if you needed." She nods this time. I smooth down her wily mane. "And clearly, I was right."

"I'm a witch?"

"You mean you didn't already know that?"

"My mom never mentioned it…"

"No, I meant your personality," I joke.

"Very funny."

"Besides, since Bethany took the last name Sloane, it's probably your father's side." I smile and pull her hair up into a ponytail. I pull mother's ribbon from my hair and wrap it around hers.

"Thank you."

"Well, we could not have the Queen Bee of this school reclaiming her throne with unkempt…"

"No. Well, yeah…but…" She takes my hand and kisses the back of it. "Thank you for being honest with me." She nods. "I have to admit…the world has seemed different since…Bethany tried to kill me." She sighs. "People…seem different." She stares into my eyes. "You seem different…but something about you told me I could trust you."

I smile. "You can…can I trust you? …to keep my secret?"

"Well, it's kind of my secret too, right?"

"No." I hold my rings up. "My other secret."

"Right. You're starting your own family." She touches my stomach. "We're going to have to take you shopping…find something that will help cover this up…at least until your third trimester." I look at her. "…my cousin."

"Come on. We should get to class."

She nods and looks at her phone. "Already third period." She goes over to the door and grabs the handle. She pulls and pulls on the handle. The door opens on her third pull. I frown…until Natavius's head crosses the threshold.

"I've been standing guard," he says simply. I nod and smile.

Meredith points at him. "So, he REALLY isn't Angela's boyfriend?" I shake my head. "So, Angela's single?" I nod. "Is she…?"

"No," Natavius says at the same time I do. Oh, that ping from his heart was so strong that it made Kya move.

"Something tells me I can trust him too," she says, staring at Natavius.

"You can." Natavius nods and smiles. "You can trust all of us."

#####

Chapter 16: Ghosts

"Jamie-Lynn?" the guy with a gun to my head grumbles. He swallows a lump and his eyes dart to her then back to me. "Jamie-Lynn, I…"

"SHUT UP!" she snaps. "Because anything you say in this moment will not cover two years of me crying myself to sleep most nights…or where you've been for the last nine years." She makes her way down the stairs. Captain Gorgeousness catches her wrist…with a super protective vibe. "LET…GO…" she groans through clenched teeth. He does.

"Everybody," she starts again, further proving who's in charge in this place. "RELAX. I need my best friend to NOT be in handcuffs, because with my dead dad being alive after nine years of thinking that he's not…I have a feeling I'm gonna need him." She looks around. "Who has the keys to Alex and Kai's cuffs?"

"That'd be me," I say. She leans so that she can see me past her father. She frowns. "Yeah, I'm a vampire…it's daytime…and I have a gun to my head. Weird day."

"I'll say," she returns. "Okay. Everybody just…stop. Okay?" She throws her hand out. "Tony, we'll start with you. Put the knife away." I look back, and the blade disappears. "Now, you…whoever you are…take…whatever that is away from my dad." Nate's eyes dart to me. I nod as much as I can. He lowers his staff. "Dad?"

He grits his teeth, and his finger wiggles on the trigger.

"DAD!" she shouts. I was expecting a whine, but she's a little firecracker. He puts the gun away. "Vampire?" I stand and slip my knife into its sheath…and show my empty hands. "Ninja?" Nate lets her go, and she stands. Her head tilts toward me for a fraction of a second. Crap. She is not going to… She drives the silver spike toward my chest! The air turns electric, and the world slows. "Ven-tu-lus," Jamie-Lynn barks, and a small tornado throws the 'ninja' toward the doors. Her spike tumbles away. "I said…relax."

Jamie-Lynn steps up to me and stares me down. My eyes bulge. "Can I help the badass, super witch?"

"No…well, introductions…maybe. Jamina Lynda Baggett…Jamie-Lynn to most…Jamie to my friends…" She tips her head back toward Captain Gorgeousness. "Jamina to him and my mom."

"You're glowing…like seriously…pale white," I mutter, before I can stop myself…I'm trying to cut my ability off, but it won't. It's like being this close to her switched it on automatically. "Sorry." I shake my head. "Angela Nicole Price." I offer my hand.

"I know," she says and shakes my hand. She knows? "Which makes you…" She looks at Nate. "…Nathan Francois."

"Dumont," Nate and I say at the same time.

She nods. "Sure." She points at the brown-haired kid, no longer looking like a red furred fox/wolf thing, in the black hoodie. "My friend?"

"Right." I slip the keys out of my pocket and go over to Nate's skinwalker. "You're not going to attack me if I undo these cuffs...right? I mean, clearly I'm the most hated person in the room."

"Second, most hated," the guy growls, glaring at Jamie's dad. I nod and undo his cuffs. I help him up. "Thanks," he says, still glaring at Jamie's dad. Clearing up which one is the best friend. I move over to the blond.

"You," Jamie snarls, pointing at her dad. "Library. Now."

"Jamie-Lynn, I'm your father and you don't..."

"Excuse me!" she rumbles, causing Captain Gorgeousness to move away from her and Tony to move away from her dad. Even Nate takes a step away. "You fake your own death...and drop out of my life for over 9 years...and now, you want to come back and play the 'dad card'...now, that I'm like a month and a half shy of 18. Really? Is that REALLY what's happening?"

"Wow," Nate gripes. "She's just like her mother."

"Tell me about it," Gorgeousness and Tony say at the same time.

"Library." She throws her arm out and points to her right. "Now."

He marches in that direction. "Good luck, James," Nate whispers.

"Boss," the ninja says staying put near the door. "I'm outside of my depth here."

"Stay frosty," Jamie's dad says. "Don't do anything until I get back." He continues into the library.

Jamie closes the doors behind them. "Verba Sonent," she says...and all sound coming from the library cuts out. I'm not even picking up anyone's breathing.

"She does that," the best friend says, as I help the other skinwalker to his feet. I nod. "I'm Alex Garner, by the way." He tips his head to blondie. "That's my cousin, Kai."

"Hey, Alex...Kai...sorry about the whole..."

"It's cool."

"No, it's not," Tony growls. "You two broke into our home..."

"We're not the only ones," Nate glares at the ninja. She turns her head away. "I recognize your scent from the woods. You were one of the hunters after me and my wife."

"Your wife...is a blood sucking monster," she growls back. "She deserves the same thing I'm gonna do to..." Her chin juts out toward me. "...that abomination first chance I get."

"Wrong answer," I whisper. Nate's on her before anyone realizes. Almost anyone. Tony's between them with his hands extended to Nate in a calming way. Alex is too…only closer to the ninja…real close. He's taking more of a protective stance though.

"Stop it, everybody," Gorgeousness says. "Jamina says stop so…"

"So, this McCabe Witch has the two of you wrapped around her little finger, too," Nate mocks. That's weird…not Nate mocking someone, he does that all the time. The weird part is that he meant it.

"Easy," Gorgeousness grumbles.

"Watch it," Tony warns.

"Besides," Alex says. "She's a Baggett Witch, not a McCabe Witch." Geez, if I didn't know that he fell into the category of best friend, I'd swear he was in love with her, too. Unless, of course, it's one of those best friends secretly pining away for her things. Geez, I'd hate to be in that situation. Oh, wait…

"Everyone's so hostile," Kai jokes, trying and failing to lighten the mood.

"Nate," I say. He looks at me. I tip my head back. "She's a hunter…if I can ignore her…I know you can."

He sighs and steps away. "So," the ninja starts. "You marry one vampire and kowtow to another one? Man, you wolves are worse than we thought."

I catch Nate's arm before he can even turn back around. I pull him back around to face me. "Ignore her. Do you hear me?" He takes a deep breath and nods as his eyes drift closed.

"Shut up, Tracy," Alex complains. "You're only making things worse"

"What?" the ninja snaps.

"Yeah," Nate adds, taking the chance to get a little payback taunting. "That's what James said your name was out in the woods. Tracy Harper…"

"Harper?" Kai asks with shock, peppering his voice. "As in Stephen Harper's sister?"

She sighs. Slips her goggles off and lowers her mask, revealing gorgeous mocha colored skin, a tiny little round nose, big brown eyes, and full pouty lips. She runs her hand over her pixie cut hair and scowls.

"How did I not know this?" Alex asks. "Does Stephen know?"

"No, and he NEVER has to…my parents either. They think I'm a student at Georgia Tech…on a full scholarship and with a full-time job to help make ends meet."

"Instead, you're out lopping the heads off vampires," I say.

"Shut up, you filthy blood-sucking parasite."

"I'm pretty human-vegan-kosher actually. Never had a drop of human blood…but you're making me seriously reconsider my stance on human blood bags."

Tracy twirls a silver dagger. "You're welcome to try it, blondie."

The library doors swing open, and Jamie storms out like a freight train. She walks directly over to Tony and slaps him so hard that I'm surprised she didn't break her hand. "YOU KNEW," she screams with tears cascading down her face. "YOU KNEW MY DAD WAS ALIVE AND YOU SAID NOTHING! YOU LOOKED ME IN THE FACE...LISTENED TO ME TELL YOU HOW MUCH IT HURT ME WHEN HE DIED...AND WITH EVERYTHING GOING ON WITH MY MOM, YOU DIDN'T THINK TO SAY A THING!" Tony opens his mouth, but nothing comes out...I think even less would come out of mine if I were in his position. She shakes her head, trying to keep in tears that get away anyway.

"We," Gorgeousness starts. "...didn't think..."

"You knew, too?" she weeps.

Gorgeousness draws his lips into his mouth and nods. "Your mom told me...in New Orleans."

"Perfect," she sighs, and her shoulders slump. She seems...broken. I can't believe it...but I just want to hug her. She wipes her eyes on her sleeve. "That's just effin' perfect..." She runs up the stairs.

A thud sounds. The room turns back to Tony...still reeling from a punch from Alex. He holds two fingers up in Tony's face. "That's twice," Alex growls. He shoves Gorgeousness aside and runs up the stairs after Jamie.

"Twice what?" I ask.

"Twice that this jerk has pulled this lie of omission crap on Jamie," Kai says, sounding almost as angry as Alex.

"So, you're lying to this one, too," Nate says, taking a jab at both brothers simultaneously.

Gorgeousness says nothing. He crosses his arms, holds his right fist up to his mouth and turns away.

"Don't start," Tony replies, wiping blood from the corner of his mouth.

"You know about the legend of these brothers right, Ange?" Nate continues, clearly starting. I nod. "Then you know about them and the town...but did my cousin tell you about their connection to the McCabe witch bloodline?"

"So," James rumbles walking out of the library with his hands behind his back. "Not only did you both fall for my wife, but now my daughter, too?"

"Ex-wife, considering," Gorgeousness says.

"Considering what?"

"Actually," Tony says with a deep, mournful voice. "Jamie was owed a favor from the Fairy Queen..."

"Fairy Queen?" I ask.

"Yes, she's actually quite nice," Nate says lacking chalance. "What was the favor?" Tony, James, and Nate all stand in a circle...equidistance from each other. Weird, the three of them act as if they hate each other, but still, they're all standing together as if they're in a huddle.

"Jamina, wished to do away with the part of the curse that makes us love her bloodline," Gorgeousness says.

"Did it work?" James asks. Gorgeousness shrugs, but Tony nods. "How can you be so sure?"

"We're back," a voice sings from the door. A gorgeous girl with honey-colored skin and light brown eyes saunters in with perfect wavy, dark red hair. Tony sees her, takes in a short, but deep breath, and his pupils dilate briefly. That's how he knows, he's really feeling this girl. She stares into a burlap shopping bag as she walks in. "Mitch and Zoe are getting the rest out of the car…" She lifts her eyes. "…and…" She checks every face. "…whoa…company…"

"Shay?" Nate says.

"Nathan?" she gasps, she actually gasped. She runs to him and throws her arms over his shoulders. He puts his around the small of her back. They separate, and she shoves him. "…you never call…you never write. I thought you died, man."

"No such luck," he whispers.

"Are you still on that insane death wish?"

"I'll admit to it, if you will." She purses her lips and shakes her head.

"So, this is what became of little Shay Hallowell?" James asks.

"James?" she whispers with just as much shock. "Wow, it's like a reunion." She hugs him.

I step over to Nate. "I thought you said that she would…"

He shakes his head. "Just because it hasn't happened yet…" He looks at me with green and gold eyes. "…doesn't mean it still won't." I frown and look down. I recognize that tone… I stare at Shay. …he only uses that tone when he's worries about a loved one. Shay separates from James and smiles. Nate thinks Shay's going to die… She looks between the pair and smiles. …and soon.

#####

"I love you too, mom. Speak soon." I end the call and slip my phone into my back pocket. "Okay," I say turning to Nate, Alex, and Kai. "Bethany, Il Cuoro Nero…or Bethany the Black-hearted…or Bethany Triste, Grand Dark Witch…former best friend of…you can't make this stuff up…Elven Princess Evangeline of the Light."

"Meghan's royalty?" Alex asks with high arching eyebrows. I nod.

"That'd explain the attitude," Kai adds.

"Hey. That's my cousin you're talking about." Kai holds his hands up. "I'm kidding. She was a total brat who got everything she wanted when we were kids. I can only assume she got worse in her late teens."

"So, you were never affected by her glamour?" Alex asks.

"Her what now?"

"Never mind."

"So, anyway…Bethany tried to be cliché and rule the world…her, apparently, former best friend Evangeline didn't agree with her. They fought. Bethany lost. She was believed dead until she resurfaced a few decades ago."

"Decades?" Nate asks. I nod, recognizing that look on his face. He's thinking about… "…like Nelfie."

"Nelfie?" Alex asks.

"Nelfala LeBeau," Nate says. "She's a friend of mine."

"Was a friend of yours," Tony says, moving into the library, big heavy book in hand.

"Was?" Nate growls, following him. I follow Nate…like always, and the boys follow me. I look around, and it's an actual library in here. Tons of books line the walls…leather sofa for lounging to my left…fully stocked bar on my right, looking like something right out of the 1950s…and across from the door a huge desk with all kinds of symbols carved into it that look vaguely familiar. It smells like a library in here, too. It smells like old books and hours spent pouring over them…and little like liquor.

"She…" Tony says, picking up a heavy-looking book from the top of the desk. I didn't realize at first, but the desk seems to be carved into the floor…as if someone cut off a tree and used the base of it to make this desk, leaving the roots intact. "…um…teamed up with Daphne and…" He examines the book and nods. He looks…I don't know. Different. He doesn't look as hard or angry as he did earlier. I'd say sad, but I don't know him that well. "…she died Nate." I gasp. Oh no… "She used blood magic and mixed it with necromancy and…" Nate trembles as if hit by a stun gun. "…she bled out while trying to kill us…I'm sorry." Tony hurries out of the library.

"Nate?"

"I'm fine," he snaps.

"You're lying…" I put my hand on his shoulder. "…and it's not your fault." He looks at me with two tear-filled eyes. I shake my head. I know how he felt about Nelfie. He feels the same way about me. She was his best friend…until she tried to be more…she tried to force her way into his heart. I guess I should take that as a warning…while I stare longingly at another woman's husband.

"Nate." I shake him at the shoulder. He says nothing. I snap my fingers in his face. "Snap out of it. I need you here, okay?"

He takes a deep breath and puts his right hand over his face. He nods and lowers his hand. "How has Bethany maintained her…youth?" He still sounds upset, but at least he was able to focus.

"Wow, just like that?" Kai whispers to Alex.

"According to my mom," I continue. "…she was discovered because she drained one of her descendants of their magic and youth."

He puts his hand on his chin. "Which is probably what she was trying to do to Merrie." I nod.

"Apparently," Alex whispers back to Kai. "The only person that calms me down that fast is Gwen."

"Do you think they're a thing?" Kai asks.

"Do you think we should warn Merrie's next of kin?" I ask, leaning against the bar and ignoring the whisper twins. Nate shakes his head. "You're thinking that Meredith was probably the cream of the crop, right?" He nods.

"She couldn't have done that good a job of draining her," Alex says. We turn to him. He stares awkwardly between us. Nate motions for him to continue. "Right." He runs his fingers through his hair. "Well, when she attacked us at Prom, she…" He shakes his head. "…I don't know. It seemed like she used up all her magic. She resorted to using this crystal thing that was basically an explosion in a bottle." Nate nods. "Then when I was brought back here…" He groans. "…after she knocked me out, Jamie said the same thing happened…she ran out of magic and resorted to summoning ghouls."

"So, while her youth remains," Nate says, using that big, beautiful brain of his…you know, not that all his parts aren't beautiful. And not that I should be thinking about ANY of his parts. "…the more she uses her magic, the faster it leaves her."

"I was gonna say," Kai jokes, warranting a glare from Nate that makes him take a step back. "Sorry. Wow, and I thought Sora had a wicked glare." Alex nods in agreement. "Speaking of which, hey, why do you seem so familiar to me?"

"Because Kai Garner," Nate says, still deep in thought. "I visited your family about ten years ago." Nate looks at Kai with just his eyes.

"After…everything with Shay and her family, I felt a need to make a new connection to my family…I knew my father's side well enough. So, I went looking for my mother's tribe again…her clan…her family."

"And you went looking for our family?" Alex asks.

"Yep. It turns out that my mother's tribe married into a larger clan of skinwalkers from the East about a century ago. They were absorbed…into an old Scottish clan, the Warnier…the Tending Warriors…or as they're called today, the Garner clan of skinwalkers."

"Are you saying…?" Kai starts.

"Yes…hello, Cousin Kai, son of Flynn…" He turns to Alex. "…which I suppose makes you, Cousin Alex, son of Riley…great, great, great, and twice removed, but yeah." He tilts his head back. "I do have to ask though…where's Sora? I figured she'd be your clan's Alpha by now."

"She's only 18," Alex whines. Nate shrugs.

"And a girl," Kai adds.

"And?" I snarl.

"Your clan is still stuck in the old ways," Nate says, sounding like a poet from the 19th century. "If the A'kani tribe ever had a girl as their eldest Mosi'son…she'd be the next Alpha. Period."

"Ah-kahn-nigh?" they ask.

"Don't you guys know anything?" I ask as if I've been doing this for years. "The A'kani tribe was the name of the original gathering of wolves that spread across the world to create the modern-day wolves like Nate and his pack and all the other packs, clans, and bloodlines of today." I flick my thumb at him. "Nate here's actually the current A'kani tribe's Alpha's brother." Nate's heart skips a beat. I look at him. I mouth a silent. 'Should I not have told them that?' He shakes his head subtly. If the fact that I told them his ancestry isn't what bothered him, I wonder what it was.

"Speaking of stuck in the old ways," Nate says, deflecting my line of thought. "…why didn't either of you use hunter's step against us…?"

"Too tight a space," Alex whines. Kai nods. "Hunter's steps good in fights…but it gets…problematic in tight spaces." Nate appears between them and flicks both their noses at the same time. "Ow!"

"Rude!" Kai snarls, covering his face.

"You two just need to learn more control." He steps back and glares at them. "Also, your attacks were shallow. You rely on your teeth and claws too much…you let your animal do too much…but your human half doesn't do enough." He tilts toward Alex. "Especially, you."

"Me? What'd I do?"

"You're an Alpha Class skinwalker...yet..." He holds up his right hand with a piece of fur between his middle and pointer fingers. "...you felt the need to use this."

Alex checks his hoodie pockets. "HEY!!!" Nate's eyes change to green and gold. He growls and focuses...the whites of his eyes slowly turn black. "Whoa...your eyes are like that Rais guy's," Alex says.

"So, you've met Rais?"

"Who?" I ask.

"Another descendant of my mother's original clan," Nate says casually. "...only along a different bloodline. He actually pointed me toward the Garners." I nod. He turns back to Alex and Kai. "If you two want, I can teach you how to fight."

"We don't need..."

Alex shoves Kai. "Considering how easy the two of them beat us?" Kai bows his head. "Why would you teach us how to fight though? I mean, you barely know us."

"Because you're his family," I say. "D'uh." Nate smirks.

"When do we start?" Kai asks.

"Now," I say with a laugh...as Nate sweeps Alex's legs out from under him while punching Kai in the kidney. They both hit the floor...hard.

"This is a library," Kai whines, holding his side in the fetal position.

Nate stands. "Yes, because an enemy would never attack in a library." He turns to me. "Ange, I'll let you take Kai...show him the basics of what Natavius showed you about speed..."

"Hunter's step?" I ask.

He nods. "It's what skinwalkers came to know Natavius's speed as." He looks at Alex. "Some skinwalkers know it naturally, most have to be taught."

"Then I guess school's in," I joke. "Crap." Nate looks at me. "Middleton Prep started a week before most schools. We've already missed two days."

"School can wait," Nate says. "We can stay a little longer to help them...besides we need to stick around and see if Bethany shows up."

"Haha," Kai bellows. "Not likely..." He points at Alex. "...I mean, who goes out of their way to see their ex."

"You dated her?" I complain.

"I was going through a bad patch," he says, standing.

"I'll say," Kai pokes.

"At least, I didn't hook up with her," Alex grumbles.

"Eeeeeewwwww. Who hooked up with her?" I look at Kai. "You?"

"I like dudes...so...no." I nod.

"That would be me," Tony says, returning with Captain Gorgeousness and Jamie's dad on his tail.

"How is she?" Alex asks.

"Calling for you," her dad says. "And refusing to talk to any of us."

"Then how…?" Nate starts.

"Zoe," Alex and Kai say at the same time. Alex hurries out of the library.

Jamie's dad glares at me. I frown, and Nate steps between us. "I'm not going to attack her, Nate. I just…" He makes a chopping motion toward me. "…she's a daywalking vampire. Do you have any idea how dangerous that is?"

"You attack her…you attack me." James and Tony look at each other before coming back to Nate. "Angela is under my protection. She's not dangerous."

"But what if this secret gets out," Tony says. "Others will want to be daywalkers like her."

"Select club," I say, simply. "Not all vampires can do it, in fact, only a handful meet the requirements." I nod, before bowing my head. Tears swim in my eyes. "And even fewer than that can do what needs to be done to make it happen." Nate puts his arm around me. I shiver as he strokes my head.

"What's going on?" Kai asks.

"This," Nate starts. "…is why I say Angela's not dangerous. THIS is her reaction to killing a daemon…imagine how bad killing a human would affect her."

"Still," Tony continues. "How could you keep this from us?"

"Me? How could the three of you keep the fact that James was alive from his daughter? If I had a daughter…" Nate's heart thuds in his chest…he does have a daughter…or he will. "…and she thought I was dead…I'd do everything in my power to let her know that I wasn't…" He glares at James. "…and get back to her."

"There were," Tony starts.

"…extenuating circumstances," James says.

Quincy nods. "…only reason we went along with Daphne's story."

"It was Daphne's idea?" The three of them nod. Nate sighs.

"Angela," Alex says from the library doorway. "Jamie wants to see you."

Nate lets go of me…without actually letting go. He holds onto my arms and rubs up to my shoulders…not fair.

"I'm fine," I say as if I'm anything but. He nods, and I step away from him…one of my least favorite things to do. I follow Alex up the stairs and to the left. We walk down this dark, hardwood hallway…with tan covering the walls at about waist height and going up to the ceiling. Cast iron chandeliers hang between every door.

Alex stops on the opposite side of the second door on the right. He tips his head inside. I walk in. Jamie sits on the edge of a huge bed with her arms around her knees. I go over to her and Tracy growls from the deep green curtains covering a massive front window. "Shut…up," I sigh, while kneeling in front of Jamie. "How are you? I mean…"

She releases her knees, slides off the bed and wraps her arms around me. I freeze. "I'm so glad you're safe," she whispers. I huff a laugh and hug her back. She lets go, and I wipe her eyes…she doesn't even flinch at the cold of my hand.

"I've never really equated vampire life with being…safe."

She smiles. "Then I guess it's a good thing that you're both witch and vampire."

"Yeah, I don't know how that worked out exactly. My mom says that the day walking ritual somehow activated my magic…but I don't get that…"

She nods. "Well, how did you become a day walking vampire?"

"I had to fight and kill a higher order daemon, if that makes sense." She nods. I sigh as the thought runs through my head for only about the fortieth time today.

"It's okay, Angela. It really is."

I nod. "How do you know me? Are you a friend of my cousin, Meghan's?"

"Yeah, but that's not how I know you." She takes a piece of paper from her back pocket. I take it and unfold it…I read over a list of…I don't know what…ending with the words *one blood flower*. I lift confused eyes.

"A few months back, when my mom went missing the first time…" It's so weird. She was such a badass downstairs with all the guys, but here…with just me, Alex, and Tracy…she seems so much younger than she is. "…I lost it, and I was looking for help anywhere I could find it. I contacted a friend of my mom's, and she gave me those potion ingredients for a locator spell."

I nod. "I hope it helped."

"Not really," she replies with a laugh. "But she was so supportive…and she called to check on me all the time and talked me down off more than a few ledges." I nod, staring into her eyes. "Tell Maria…tell your mom, I said, 'thank you.'"

I gasp. "My mom…?" She nods. "She is kind of awesome, isn't she?"

Jamie nods again and wipes her eyes. "She was so worried about you…but she helped me…even with everything she was going through…probably because of everything she was going through. I don't think I could've done it without her."

"That's the same thing you said about me," a voice says from the door.

"ZO!" Jamie says. She stands and runs to the pretty girl with the mocha complexion, gorgeous high cheekbones, and jet-black hair. She wraps her arms around Jamie. "Zo, I know this is going over quota but…"

"Don't worry about it," Zo, who I guess was Zoe who Shay mentioned, says. "Quincy told me what happened…" Jamie nods into her shoulder.

"Zoe?" Tracy says.

"Hey, Trace," Zoe hums. "Quincy gave me the rundown about you, too." Tracy nods and retreats a bit.

"Okay, this is getting too weird even for me."

"What did you say, vampire?" Tracy snarls.

"Vampire?" Zoe asks.

"I'll tell you later," Jamie says. "What is it, Angela?"

"All of this." I point at Jamie. "Our moms…my cousin…your dad…" I flick my thumb at Tracy. "…her…" I throw my hand toward Alex. "…him…Nate…the brother's…all of it." I shake my head, ignoring all the eyes staring at me. "It's weird, but we've all been crisscrossing for years…" Jamie frowns. "…it's kind of like we're all one big family…and we're coming up on a reunion."

Alex steps into the room. "Kind of like…it's all fate…?" I nod…slowly.

#####

Chapter 18: Circle

"Trust me," Natavius says, climbing the brownstone's stairs. "If anyone can help, it'll be her." I barely register his words…I stare at the sun…I've never seen it without protection before that day at the cabin. I sigh. "Lana?"

"Anna?" Meredith calls from the third step. "Are you alright?" I nod. "Why aren't you glittering or whatever?" I frown. "You're a…" She looks around and puts her hand next her mouth. "…vampire, right?" she whispers. "Shouldn't you look like you have diamonds embedded in your skin in the sunlight or something?"

"Why on God's green Earth would a vampire do that in the sunlight?"

Natavius snickers. "Um…that book…remember…"

"Oh…right. Those books where a vampire fell in love with a human." I shake my head. "No more ridiculous than a vampire falling in love with a wolf, I suppose." Meredith smiles. "Well, rest assured that if not for extenuating circumstances…I would not be glittering in the sunlight, I'd be burning in it…" I steal one more glance at the sun. "…instead of standing here in awe of it."

Meredith bobs her head. "Got it. Vampires burn in sunlight."

"Normally," I murmur, tilting my head back to bask in the rays of the sun. Odd, Kya feels at peace. Vance said that my immunity to sunlight has not negatively affected her growth or development, but… I sigh. …do I really wish to press my luck?

The call box buzzes as Natavius leans into the button with his thumb. "Yes," a mature woman's voice answers.

"It's me."

"Come on up," she replies.

Another buzz sounds, followed by a mechanical clack. I sigh and trudge up the stairs. I thought I enjoyed storms, but clearly, I enjoy being outside during the day without protective covering. I step into the building as Natavius and Meredith reach the top of the ground floor. I follow, keeping their scents as a guiding marker. We reach the third floor, and they stand just outside of flat 4A as opposed to 4B, directly across the hall.

The door opens. I frown. A woman who appears to be a slightly older version of Angela with dark brown hair steps out into the portal. She wraps both arms around Natavius, and he reciprocates. "Oh," she hums. "How much do you miss that daughter of mine?"

"A ton already," Natavius admits. Her daughter…? So, this IS Angela's mother. Natavius has brought us to Maria Price's flat.

"Aw, then I really have bad news for you, sweetheart. I just talked to her. She says that she and Nathan will be staying down in North Carolina for a few days longer." Natavius nods.

"They will?" I ask absently. She nods, never removing her eyes from Natavius. "He didn't tell me that." I stare at my mobile. I sigh. He made me promise to check in only every four hours or in case of emergencies…otherwise, he knew I'd be calling him every other minute. Almost an hour until the next call.

"Is this her?" Maria asks. I lift my eyes, expecting to meet hers. She stares at Meredith. Natavius nods. "Oh, I could tell…look at you, as new as a shiny penny." She steps back into her doorway. "Come in, come in," she says, beckoning us forward. Natavius enters after Meredith. Maria stops me at the threshold. "Not you." I frown. "I know exactly who you are little miss 'Midnight Princess.'"

"Pardon?"

"Just like I know the hell you've put my daughter through." I shake my head. "Don't deny it. I get that she's in love with the guy you're in love with…"

"She is?" Meredith asks.

"…but that's no excuse for you treating her that way. You can't help who you fall in love with…even if they're taken." I nod with tears welling in my eyes. Up until a second ago, I was fully prepared to defend myself…defend my actions…but one mood swing later and…

I weep. "I'm so, so sorry," I sob. "I promise I did not mean to treat her so poorly. I love her, I swear."

"Oh," Maria whispers, stepping out into the hall. "I didn't mean it. I was just pulling your leg." She wraps her arms around me. "It's okay. Shhh," she attempts to soothe me, but it's too late. The floodgates have opened, and Kya is only adding fuel to the fire. "What's wrong? Is she alright?"

"Um," Natavius purrs.

"Mood swing," Meredith suggests accurately.

Maria gasps. "Oh, you're pregnant!" I sniff and nod, trying to clear away some of the mess on my face. More follows its dismissal immediately. "Come in, come in." She ushers me inside. "Get off your feet. Natavius, bring a…" Before she can finish, a chair slides in behind my legs. She lowers me onto it. "There. Are you alright, dear?" I nod, although my continued tears say otherwise. "Do you need a pillow for your back? An ottoman for your feet?"

I shake my head. "I'm sorry," I repeat. "My daughter…is part Aldien…and part wolf…her emotions affect and often act as a catalyst to my own…" My eyes swell. "…and they are soooo intense for someone so small."

Maria nods and caresses my cheek. "Sweetie, that'd be true if you were part angel or not." I smile. Natavius offers a box of tissues.

"Thank you," I whisper, while taking one…and then another…and then four more. The three of them continue focusing on me. "I'll be fine, I promise. We're not here to help me…" I sniff and wipe my nose. "…we're here for you, Meredith."

"But we can take a minute to focus on you, Anna."

"Who's Anna?" Maria asks.

"Me."

"I thought your name was Alana."

"It is." My eyes dart to Meredith. "Bit of an inside joke." Maria laughs with a nod. "And for what it's worth, I am sorry for how I've treated Angela. My…empathic abilities are a bit of a blessing and a curse. I felt her emotions for my Nathan unintentionally and that was a terrible invasion of her privacy. And worse, I used that information against her and that is unfair."

"Wow."

"What?"

"Angela wasn't lying. You are the real deal, aren't you?"

"Real…deal?"

"An Aldien," Natavius submits. "Angel-kind. Nephilim."

"I suppose."

Maria nods. "Forgive me, it's just…to actually meet one of you…once in a lifetime thing."

"I am the last, yes."

"Really?" Meredith asks. I nod. "That's so sad."

"Not even the half of it," Natavius says. "She's also the last original vampire." Meredith gasps.

"The last of two noble houses," I complain…my mood sinks. Kya's follows and with it more tears. I sigh. "Meredith. We are here to aid you…in your adaptation to this new life that has been thrust upon you."

Maria nods. "Alright, maybe if we change subject your and your daughter's moods will lift." I nod. She turns to Meredith. "Alright, sweetie, give me your hands." Meredith places both hands in Maria's. "Whew. Oh yeah, you definitely have the gift…it seems you've had a seal recently removed." Meredith frowns. "Should I tell you about your…" She makes air quotes. "…'cousin' Bethany?"

Meredith nods. Maria tells us the story of the 400-year-old dark witch who tried to conquer the world only to be stopped by the elf who she considered her best friend. She follows by telling us that after their epic battle Bethany was believed to have died, but four decades ago, she resurfaced while draining the life force of one of her own descendants.

"So," Meredith starts with a shiver. "Bethany's…not my cousin…she's what…my great-great-great-great-grandmother?"

"Add a coupla more greats," Natavius suggests. "But yeah." He nods. "I remember hearing about the story. They fought in France…Evangeline of the Light was from Rome…her family ruled from the shadows…ironically enough." He sighs. "From what I understand, Bethany had amassed a secret army before Evangeline confronted her. After the battle though…" He frowns. "…those people…her servants…they vanished."

"Natavius?"

He looks to me. "There was a girl…" He wipes his mouth. "…her name was Amelia…she was my friend but fell under Bethany's thrall. I tried to find her after Bethany fell…but most of her village was gone." I extend my hand to him. He takes it, and I caress his with my other. He sighs.

"But," Meredith starts. "Does that mean that I'm evil?" Maria frowns. "I mean, my ancestor Bethany was a Dark Witch…" She shivers again. "…from the sound of it, she was the boogie woman of the witch world…and I have her magic in me."

Maria laughs. "No, sweetheart…" She wraps her arms around Meredith. "No." She sighs. "What you are…Witch of Shadow or Witch of Light…has no bearing on the person that you are. It's only the type of magic you wield."

Maria motions to me. "Take Alana and my daughter for instance. They're both vampires. By definition what they are means that they should take life to sustain their own existence." She nods. "But my daughter and Alana are both good people. They deny those urges to do good in the world."

Meredith huffs a laugh. "I'm not exactly the poster child for good behavior," she jokes. "I've been kind of a mean girl…bully…all my life…" She scoffs. "…oh, and a closet lesbian." Natavius arches his eyebrows. "Yeah," she adds, becoming agitated. "I'm a big d-"

"Stop that right now," Maria warns. "Don't you dare let labels affect the person you are." Meredith frowns. "You're a high school mean girl…so what? You've still got an honest to goodness angel routing for you." Meredith looks to me. I smile. "You have friends who support you." Meredith nods. "Then don't let anything else ever stop you from being what you want to be."

Maria steps away and goes to the kitchen. "They're just labels…labels are for cans of soup…or tea…" She comes back. "…speaking of which, who wants some." Natavius and Meredith raise their hands. Kya prompts me to raise mine as well.

Maria returns from the kitchen after a few minutes. "It'll be ready in a few. Now, Meredith. You won't be able to use healing spells or spirit magic as well as a Witch of Light could…but I can help you with some basic defensive and offensive spells if you'd like."

Meredith nods. "I would."

"And Anna," Maria jokes. "I'd also like to teach you some spirit magic, too."

"Me? I'm a vampire. Vampires can't use magic."

"My daughter's a vampire and if anything, it activated her magic. Besides, you're part-Aldien, too…and Aldiens are basically beings of pure spirit magic." I frown. "How do you think you're able to feel the emotions of others and compel people?"

I gasp.

"Yes, Angela told me about that, too."

"What?" Meredith asks.

"Aldiens," Maria continues. "Have the ability to manipulate the minds of others with their spirit magic. It's a mind compulsion that pushes others to do as the Aldien wishes. Alana used that same ability to make sure that Angela would never be affected by another's compulsion again…including her own."

"You did?" Meredith asks.

I sigh. "I did something horrible to her…and she was afraid of me. I wanted to set her mind at ease."

"And you did. So, let me help you learn to control your gift." I nod. "Good. My daughter will do anything for you…to keep you and your husband safe." She caresses my cheek. "Which means that you have another layer of protection…because I'll do anything to keep my daughter safe…and that includes keeping you safe."

"Me too, Anna," Meredith declares.

"You know, I've got you," Natavius says.

I huff a laugh as happy tears fill my eyes. I hold my stomach. "Do you hear that Kya? Our family just keeps growing all the time."

#####

Chapter 19: Assault

"It...it is...just..." I sigh. He repeats the sound on the other end. I absently play with my school tie. "...with this training that Maria Price and I have been undergoing...I feel you clearer...even with you there."

"I feel you, too...both of you."

I caress my belly and smile. "We miss you so much."

"You have no idea."

I laugh. "I think you know that we do." He laughs too. "Love you."

"Love you more...both of you."

"How goes your fact-finding mission?"

"I told Raven everything that we found..."

"I am NOT Raven. I AM your wife who misses the sound of your voice..." I clear my throat. "...and other things. Please remember that our honeymoon was cut short."

He laughs. "Oh, believe me, I remember." He inhales deeply. "I reconnected with Tony and James."

"Oh," I hum, remembering the emotion that flowed from him when he told me about his former friends. "Was it...bad?"

"Worse than you'd think..." He groans. "...James, who's a member of the vampire hunter's order, almost killed Angela, I almost killed James, and Tony almost killed me."

"Then I feel it is only fair that I make my very best effort to kill Tony."

"Mood swing?"

I laugh. "Not as much as you would hope." I play with a stitch along Angela's comforter. "He almost killed the love of my life, after all," I pout.

"I'm fine. After things settled down, James contacted a former member of the order here in town. Hugh Taylor and James shared what information they'd gathered on things here in town. It seems a rogue member of their order had been killing supernatural beings whether they were deemed dangerous or not. He was stopped by a group of kids here."

"I do not like it."

"What?"

"I do not trust this order." I nod. "If they're all as zealous as Jeremiah was in his mission."

"Yeah. I'm staying on my guard. Trust me."

"With my life," I whisper. Kya moves ever so slightly. I groan.

"What's wrong?"

"Kya's a little uncomfortable. I think she misses the sound of your voice."

"She'll hear it again soon. I promise."

"Take care of yourself…and Angela."

"I will. Take care of yourself and our daughter…"

"I will."

He huffs a laugh. "…put the phone to your stomach please…"

"Nathan," I laugh in the form of a whine.

"Do it, princess."

"Fine." I do as he requests.

"…Anara," he whispers.

"Her name is Kya."

"Whatever, princess." I laugh. "…be a good girl and protect your mother for me." I shed a happy tear. "Alana?"

I return the phone to my ear. "Yes?"

"I have to go." I nod, and my happy tears turn bitter. "Good bye, my love."

"Good bye, my Nathan." I end the call to the sound of metal striking metal.

I sniff and wipe my eyes. I hurry out into the foyer phone still in hand. The sound repeats as I peer over the railing…at my niece, Mary Margaret, putting on a demonstration against the twins…at the same time. Maggie twirls a metal baton in each hand. The twins repeat the maneuver, circling her at opposite positions.

Kimiko moves toward her silently, from her blindside. She has Maggie. She swings, and Maggie kneels, holding a baton above her head. She deflects the blow. Mimiko takes the opportunity to attack. Maggie blocks her strike, slides her baton along Kimiko's and uses the space to launch an attack against Mimiko.

Mimiko leaps back while blocking the blow. Maggie spins and sweeps the legs out from Kimiko. She manages to get a baton-filled hand down and handsprings away. Maggie pushes off and springs toward Mimiko with dizzying speed. She drives her left baton against both of Mimiko's. She forces both batons skyward and strikes with the right one, landing a crushing blow to Mimiko's left rib cage. Mimiko falls with a whimper, sliding to a stop by the doors.

Maggie turns just in time to prevent Kimiko's next volley. Kimiko strikes and Maggie counters. They repeat this dance, each baton striking its opposite number. Mimiko recovers. She springs to her feet and reclaims her lost weapons. She joins her sister and Maggie, who incorporates the other twin into the ballet. She dispatches each of the sister's attacks effortlessly…she's toying with them. She moves at only half of the speed that she used only a moment ago to give them some chance.

I sense her mood though. She grows tired of the game. She disarms them one weapon at a time…she sweeps both legs out from under Kimiko…and then brings the batons down across her abdomen. She then crushes Mimiko over the knee…before smacking her over the back of the head. Maggie stands and checks on Kimiko…she yields. Mimiko…rises to her hands and knees but extends her hand to Maggie. She yields as well.

I clap, before placing my hands on the railing. She looks up at me and wipes her brow…tickling the tiny tufts of blond hair. "You truly are your mother's daughter." She smiles with a nod.

"T'ank ya, Alana. Comin' from ya, I consider t'at high praise indeed." I laugh. Her accent is as endearing as her sire-mother's. I sigh because it also reminds me that Alexander…is gone as well. Oh, Kya…I love you already, but these mood swings may be giving me whiplash. "Are ya a'ight?"

"Fine. I'm fine. Thank you." She laughs. "What?"

"Yer accent's adorable!"

I shake my head and return to my bedroom. "Oh, my daughter you're…" I frown. "…upset…on edge…angry." I turn back to the doorway. "No, it's not you…that's coming from outside…" I close my eyes. Remember the first lesson that Maria Price gave me. I clasp my hands together in front of my heart. "Quies," I whisper to my daughter. Now, I have to focus on the emotions coming from outside. My eyes shift to silver. "Jacio."

I feel it…it sweeps out of my body in a wave…washing over everything…inanimate objects feel as cold as stone no matter what their actual composition is. I feel the twins and Maggie in the foyer…the twins feel cooler than Maggie does…I sense the others, all in their bedrooms along the first floor. Odd, Kyle and Elizabeth are…ahem…ignore THAT…and keep searching. I do not sense Raven, but I thought she was in her office…she may have taken her secret exit through the bookcase to visit…

"No," I protest, feeling the malevolence just outside of our very door. I hurry back out into the foyer, where Maggie and the twins prepare to square off again. "MAGGIE! KIMIKO! MIMIKO!" They peer at me. "Get away from…" Before I can finish, the front door evaporates into a pile of splinters flying inward, throwing the three of them to the floor with a deafening bang.

Three men…no, hunters dressed in their head-to-toe riot gear, carrying automatic weapons rush through the vacant portal. Did they find me? Did they investigate Amber's murder and concluded that it must be me?

They take aim at Margaret and the twins. "NO." Two of them aim at me. I duck.

"Hold. She's the target. We take her alive." What? "Open fire."

I stand as Margaret recovers. She throws the baton in her right hand at the hunter in the center. It collides with the center of his forehead, dropping him instantly. The other two look at his unconscious form and then fire at the three of them. The rhythmic pop of their gunfire sounds like rolling thunder echoing off the foyer walls. Margaret moves with the speed that Raven taught her…but the twins…aren't as lucky.

"Argh," Kimiko wails, but I can't see her. I look around for a weapon…for anything useful, but I only have my phone. I take one of the balusters in front of me and pluck it free to the sound of disgruntled lumber splintering. I throw the makeshift wooden stake at the one closest to me…knocking the gun out of his hand and distracting the other. Margaret rushes toward them. She leaps at them, wrapping her legs around the armed one's neck…and her arms around the other's. She spins and hurls the men in two different directions. The gun-wielder flies, crashing into the opposite staircase. The other hits the railing along the first-floor walkway only to fall to the marble below.

Margaret kneels and examines the two unconscious assailants. Five more rush through the door with their weapons ready. Everything slows as Margaret looks to me. I point downward. "GET THE TWINS OUT OF HERE." Her eyes dart to the men and then to me. "GO!" She nods and vanishes in a blur.

Demitri, Kyle, Elizabeth, and Michael rush out of their bedrooms. "NO! Go back inside!" I warn, flailing my arms in front of me as if pushing them back. They ignore me in favor of drawing their weapons. A hail of gunfire, rolling thunder, and the smell of silver cuts through the air. They duck behind the railing taking limited dam-

NO! Michael was not fast enough. He's on the floor…bleeding and…the emotions coming from him…his pain…his stomach…his chest. They nicked his heart. I shed a tear. He's a New Blood. New Blood's aren't capable of healing on that level yet. More tears. He's going to die, and he knows it. I shiver. He's so afraid.

My daughter steels my resolve. I have to keep her safe. I promised Nathan I would do what any good mother would. Protect her child with my last. I do not know if they came here as a result of Amber's death or not…but they have hunted me during my honeymoon and now to my home. They came here prepared for a fight... I stand and return to my room. …but I will give them a war.

I throw my door open to find two soldiers with their weapons aimed at me as a third, climbs through my window.

"Hold," the woman in front says with a clenched fist aimed skyward. "She's the target." She returns her hand to her weapon. "Come with us and you won't be harmed."

"Why?"

"We were told to capture you," the man next to her barks. "That's all you need to know vampire."

"And you expect me to comply while you slaughter my coven...my friends...my family...?"

"It's that or we shoot you," she returns.

"Then you leave me little choice, it would seem."

"Good," she adds and tips her head toward me. The man lowers his weapon and claims a pair of handcuffs from his hip. I inhale deeply, and the air turns electric around me. I move forward, passing the gun wielders and kick their third back out of the window, shattering it in the process.

"What the...?" the man says, turning to me.

"Shoot her!" I claim my sword and cut his gun strap before he can reclaim his weapon. It falls to the floor, and I kick him in the knee. I follow-up by throwing my elbow into his neck. He groans and clutches his throat. I toss my sword at her, hilt first...it collides with her nose, and she falls to the floor. I take my weapon from the floor and stand. I inhale deeply again. I feel exhausted...and queasy from moving so much.

"You..." the man groans in a gruff voice, still holding his throat. "...won't...escape..."

"We'll see." I kick him as hard as I can, sending him flying out of the bedroom door. He crashes into the railing and tumbles over the side to the first floor...the scent of blood trailing behind him. I put my hand on my belly. "Kya..." I pant trying to calm her. "...bear with me...a bit longer." I march out of my room and scan the first-floor railing. The rest of the coven...is...

"No," I mutter, sensing no emotions from any of them. My stomach turns, and Kya complains along with it. "Please...goodness no..."

"We have the target, sir," one of the men snarls running up the opposite stairwell. I can barely focus enough to see them. Pain rips through me viciously. "She's armed, sir. Please advise. Do we still take her alive?"

"We have orders...we take her alive."

I lift my sword. "Not a bloody one of you will survive this encounter."

"Well said, sister," Raven says, marching out of her office.

"SIR, ANOTHER ONE!" Raven slips two daggers off her belt. Her long coat comes to a rest as she surveys the foyer. "OPEN FIRE!" Pain...flickers through my sister...and just as quickly something else replaces it. Something dark and menacing replaces all the anguish that welled up in her until a fraction of a second ago. I caught a glimpse of this emotion in her once before...as I lay on the ground...in my Nathan's arms, bleeding out...and fearing that I'd breathed my last breath. Then as now...that darkness turns into something else. Cold clarity...she has turned off all parts of herself that feel sympathy or empathy.

She moves faster than my eyes can keep track…she cuts each one of them several dozen times, before moving onto the next…

"SIR?" barks a woman.

"OPEN FIRE! SHE'S GOING TO KILL THEM ANYWAY!" The men gathered on both stairs take aim and fire on my sister and their fellows alike. Raven grabs a pair of her assailants and uses them as human shields.

"RAVEN!" I leap the railing, coming down on the stairs. I slice one across the back, cutting through his body armor and separating him from his weapon. He yells in pain. I kick him and he tumbles down the stairs knocking down several of the others. I claim his weapon and open fire on the opposite staircase. Several of them fall…more of them leap the opposite side of the railing. I toss the empty weapon aside as Raven throws her lifeless shields aside in the same manner.

"Lana, we have to get ya outta here." Raven puts her phone up to her ear. I nod and move down the stairs. One of the men grabs my leg and I kick him in the face. "We need ya here…NOW," Raven says into the phone.

I move down to her side…as more men swarm the door. I ready my sword…and Raven…ends her call. I step between her and them. "They will not shoot me…they want me alive…"

"T'ey what?"

I feel it…before it occurs to me what is happening. My hair seems to lift, and the hairs on my arm stand on end. The air doesn't feel electric around me…it becomes electricity…and it doesn't fill the air, it ignites it. The men running through the door all fall at the same time…and in their place, stands Natavius. He flicks his wrist, and his blade slides back into its position in his long sleeve. He scowls and looks around.

"What happened here?" he says in more of a gasp than actual words.

"Don't know," Raven admits. She aims her phone at him. "Glad you came." He nods. "More of t'em are comin'. By now, t'ey've taken t'e garage…"

"Sun doesn't go down for another hour." They look at me. "I'm fine…but Raven." Natavius nods as a roar comes from the open doorway. Raven's red Lamborghini idles at the bottom of the stairs. The driver side window lowers and Mona glares at us. "Did she…?"

"COME ON!" The passenger side door opens.

I look to Natavius and Raven. They nod. I hurry out the door and move to the passenger side. I dive into the minuscule back seat…and wait…I stare at my sister as she whispers something to Natavius. He nods and shoves her out the door. She moves as a blur and slides into the front seat…a trail of smoke following her. She jerks the door down, closing it as Mona speeds away.

"Why are you helping us?" I ask. "You hate us."

"Yes," she groans. "But I love my son and without Raven making her monthly call to Denisoff, he's as good as dead." She glares at Raven.

"Consider you and yer son in my good graces." Mona nods, shifts the plotter, and pushes down on the accelerator, propelling the automobile forward…towards the iron gate…which is NOT opening. "RAM IT!" Raven yells. "T'is car is reinforced…" She looks at Mona. "…it's tank proof."

Mona nods and speeds forward. The car knocks the gates off their hinges. They clang against the ground and scrape the streets before sliding to a stop. She speeds through the city streets. "Why is this happening?" Mona asks

"Me. They were after me…" I sob. "…and because of me…Demitri, Kyle, Elizabeth…Michael…Dan, Jack…possibly even the twins and Maggie…"

"No," Mona says. "I saw them." She looks at Raven. "The blonde…she put them in the silver Jaguar and threw me the keys to this." She nods. "They got out just before those guys took the garage."

"Where will they go?"

Raven sighs. "I know exactly where Maggie would go in t'is situation…" I catch her eyes in the rearview mirror. "…she'd go ta someone she trusts…she'd go ta see her sire-father…me husband."

#####

Chapter 20: Siege

"Nate?" He frowns and looks at me as if coming out of a daydream. "Are you alright? We kinda lost you there for a second." He nods and rubs his head. "Are you sure?"

"Yeah," he growls. Kai and Alex take the opportunity to try the pincer move he taught them on him. He catches each of their left wrists, twists and throws them down to the gray stone patio at the top of the stairs.

"Ow," Kai whines, holding his back. Alex is already on his feet again...ready...but he waits...he's smart. He may not have been an awakened skinwalker as long as Kai, but I'm guessing he's been in a lot more fights than his cousin has.

"You both still lead with your claws..." He nods. "You let the wolf and tiger lead you still. Don't get me wrong, both have good instincts...but when you're going up against someone with those same instincts...someone who thinks every move through..." Nate nods. "...you will lose, every time."

Alex nods.

"That's enough for today," Nate says. Alex inhales deeply and his fur vanishes in a ripple that moves up his body. "You've gotten better at phasing...without your fur."

"Still feels weird."

"You just have to get used to it."

Jamie laughs next to me. "What?" I ask.

"It's just funny watching Alex getting his butt kicked..." She looks at me. "...by his long-lost cousin."

I snicker. "Nate's pretty good at kicking your butt and teaching you a lesson while doing it."

"Like this," she snaps and moves her clawed hand out toward me. My power kicks in before the rest of me can react...she didn't put any magic behind it. "Huh, you didn't do anything?"

"Eh, if you'd thrown fire at me, I'd've caught it."

"Yeah, you're good at catching things..." I frown. She giggles. "...it's throwing it back that's the problem." I nod. "I'm hinting at the fact that you're completely and totally in love with your best friend and can't get over it." I scoff. "The catching was referring to feelings and..."

"I got it...and thanks," I whine. "It's not like he has super hearing or can hear us from here." She smiles. "How about you...? I mean...that Tony-guy switched up pretty quick after your wish thingy kicked in...right?"

"What?"

"Tony and Shay pretty much started making out as soon as he realized he wasn't in love with you anymore and despite the fact that you deny it, you're still in love with him a little bit," I say quickly, trying to cram it all in. She looks like I just shot her puppy…and forced her to watch. "I'm sorry…I'm sorry…I'm so sorry. It's just…" I stare at him. "…Nate's kind of a sore subject for me…and when someone starts in on my feelings toward him, I get…" Nate holds his phone up to his ear. "…kind of…"

"…bitchy?" I come back to her. I'd argue the point, but her face tells me just how bitchy I was being. I nod. "I get that. I get kind of…that way…about Tony…and Quincy…and Rais…" She fidgets, playing with her hands. "…and Alex if I think someone's going to hurt him."

"Oddly enough, I get all of that," I say, distractedly. "Hey…speaking of witch, I'm gonna go and talk to…" She nods, I think, as I hurry up the stairs, leading to the gray stone patio. He takes the phone away from his ear and ends the call…and almost the phone. I snatch it out of his hand before he crushes it. "HEY…what'd the innocent, little phone ever do to you?"

"She's not answering," he growls, marching toward the house.

"What?"

He pulls the left door open and marches into the vestibule. "She's…" He throws his arm out. "…not answering. I sensed something…panic…then fear…then dread…then anger…and relief…and then sadness…lots of sadness." He stops in front of the stairs and turns back to me. "And now, she's not answering the phone."

"Well, I'm sure there's a reason for that. I mean, she's been on the mood swing rollercoaster and…and…she's been calling you every four hours on the hour, so…" He peers at me over his shoulder. I nod, trailing off, realizing that I'm trying to get him to calm down, but everything I'm saying's making me panic. "…something might be wrong," I mutter. He nods and plucks his phone out of my hand. He turns and calls her all over again.

"What the…?" An arm wraps around my waist. I look down…and don't see anything. I look up…and I'm on the second-floor hallway. The arm releases me, and I step away. "BAL," I growl, turning to him and before my power even kicks in.

His outline comes into view, and he steps forward, putting two fingers over my lips. "Shhhh. Do you want your wolf to hear?"

"What I want is for you to explain what you're doing here and why I shouldn't yell for him?" I hiss in the form of a whisper.

"I missed you."

"Bal!"

"You've shortened my name…a sure sign that you're attracted to me."

"BAL!" I snap.

"Fine," he croons. "You are NOT the only reason, I'm here…well, here in Edenton…" He said the name with…I don't know…reverence in his voice. "…you ARE the reason that I am here on the second floor of this manor."

"Why?"

"Because I wanted a moment alone with you."

"No. Why are you here in Edenton?"

He taps the underside of my chin, tilting my head back. "I don't want to say," he whispers against my lips…when did he get that close. "…because I want you to kiss me, and I don't think you will after I tell you."

"Now I won't, if you don't." His lips curl up into a smile. "Come on…tell me, Bal."

He sighs. "We've come to retrieve a very important crystal that the fiery, young witch took from us."

"We? Us?"

He nods. "You already know who 'us' is." I nod. "I…" He hedges. "…wanted to remove you…to keep you safe."

"Safe from what?" He swallows a lump. "Safe from what, Bal?" He shakes his head. I step back. "Bal, you can't…"

"I have to, and you know it." I grit my teeth and hurry over to the stairs. He catches my arm. "Angel, please…"

"My name is Angela…and I need you to let me go. Right now. Or we will have a problem." He does. I hurry down the stairs. "NATE!" I reach the landing, and he's at the bottom with Kai and Alex. They stare at me. Nate frowns. He gets it already. His eyes shift to green and gold. He looks at Alex then Kai. His frown intensifies, and he follows the trail of malevolence…that is coming from them…to the…front door.

It explodes… All three of them fall to the ground. I crouch and cover my eyes. I stand and hurry down the stairs and help Nate to his feet. "You okay?"

"Not even a little," he growls. "Ghouls."

"What?"

Alex springs to his feet, covered in fur. "Ghouls? Man, I hate ghouls," he rumbles, his voice sounding deeper, scarier than ever. A skittering, sort of clicking noise sounds…and the air smells like an open sewer. A pile of white, round things tumbles out of the smoke, through the missing door. "Here they come."

"Ewww," I whine, realizing that the little round things have tiny, slimy bodies connected…and open their mouths to reveal a bunch of little needle-like teeth.

"Oh please, eat that bitch alive," an annoying, nasally voice whines. I look up from them to find Bethany standing in the middle of the doorway.

"Or...ooooo...drag her out to the front yard...it's the middle of the day...let the blond vampire burn."

"What's the matter?" I taunt. "Can't get it up enough to burn me yourself."

She snarls and tries to step forward...but someone stops her. "Focus," that woman we ran into in New Orleans...Daphne says, stepping up behind her. She sighs and looks around. "We're here to get the crystal back."

"Daphne?" Alex and Nate say at the same time.

"Alex...? Nathan...?" She nods. "I wasn't expecting to see either of you...just give us the crystal, and we'll leave. No one has to get hurt here."

"Oh, I think," Tony starts, standing in the library door. "...at least, one person...NEEDS to get hurt."

"Hello, lover," Bethany says, full on nasal. Tony snarls as a response.

"I can agree with that, little brother," Quincy says, coming out of the door opposite the library. "...and your previous statement." Daphne sighs and looks at them, before settling on the older brother. "Jamina told me what you did...you actually went and did it, huh? You went and attacked the LAST person still on YOUR side."

"I did what I had to."

"Attacking your own daughter?" I ask.

"You wouldn't understand."

"I'm vampire...and my mom, a witch, still hugged me when she saw me again...and she held me just like she always has....so believe me...I understand." I slip my knife out from behind my back. "You're clearly a whack-a-doo who drank too much of the En Quosque Kool-Aid."

"Agreed," Tony says pulling his knife from the small of his back.

"I triple that," Quincy says, stepping forward.

"I quadruple it," Jamie says, moving out from behind the stairs on the library side. She shakes her head. "Hello, Daphne."

"I'm still your mother."

"My mom would never attack me. I always thought I was the line you wouldn't cross, Daphne..."

"Jamina Lynda Baggett, give me the crystal..."

"Or what? You'll attack me. Lie to me. Manipulate me...or tell me you can bring my dad back?" Daphne gasps. "Yeah, he came back all on his own, thanks. We had a nice little chat about how you convinced him to stay away...because I have a half-sister out there somewhere."

"That lying, cheating bastard went back on his word."

"You're one to talk," Jamie snarls.

"ENOUGH OF THIS FAMILY DRAMA," Bethany whines. "GOD!" She throws her hand forward. "Destroy them." The little ghouls rush forward…and Kai and Alex meet them head on…busting their huge heads open.

I step forward, and Nate catches my wrist. "Not yet," he whispers. I nod.

Daphne opens both of her hands. "FLAMMA! VINTUS!" A fire tornado spins out of her hand.

Jamie extends her hand and Quincy appears next to her, doing the same thing. "Igneum globum," she barks…and a wall of flames appears between mother and daughter, colliding and mixing with the tornado. Whoa, they're using spells that are definitely way out of my pay grade.

"Invite…" Bethany says. "…lupus…" She holds a diamond between her thumb and pointer and water flows out of it…it starts to take shape and freeze…but before it can…Tony smashes it with his knife.

"What else ya got?" he barks with a scary-cool demeanor. Man, he really does remind me of Nate.

"How about this, sexy?" Bethany replies. She lifts the diamond above her head. "Invite… vivente igne."

"WHAT ARE YOU DOING?" Daphne yells, while tossing a lightning bolt at Jamie's…wall of water. When did they switch up?

"WHAT YOU WON'T!" A light emanates from the rock above Bethany's head. It becomes a swirling fireball, that's growing bigger. Tony takes a step back and repositions his knife.

"Ange," Nate says. "See what you can do to help Tony…I'll help Kai and Alex clear the rest of these things." I nod…why am I nodding? What can I do against a giant fireball when a guy that's been practicing magic since he could crawl…over a hundred years ago…is backing away from it? Nate vanishes in a step, and three ghouls shatter.

"Angela," Tony says, continuing his Nate impression. "See if you can stop it."

"What?"

"Use your fire magic to stop it."

I swallow a lump. "I'll try." I hold my hand out to it. "Flamma?" It continues growing…sprouting…what looks like…arms, legs, and a head.

"MAGIC REQUIRES CONFIDENCE," Tony barks. "You have to know what you want to happen and know that you can make it happen. Now, do you believe you can stop it?"

"I…"

He grabs me by the arm. "CAN YOU?"

"YES."

He points his knife at it. "THEN MAKE IT HAPPEN!"

I nod as the air heats up and swirls around me. The air smells less like a sewer and more like burning…rotten eggs, although I can't say if that's better.

Stop focusing on that, you idiot…and focus on the fire man. I put my knife away and hold both hands out to it. "FLAMMA!" The fire man floats down to the floor and stops… I keep my hands out…and it's weird. It's as if I can feel him…as if I'm actually holding him in place. It's kinda like how fireballs feel like hefty softballs in my hand.

"Like that would work," Bethany taunts. "Roast her." The fire man doesn't move. "DESTROY HER!" Nothing. She shakes the diamond violently. "I'M YOUR MASTER, AND I SAID DESTROY HER!"

"What's the matter?" I mock. "Can't control your, man."

"No," Tony says and then Alex repeats in a bark, rushing past me with half of a ghoul in his hands.

"SHUT UP!" Bethany screams in a whine.

"We don't have time for this," a kindly, authoritative, older man's voice says from the door. Bethany frowns and turns to it as an old guy with silver hair and a glowing white, pristine suit…and skin to match enters. His hands rest behind his back, one in the other from the look of it. He looks like a vampire…but… "It's time this little skirmish ended; wouldn't you say?"

"Nate?" He looks at me. "This old man…" I turn back to him…taking in his bluish-silver aura. "…he reads like Alana." Nate growls, and his eye change to green and gold with black replacing the whites.

The white-haired man…no, the Aldien's eyes change over to silver. He takes in Nate's appearance. "I was hoping that I wouldn't have to use this on you so soon." Nate stumbles…just in front of the old man…falls to his knees and then passes out.

"NATE," I yell and then stare at the old Aldien. He glares at Alex…and he falls, unconscious. Definitely Aldien. He turns to Kai…same. He looks at Tony…and then Quincy…they both fall.

"Now, you," he says coming to me…I wince, remembering how Alana almost made me punch my way to China…or Australia. Our eyes meet…and…nothing. "What?" he grumbles. "Sleep." I shake my head. "SLEEP, DAMN IT!"

"BITE ME!"

"You tell 'em," Jamie groans as her mom directs a steady stream of lightning at her. Jamie holds the electricity back with a shield the size of an SUV. "Lil' help?" She's trying to put on a brave face. I know this is killing her…not literally, but still…

"I was gonna ask you…" Holding this fire man in place is…

"Hmm," Jamie replies. She pushes out with her left hand and points at her shield with her right pointer and middle fingers. She draws a triangle on the shield…and then turns so that she's facing Bethany, angling the shield with her. The lightning ricochets off and flies toward Bethany. It hits and sends her spinning like a top. The diamond falls out of her hand and rolls toward me. It taps my boot…and I notice…that the fire man, stopped pulling against me.

"Huh?" I bend and pick up the diamond. The fire man turns to me.

"Give that back!" Bethany shrieks. God, her voice is annoying.

"Sure." I extend it toward her. "Where do you want it?" The fire man has his hand extend toward her just like I do. "So, this thing controls you?" The fire man nods. I smile. "Jamie, is he as strong as I think he is?"

"Oh-ho, yeah!"

"The boys…"

"GOT 'EM!" She kneels and puts her hand on Quincy. She points at Nate, Kai, Alex, and Tony lying at the bottom of the stairs. She draws a square in mid-air. "Concustodio," she whispers…and her magic flows over the boys.

I come back to Bethany and the man in white. "Don't do this," Balthazar whispers in my ear.

"You drew the lines between us, Bal…not me. You picked your side…I picked my family and friends." I lift the diamond. "DESTROY THEM." The fire man lifts his hands above his head and creates a huge fire ball. It grows bigger and bigger…

"Daphne?" the Aldien questions.

"I don't think even you could survive this hit. Retreat," she complains.

"NO," Bethany whines.

"Think you can take that without my help?" Daphne asks. Bethany frets, but backs up, moving toward the doorway.

The fire man draws back…heaving the ball of destruction above his head…burning the wood beam in front of the stairs. I frown. "Are you going to…?" He throws it forward and it…well, I lose everything in the blast…and the ensuing smoke and dust. I groan…I hit my head…and everything goes white for a second…wait, I'm on the floor…and I think a splinter is literally impaling my left arm and right thigh. "GAH," I pant as something yanks the one out of my arm. "Nate…?" I whisper.

"Are you alright?" Balthazar asks.

"Bal…? What are you…?"

"I just wanted to be the one to tell you that I took the crystal while you were all fighting down here."

I can't see him, but I clutch at his arm desperately. "Bal, how could you…?"

"Sleep, my love."

He pulls the one out of my thigh. "ARGH!"

"You've lost a lot of blood and using the Living Flame drains you even with the Summoner's Stone."

"What...the what?" I feel his lips against mine. He tugs on my lower lip, pulling it between the two of his. I groan. I can't help it. It's a good kiss. I move my uninjured hand away from his arm and up into his hair. We part, and I pant...wanting to ask for another.

He lays me down gently. "Rest. I'll see you back in New York."

"Okay," I mutter and close my eyes...

#####

Chapter 21: Fallout

"Ange?"

"Nate?" I clear my throat with a groan. My eyes flutter open, feeling dry and a little sore. He hovers over me, just two or three inches from my…my big stupid mouth, that's hanging open now. Stupid because I actually feel like I'm cheating on the married man by letting Bal kiss me.

He flashes a huge fake smile, while moving the hair back from my forehead. "There she is." He's such a good actor. His smile looks so genuine, and his voice sounded just happy enough to fool most people. I'm not most people though. I stared at this face for days in Paris…I know it better than the back of my hand. He's worried and…scared. "You okay?"

"Yeah," I sigh. He pulls me up to a seated position, so that I can see the huge gaping hole that used to be the front of the Blackshear brother's home. "Holy crap…" I point. "…did I do that?"

"Sort of," he whispers. "The…Living Flame…that creature you were controlling, did it." I nod. "Are you sure you're okay?" I look at him and nod. He hugs me…and holds me so tight that all the air rushes out of me…and I feel like I can't breathe…but not because he's holding on too hard…because I don't want him to let me go, but he has to…because I'm not his and worse yet, he's not mine. "You scared the hell out of me."

"Scared me too."

"Me three." I turn to Jamie sitting on the stairs behind us. Her knees are under her chin and tear streaks move away from her eyes.

"Is everyone alright?"

"More or less," she says. "The crystal is gone. They got it."

"I know."

"You know?" Nate asks. I nod. "How could you…?"

"Balthazar was here." Nate frowns. He lets go of me and stands. He paces away, turns back as if he's going to say something, only to turn again and walk out of the big hole.

"Who's Balthazar?" Jamie asks.

"En Quosque's daemon…the one who can make himself disappear…" She nods. "…well, even when he disappears, I can still see him…because my ability allows me to see the glamour that coats him."

"Okay," she says, putting her feet on the step below her. "So, what did he grab it in the confusion? You saw him when he made a break for it?"

"No. He…" I mess my hair…which I'm sure was already a mess. "…he tried to warn me about the attack."

Jamie jumps to her feet. "What? Why would he do that?" She storms down the stairs. "Why didn't you warn us?"

"I did. As soon as he told me what was coming, I came down to warn Nate."

"It's true," Alex says from the landing. "She vanished and when she came back downstairs…Nate just looked at her…and knew something was up."

I nod. "Okay," Jamie says, moving from Alex to me. "Why would he warn you?"

"He…claims he's in love with me."

"WHAT?" Alex and Jamie yell at the same time.

I shrug. "I don't know. I mean, he told me I was beautiful when we first met. He claimed he couldn't stay away after tracking me down at a party. He came to see me before we came down here…" I mumble. "…and he might've…kissed me a little."

"What?" Jamie says.

"He kissed you?" Alex asks. I draw my lips into my mouth and nod. I close one eye and hold up two fingers. "Twice?" I close the other eye and nod again.

"Do you care about him?" Jamie asks.

I open my eyes. "Wha- No! Why do you ask?"

"Because if you did, I'd understand." She looks past me, toward the library. Quincy and Tony argue about something, Tony with lots of arm movements and angry gestures and Quincy with his arms crossed and his eyes focusing on her. She comes back to me. "Because I know better than most people…how much you can't control who you fall in love with…" She sighs.

"I don't know," I admit. "I mean…I let him kiss me and…when he talks to me, it does weird things to my heart and stomach…but…I don't know."

"Why not?" Alex asks.

I open my mouth. "Ange." I turn quickly to Nate, marching back in through the hole with his phone to his ear. He's seething…but not his, I'm angry seething. His 'I'm worried' seething. He stops and purses his lips. He takes the phone away from his ear and shakes it like a saltshaker…and as if he's going to crush it…again. I snatch it out of his hand.

"Hello, whoever this is upsetting Nate so severely. Who are you, and why are you making him make this face?"

"Angela," Alana's voice sings back. "Thank the Heavens that you're safe, too."

"Lana, what's going on? I've only seen Nate this upset when you vomited blood. Are you and…?" My eyes dart around the vestibule. "…things…okay?"

"The baby and I are fine." Her voice trembles.

"Lana, what's wrong?" My eyes dart to Nate, who's in full-on angry pace mode.

"I…" She weeps and breaks off. "…the manor was attacked…by a group of vampire hunters."

"Raven?" I whimper.

"She's…fine…" Alana swallows a lump. "…but…I'm not sure about the twins and Margaret…" She pauses with a pant. "…but…Demitri…Kyle…" She sobs. "…Elizabeth…" Stuttering sigh. "…even poor Michael…"

"Mike…? You mean that New Blood I brought in two months ago?"

"Yes. …they're all…"

"Who…? Why would…?"

"Vampire hunters," Nate growls.

"We'll be fine…" Alana sighs again. "…just…be careful…the two of you get back here safely, yes?"

"Alana…?"

"Promise me!"

"We will." I stare at Nate…who's trembling, probably as violently as his wife is now. "I'll bring him back to you. Just take care of yourself. Okay? And tell Raven, I love her."

"I will."

"Love you, too."

"And you. Ta." She ends the call. I take the phone away and stare at Nate still seething.

"What happened here?" James says at probably the worst possible moment EVER. Nate lifts his head, and his eyes phase green and gold as he does…the whites of his eyes fade to black and if I didn't know better, I'd swear he just grew to twice his normal size…muscle wise anyway. He vanishes and reappears, holding James horizontally about four feet off the ground…by the throat, just before slamming him down on his back. James gets both hands around Nate's wrist. "WHAT THE HELL?"

"DAD?" Jamie shouts, rushing forward.

Nate growls as a response. Tracy puts her gun to Nate's temple. "LET HIM GO!" Nate glares at her.

I run, doing that fast-moving thing to put myself between them. I hold both hands up to let her know, I don't have anything. "STOP!" I shake my head. "He's…I'll get him!" Tracy looks at me and lowers her gun a little. I nod and turn to Nate. "Nate? Let him go…he had nothing to do with it!"

"He's one of them!" Nate roars with sweat beading around his forehead…and slather building at the corners of his mouth. He grits and bares his teeth, exposing his growing canines and incisors.

"I know. I know...but he was here." I shake my head again. "There's no way he could've been the one who attacked her."

"Attacked who?" James grunts.

I look at him and lean forward. "A group of your vampire hunters attacked the Chief Magistrates' manor a little while ago...killing..." I nearly choke, because talking to Alana...I could focus on Alana...but now, they're faces move through my head. Demetri always working out despite being a vampire. Kyle always obsessing over his hair...which was always gorgeous. Liz who got a little crazy when she and Kyle broke up, but still managed to stay friends with him. Mike...little new blood Mike... "...they killed most of her coven."

"What?" Tracy asks sounding as shocked as I sound sad. "We didn't hear anything about..."

"WELL, THEY DID!" Nate thunders. I reach around him and grab his arm...just above James's hands. I pull on his arm as hard as I can...and he doesn't budge, I might as well try pulling the Earth up for all the good it does me. He doesn't yield at all...unlike James's throat under his hand...a hand that's tightening still. I pull again. "YOU ATTACKED US IN THE WOODS ON OUR HONEYMOON! AND NOW YOU ATTACK HER AT HER SISTER'S HOME!" He squeezes harder.

"Nate!" Jamie says. "I like you...you seem cool...and I get that you're Alex's cousin and all...and I'm sorry that your wife was attacked...but I will drop you where you stand if you don't let go of my dad right now."

I turn to her. "Just..." I nod. "...give me a minute." She nods and lowers her hand. "Nate, seriously, I need you to let him go!" I wrap both hands around his arm again. Think, Ange...think. Fire. I slip my lighter out of my jacket pocket and light it with my left hand. "Extermino," I whisper, focusing the heat into the palm of my right hand. I singe his arm...he hisses, and then he lets go.

I pull him back and then shove him away from James. He opens his mouth, and I hold a finger up in his face. "You were being an ass. I'm the best friend. I get to make that call." He growls while closing his eyes. He puts his right hand over the bridge of his nose, shielding his eyes and his left hand on top of mine. He nods and slowly loses some of the excess muscle he spontaneously packed on...too bad...made him even hotter.

He drags his hand, tugging his face down. I put my free fingers over his ear, with my palm cupping his cheek. "Listen to me. Some of the vampires died...and that sucks...and we'll deal with that..." He nods with me. I sigh with tears swimming in my eyes, matching his. "...and it was done by the people who James is...associated with..."

He clenches his jaw. "...associated with...?"

"Shush." He huffs but follows it up with a deep breath. "...but the fact remains. Your wife is fine...all right? Your child...is fine." He sighs in relief and nods.

"Child?" Alex asks.

Nate nods and pinches the bridge of his nose again. "Yeah," he grumbles. "...I..." He motions to himself and then moves his hand outward making a circle. "Alana and I are going to have a little girl."

"Impossible," Tracy says. "Vampires can't have children."

"The Original Vampire race could," Jamie says. "...but still...one having a child with a wolf?"

"Nate's not a normal wolf, Jamie-Lynn," James says.

"He's half-daemon and half-wolf," Jamie says with a nod. "Right...skinwalker...I keep forgetting that you guys are technically daemons." She shoves Alex at the shoulder. Don't blame her. I look at Nate and I just can't put him in the same category as Ephraim, Devon...or even Balthazar.

James clears his throat and follows it up with a nod. "And furthermore, his wife's no normal vampire...even for an Original vampire. She's half-Aldien."

"You're awfully well informed," Nate complains.

"We have to be," James returns.

"So, it's true," Jamie says. "Twee told me about the last vampire...I..." She shakes her head. "...put it together that the last Aldien and the last original vampire had a kid, but..."

"Clearly, not the last," Nate complains. He rubs his head. "His power worked on me...Alana's eyes haven't worked on me since the first time she used them on me."

"Skinwalkers are highly adaptable," Tracy says as if giving a school report. "The link between skinwalker the human and skinwalker the animal has some benefits that were unforeseen. The two minds work in..." She brings her hands together. "...concert to shield one another...now that you've experienced an Aldien's silver-eyed empathic attack...it'll never work on you again, unless you want it to."

"Like the Alpha's bark," I suggest. Nate nods slowly with a scowl. "We should head back to New York, Nate. Check on Alana and Raven...find out about the twins."

"Wait," James says. "Give me a few days...to find out what exactly happened in New York." He crosses his arms and nods. "I haven't really understood a lot of the orders coming down from the top lately and I definitely don't like that."

"Sir?" Tracy says.

"I mean, come on, Trace. Think about it. You've gone over the simulations at the Academy. You know the drill. The Order calculated how many members we'd need to pull off an assault on the Chief Magistrate's Coven…" He nods and paces…like Nate does, hand on his chin, working it over in his head. I think I seriously underestimated how close James, Tony, and Nate were before falling out over…a girl.

"Yes," Tracy says. "We surmised that we'd need at least twice as many as the number of vampires in the coven." She nods. "Then taking into account the likelihood of the Chief Magistrate drawing several vampires with special abilities to her side…add two additional for each of those variables…the Halfling vampire…" Nate growls. "…sorry, the Midnight Princess was considered negligible since our goggles negate the effect of her abilities…and six additional soldiers for the Chief Magistrate."

"Exactly. You'd be looking at committing 60 men to a mission that has no guarantee of success." Tracy bobs her head. "Add to that the fallout of such an undertaking."

"Fallout?" Quincy asks, Tony and him having come out of the library at some point.

"Think about it," Nate says with his calculating face on…weird because Tony wears the same expression. You'd swear they were all one guy at some point, considering their matching postures and expressions. "You attack a coven of vampires; you might bring down the ire of a senator, possibly the magistrate presiding over that region." He shakes his head. "But if you go after the Chief Magistrate…"

"…then you're asking for every loyal vampire," I start. "…and even some that aren't quite as loyal, to come down on you."

"Why?" Alex asks.

"Survival," Tony says. "If they're big and bold enough to take on the top of the food chain…what would a nobody vampire standing alone do against them?"

"So, why would the order risk it?" Alex asks.

"I don't know," James admits. "The order came down to track a vampire in the Canadian Wilderness. I was brought in because…" He sighs and looks at Jamie. "…having been married to a witch, I'm good with weird and they said that more than likely this vampire would have a protector with unusual abilities. I assembled a team, and we were told to catalogue and capture."

"She's not a moose," Nate grumbles.

"I know," James says.

"That's his point, though," Tracy says. She sighs. "Occasionally, vampires are determined to be harmless before we approach them. In those cases, the protocol is to capture, catalogue, and then release."

"Like a migrating swan," I jab.

"Good one," Nate says, extending his fist to me. I bump it with mine.

"No," James says. "The bio-markers that we use on them warn off other vampire hunters. It's for the vampires own good."

"You guys didn't seem to care too much for my 'own good.'"

"Protocol says that unknown vampires," Tracy says in book report tone. "…and vampire anomalies are to be treated as hostile and dangerous until proven differently."

I motion to myself. "What part of the little blond vampire says dangerous?"

"Knife at the small of your back, your speed, your fighting ability, the fact that you can walk in sunlight without a problem," she counts off quickly. "Take your pick."

I step forward. Nate catches my arm, hooking it with his. "Oh, I will end her," I warn. He pulls me back to his side.

"So, why is this so interesting," Nate says, bringing me to a stop. "I mean, your order has been aware of my wife for a while now, right?" James nods. "…about her parentage and what that most likely means in terms of abilities, right?" Another nod. "…so why try to catalogue her now?"

I frown. "Because she's pregnant now." All eyes turn to me. "I mean I have NO CLUE how the Order's higher ups know that…but clearly they do."

James frowns and clenches his jaw. "Kind of like how they knew the two of you would be in the Canadian Wilderness…alone…for your honeymoon."

"A traitor?" Tony suggests.

"No," I dismiss quickly. "We had one…and he's dea…wait, Mona?"

"No," Nate says. "Mona's hands are tied by her love for her son. She wouldn't…"

"You're holding her son hostage?" Jamie complains. "What is wrong with you guys?"

I step forward and count off. "Her son, Joey, who is her biological and sire-son, was working with a coven of vampires who tried to kill and overthrow Raven, the Chief Magistrate. Thanks to Alana and Nate's pack, they beat the vampires killing all of them except Joey, Mona…and the leader, who got away but, Alana swears is dead now too…" I frown. "…killed by your mom for failing…" Jamie frowns. "…when Raven found out about the connection between the two, she sent Joey to Russia to serve another magistrate and kept Mona here under the belief of *keeping your friends close and your enemies closer.*"

"Oh," Jamie says, sounding depressed.

"But failure's not the reason, Daphne killed the traitor," Nate supplies. "Alana went dream walking…a talent that members of her maternal grandmother's bloodline were capable of doing…" Jamie nibbles her bottom lip. "…apparently, your mom was pissed because of his obsession with Alana, despite her rejection of him. She said that if he did that with her daughter…then…" Nate 'blows up' his hand. "…poof turned him to ash."

"That sounds like Daphne," James, Tony, and Quincy all say at the same time.

Jamie huffs a laugh and wipes a tear from the corner of her eye. "Thanks, for that." Nate nods. "The human," she says after another sniff. She smacks herself on the forehead. "OMG, how do we always forget about the human?"

"What human?" Tracy asks.

"The human member of En Quosque," Nate says, catching her meaning automatically. Jamie nods. "He has near-perfect future sight. He could've foreseen all of it…shaped events so that…" Nate's eyes swell. He grabs my arm and drags me toward the front yard. "WE HAVE TO GO…"

"Nate?" James says. "What are you…?"

He stops after we make it halfway through the huge hole. He half turns to James. "Don't you get it, Baggett? If your Order knows when my wife got pregnant…where we would be on our honeymoon…and to attack the Chief Magistrate's home…" He motions to himself. "…exactly when I was out of town, which would put Alana back at her sister's…" He points at James. "…you have to realize what that means."

James shakes his head as if hearing something he doesn't belief. "How could we not have seen it?" Tony complains.

"What?" I ask at the same time Tracy does.

"Guys," Jamie says, clearly proving she's as smart as her dad is, because she caught it, too. "If the Order knows all of that, only one of two things is happening…" She holds up her right index finger. "…either the human is supplying the Order with information to further En Quosque's goal…" She lifts her other finger and swallows a lump. "…or, and this is so much worse, the Order has been working for En Quosque all along."

#####

Chapter 22: Da

"Where are we?" I ask, staring up at the small building facing Central Park West.

"We," Raven starts, lifting her door. "…are at…" She stares at the building with a bit of a frown. She slips out of the auto, thankfully this time of day the gray and tan building casts a shadow over her. "…a flat of someone who I trust explicitly, sister. Me husband…" A valet tips his hat to her and moves toward the auto. Mona lifts her door as he comes to her side.

"Ma'am," he says, catching my eyes in the rearview.

"Yes," I hum, sliding toward the passenger doorway.

"Oh, you're…" I pull my cardigan closed around my swollen belly. He climbs out. "…hey, she could use a hand."

"I have her," Raven says, lifting the seat. She offers me a hand and helps me out. I try to hide my sword as best I can. "Don't mind that, sister. They never do." I frown as she turns toward the door. Her car speeds away as the three of us make our way to the entrance.

"Mrs. Gregory," the doorman says just before performing his title duty. "Good to see you again. We don't usually see you this early in the day."

"Well, special circumstances, Ralph." He nods. "How'd yer son do on his exam?"

"He did fine," the brown skinned, heavyset man returns, holding the door open, stretching his maroon overcoat over his belly. He tips his matching hat with gold trim to Mona and me as we pass. "…not as good as he was hoping, but still pretty good."

"Och, I told ya. No one's harder on t'at boy of yers t'an himself." Ralph laughs and issues a dismiss wave. "Talk to ya later."

"Later, Mrs. Gregory."

We cross the overly modern lobby…weapons in hand heading toward the elevators. Several of the bellhops, custodians, and various other employees…well, they ignore our weapons, but tip their heads to Raven all the same. We reach the elevator, and she presses twelve inside.

"What is going on?" I ask. "We are carrying weapons of all things and they…"

"They think that I'm a collector of antique an' modern weaponry," Raven returns watching the numbers change above the doors. She looks at me and shrugs. "Sort of a truth within the lie."

"You must come here a lot," Mona says. "Not one soul batted an eyelid at the fact that Alana's carrying a sword or the chakram in my hand."

"Aye. They probably noticed more that she's a pregnant school girl than that she's armed." Mona bobs her head. The elevator dings, the doors slide open, and Raven marches out with a confident bop to her step. Mona and I follow. She moves quickly to the third door on the right and knocks twice, pauses, knocks once more, pauses, and then knocks three times.

I inhale deeply, trying to get some sense of who will be on the other side of the door. I smell Maggie's scent…and the twins…and… I gasp and stare at my sister, who seems to be trying very hard not to return my gaze.

The door opens abruptly. "Come in, come in," Maggie says, beckoning us. She wraps her arm around Raven and then moves aside to allow us to enter. "Who else made it out?" She pushes the door closed behind us.

Raven sighs. "We haven't heard from anyone else." She nods. "I called Richard and told him to warn the others off…and to take the New Bloods with him to a safe house."

"Good, good," Maggie sighs.

"How are the twins?" I ask.

"Well," Vance says, coming out of the hallway to our right. He wipes his blood-covered hands on a white towel, staining it. He takes a deep breath and stops. "Mimiko is fine. I managed to remove all of the bullets from her body…but…" He clenches his jaw. "…Kimiko's left arm isn't healing." I cover my mouth with both hands. "…I've removed all of the silver that I could find and gave her two transfusions, but the damage may have been too extensive."

"What do you mean?" Mona asks.

"If her arm is…" he sighs again. "…if it is silver poisoning that's stopping her regeneration, then I may have to amputate her arm."

"Will it…grow back?" Vance looks at me and shakes his head slowly. "No," I cry, down to my chest.

Raven issues a stuttering sigh and wraps her arms around herself. Vance takes half a step toward her and stops himself…his eyes dart between Mona and me. I move to his side and put my hand on his shoulder. "Go and hug your wife. She needs it."

He purses his lips and nods. He goes over to Raven and puts his arms around her waist. She slips hers over his shoulders and grips at his shirt.

"What?" Mona asks. "You two are…? I guess vampire and wolf pairings run in the family?"

"Hey," Maggie snarls. "Mind yer manners. Yer talkin' bout me ma and da there. Show sum respect."

"Sorry."

"It's fine," Raven says, wiping her eyes. She separates from Vance and looks at Mona. "Mona, t'ank ya. I have no doubt t'at you saved me and my sister's lives today." Mona frowns. "Despite…t'e fact that I give Denisoff regular calls…" She shakes her head. "…I don't do it to keep Joseph alive. I do it to check on him." She smiles. "Denisoff says he's progressing nicely and t'at's high praise comin' from him."

"Progressing nicely?"

"Ya never told her?" Maggie asks. Raven shakes her head. "Ma saw t'e potential in yer boy. T'e report we received from me sister, said t'at he willingly slipped inta bloodlust…doin' it at will to beat Angela. T'at's a very advanced ability…wit' training he could be taught to maintain his cognizance while using the strengt' and speed associated wit' bloodlust."

Mona sighs. "So, he's alright?"

"Not only t'at," Raven says. "But I'll have Denisoff send him home…" She lifts one finger. "…provided, you bot' remain in…" A tear falls from her left eye. "…what's left of me coven."

Mona nods as tears stream down her face. "Of course, Chief Magistrate."

Raven nods. "I have some phone calls to make." She turns to Vance. "Dear, have ya heard from Natavius yet?"

"Heard from him? He beat you three here." I gasp. "How do you think I got enough blood for all three of them?"

Maggie sighs. "Sorry, ma…" She looks at Vance. "…da, using my speed during a fight still drains me way too much." She puts her hands behind her head and tilts her head back. "It's a little embarrassin' admittin' t'at with me sensei in t'e house."

"Raven?" I ask.

She shakes her head. "Same one who taught you…and ma too."

"Natavius." She nods. "Vance, where is Natavius now?"

He points down the hallway with his thumb. "He's sitting with the twins." Vance turns to Mona. "There's some blood bags in the fridge…" He looks at me. "…and roasted lamb." I nod as my stomach…and my daughter…rumble in unison at the mention of the word. "You should also call Nathan again." I gasp. "He's in a bit of a panic, and he's heading for the airport now."

I nod as Raven and Vance wander down the hallway. Maggie collapses on the couch and Mona and I make our way to the kitchen. "How are you holding up?" She opens the refrigerator door and looks at me. "I mean, you were closer to the others…" Her eyes move lower. "…and you're pregnant." She peers into the refrigerator. "I know I was an emotional mess when I was carrying Joseph. I can't imagine doing that with all the heightened senses and emotions of being a vamp…" She stands with a blood bag in hand and looks at me. "Oooooohhhh," she purrs.

"What?"

She places the blood bag on Vance's marble countertop. She reaches for…and claims my sword. I resist, for a moment and then give it up. She places it on the counter next to her blood bag. She comes back to me and produces a handkerchief from her jacket pocket. She wipes my face…she wipes the tears from my face gently. She then hugs me. "It's going to be alright," she whispers into my ear, while stroking my hair. I sigh. "It's going to be alright," she repeats. I nod and put my arms under hers. "It's going to be alright."

"Why do you keep saying that?"

"It's going to be alright." I shudder. "It's going to be alright." I sob. "It's going to be alright." My knees buckle. "It's going to be alright." I groan as the pain of our friends dying washes over me. "It's going to be alright." I feel an awful ache in the center of my chest as their vacancy becomes a hollow swirling of winds…scrapping my heart…leaving tiny scratches in the wall…until it breaks…and re-breaks and breaks again…and I cry… "It's going to be alright." …it's all that I can do…weep for their memory…and transcribe the pain of their absence… "It's going to be alright." …on the shattered pieces of my fragmented heart.

#####

Chapter 23: Mother

I have no idea what to do here. "You look lost," Natavius whispers. I nod. We return to the twins, Mimiko holding her sister's unconscious head in her hand. "You don't have to do anything when you're outside your depth." I frown. "Take me for instance…I'm good at running fast. I went to get the blood for the transfusions and my parts done."

I laugh soundlessly, trying not to let it go. "Awww, Auntie Lana," Maggie whispers. "Yer cryin' again." She kneels next to me and gives me a hug.

"I can't seem to help it." I wipe my eyes again. "I'm surprised I haven't cried myself dry yet."

"You'll feel better once Nathan gets here," Natavius suggests.

"I hope so."

"Aye," Maggie says, rounding the bottom of the bed. She sits down next to Mimiko. "Ya'd be surprised how much bein' round t'e right person makes everyt'in' t'at much better." Her hand slides across the comforter until it reaches Mimiko's hand…outstretched towards her. Their fingers intertwine. Mimiko kisses Kimiko on the forehead and tilts her head so that she can see Maggie. She offers a weak smile. Maggie, in turn, bows her head to kiss Mimiko's fingers.

"How long has this been going on?" I whisper to Natavius.

"At least as long as the mute sister's been awake, before that I couldn't tell ya." I nod. "When Mimiko woke up, Maggie's face was the first thing she saw…" I sniff. "…they hugged…" A tear tracks down my left cheek. "…did a little more than hugged…"

"…wondered why her sensei and her sire-aunt are talkin' bout her as if she's not in tha room."

"Sorry," we whisper. Natavius stands, and I reach for him. He gives me his hand and helps me out of the chair. Kya has played havoc with my balance lately and that fight with the vampire hunters only hindered me regaining my equilibrium. Natavius opens the door and holds it for me. I step out into the hallway. Natavius steps out behind me and closes the door.

I sigh. "What's wrong?" I shake my head. "Come on. You can tell me."

"I miss Nathan. If he were here right now, I might actually bite him!"

"Awkward," he hums.

"Sorry. It is…my hormones are all over the place. I've been overly emotional…" He wipes a tear away. "…exactly. And when I haven't been that or maddeningly hungry and for the strangest combinations of blood and meats…I've been fighting the insane bouts of…" I lean closer. "…randiness."

"Okay…can we talk about LITERALLY anything else?"

"Sorry. I did not mean to make you feel uncomfortable." I caress my stomach. "Our child has been driving me mad…and I am talking to you about it. Is that insensitive?"

"No, I mean…" He motions to himself. "…I said what I said…and did the stuff that I did…" He motions to me. "…and you said the things you said and did the rejecting thing and…"

"I know that you are in love with Angela," I blurt out. His mouth hangs open. "For someone who moves so fast…" I wave my hand in his face. "…I think that one stunned you to the point of forcing you to stop."

"I…I…"

"Oh no…" His emotions envelope me like a warm blanket. He is open again, not hiding his emotions at all. "…it is more than that." I gasp. It is not that he is not hiding his emotions. He cannot hide them. "You are scent-bonded to her?"

His mouth snaps shut. He nods. "I couldn't've hidden that one from you if I wanted to." I nod. "Honestly, I'm tired of hiding…"

"Tell her."

"Not that." He looks around and then comes back to me. He pulls his shirt up and turns his back to me. There's a mark that looks like three feathers…two beside one another and a third above them, spreading wide on the lower right portion of his back…just above his cheek…no, it is not three feathers…it looks more like an apple…with a leaf. "This. This is the Mark of Eden." He lowers his shirt and returns to me. "I am…En Quosque's wolf."

"I know." He bows his head. "Well, Nathan and I know…we have not exactly made it public knowledge but…" I sigh. "…we assumed as much given that Nicholas was told to find a 2000-year-old wolf…and according to Nathan…you and Mosif are the only two who fit that description." He frowns. "Although, most wolves age extraordinarily slowly…you do not seem to age at all."

"Eden…when I tore him apart…" He motions to himself. "…a part of him, imprinted on me. When I matured…the aging thing…sort of just stopped…"

"…matured?"

"I was ten, when the original Witch of Light, Alaya, convinced me and Sharon…that's the translated name of the 3rd Fairy Queen…to turn against our master." He passes me, heading toward the living room. I catch up to him. "I was so young…and I loved Alaya like she was my mother. Her hair burned like fire…or that's how it looked in sunlight."

"You have kept this from them…from the wolves for so long."

"I didn't keep anything from them." He sighs. "My first memories…were of waking up in the desert…I had no idea how I got there, my name…anything about my past…" He lifts his eyes to me. "…It turns out that the First Alpha…Mosi didn't find me…the fairies delivered me to him…" He shakes his head. "…I've served the Mosi'son Clan ever since."

"Then how…do you know of your life before the tribe, if…"

"You. When you hit me with your silver eyes…back at the safe house when you Nathan were trying to run away together…" I shake my head. "…inadvertently, I know, but still…it brought back ALL of my memories. So, yeah…I've been hiding the truth for the last year…but that's it. I promise."

"I know." I put my hand on his shoulder. "Will you rejoin your brothers?"

"My…"

"I sensed it, when you thought of Ezekiel…and of this, Balthazar, they're two of your original 'brothers,' yes?"

"Yeah. Along with one other from the original En Quosque…" He lifts his eyes to me, but they seem dangerous, fearsome. They cause a quiver in my spine and even Kya trembles. "…the Aldien."

"Impossible…I'm the last."

He shakes his head. "Even when Anara was alive, she wasn't the last. Her father…your grandfather, Anaras…placed himself into a deep sleep, so that he would be at full strength when we were ready to revive Eden."

"We were ready…?"

"They." He nods. "They…Balthazar, Ezekiel, and Anaras…were my brothers in the past…" He nods, and the corners of his mouth turn down. "…Christopher, Vance…and Nathan…are my brothers now. I would fight any enemy for them." He shakes his head. "I told Ezekiel as much…the Eye…they're his puppets. So, if they're coming after you. It's for En Quosque."

My hand moves to Kya instantly. "Yes, I think Nathan surmised as much as well, given what he learned in Edenton."

"Huh," he complains. "So, that little pup's smarter than even I realized he was…no wonder Quinton's always saying he'd make a better Alpha."

"Bite your tongue. Alpha Quinton is a fine Alpha."

"How would you know?" he asks, starting to regain some of the humor in his voice. "You've only known one…I've known 'em all. Ranking…" He closes one eye. "From favorite to least…I'd definitely have to go 1st, 5th…no offense to Mosif…2nd, 4th and then 3rd." He puts his hand next to his mouth in a secretive way. "…and Quinton's grandfather only got ranked below Nathaniel because he was only the Alpha for half a day…before that jerk son of his killed him."

"You know, talking about an Alpha that way…past or present…could get you killed."

"They'd have to catch me first." He frowns. "What's going on with your eyes?"

"Why am I crying again?"

"No. They're silver"

"But I'm not..."

"I am," I hear...in my voice. No, it's not my voice. It's older, more mature than my voice.

"Mother?"

"Alana?" Natavius calls.

"Natavius?"

"Alana, can you hear me?"

"Yes, Natavius, I can...are you...?"

"You can't speak or at least, you can't speak in a way that he'll hear you," mother says. She sighs. My vision phases through a blinding light, leaving me in a white space. "I hope this works." I gasp. I turn to...my face...on a taller woman with longer, darker hair. I swallow a lump. "The visions you gave me said that it would." She shakes her head. "And you gave me perfect vision, my daughter."

"Mother?"

"Yes. How are you my little Isis?"

"My name is Alana," I complain.

"Oh?" she laughs. "Your father was so certain that you would choose to go by the name he chose for you." She walks to her right, revealing a swollen stomach beneath her simple white dress. She plays with the gold chain rope dangling from her waist. "You must have so many questions, starting with how we're talking now?" She puts her hand over her heart. "Speaking of...well, speaking...how is my vernacular? Is my speech pattern...?"

"Mother," I complain.

"Oh, you use the King's English."

"Queen's. England has a Queen as her ruling monarch now." Mother nods. "How are we talking?"

"Ah," she hums. "Your...hm..." She looks at my belly, which is not quite as swollen as hers is. "...by this point in my visions, husband...when I encountered him in the forest, I put to use to that big, beautiful mind of his. You see the dichotomy of the skinwalker's mind is what gives them the ability to resist even the Aldien's mind compulsion after some time, but it also allows for things like this. You see I stowed a portion of my consciousness in the skinwalker side of his mind. The more the two of you communicate using your empathic abilities the more of my consciousness the two of you will be able to access."

"You still did not explain *the* how. You explained what is happening…not how it is happening."

"Oh, my clever girl," she breathes. "…but that's the beauty of our race…most of our empathic abilities, seem to teach themselves to us…like your and your grandmother's dreamwalking."

"You know about that?"

She nods and caresses her belly…with me inside. I gasp and caress my daughter. "You, my darling daughter, gave me visions of the first one hundred years or so of your life…none of it seemed as clear…" She smiles. "…as vibrant as the moments that you spent with Nathan." I smile. Her silver eyes move down to my belly. "What will you name your daughter?"

I laugh. "My Nathan and I have agreed that we will name her after…his mother and…" I throw my hand out toward her. "…you…his mother and you."

"Anara?"

"She'll go by Kya," I insist.

"How much of her life has she shown you?" I tremble…and all happiness garnered from this…this impossible moment to speak with my mother goes. "What's wrong, my love?"

"I see our daughter. She's beautiful…she grows up surrounded by so much warmth and love and she is greatly cared for…as she grows into a beautiful young woman…" I shake my head. "…but my husband…is never with her." I lift tear-filled eyes to her. "What does that mean?"

Her head bows. "I'm so sorry, my love…" I shake my head. "…but I never saw myself with you."

"No," I howl, breathlessly. She nods and walks over to me. She claims my hands…and I feel it…I feel the warmth of hers…somehow, she made this encounter as real as possible. "Please, mother. Tell me there is something that I can do to avoid this…this fate."

"I can't." She pulls my hands up to her mouth. "If I could take this pain, this burden from you I would…but if you do something to save Nathan…then you may hurt your daughter in some way."

"My daughter or my husband…" I snatch my hands away from her and step back…my pain…my anguish, turning to anger so intense that I see red briefly, and a stabbing pain moves through my temples. "…fate cannot possibly be that cruel."

She stares at me, and tears roll down her cheeks. "Yes. It can." The back of her right hand moves down the side of my face, and her skin fills like warm silk to the touch. "I never got to hold you once. I never even got to experience this part of your life…and I was killed by my husband…who I loved almost as much as I love you…so you see…fate can be that cruel."

I nod, and the anger dissipates, replaced by a deep chasm of pain…some my own…some my mother's. "Was this our fate all along? To suffer so much?"

"You will be happy again my daughter. You will find great joy in your daughter…she will not remove the pain of losing Nathan…but focus on her, the gift that he will leave behind." She lifts her head and looks up. "It seems my time is running out."

"No," I weep and wrap my arms around her. "Mum, please…stay a bit longer. I need you. I have needed you so much over the last century." I sniff as tears pour from my eyes.

She strokes the back of my hair. "No, you haven't. Look at you. You are so strong, so smart…so beautiful…Raven and Alexander did exactly as promised. They raised my beautiful girl in my stead." I nod against her heart. "I have to go…but…there is more…" A fierce wind sweeps in. "…you will see me again…"

"Please…"

"…and know that I will love you, my darling Alana, always."

"…mummy, don't go."

"Alana?" Natavius calls.

"MOTHER!?" I sit up. I am on Vance's couch. I touch my face…my tear-soaked face.

"Ya were callin' fer yer mother," Raven says. "What happened?"

"I saw her," I whisper. "Somehow, she implanted memories in Nathan…and the more I communicate with him empathically, the more they transfer to me."

"So, she was nae lyin' about t'at?"

"You knew?"

Raven nods and crosses her arms. "I t'ought ya mother was mad. She started talkin' about all t'ese t'ings that would happen after you were born…her deat'…Alexander bein' t'e first to hold ya…she saw…" Raven laughs. "…each and every time ya escaped and went out explorin'…she told Alexander an' me not to be too hard on ya…because ya were like her…someone who wanted to see people, experience new t'ings…"

I laugh through happy tears.

"…she saw Nat'an." Raven bows her head. "After seeing what he did to t'at town…and what he did to that troop of vampires wit' his bare hands…I could nae believe it." She sits on the coffee table across from me and Vance puts both hands on her shoulders. "She said t'at Nat'an was t'e key to yer happiness…t'at when ya met him…you'd fall in love instantly, but most of all…he'd give ya what ya always wanted…" She touches my stomach. "…a family of yer own."

I sigh into another bout of happy tears…until I remember that my happiness…the love of my life…won't be a part of that family. I sob…

"Lana?" Vance and Natavius say at the same time, but it's too late. The floodgates are open…and I…and Kya…weep for her lost father…my world…my Nathan.

#####

Chapter 24: Relocation

"Nate, are you okay?" He frowns, but his eyes remain on traffic. His thumbs rhythmically strum the steering wheel in place of the music he refuses to turn on. "I mean, you know besides the evil organization targeting your wife and child and hoping to bring about the end of the world." His head bows. "Ba dum ping," I imitate a rim shot.

"You're better than that," he grumbles. He looks at me. "Try again."

"So, a vampire, a wolf, and a witch walk into a bar…"

He shakes his head. "Something's…off. I noticed it as soon as we landed."

"Not exactly comforting to know that they have one member who can be around, and you not even know it and another member who can see every move you make before you make it."

"Stick to jokes," he warns. "Because cheering people up with observation…not your strong suit." I shrug. "No, it's just. It's all over us." He looks at me. "The malevolence…" He averts his eyes. "…it's even got you now."

"Yay." I give two big, over exaggerated thumbs up. "I'm on their radar." I nod. "You know I was just thinking that if I'm not careful, I might not almost die at all this half of the year." He smirks, fighting off a laugh. "I'll save the good stuff for after you see Alana." He looks at me. "Because I know you won't be able to laugh for real until you see her with your own eyes."

He exhales loudly through his nose. "How the hell is it that you get me better than people I've known for almost two centuries?"

I shrug again. "I'm more of a people person?"

He smiles. "Thank you."

"You're welcome." God, I love him so much. I never thought I'd settle for being a guy's best friend as opposed to being his girlfriend…but even this doesn't feel like settling with Nate. I love him, and I'd do anything for him…even if it breaks my heart for the rest of my very long life.

I readjust in my seat, and I feel something. "Crap."

"What?"

I squirm. "Knife came out of its sheath." He snickers. "Fine, I'll fix it with my hands." I reach back…that's weird though, it's never done that before. What is this? A piece of paper? I take it out and unfold it. Was this stuck down in my sheath?

"What's that?"

"Receipt?" I unfold it.

My dearest Angel,

I frown.

"What?"

"Nothing." I shake my head and crumple the note.

"Are you sure?" I nod. He focuses on the road, and I flatten out the note.

"You know, for that note to be 'nothing,' you're paying an awful lot of attention to it."

I wad it up again. "You can tell I'm lying, can't you?"

He nods and shifts the car into park. "You can tell me the truth later." I frown and look at the tiny building across the street from the park. I look down the rest of 8th Avenue. Well, tiny compared to the rest of the buildings here. "We're here." The door opens behind me. I climb out and catch the scent of the human wearing the ridiculous maroon coat with 8 equally ridiculous giant gold buttons. He tips his hat to me.

"Thanks, dude." He nods and pushes the door closed. A guy in a vest the same color falls into the driver side of Nate's car. He pulls away as Nate makes his way toward me. "So, whose place is this?"

Nate sighs and keeps walking. We walk through the sick lobby with marble floor and gray marble reception desk. He tips his head to the concierge as if he knows him, which makes sense since the guy with light almond skin and a buzz cut nods back. We reach the elevators and wait.

"Seriously, dude. Even you can't afford a Central Park West apartment. Whose place is this?"

"Okay, first of all, I can. Second, I prefer Brooklyn and that was even before they moved out all the interesting people, slapped a fresh coat paint on everything, and started charging quadruple for the same spaces. And third…" The elevator dings. "…you wouldn't believe me if I told ya, so you'll just have to see it for yourself."

We step inside, and he presses 12. He crosses his arms and turns toward the doors. I cross my arms and imitate his stance. "I'm Nate," I groan, trying to recreate his tense voice to go with the stance. "…and I stand like this in elevators because it makes me look like a badass."

He laughs…really laughs, showing teeth and all. "I thought you were gonna save the good stuff for after I saw Alana."

"You don't need to see your wife again after three weeks away when you're a tense little ball of fur."

He turns to me with a bemused frown as the elevator dings for the twelfth time. "…little…?" I shove him in the back, and he stumbles out of the elevator. He walks down the hall, not before glaring at me over his shoulder one good time, until he comes to apartment 12F. He knocks with two hard raps on the door.

The door opens and Maggie smiles at us. "Nat'an!" She wraps her arms around him. How does she…? "I have nae seen ya in so long. How many decades has it been, man?" Nate shrugs. "We'll catch me up later. Yer wife's inside. Go." He steps past me into the apartment. I step up to the threshold, and she hugs me.

I freeze. "Um, what are ya doin' there, Mary Margaret?"

"I know we don' know each ot'er well, lil' sis, but…" She leans back and looks me in the eye. "…t'e blood makes us family. An' I take t'at very seriously."

"I guess." She nods and steps inside. I push the door closed behind us and turn to the living room and… "MONA!" She sits on the sofa with Alana's head in her lap. She strokes the side of Alana's hair and puts her free pointer finger up to her mouth as if to shush us. "What are you doing here?" I stage whisper. "Did you have something to do with the attack on the…?" Maggie punches me on the shoulder. "Ow."

"She said shush," Maggie issues matching my volume. "Alana just fell asleep…she…" Maggie's eyes meet Nate's eyes. "…she cried herself ta sleep. Not'in' could console her."

Nate sighs and nods.

Maggie turns back to me. "Now, go down t'ere. Second door on t'e right." She points down the hallway to my right. "Raven's waitin' fer ya." I open my mouth to respond with an angry finger pointed at that traitorous hoe-bag holding my sire-aunt. "Uh, uh. Go. Now." I scowl.

Nate ignores Mona altogether and goes over to Alana. He kneels in front of her and collects her hand. She whimpers and opens her eyes slowly. "Hey, Princess," he whispers, moving a stray strand of hair away from her forehead in that super sweet way guys do sometimes.

"Our Nathan," she sighs back. She caresses his cheek, while lifting her head. "Oh, you look so tired," she whispers. "Did you even sleep on the plane?"

"I can sleep when I'm dead..." Alana gasps and shivers...with tears swimming in her eyes. "...and not worried about my wife and child." He smiles...and kisses the back of her hand.

She huffs a laugh...but it feels forced...fake. She leans forward. She and Nathan kiss and then he wraps his arms around her and holds her close. He kneels again and puts his hands on either side of her completely noticeable stomach. She puts her hands on top. "We've gotten so big," she complains, holding her larger stomach.

Nate leans forward and kisses her belly. "You have?" he asks as if he hadn't noticed. Pfft, knowing him, he really didn't notice. "How are you doing my darling little Anara?"

"Her name is Kya," Alana says as a laugh.

Nathan looks up at her. "Uh uh, she just kicked when I said Anara...nothing when you said Kya."

"We'll see."

Mona slides out of the way, tipping her head to Nate. He returns the nod, and then takes her place on the sofa, and Alana nuzzles up against him. "Oh," she whines. "We're so big it is harder to get close to you."

Nate pulls her closer with little effort. "You...two...still just look like the most beautiful mother and child I've ever seen to me, Princess." She hums an aww and kisses him on the cheek. "How are you feeling?"

"Would you like the honest straightforward answer or the PC response...?" She tips her head toward Maggie and me. "...for the audience?"

"We vowed only honesty with each other, Princess."

"I have been extraordinarily randy since you have been gone and I would really like to be alone with you so that I can tear every stitch of clothing from your body." Nate smirks and nibbles his lower lip. "I am talking..." Alana pauses to think. "...well, do you remember after we went to that concert in the park, and we drank those six bottles of champagne?" Nate nods. "Like that." Nate smiles. He tries to fight it off, but it just keeps coming back until he bends to kiss Alana.

And I have officially heard and seen enough. I sigh and walk down the hall.

"I think we should find some privacy," Nate says.

I speed up. I think Maggie said it was the second door on the right. I reach it and knock. "Come in," Raven calls. I open the door and it's a bedroom. It's simply decorated but has a huge bed in the center with a black wooden base. One of the twins lies in the bed with her bandaged arm above the covers. The other twin…I suck for not being able to tell the difference between them before they talk or don't talk…lies beside her on the bed. Raven stands at the window peering out…and Vance, Nate's pack brother, has his arm around her.

"Raven," I say. "You wanted to see me?" Raven and Vance turn to me. She appears in front of me and wraps her arms around me. I hug her back. "Is she going to be okay?"

"We're still waiting," Vance says. "I have Natavius out retrieving more blood for her, but it's still too soon to say. One of the vampire hunters was using silver nitrate laced rounds while the others were using standard issue and shredders."

"Can I get that recap in English?"

"Silver…in liquid form," Raven says. "It buried itself inta t'a tissue of her arm…shredders hit flesh and shatter, making t'em difficult to remove fer t'a patient and dangerous fer t'a doctor." I nod. "Mimiko's been by her side since Vance got her outta critical condition." I nod. Mimiko lifts her head and nods. I wave.

"What did we find out about the vampire hunters?" I ask.

"Natavius says that they cleared out as soon as Raven and Alana got away." Vance sighs and crosses his arms. "Unfortunately, Maggie, the twins, Raven, Alana, and Mona were the only survivors from the house."

"Well, isn't that convenient," I complain.

"Hey," Raven snaps with an actual snap of her fingers in my face. "Lana cleared Mona…compelled her and everyt'ing." I nod. "Fer now, we have ta regroup. We'll scatter for the most part. Alana's going home with Nat'an…and Natavius and Mona will stay with them." Jealous twinge. "I'll stay here with Vance, Maggie, and the twins." She points to me. "And you…I want you to stay wit' yer mot'er."

"Yer me mother," I imitate her.

She smiles. "Yer bio mom t'en." I nod. Raven shivers. "The Magistrates are comin' in day after tomorrow for a meeting."

"Why not tomorrow?" I whine. "What do they have something better to do than come to the aid of their leader?"

"Sadly," Raven says. "Yes. In the case of Prefect Xiao, he's attending a wedding in Japan on my behalf and is seeing to some other affairs there. He won't be able to fly out until tomorrow our time. Late in t'a day, his time. He won't be back state side until the early morning. I have Michael investigating…" Raven sighs and clenches her jaw. "…somet'ing for me."

She sounds exhausted. Then again, her coven was attacked in her home…most of them were killed…it is almost nine at night and she's been up for at least a day…and unlike her sister and me, she doesn't keep a school schedule to keep her awake during the day. "You, okay?"

"Just wonderin' how t'is all happened," she sighs.

"I can give you the report on what we found in Edenton."

"Nathan called me from the plane."

"When?"

"When you were asleep," Vance says…and wraps his arms around Raven's waist. I arch one eyebrow as she leans back into him.

"Um…what's going on?"

"Och," Raven complains with a facepalm. "I'm so forgetful. I'd forget me head if'n it was nae attached." She motions to Vance. "Angela, meet yer sire-father, me husband Vance Purdue."

"Your what?" Raven wiggles the fingers of her left hand in my face, showing off her emerald engagement ring next to her platinum wedding band. "Did you two just get…? How…long have you…?"

"This October," Vance starts. "…will make our 139th anniversary."

"139th?" Raven asks. "I thought it was only 137th?"

"Ah," Vance hums. "Remember? You count from our actual wedding day, but I count from the day I brought Mary Margaret back to you."

"Aye," Raven hums, happily with a nod. "She's been callin' ya 'da' ever since." He kisses her on the cheek.

"Whoa," I fuss. They look at me. "I mean, Natavius and Alana hinted at…but…" I nod and offer my hand. "Nice to meet you…" I frown. "…da."

He laughs and claims my hand. "You seemed so shaken up after your run in with Balthazar at the reception, that I almost told you right then and there…if for no other reason than to hug you." I laugh this time. "The blood makes family…" Vance looks at Raven then comes back to me. "…in this case, the family that you choose."

"Sounds nice. I didn't get to choose though," I say, sounding more bitter than I meant to sound. "Sorry. I know that wasn't your fault."

Raven shakes her head. Her phone starts to ring with a heavy metal tune. "I have ta take t'is, love." She kisses Vance. She points at me. "You…stay here wit' t'e twins fer now." I nod as she moves over to the door. She opens it. "Hello, Michael…what do ya have fer me?" She paces down the hall.

"It's a little shocking, isn't it?"

"Naw," I say, turning back to him. "After NOLA, Paris…and…" I shrug. "…Edenton of all places…I've pretty much seen it all."

"So," Vance starts. "You've seen Nate fight for real?"

I bob my head. "Yeah, I mean, he fought Ephraim in New Orleans and…"

Vance shakes his. "No, I mean, REALLY seen him fight." He steps closer…and his scent sweeps over me, like fresh soil and clover. Amazing, I've smell it a couple of hundred times on Raven…but I never noticed it before now. I thought, maybe she'd built a shrine to Ireland or something but… "Angela?"

"Oh, sorry. No, I guess not."

"You haven't seen it," Natavius says from the door.

"Hey…" Before I can even finish, he has his arms around me. I sigh and put my arms over his shoulders. "…I take it you missed me a little."

"Only a little," he whispers. He holds me tight…like I might break if he lets go of me. I take my arms away, but he continues holding on. I replace my arms and peer over his shoulder awkwardly. "Okay," he sighs. "Maybe more than a little."

He lets go. I shove him at the shoulder. "Well, what's a fake boyfriend without his fake girlfriend?" He laughs. "So, what's so special about seeing Nate REALLY fight?"

"Let's just say," Natavius starts.

"When he REALLY gets going," Vance picks up for him. "…you don't want to be anywhere near him. Trust us." I nod, believing the sincerity in their voices. "Also, no offense to my lovely wife, but I think she may have made an error in judgement. I don't think you should stay with your biological mother. I think you should stay here with us."

"What? Why?"

"Alana and Nate are going to their place with Natavius and Mona…" Jealous ping. "…and while they can't see him, they can detect this daemon…"

"Balthazar," I say. Vance frowns and stares at me. "What?" He steps forward and takes my chin. He tips my head back and peers into my right eye and then my left.

"Oh no."

"What?"

"RAVEN!" Vance hurries out of the room.

"What was that all about?" Natavius shrugs. Raven storms into the room with Vance behind her. I swallow a lump as she comes to a stop in front of me. "Wha-what's going on?"

"Tell me about Balt'azar."

"Well, he…"

"No. Say his name."

"Balthazar," I say. She glares at me. "What?"

"Are ya…" She breaks off to scoff. "…are ya fallin' for t'is daemon?"

"What?" Natavius barks.

"I…I don't know…" I admit. "I…honestly, don't know…"

#####

Chapter 25: Tryst

I look down at Balthazar's handwritten note. I can't believe I kept this, then again, I can't believe I'm doing this. I mean, I should've thrown it away as soon as I found it...and I REALLY should've thrown it away considering what happened and the way he stalked me in Edenton...only to attack Nate and the others.

I sigh. He tried to warn me off though...and he kissed me again. I mean, I practically blew off the front of Blackshears' house. Then, in the middle of that chaos, I let him kiss me. That must mean something, right?

"Smart, Ange," I mumble to myself. No matter what...even if he is serious and really is...in love with me, he's the bad guy. There's no getting around that. He's the 2000-year-old daemon who serves a demigod trying to take over the world.

"You came?" I turn...to him. Just him, not his glamour or anything.

"I came."

"Come on. This way," he says, walking over to the huge apartment building on my left. "Hey, Manny," he says, casually to the doorman.

The doorman tips his hat to us. "Hey Mr. Balthazar. How are you today?"

"Good. How about yourself?"

"Not too bad. Not like you to bring a lady home, sir."

Balthazar looks at me. "Yeah, well..." He goes back to Manny. "...I haven't met many women as special as Ms. Price here."

"Ms. Price," Manny says with a tip of his hat.

"Manny. Nice to meet you." He holds the door open. Balthazar walks through, and I follow. Why am I following?

"Problem?"

"Well, you're a member of En Quosque. You're the bad guy, and you've been posing as a normal dude."

"I'm sorry." He turns to me near the gold tinted elevators. "Should I have been waving my En Quosque flag and wearing my *I heart Eden* t-shirt?" I frown. "We're a secret organization...you don't remain a secret if you draw attention to yourself, i.e., if you don't act like a..." He pauses to think. "...*normal dude.*"

I scoff and turn to walk out the door. He appears in front of me, his eyes darting around the lobby. "I knew this was a mistake." He sighs. "Move."

"No."

"Move, or I'll move you."

"I'm faster than you, and I have 25 hundred years of experience over you." My back tenses, and all my senses open wide. Is he threatening me?

"But…" He steps to his left. "…if you really want to leave, I won't stop you. I'll ask…or even beg you to stay…" I glare at him. "…but I won't stop you if you choose not to."

"You're serious?"

He nods. "I wasn't mocking you earlier…and just because I'm…" He makes air quotes. "…*the bad guy*…all a matter of perspective by the way, that doesn't mean I can't get to know my doorman or show interest in him and his life." He shuffles and slides his hands into the pockets of his slim gray slacks. He notices me, noticing him and smooths down his deep blue tie over his matching shirt. "For the record, Manuel has a long-term girlfriend who he's saving up to buy a ring for…and with whom he shares an apartment…well with her and their two children in the Bronx.

"Angela, please believe that even a bad guy…even a 2000-year-old bad guy…can be taken aback by a woman." He steps closer and collects my left hand, and of course, I'm an idiot and let him. "…can be caught off guard by her beauty…find out more about her and find that he only wants to know more…" He slips his left hand up and caresses my cheek. "…and then find that every moment that he spends with her makes him want to spend two more in exchange."

"True…if it's true, that is."

I look away…or try to, but I stupidly turned into his hand. He pulls my face back to meet his. "It is." I look into his eyes. "Kiss me," he whispers. I look around taking in all of the people already staring at us. I shake my head, subtly but quickly. "Them?" I nod. "I don't care about them. I care about you."

"But…"

"If you want to come upstairs with me, kiss me. If not…" He releases me and takes a step back. "…don't and you'll never have to worry about me again."

"Never?"

"Never," he mouths in return. I swallow a lump, and he takes another step back with his hands up like I'm mugging him. I stare at the floor between us. "Fine. I understand." He walks to my left. "It was nice getting to know you, Ang-"

I catch his arm, before he can finish and pull him back around to me. What are my options? I haven't been interested in a vampire since Stephen, and I'm in love with my sire-aunt's husband, who happens to be my best friend. Then there's Bal…who's…

"Well?" he says, pointing out that I'm just standing here holding his arm like a little kid.

"Be honest with me."

154 | Midnight Princess

"Ask me anything."

"No. I mean, that's my condition. You have to be honest with me at all times. Even if you think, it'll make me think you're a monster. Even if you think that it'll make me hate you…I want you to tell me the truth all the time. Clear?"

He nods without hesitation. I pull him around and drape my arms over his shoulders. He puts his hands on the small of my back and kisses me. He's such a good kiss…it's so good a kiss that I feel a tingle in my toes and my eyebrows arch on their own. It's so good a kiss that I don't even realize we're moving until my back collides with the elevator wall. He takes my arms away from his shoulders and pins them to the wall. He moves away from my lips and kisses my neck…and… "Mmmm," I moan…I'm actually moaning…but those lips of his are like magic against my skin.

Our palms slide together, and he puts his fingers between mine. He returns to my lips, and our tongues meet…his is soft, but he applies just the right amount of pressure. I squeeze his hands and lean back…or he leans forward. We part…both panting heavily. He rests his right cheek against my left.

"Do you see what you do to me?"

"The same thing you do to me?" He laughs, his warm breath caressing my ear. His hands move achingly slowly down my wrist…his left stays at my wrist and move over to take the other…but his right keeps going. It moves down toward my… "Stop," I snap, not quite ready to go there…yet. His fingers dance along my collarbone. "Sorry," I say in the form of a throaty whisper.

"No," he replies, matching my voice. The elevator dings, and I assume the doors open behind us. I have to assume because I can't tear my eyes away from the two emeralds staring back at me. "It was my fault. I shouldn't have been so presumptuous." I nod with a tense jaw and lips wanting to kiss his again.

He steps back, pulling both of my hands along with him. "Come." I nod, and he pulls me out of the elevator. We reach the third door on the right, and he just pushes it open…no, doorknob turning or anything.

"You felt pretty confident that I was coming, huh?"

He smiles. "Yes…but I always leave it open." He steps inside, and I shove him. He stumbles backward and tugs on my hand. He pulls me into him and wraps his arms around me as he drops onto a plush white sofa. I kiss him as if I haven't seen him in weeks…we slide and fall off the couch.

"Ugh," I complain when he hits the floor, and I hit him. He laughs…I laugh, until I bring it down with a sigh, because I'm realizing that the guy,

I'm making out with is not only the bad guy, but I hardly know anything about him.

"What?"

"What's your favorite color?"

"What?" he laughs.

"I don't know you. So…"

"What's your favorite color?"

"Nuh-uh…I asked you first."

"Green."

"Makes sense."

"How so?"

"You own a mirror…and you see what I'm staring into anytime you want." He huffs a laugh, then tips his head toward me. I sigh…put one hand on top of the other on his chest and rest my chin on my hands. "My favorite color to wear is black, but my favorite color is blue because it's the color of the ocean…" He smiles. "…and the color of my father's eyes."

"Are you and your father close?"

"We were."

"I'm sorry."

"Don't be. He left…and after he died, I found out that he was just as awesome as I remembered. What about you? Your father…?"

"Died well over two thousand years ago."

"I'm sorry."

"I'm not. I killed him." I frown. "You said you wanted honesty." I nod. "He didn't agree with my choice…and attempted to stop me from following Eden's path. He tracked me through what is now Northern China…" His eyes seem miles away. "…like you, he could see me, even through my glamour.

"He found me one morning just before sunrise." He looks at me. "…but I wasn't alone. I'd been avoiding him so that I wouldn't have to hurt him…but there he was…there she was…bloodied at his feet. He looked at me with such condescension…such arrogance…and he said to me, 'This is the ruin that Eden wrought.'" He sighs. "I slew him where he stood. I burned the hovel and never looked back."

"You didn't bury her?"

His eyes snap back into focus as if he didn't even know I was there. "No. It wasn't our way. We burned our honored dead back then. So, I burned them both to show that I loved them. My wife and my father…"

He moves forward. I sit back, and he sits up, sliding out from under me. He stands and paces away. "Bal?" He pauses at the hallway, undoes his tie, and pulls it away with a fabric scraping zip. "Are you alright?"

"Over two thousand years, you'd think I'd be over it by now."

156 | Midnight Princess

I move over to him and tug at the back of his sport coat. He looks at me over his shoulder. "Two thousand years or a single day…" I begin, paraphrasing Nate. "…to your heart…a loss, is a loss." He nods and walks down the hall. I stare after him for a minute. If I had a heartbeat, it'd be racing right now. I follow him. The darkened hallway lets little light out…except the last door on the right…left cracked open with a beam of light slicing the darkness.

I go over to the door and peak in. He slips his jacket off and tosses it onto a chair at the window. "Can I…?" Before I finish, he pulls the door open and motions for me to enter. I step inside of his bedroom with its huge California King-sized bed with black…silky looking sheets and no comforter. I walk toward the chair. He steps in front of me and motions to the bed. "So, you expect to get me into bed on the first date?"

"On the bed, maybe."

I laugh, slip my coat off, and crawl across the bed before lying down on it. "Are you okay?"

"I'm here with you, aren't I?"

I readjust on the bed. His silk sheets tickle my stomach between the top of my jeans and the bottom of my t-shirt. He traces one unbearably warm finger along the back of my thigh, across my butt, and then runs it parallel to my spine. Every inch that he caresses still burns with his touch. God, I sound like one of those cheesy romance books. It sucks because for the first time, I get it. I get why writer's write that crap… I glance back at him. He smiles his Earth-shattering, heart-rending smile. A flirtatious grin appears on my face before I even realize it. …they write that crap because it's all true.

"What?" he sighs as four fingers sweep from one of my shoulder blades to the other. "You look like you have something on your mind." Sunlight shines through his brunette locks throwing a shadow over his eyes. Those emeralds he calls pupils feel like they just rip right through me. He arches eyebrows that are more perfectly trimmed than anything any cosmetology student could've dreamed of doing.

"I hate you," I complain in a breath. His smile turns flirty. A glint beams across my eyes from his pearly white teeth. My chin rests uncomfortably in the palm of my hand. I exhale loudly through my nose and turn to his blank flat screen.

"You don't hate me."

"Yeah, I do," I snap before turning back to his face. "I hate you…because I don't hate you. I should hate you. I really should, but I don't." I roll over onto my back, propping myself up on my elbows. He moves beside me and drapes one arm over my exposed bellybutton. "In fact," I start again staring at him, staring at me. "I kind of…love you." His hand touches the small of my back and lifts me. Our lips almost touch, and I feel like I'm gonna pass out if he doesn't kiss me soon.

"That's a good thing," he reassures. "…because I love you too, Angela." He delivers a quick peck to my lips, and I undo the top button of his shirt. I inhale deeply as he leans in for another kiss, and I undo another one.

I stop and lean away. "Ugh. What the hell is wrong with me?" I whine to those beautiful eyes. He tweaks his head, and I tilt back a little. I can't help but watch his lips as he moves away, too.

"What…?"

"I was human…and I fell for a vampire. I'm a vampire, and I'm falling in love with a daemon. If I were a daemon, what then? Would I be trying to hook up with the devil himself?"

Balthazar laughs dryly. "You do realize that daemon, the word for our race, was only derived from the word demon and didn't originally mean 'evil' right," he asks, moving closer to me. I press my lips into a line and nod. His free hand cups my chin. "And as far as 'what's wrong with you,'" he breathes sending a shiver down my spine.

"Yeah?" I whisper.

He shakes his head, causing his lips to sweep across mine back and forth. "I can't find a single thing that's 'wrong with you.'" I swallow deeply, his warm sweet breath still caressing my lips. "Because to me, you're perfect." I manage to crack a smile before he pulls me in for a kiss.

#####

Chapter 26: Impossible

"No, we haven't seen her," Nathan says. He looks to me and even if not for my empathic abilities, I could see it plain on his face. He's worried about her. Raven said that she fled from Vance's flat after they accused her of having feelings for Balthazar, En Quosque's daemon. "We'll call if we hear anything." He nods. "Alright." He ends the call and turns to me. He grips his phone, and I take it from him. "Will you two stop doing that?"

"Angela takes this from you for the same reason that I do. So that you will not break it." He sighs into a nod. "You are worried about her. You should go find her." He shakes his head, holding my wrists. "Natavius and Mona are here."

"Natavius left," Mona says.

"What?" She nods. "Did he say where he was going?" She shakes her head. He must be in agony. If Angela truly has feelings for another, and he is scent-bonded to her…

"Love?" I hum a response that is neither negative nor positive. "How are you?" I shake my head. "Mona, would you give us a minute?" She nods. "We have two guest bedrooms, feel free to take which ever you like." She hurries down the hall.

My Nathan ushers me into the kitchen and turns the radio on. It plays a jazz song with a trumpet that eases Kya's mind. "Honesty," he says.

"She may be in love with this daemon, and he's scent-bonded to her, but she doesn't know, because he's been too unsure to tell her, because he's never been scent-bonded to someone romantically before and…"

"Love, Love, Love…slow down. What are you talking about?"

"Natavius is scent-bonded to Angela." He frowns. "I…" I clear my throat. "…do not get angry."

"I'm not making any promises."

I nod. "I am only telling you this because we promised that we would be honest with one another at all times." I swallow a knot, and the easiness that the jazz music gave Kya evaporates as she synchronizes with my emotion. "Natavius…had…" I extend my hand to him to calm him. "…emphasis on HAD…feelings for me."

"He what?"

"HAD," I reiterate. "He expressed them to me while you were…" I motion between us. "…while we were…" He growls and closes his eyes. "Nathan," I snap. He looks at me. I point at him. "Please remember that you created that situation by leaving without telling me, your fiancée, or him, your best friend, where you were going or what you were planning."

"And that makes it my fault?"

"No, but…you cannot control with whom you fall in love…" I sigh and turn away. "…if I could…" I come back fighting silver tears back. "…I would have given up on loving you while you were gone."

"I know." He groans and backs into the refrigerator causing it to smash against the wall.

"I am not saying that to hurt you; I am saying it to give you some perspective."

He wipes his nose and nods. He motions for me to continue.

"Nothing happened. We talked…and he expressed his feelings, which I believe were a manifestation of the affection he felt for my mother." He nods. "He…" I reach out and claim my Nathan's arm. "…we would never do anything to hurt you with such malice. You have to believe that, my Nathan."

"Yeah," he rumbles. "It's like you said…if people could control who they love…"

"We wouldn't be standing here worried about Ange," Natavius says from the kitchen doorway. I turn to him and put my arms over his shoulders. He puts one arm around my back. I cannot see his face, but if I'm reading his and Nathan's emotions correctly, they're glaring at each other.

"Stop it," I nag. I release Natavius and return to my Nathan's side. He puts his arm over my shoulder. "We have to focus on the here and now. Did you find her?"

"I didn't…"

"Natavius," Nathan and I say at the same time with the same disapproving tones.

"No. She has to be with…HIM…" He tosses his hands up. "…I tracked her to the Upper West side of Manhattan and then…nothing. Only Balthazar can make someone's scent disappear so completely."

"What about those grenades that the Order uses?" Nathan asks.

Natavius shakes his head. "The stuff inside of them is probably derived from his pheromones…and they're watered down compared to what Balthazar can do." Nathan nods. "Did you tell him?" Natavius asks.

"No. I did not feel it was my place."

"There's more?" Nathan says with a rumble to his voice that suggests he's trying to stay calm.

"Natavius?"

"I got my memories back," he admits. "I was En Quosque's wolf. I remember everything about Balthazar, Ezekiel, and Anaras…Alana's grandfather."

"And you didn't think…?"

"Nathan, no." He frowns. "Put yourself in his place. En Quosque started a war against the world. A war so all-encompassing that vampire and wolf are willing to work together without question or hesitation. Would you really like him to announce to everyone that he was…WAS a member of their number?" Nathan frowns. "What would happen to him?"

Nathan steps forward. Natavius stares at him with concern. Nathan slips his arm around Natavius's shoulders. "…nothing that I'd want to happen to him," he answers. He nods and puts his other arm around his pack brother, while patting him on the back. "Not even the annoyance of being asked about it."

"Thanks," Natavius says. They part. "I was gonna make a blood, steak, and coffee run. Who wants? I'm buying."

"You do not have to do that," I say.

"Yeah. I do. Either I keep moving out there or I pace a hole in the floor here…because every time I think about something happening to her…about her being with HIM…I just…" He sighs. "…wanna break something."

"Nathan, why don't you go with Natavius on his supply run?" My Nathan frowns. "I am fine. Mona is here, and there are plenty of weapons stashed around the flat. If En Quosque or the Order comes anywhere near…I'll sense them and call you both back immediately." I turn to Natavius. "And if I hear anything, I'll ring you both instantly. Yes?"

"I…" Nathan starts.

"Ooohh…you know what I would fancy right now? Streaky bacon and ice cream." I purr. "Just thinking about it…" I pat my Nathan's chest. "…please go and get your very pregnant wife some." He sighs. "Thank you, dear."

"You're welcome, Love." He kisses me and steps away. Natavius follows, and I pat his shoulder as he moves past me.

I step into the living room as they exit the flat. I wave to my Nathan as he pulls the door closed behind them. He stops and holds in the door. "Go. Talk to him." He nods and steps out. My heart plunges. I should be spending every moment that I can with him, but his brother needs him now.

Mona returns from the hallway. "Did you find a room to your liking?"

"Yeah. It's pretty big…especially for a spare room."

"My Nathan likes his space." I note the mobile in her hand. "Were you talking to Joseph?"

She nods. "He's…actually, starting to grow on Denisoff. He's already been promoted twice and he's almost fluent in Russian." She sighs.

"Are you alright? Do you miss him?"

"Of course, but that's not it." I move to the sofa and tap the spot next to me. She sits with another sigh. "This…isn't the life I would've chosen for him. Not just, living in Russia…" She smiles. "…actually, I think getting out of the country did him some good. Vampirism doesn't suit him." She laughs humorlessly. "You know that better than most."

"His susceptibility towards blood-lust?"

She nods. "I still remember the day he was born. He was so beautiful, so perfect. His little streak of blond hair…his bright blue eyes." I smile feeling the warmth, radiating from her. She sighs. "I'll never get to hold a child like that again."

"Perhaps, you can." She frowns. "How would you like to play nanny to…?" I caress her. "…my daughter?"

"You would let me…?"

"Of course," I breathe…and something ripples up my spine. My eyes move over to silver on their own.

"Alana?"

I turn to Mona…or where she was…I cannot say for sure, because I can no longer see her. I only see the white space that I visited during my time with my mother. "It's alright, Mona. I believe I'm getting a vision."

"Should I call Raven?"

"No, no. I'll be fine. Just give me a moment and ignore me for a time."

"Okay," she says. She moves away from the sofa.

I lean back and try to get comfortable. I wonder what mother has to tell me this time. I sigh, considering her news last time.

"So…wife and the kid all in less than a few months." Natavius? "How does it feel?" My eyes come into focus…or more accurately, my Nathan's eyes…I see Natavius sitting across a café table from him.

Nathan nods and sips his overpriced coffee drink. "Are we really going to do this?" Oh no, please tell me that they are not going to fight.

"Do what?" Natavius inquires. I sigh and roll my neck trying not to let how I feel get in the way of hearing what needs to be said.

"En Quosque…Alana." My jaw clenches. I inhale deeply and try to focus on the words not the emotions. "When Alana started convulsing at our first wedding, you whispered that you loved her." He did? Natavius looks away. "Nate…just tell me…"

"I was never scent-bonded to her," he says. I…Nathan looks at our pack brother. His expression is heartbreaking…no, he looks as though his heart has been torn out. "I don't know how it happened though. I loved her…and not like, I love a pack sister.

"You know, you never had anything to worry about though, right?" Natavius asks with a punch delivered to Nathan's shoulder. "And I'm not just talking about the way that she feels about you. You're my pack brother and before that, I looked after you as if you were my own cub. I would never do anything to hurt you."

"I know," I utter at the same time my Nathan does.

"This thing…those feelings that I had for Alana; they were my burden to bear. I just feel suckish about making it hers, by telling her about it." Nathan takes another drink. Natavius smiles. "You still don't know how to have the difficult conversations, do you?" My Nathan shakes his head. I suppose that makes two of us, my love.

"Alright," Natavius chuckles. "I'll let you off the hook. How is Lana doing anyway?"

"She's great. No injuries from the attacks…but…mentally…I don't know." Natavius frowns and leans forward. "Ever since I got back, I feel like she's holding something back. It sucks because we promised to be honest with each other and I have." He's right. It's not fair.

"Do you think maybe it has something to do with the baby? Like she's having visions like her mother did?"

"I don't know. Maybe. I just hope she's not dreaming about her own death again." No, my heart…it's yours…or rather, the absence that yours leaves in its wake. My Nathan sighs. I can feel some of his emotion. He doesn't want to think that I am deceiving him, but he feels my emotions just as strongly.

"So," my Nathan starts again. "Angela?"

"How about that?" Natavius says.

"Yeah, how about that." Good. They are on to a cheerier subject…if we knew where she was it would be… "My two best friends coming together would be…"

A gentle breeze rolls in and takes me off guard. Nathan gasps. Natavius almost gags on his tea and puts his cup down. He sniffs again. Nathan does the same. His nose twitches…he recognizes but does not recognize the scent he detects.

Natavius leans forward and sniffs again several times. "No way," he sighs. Nathan groans and leans back. I feel his pain. His head feels as if it's about burst. "There is something weird going," Natavius breathes.

Nathan examines the people nearby. They seem to swirl around him. "I can't focus," he grumbles into his coffee. He exhales a gruff breath. I feel it. His skinwalker side and his wolf sides are clashing. His eyes faze to honey and emerald as surely as mine would move to silver.

Natavius puts his hand on Nathan's shoulder. "Something…smells familiar," Nathan growls. His fingers wrap around his forehead, and his thumbs attempt to bore into his temples.

"I know," Natavius replies. His eyes scan the people as well. "It…can't be though." Nathan shakes his head. "Right?" Nathan's confused. He doesn't know what Natavius hints at, and I don't recognize the scent I'm detecting through Nathan. "You," Natavius begins but breaks off. "You don't recognize the scent?"

"No," Nathan replies, his headache raging. Nathan puts his hand on the table's edge and crushes it. The steel warps under his grip. "Sh-should I?"

Natavius's hand snaps to Nathan's wrist. He squeezes and pulls at the same time. "Okay," he whispers. "I'm going to need you to let go of the table." Nathan growls. "Please. I'm not as strong as you are. I can't make you."

Nathan releases. Natavius lets go as well. "Who? WHO?" The women at the next table glare at them.

"Breathe, damn it," Natavius whispers. "I need you to keep it together. At least until no one's paying enough attention to us so that I can make us…Nate," he cuts short as Nathan's head hits the table. "Nate," he says through gritted teeth.

"Can't…help it…" The scent's swirling around him, tilting and turning his world. "Who is it?"

"It's…no way," Natavius gasps. He says several cuss words that only wolves would understand and leaps back from his chair.

Nathan looks up. A woman stands across the table from them. Her eyes covered by large sunglasses. Her dark hair falls in curls across her shoulders. Her white silk blouse is open just enough to give the briefest hint of skin. Her crimson lips part slightly. I cannot see her eyes, but I can tell that she is staring at me…at my Nathan. She marvels at his excruciating pain.

"Who are you?" I whisper, trying to regain some form of composure myself.

"Let me give you a hint," a voice sounds out ripping through my Nathan's dreams and nightmares of the last century. I see a wash of memories flood through his mind. "'I'll love you…until the stars no longer remain in the sky.'"

Nathan's mind snaps back into focus. He stands and glares at the woman. He leans forward, reaching across the table. He hopes to touch the phantasm before she vanishes. "R-Rosalind?" he stammers.

She smiles and removes her sunglasses. Her eyes are still the amazing hazel colour he remembers. Her scent is off, but his body reacted to it all the same.

"Hey lover," she returns without any trace of her Spanish accent. "Did you miss me? Or did you just spend the last hundred years running away from the memory of me?"

The words ring true on both fronts…and on both fronts…I feel it. It cuts through me like a knife. "I thought…" I swallow a large knot. "…I thought," my Nathan repeats.

"You thought I was dead?" she says. "Well, not quite…not exactly." My hands clench into fists. "…but the fact remains you left me to die." The stress that permeated my entire body has now taken residence in my lower back. My arms twitch from the pain.

"Hello, Natavius," she exclaims, turning towards him. "How have you been?"

"Oh, you know, not dead," Natavius says with an incredulous tone.

"What a coincidence," Rosalind says.

"What? How?" Nathan pants.

"You'll have to catch me to find out." With that, Rosalind vanishes…much to the dismay of the women at the next table.

Nathan…my Nathan leans forward. He catches her scent, and the world tilts, becoming electric around him. He is going to follow her.

I gasp as I snap back to our flat. "Mona?" I pant. I rise… "Ugh," I groan and hold our daughter as something moves her. "What's wrong, my lovely?" I breathe.

"This," chimes a familiar voice. I turn… THUD! …and everything goes dark…something…struck…me…and…

#####

"Ugh," I complain and hold my hand to my forehead. I groan.

"Alana," Mona calls. "Are you alright? Is the baby?"

"No...it is..." I open my eyes to absolute darkness. It has to be if even vampire eyes cannot see anything. "Where are we? What happened?"

"I don't know. You called for me and when I returned to the front room..."

"Someone knocked you unconscious?" I suppose.

"Yes. I woke up here. Wherever here is."

"Umm," I hum.

"Alana?"

"Fine." My eyes switch to silver...skipping the vampire's blue altogether. "...it is..." Something comes into focus... "I see silver eyes staring back at me..."

"Ah," an older man's soothing voice hums. "There's my girl...I knew that the two of you were so connected that I could commune with you through your..." He laughs. "...mate?"

"Who are you?"

"Who's who?" Mona asks.

"I am...seeing through Nathan's eyes."

"Really? Is that what you were doing earlier?"

"Yes." I ponder what it could mean to do this twice in one day; especially since I have not been able to do it since father...since Adamar nearly killed me.

"Are you done with your silent contemplation?" the man asks, his silver hair shimmering in the fading daylight. "I'm talking to both of you now." He points at my Nathan. "...the wolf before me and my granddaughter...so near...yet so far."

"Where's Rosalind?" I ask at the same time Nathan does.

The man smiles and turns to the right. His pristine white suit barely registers the changes in his stance though it moves like normal fabric with him. It is like mother's dress from my visions of her... it is of him, but not on him.

"Oh, that pretty skinwalker?"

"Skinwalker?" Nathan asks. "Rosalind's not a skinwalker...and even if she were, she would've..."

"Been an un-awakened skinwalker until she encountered her totem animal?" He smirks and points at my Nathan. "Imagine the likelihood that a wolf-totem skinwalker would encounter another wolf-totem skinwalker."

I feel Nathan's tension from here. I smell the salt-spray of the ocean. He must be near the docks. I don't sense Natavius near him though. Beyond my…my grandfather, I see a few ships…no, yachts and other personal vessels docked. Are they at a marina, perhaps? Did Rosalind lead my Nathan into a trap? Does she work for En Quosque?

"You're the Aldien of En Quosque," my Nathan says. "I remember you from Edenton. You're the only Aldien left…other than Alana."

"Alana?" The old Aldien nods. "So, Anara named her after her mother. Names run in our family." He motions to himself. "My name is Anaras…" He nods. "Nathan Mosi'son…Alana…" He scoffs a laugh. "…Arkhram… your vampire ilk never had a true familial name…even that one, they stole." He sighs. "We had one, but after I joined En Quosque and championed Eden's cause…" He takes a deep breath. "…our kind banished me…stripped me of title and familial name."

He points at my Nathan. "I know you know that feeling, young Nathan," Anaras taunts, calling him what my father used to…strange, it carries so much more weight now. He scoffs. "…but you have no idea of the pain that awaits you."

"If you came to fight," my Nathan snarls. He takes a fighting stance. "I'll crush you."

"Nathan, remain calm."

"I promise nothing," he whispers.

"So, you can hear me…?" He nods.

"So, can I," Anaras says, leaning towards my Nathan. "That's the point of the link that I established between the three of us. In a way, I'm glad that you've been practicing your spirit magic." He holds his hands over his eyes. "I thought it was a lost art."

"WHY ARE YOU THERE?" I demand. "WHY ARE YOU TORMENTING MY HUSBAND?"

"Now, who needs to be calm?" my Nathan murmurs.

"Ah, the direct approach," Anaras purrs. "You truly are your mother's daughter."

"My wife asked you a question."

Anaras chuckles to himself. "I merely wanted to meet the father of my great-grand…hmm…daughter…" He laughs again…and with every chortle, my Nathan's anger increases. "…and you're planning to name her, Kya…"

"So, you can read me…but can't read my Nathan if he doesn't want you to?" I taunt.

"Yes, because of our earlier encounter. His retched skinwalker side…keeps him between beast and human…making it difficult to manipulate the two…made one."

"You're hiding something," Nathan says. The ability that Nathan received from his mother. I've never seen it through his eyes…not like this. Cascading waves of darkness radiate from Anaras toward my Nathan. "What aren't you saying?"

"You're the direct sort, too. Ezekiel didn't tell us that part. Just that you two were so suited to each other that if you met you would certainly and instantly fall in love." He sighs. "Eighty…" He looks away. "…six."

"WHAT?" Nathan and I gasp at the same time.

"How do you think Natavius knew where to send you, young Nathan? And it was a simple matter to implant the suggestion in the vampire… What was his name? …ah, Irving's head."

"You brought us together?" Nathan asks.

"Why?"

"If the two of you haven't figured that out yet…then perhaps you're not as smart as Ezekiel thought you were."

"Anara," Nathan says.

"You want our daughter? Is that why the Eye of Ezekiel has been pursuing us?"

"Of course."

"Why?" Nathan demands.

"Why have we put effort into anything we've done? The resurrection of our master, of course." Nathan trembles, rage swells in him all at once. "The great Eden has been defeated three times before because of the limitations of flesh."

He glares at my Nathan. "Despite my complaints…the unions of your four bloodlines have created beneficial advantages for the two of you…it only stands to reason that combining those four into one being would create…well…" He sighs and stares at the sky. "…a vessel worthy of Eden."

"You intend to use your ability," I start. "Your spirit magic…to implant Eden's mind into our daughter's body."

"YOU WHAT?" Nathan yells.

"Think of it. Eden would no longer be a demigod among mortals…but with the power and longevity of those four bloodlines, combined with Eden's awesome might…EDEN…would be a God!"

He laughs maniacally and stops abruptly. "Which brings me to my next point…" He turns cold silver eyes on my Nathan. "A true God…has no parents…so, once we have retrieved the child from you, granddaughter, you will die." I tremble.

"OVER MY DEAD BODY!" Nathan roars.

"Exactly." Nathan frowns. "Enough talk," Anaras sighs. He turns and strikes my Nathan with a palm to the diaphragm. All the air rushes out of him at once. He's an Aldien…how can he possibly be this physically strong? My Nathan bends…his vision blurs. "To have such a weakness," Anaras gloats. "I studied martial arts before there even was such a thing. It was child's play to pinpoint that spot…especially after gleaning it from your mind, Alana."

"No," I weep.

He steps to one side and draws back.

"NATHAN!"

He tries to prepare himself for the hit. Anaras's fist sails through the air like a hot scalpel cutting through warm butter. I can actually hear the air scraping against his knuckle. His fist collides with the side of my Nathan's head. "ARGH!" I yell out feeling as if my skull should have exploded.

My Nathan flies. His body skims the water so fast that it feels like hitting solid rock. A second later, he crashes into the neighboring dock. I was saved that physical pain…the emotional pain on the other hand, rips through my body. He skips off the water once again and then crashes into it in earnest.

He sinks…and with him my heart…and every fear in my mind of late. Images of a father-less Kya flash through my mind. The water is frigid. So, cold I feel as if it enters my body.

Crimson streaks across my murky vision. No, my Nathan must have a gaping wound. His eyes are open. Is he conscious?

"NATHAN! NATHAN!" What's that? Did I see something above…?

My eyes come into focus as a light pierces the darkened space. "Nathan?"

"Not even close," my Nathan's nephew, Quinn, says. He stands next to the door, wearing a pastel gray suit, a huge smile, and sunglasses…that are eerily like the goggles warn by members of the Eye of Ezekiel Order that have been hunting me.

"Quinn? What are you…?"

"Let me be the first to tell you about a death in the family." I gasp. He touches his chin. "Well, two if the old man's true to his word." He smiles. "By now, my uncle Nathan's on his way to a watery grave." I tremble.

"What do we do with the extra?" a husky voice, vaguely reminiscent of Vance's asks.

"What else? Kill her. We only need this one," Quinn says. The voice answers with a laugh.

"What are you talking ab-?"

"Well, now I guess that makes three," Quinn says.

"Who's there?" Mona calls. "No! Please! NO! I HAVE A SON!" A gunshot rings out, echoing off the walls…and then two more…causing spastic twitches along my spine.

"As if a vampire could have a child," the other voice says.

"This one can," Quinn laughs. I baulk at him, and he points a silver-tinted revolver at me. The smell of silver wafts from the barrel. I remain seated in this tiny cell.

I do not even bother using my eyes, because I know the glasses are for that purpose. He works for En Quosque, which means he has access to the Order's ordinances. He will turn Kya and me over to them.

I will weep for Mona later…and give Joseph my condolences. I have to focus on me now. I hope my Nathan will find a way to survive…but there was a third.

"And the other?" I grumble, holding back tears. "You mentioned three deaths…for all of which I'm certain there's a special place in Hell reserved for you."

"Oh, right…" He scratches the side of his head with his gun barrel. "How could I forget? Alpha Quinton's dead," he says with a menacing timber. He glares at me, motioning to himself. "…long live the Alpha."

#####

Chapter 28: Calamity

"Bal?" I sit up. "BAL?" My eyes switch over, and my ability turns on. His aura moves from the bed to the closet and then out into the hall. I sigh. "So much for romance." I climb out of bed and gather my clothes. I head for the shower. "No walk of shame for this girl."

I sigh, standing under the warm spray. I still feel like an idiot because he could've killed me at any time. I don't have any idea where he went or what he's up to, bad part about dating a bad boy, who's an actual bad guy. Good water pressure, at least.

I dress in a hurry and head downstairs, following the trail of his aura. "Ms. Price," Manny says.

I wipe my eyes and turn away. I come back to him. "Hey, Manny. Have you seen…?"

"Mr. Balthazar gave me a message for you. He said he had to handle some business and that you knew what he meant and that he hoped you wouldn't follow him." I frown. "Don't shoot the messenger. You could probably call him or text him."

To do that, I'd have to turn on my phone. Raven would find me fast and reach me even faster. I sigh. I ran away like some little kid. I guess I should face the music like an adult. "No, it's okay. Thanks, Manny. Could you call me a cab?"

"No problem." He walks over to the curb and extends his hand. He whistles. "TAXI!" A yellow SUV screeches to a stop in front of him. He opens the door.

"Thanks again, Manny," I say, slipping him a twenty while climbing inside. He closes the door behind me, and we pull away.

"Where to miss?"

I almost give him mom's address…then I almost give him the manor's address. Damn, I'm basically homeless. "I'll tell you in a sec. Just drive, okay?"

I take out my phone and turn it on. I sigh. "At least, I didn't bite him like I thought I would." My head tilts back…wet strands of hair tickle my neck. I touch my collarbone. I can still feel his hands…his lips…his… My phone buzzes…and then again…and again…and then two dozen times after that. A string of texts from Raven and Nate…a couple from my mom and Natavius and…

The phone starts ringing, and Natavius's picture pops up. "Hello?"

"ANGE! Finally!"

"Natavius? What's going on?"

"Can't go into too many details now, but I need you to do your thing and find Nate!"

"What? Why? Can't you just sniff him out?"

"JUST DO IT!"

"Stop the car!" He pulls over, and I toss a ten through the little window. "Keep it."

"But your tabs only…"

I kick the door open and climb out. "Natavius, what's going on?"

"Long story short…the dead came back to life in the form of Nate's first wife."

"Rosalind? She died…burned to death in a…"

"Yeah, not so much. Nate went to find her, and she left one of those scent-less grenades behind. I can't track him."

"That's where I come in." My eyes phase over. "But I've never used it to try and find someone with this level of pinpoint accuracy from so far out…"

"You have to."

I take a deep breath and focus…I think of Nate…his black aura that seems to shine, like moonlight reflecting off the surface of the ocean at midnight. I open my eyes. "I see it," I say, commenting on Nate's trail about three blocks away. "He definitely came by here…" I turn to the left. "…and it looks like he was heading east…toward the water."

I shake my head, snapping out of it. "Where are you?" My damp hair flies over my shoulders. "You're behind me, aren't you?"

"Yeah." I end the call and turn around. He glares at me. I look down. "We can talk later."

"Yeah." He's pissed. He thinks I joined En Quosque. "Can you pick up his scent now?" He nods. "I'll follow you." He vanishes…too fast. I kick my ability back on and follow his trail. The air sizzles around me…my hair feels as if it dries out before I even take my first step. I come to a stop…on the dock…behind Natavius.

"What's going on?" I ask. He stares at the water. "Natavius?" He looks to his left…at the next dock…that looks like a missile hit it. "What happened here?"

"Catch." He tosses his phone to me and dives into the water.

"NATAVIUS?" I run to the end of the dock…and only find bubbles, bursting at the surface. "Natavius?" His head comes up a second later and then… "NATE!"

"Grab him," Natavius says, moving closer to the dock. I reach for him and catch his collar. I pull him up, get a hand under his arm and drag him onto the dock with me. Natavius moves around to the ladder at the side. "How is he?"

His mangled arm hangs out of his left sleeve...and there's so much blood. His jaw seems off...like it's dislocated, and he's barely breathing. I tremble. How could I have turned my back on him? I wrap my arms around him. "Not good," I whisper.

"Nate?" Natavius says. "Nate?"

Nate's eyes flutter and then open. His eyes seem to dance...he must be in excruciating pain. He groans, trying to sit up. "Nate? Take it easy. We've got you."

"A-lah-na," he mumbles.

"You can't worry about her now," I say. "You need to heal first." He reaches up with his right hand and shoves his jaw back with a disturbing crunching noise. I turn away.

"I feel..." He pants. "...her distress..."

I come back to green and gold eyes with black eclipsing the whites. "Uh oh," Natavius hums. "He's going full-on wolf mode."

"What?"

"His skinwalker side is a wolf...and his wolf side is well..." He nods. "...when Nate uses both together..."

"He fights for real?" I suggest, staring at him. Natavius nods and grabs my arm. He pulls me away from Nate and wraps me up. "He won't hurt me."

"No guarantees when he's not holding back anymore."

"Nate," I say, pulling away from Natavius. "Nate, listen..." He glares at me. My heart hurts...just from him looking at me like that. "...you heal...I'll find her." I put Natavius's phone in his hand. "I'll call with a location." The black drains away, but his pupils remain two-toned.

"Promise?"

I kneel and wrap my arms around him. "Just finish healing, and I'll call you as soon as I lay eyes on her." He nods and strokes the back of my head with his good arm. I stand, my ability turning on.

"Ange," Natavius says, stepping into my path.

"Nata..." He kisses me...before I can get another word out. We part...my lips still hum with the warmth of his. "Natavius?" I moan. "I thought you were...I mean, you..."

"I don't care where you went, who you were with, or what you did. Be careful. And don't do anything that puts you in any danger needlessly. Clear?" I nod with a blank expression. He tips his head to the right. "Go. I'll keep an eye on our boy."

I run past him at a normal human pace...better than stopping and looking at him, which is what I want to do. He kissed me...and not fake out boyfriend kissed me. I'm stuck...stuck between the guy I want, who's married to someone else…the guy who wants me, who I might see a chance with if he wasn't evil…and the guy who…does Natavius want me, too?

Don't think about that, Ange. You made Nate a promise. I focus. I'll start at Nate's apartment…track her from there…all the way out in Brooklyn. I haven't fed in two days. This is gonna suck…but I owe them. I owe Nate and Alana this…I may be giving up on my feelings for Nate…but that doesn't mean I'm going to act as if they didn't exist. They don't still exist.

It's broad daylight. I'll have to move faster than I ever have before. I pant, puff, and breathe heavily racing across the bridge. Ignore it, Ange. You love her. You love him…you're doing it for them… My phone buzzes. Ignore it and keep running.

#####

Chapter 29: Tracking

I reach the stoop in front of his house…hands on my knees, woofing it up like a big dog. Much bigger deal now that I know an actual wolf. Breathe on your own time. Nate needs you. My eyes switch over to my special witchy vision. I see the shining black of Nathan's aura with the vibrant red of Natavius's. Then I see…five auras…all varying shades of brown…wolves from the way they move. They come back…carrying Alana's pale blue with its splash of silver…and Mona's purple.

They piled into a car… "Ugh," I groan, feeling the strain of using my power too much…especially, after moving so far, so fast and running on the fumes of a two-day-old feed. Definitely, wouldn't be able to use fire magic now. I have to find her though. "You can do this, Ange."

"Yes, you can," mom…bio-mom says behind me.

"Mom, what are you…?"

She offers me a thermos. "I felt you coming like a bright, shining beacon, baby. I figured, moving that fast…you'd need this for something important."

"Mom?" I sigh on the verge of crying.

"You can explain this whole mess with En Quosque and this daemon boy later."

I wrap my arms around her and then take the thermos. I nearly rip the top off and throw it back. It's cow…and it's a little warm. She knows I miss my cheeseburgers. I guzzle it down in nothing flat and wipe my mouth. I lower the thermos, breathing heavily. I wipe my lip again and stare at the woman who gave birth to me.

"Sorry, mom." She makes the gimme motion. I place the thermos in her hand. "I'll explain everything later. I promise."

"Go. Take care of your friends."

I give her another quick hug and step away. My mom has been so supportive with everything in my life, my new life. I run…following the wolves trail back into Manhattan. It goes uptown and heads into the…the financial district…? I come to a stop…not nearly as winded thanks to the blood…and the awesomest birth mom ever.

I look up at the building in front of me…and take out my phone. "Hello?" Nate's voice comes through Natavius's phone.

"Dude…you won't believe where I tracked her to."

"Does En Quosque have her?"

"No. I-I don't think so…she's in your cousin's building."

"What?"

I look up…following their auras. "I can't tell what floor, but they're definitely still here."

The phone creaks and a weird screeching sound comes through. "I'm on my way," Nate growls.

"Hey, you broke my phone," Natavius snaps as the call ends.

I walk into the lobby that's so heavy with the smell of wolves that I nearly gag…not from the stench, because being around Nate and Natavius all the time, I'm actually pretty used to that. No, the number of different wolf scents is what floors me. There's at least 60 recent scents and I'm talking just walked through the lobby.

Alana and Mona's scents don't go this way though. Neither do their auras. They must've brought them in through that underground elevator. I march toward the elevators trying to get a bead on…

"Excuse me," a wolf, wearing a security guard's uniform, growls, stepping between the bank of eight silver elevator doors and me. "Do you have…an appointment, vampire?"

"No, but…"

"Then leave…before I rip your head off."

"Okay," I start, fanning my face. "First of all, you have serious lamb breathe. Ugh." He cups his hand in front of his mouth and sniffs. "Second of all, I'm Angela Price, the Chief Magistrate's personal assistant and third of all, I need to see Christopher Dumont. It's an emergency."

He shakes his head and points to the doors. I don't move. He frowns and glowers at me with his lamb-breath mouth hanging open. "Yeah, yeah…daylight, blah, blah, blah. Seriously, I need to get upstairs."

"What part of 'no' don't you understand, vampire?"

I step back. "Was it the lamb breathe comment?" He renews his point. "Fine." I turn and walk away. I could've taken him…left his throat, diaphragm, and groin exposed. I could've had him on the ground in no time… Focus, Ange. I look around. Two wolves at the reception desk, watching me the entire way. They probably heard our entire conversation…maybe I can pay back the favor.

"The leech actually thought that tossing around that blood-sucker's name would get her upstairs."

"I know right. Even if Dumont wanted to let her up, Quinn Dumont has barred anyone not on staff from going upstairs."

Why would that little weasel do that…? Unless. I stop by the door. I take a deep breath. Wait for it, Ange. The elevator dings in the distance. I move through the lobby so fast that they don't even register me. Not with their eyes and ears, at least, it'll take their noses a sec to catch on.

"Do you smell…?" one of the wolves behind the receptionist's desk growls. Okay, that was less than a sec.

I hit the back of the elevator and turn. I punch 22 and tap it repeatedly. That's Midnight's floor…the vampire friendly level.

"Vampire?" the guard, who stopped me, growls. He runs for the elevator as the doors close.

I breathe a sigh of relief. Haven't had to fight anyone yet, that's a good sign. My eyes phase, and my ability flares. I'm getting closer to Alana and a group of wolves…but I don't read Mona anymore. Did they take her somewhere else or…? Shake it off. Can't be. They wouldn't, would they…?

The elevator dings on Midnight. I read Alana, three floors up. I press 26 and the doors close. I take out my phone and quickly text, "25th floor" to Natavius. I slip my phone into my pocket. I step off the elevator and…geez, is there a floor in this building that doesn't have at least 2 wolves working on it? I hurry past the cubicle farm and find a supply closet. I switch on my ability again and…I was right, Alana's on the floor below…not too far from me either.

I wedge a cabinet between the opposite wall and the door, tipping it on its side. "Hello?" comes from the door as the handle rattles. Ignore it. I pull out my iron spike and start carving out a hole in the floor. I'm sure Raven can reimburse the scowly wolf for the floor…besides, I'm trying to save his cousin's life…technically, his cousin's wife…but with Nate, same difference.

I crawl into the tiny opening and find a support beam as someone pounds on the door. Why don't they make ventilation ducts as sturdy as they are in the movies? I could fit through one of those a lot easier. I move along the beam on my belly…going between floors.

"How long are we supposed to hold her here?" an angered voice snarls.

"Just until Rose comes back," Quinn says. *Rose*…as in *Rosalind*? I can't believe this little turd burglar really did kidnap Alana.

"Keeping me will gain you nothing," Alana says.

"I thought I told you to shut up," the angry one says.

"Hey," a girl chimes. "Do you guys smell vampire?"

"What do you think she is?" angry carps.

"No, like…another one."

"Impossible," Quinn says. "You must smell the dead one." I cover my mouth. Dead one? They killed Mona. "Ugh," Quinn groans. "STOP THAT!" I feel what he meant a second later. That was Alana, projecting her pain over Mona's death to everyone in the immediate area.

Alana pants. "Now, you are in trouble."

"You have it backwards," angry snarls. "You're the one that's in trouble."

"And I would have agreed with you…until 10 seconds ago…and in 10 more seconds, you will realize what I mean.

My ability kicks in. I see Alana's aura, surrounded by Quinn and six other wolves. I look past her, and I see Nate…Nate's coming like a freight train with no brakes. I wonder where Natavius is. Why didn't he come with Nate?

#####

Chapter 30: Insult

My Nathan throws open the wooden double doors and marches in with a purpose…and that purpose is reclaiming his wife and child. He seethes. "Alana."

"Nathan."

"Restrain him," Quinn says.

Two wolves, including the one who was yelling at me take his arms. "Corey?" Nathan growls, staring at that one. "Does Vance know you're…? What are you doing here?"

"What my brother refused to," Corey returns. "Serving a true Alpha."

Nathan glares at Quinn. "I heard…" He baulks at his nephew. "How could you do that? He was your father…he loved you!"

"HE LOVED YOU MORE!" Quinn yells, pointing his gun at Nathan. Their heavy breaths fall rhythmically inline. "Do you have any idea how much of my life that doddering old wolf ignored in favor of keeping an eye on you?" He beats the weapon again his chest. "Son should come before brother! Especially some half-breed mutt like you!"

"Careful," Rosalind chimes. She marches past Nathan and goes over to Quinn. "You're talking about my race." Quinn inhales deeply and wraps an arm around her. They kiss. My Nathan swallows a lump.

I stand. Quinn's gun trains on me. "Hold her."

"Don't touch her, Kyra," Nathan snarls.

"I have to," the pretty wolf with blood red hair chimes behind me. "Alpha's orders."

"You used the bark on your own people?" Nathan says.

"I had to. Some came willing." Quinn tips his head towards a smirking Corey. "Others…felt too much familial loyalty," he looks to me, or more precisely, to the wolf holding me.

"So, you turned Vance's brother and Natavius's sister against us?"

"Well, when you're in line to be the next Alpha, you'll find that it doesn't take much convincing."

"How did you do it?" I ask. "How could YOU have beaten Quinton? He was four times the wolf you will ever be!"

"Careful," Quinn says. "Talking about an Alpha like that…past or present…could get you killed." He purses his lips. "Fortunately for you, my wife's associates have gone to great lengths to make sure that they get that…thing growing inside of you. So, for now, you live."

Rosalind saunters over to me. Every lustrous auburn curl seems to bob as if obeying a command. "So," she begins, coming impossibly close. She inhales my scent. "You're Nathan's new…thing." At this word, all the other wolves in the room snicker.

Nathan roars and almost pulls away from Corey and the other wolf. "I SAID RESTRAIN HIM," Quinn says with the bark of the Alpha. The other girl wolf grabs a small statue and clubs Nathan on the back of his head.

"Nathan!" I yell. He groans. His head rolls, and he lifts it just enough to see us. Blood tracks over his ears and around his neck. My still heart quivers and is only matched by the pain coming from…next to me.

Rosalind looks between the two of us as if astounded by something. Her mouth contorts and then pulls down at the corners, taking one last glance into Nathan's honey and emerald eyes before returning to me.

She caresses my cheek with the back of her hand. "Well, I suppose Nathan was pretty desperate after he lost me." Her eyes move back to him, and a wicked smile stretches across her face. "He was probably deeply depressed." Nathan grimaces. "Then he…most likely…killed everyone who was responsible for my 'death.'" He reacts again. "Finally, he…almost certainly…traveled the world for the last century in search of that missing piece of himself." Her eyes come back, and they are ice cold. She taps my chin, tilting my head up. She's nearly a head taller than I am. "That's why he settled for you…he was just tired of looking."

My Nathan reacts again…not with words this time but there is so much pain in him now that I cannot stand it. The emotion almost matches the feeling he experienced…when I almost died. I remember how I never wanted to feel that kind of pain coming from him ever again.

I become furious. "Shut up. Shut up, you stupid bloody cow!" I shriek, my lips still quivering. "He missed you terribly and instead of going to find the man you professed to love, you…you joined En Quosque and concocted this insane revenge plot with his nephew of all people."

The wolves growl. Some voices are lower than others are. None growl louder than Quinn. Kyra renews her grip on my shoulders. Rosalind steps closer and tilts my head back by pulling up on my hair this time. I hiss at the eye-tweaking pinch. She smiles that wicked smile again and then slaps me. A sting sets in against my cheekbone.

Nathan roars and lunges forward so much that the last two wolves join the two restraining him. The girl hefts her large blunt weapon and strikes my Nathan in the back again. I yelp, but seemingly in vain. He does not even react to the blow. He roars again and snaps at the wolves holding him back. Rosalind looks at him with fear in her eyes. His eyes have changed to honey and emerald, and the whites vanish, giving way to inky darkness. His canines and incisors descend. I cannot tell if he is fighting the change to be honest.

"Hold him," Quinn bellows stepping around his uncle. Nathan watches him taking in every movement that he makes. Quinn points his gun at Nathan and one stern finger at me. "This…this is what you would fight me for uncle. This is what you would fight your own kind for…this thing." Nathan does not respond. He continues struggling against the wolves clutching him as the girl strikes him in the back again and again. "We should destroy it right now," Quinn continues as he wraps one arm around Rosalind's waist. She shifts, her discomfort is apparent, and then settles into his embrace.

"IF EITHER OF YOU TOUCHES MY WIFE AGAIN," Nathan snarls in a voice not quite his. It's deeper, throatier, more menacing…like the two wolves within him sharing a thought. "I WON'T HESITATE TO KILL YOU BOTH AND EVERY OTHER WOLF IN THIS ROOM!"

Rosalind takes a step back. Quinn releases her and takes a defiant step forward. One-step is all he manages; he realizes that one more step may provoke his uncle enough for him to escape. Rosalind's hand snaps over her agape mouth.

"Shock, fear…," I explain Rosalind's mood to the rest of the room. With great personal satisfaction, I conclude, "…and jealously." Her head whips around to me. She comes close to my face again and emits a low timber.

She tosses her hair to one side, smacking me in the face, and whispers so low that I only just hear her, "He was mine…first." I baulk at her again to little good. "I will have him again…only this time…" She peers over her shoulder. "'…until the stars no longer remain in the sky.'"

I bare my fangs, and she whips back around to see what I am doing. Silver reflects in her eyes. Before even I realize it, I rip through her mind as if it were an open book. I watch as several men approach her from the town where she and Nathan lived. They spew several disparaging remarks at her with regard to his skin color. She retreats into their shared home.

They barge through the front door. I gasp. They beat her without mercy or sympathy. My stomach turns as each one takes their time having their way with her. I almost fall to my knees as they douse her with kerosene as well as the rest of their home. They set the blaze and scurry away like the cowards they are.

"I have to live…" I am hearing her thoughts. "…I have to see him again." She crawls…dragging her beaten body from the house…the fire catches…flames engulf her. The searing pain is unimaginable…blinding even. She continues pulling herself forward.

She reaches the snow just outside and puts the blaze out. Her eyes cannot focus…she cannot hear anything…the pain has made her mute and dumb…something begins licking my outstretched fingers as I lay dying in the snow…I see a pair of wolf eyes and dark gray fur…before nibbling starts…the cold sets in…but her body feels electrically, tinglingly numb…she goes into shock…the only thing that I can think of is my Nathan's handsome face telling me that he will love me, "'…until the stars no longer remain in the sky.'"

"What did you say?" Quinn growls, taking me away from the torment of her memories. Tears stream down my face. I look at his enraged expression and then at Rosalind. Tears well in her eyes and fear laced with maddening sadness stream off her. "WHAT DID YOU SAY?" Quinn snaps again stepping closer.

I swallow and stare at my Nathan. "…un-until the stars no longer remain in the sky," I repeat…meaning every word to my Nathan.

Quinn growls and stares Rosalind down. "Funny," he starts, taking her by the arm. "That sounds terribly familiar." Rosalind places one hand on his cheek trying to pacify him. He moves it away with his gun-wielding hand. He returns to me. "What does it mean vampire?"

"It…," I begin, still staring at my Nathan. "It was something that my Nathan used to say to her often." I look at Rosalind. Sullen tears move across her perfect cheekbones and drip from her flawless jaw. "He would tell her that he loved her…and that he would continue to…until the stars no longer remained in the sky." I nod. "He would say it to her…to reassure her, whenever he had to go away."

"And you use this same phrase with me?" Quinn says, pointing his gun at her.

"Because…she still loves him. She hopes that after En Quosque kills me that she will be able to go back to him."

"Shut up!" Rosalind snarls.

"She is using you to further her own petty agenda…something that she could have accomplished on her own long ago!"

She storms over to me. "I said, shut up!"

"And all the while, hoping to cast you aside as an afterthought when she gets the person she truly wants!" My eyes dart to Quinn and back. "Just like Alpha Quinton, another soul who loves Nathan more than you!"

"Shut up!"

"Sad, truly! Considering that Nathan loves me and only…"

Rosalind's eyes flash bright amber as her hand wraps around my throat. "SHUT UP! SHUT UP! SHUT UP! YOU ARE NOTHING! YOU ARE A DISGUSTING PARASITE! A BLOOD GUZZLING WHORE, WHO SEDUCED MY HUSBAND!" She gasps and releases me, while stepping back.

"And the truth comes out," Quinn says, putting his gun…that he has put so much weight behind this entire time…to the back of her head. He refuses to relinquish it as if it were affixed to his right hand. I gasp this time. He glares at me.

"The truth comes out indeed," I say, staring at the weapon. "That is how you beat him."

"What?" my Nathan groans.

"Nathan," I sob as pain racks my body, because I know what I am about to say will hurt my Nathan all the same. "He shot him. He shot Quinton. That is how he beat him."

My Nathan's head bows forward. He drops to his knees as if defeated. Everything within him seems to go all at once. I tremble…because it is not gone…it is being forced down…and in its place…

He lifts his head…his eyes glow honey and emerald and the whites are gone, replaced by the inkiest blackness. His skin becomes a few shades darker and his muscles bulge and threaten to rip through his tattered clothing.

…and in place of Nathan's love…his sadness…his pain, something else stirs… He roars. …rage fills him…overwhelming, all-eclipsing rage.

#####

Chapter 31: Injury

"Well, I've heard enough," comes from behind me. The ceiling tiles give way as Angela comes down.

"Angela?" Kyra says.

"Sorry, K," Angela says, cartwheeling off the desk. Her feet collide with Kyra's head, knocking her away. Angela twirls, drawing her knife. She slices up, cutting Quinn's gun arm. He drops the weapon. She spins into him and drives the knife into his stomach with her back to him. "Non-life-threatening blow," she says to herself, while pulling the blade out.

"Ugh," Quinn groans and falls backwards. Rosalind takes the opportunity to run past Nathan, still on the floor, still seething.

The other girl wolf runs toward Angela, who tosses her knife in the air. She catches the blade, causing her fingers to sizzle. She hisses but throws the knife at the wolf handle first. She hits the girl in the face, flooring her.

"Lana, run!" I do as best I can in a waddle.

The last wolf standing…not holding Nathan leaps in front of me. "You're not going any…ugh!" he groans as Kyra lands on top of him. Angela scoops me up and tosses me over Nathan's arched back. I twist and land on my feet. The wolf holding Nathan's right arm stands and Angela kicks him in the chest.

Corey releases Nathan and steps forward. "You're just a vampire."

"A dead vampire," Quinn says, scrambling for his gun.

Corey throws a punch at Angela. She catches his arm, turns, and hurls him out the door, past me.

"Get…out…!"

"What?" Angela asks Nathan.

"…get…" Nathan repeats. "…OUT!" Angela's eyes swell, staring at him.

"Angela! Come on!" She nods, collects Kyra, and bolts out the door. I close it behind her as Nathan rises to his feet.

"What are you…?" Corey starts, as Nathan snarls behind the door. His rage seems to pulsate through the room, radiating out with such intensity that I step back. "What's going on in there…?" Corey says approaching the door.

Angela catches his wrist, twists his arm behind his back, slamming him against the wall. "You do NOT want to go in there," she warns. "…Uncle Corey."

"Uncle…?" The sound of a freight train moving through the room cuts off Corey's question. Several screams sound, followed by a gunshot. I clutch my heart. Two more go off and then Quinn releases a blood-curdling shriek that cuts off with a gurgle. Corey trembles, giving up his struggle. Angela begins to cry.

"Angela?" She looks at me. "What is it?"

"I only sense two people still alive in that room…barely." I approach the door. She releases Corey and grabs my hand. I turn to her, and she shakes her head. "No…Lana don't…"

I snatch my hand away. "I have to…he is my husband…the father of my child…" She nods and more tears fall away. I return to the doors and take a deep breath. I throw them open and find Nathan, on his knees, in a collapsed heap in the center of the blood-spattered room.

"Nathan?" His head lifts, but he does not turn to me. "My Nathan," I sing. "It is your Alana…"

"La…na…?"

I move to his side. "Yes, my love, it is me." I kneel next to him and claim his blood-covered right hand. "Are you alright?" He lifts his head…honey and emerald over black stares back at me. He shakes his head as tears fall away. "I know. I know. Quinton…?" He quivers and more tears escape. I kiss the back of his hand. "I am so, so sorry, my love." He shakes again, and I put my arms around him.

He rests his head against my heart and sobs. "ARGH," he cries and moves his arms around me in return.

"Lana?" Angela calls from the door. I put a finger to my mouth but beckon her forward a moment later. She enters the room on soundless steps, peering around at the devastation my Nathan wrought. "Is he…?" I shake my head and stroke the back of his.

"My God," Corey says from the door. "He did this to five wolves…with his bare hands?"

"Quiet," Angela snaps. "This is your boss's fault. He…" She turns back to us. "…where is he? He's the other life I sensed." Her eyes phase dark blue. "There! He's behind the desk!" She glares at Corey. "Come on!" The pair hurries over to Quinn, whose panic I sense, despite feeling that he deserves it.

"Oh God!" Corey mumbles, covering his mouth.

"Get him out of here," I say. "Make sure he is cared for and…"

"What's the commotion here?" Christopher says. He stands in the doorway, flanked by guards from Midnight, covered in police issue riot gear. He has Kyra's arm draped over his shoulders. She holds her aching head.

"Christopher?"

"Alana? Nathan? What are you guys doing here? What happened here?"

"Never mind that now." Christopher frowns. "Do you have a doctor in the building?"

"Why?" He passes Kyra to one of his guards. "Is Nathan hurt?" He runs to us.

"No, but Quinn is. Severely."

"Quinn?" Angela waves Christopher down, then signals for him to come closer. He snaps his fingers and three of the guards move to their location.

"Sir," one of the guards snaps. "Massive trauma to the chest and neck. He needs immediate medical attention."

"Then it's a good thing I'm here," Vance says, walking in with a medical bag. "You," he says to one of the guards near Quinn. "Go and find me a couple of first aid kits…I'm definitely going to need more bandages than I have here." The guard nods and exits.

"You," he says to the one near the door. "Take Kyra to Christopher's office. She doesn't look too banged up, but I'll examine her later." The guard nods, sweeps Kyra off her feet, and walks out. "You," Vance says to his brother. "I'll deal with later." Corey swallows a lump but does not break his vigil over Quinn.

"You two," Vance says, parting the last two guards. "I need this space cleared." They nod and work to move the desk and overturned office equipment away…one stumbles over… I work to contain Kya's lunch. …a severed arm. I suppose I should be grateful that he did not do that spine removal maneuver he brags about so often.

"You," Vance ends, kneeling next to Quinn, and with one finger pointed at Angela. "I understand you were a Poli Sci major at Columbia." Angela nods, staring at Quinn. He lays on his back gasping for air, hands hovering above his gaping chest wound. Vance opens his black leather medical bag and searches through it. "Did you ever consider going into medicine?"

Angela swallows a knot as Vance removes several forceps from his bag. He threads a curved needle on the first try. Angela shakes her head.

"You should," he says. "My sire-granddaughter told me what you did for her down in Edenton. Field medic and rough…but she says you were calm and removed that bullet from her easily enough."

"You-you know, Marisa?"

"Of course, I do. Hold this." He gives Angela the needle. She holds it. He applies forceps to the top of Quinn's injury and repeats every few inches with another and another. "You'd be surprised how adept you can become at it…" He applies the last forceps. "Uh oh…" He touches the left side of Quinn's rib cage. "…that one's broken." He removes the bottom forceps and the two above it, rolls up his right sleeve, and… I swallow regurgitated blood. …reaches into Quinn's chest.

"Where was I?" he continues, his arm disappearing up to the elbow in Quinn's chest.

"Um, um…" Angela says.

"...adept you can become at it," Christopher says, looking over Vance's work.

"Right. ...how adept you can become at it when you have decades to practice. There...it's set, and I think it'll heal properly on its own." Vance removes his arm and Quinn's breathing becomes less erratic.

"Wow," Angela breathes.

"Wow, indeed," Vance says, reapplying the lower forceps. "Suture, please." Angela places the needle in his blood-covered hand. He begins, sewing Quinn up, moving between forceps. "I definitely think you have the eye for it."

"Vance," Angela says with a weak voice. "Is Raven...?"

"She'll always forgive you. You know that, right?" He peers at her over his shoulder and continues sewing. "That's what mother's do...they try to understand their kids' rebellious phase...help them learn from their mistakes and..." He finishes the stitch and bites the thread. He makes a knot at the end. He removes the forceps quickly one by one. "...support them...no matter what they decide." He reaches into his bag and retrieves a rather large syringe and then another. "Christopher?"

Christopher steps forward, rolling up his sleeve. He kneels next to Vance and offers his exposed arm. Vance forces the plunger all the way down on the first syringe and inserts the needle in Christopher's arm. He fills the syringe with Christopher's blood before removing the needle.

"Angela, do you have something I can tie off Quinn's arm with? I'm afraid his blood pressure has dropped incredibly...it'd be hard to find a vein."

"Here," my Nathan says in a gruff voice. He pulls mother's ribbon from my hair. He stares into my eyes with his normal, beautiful mahogany pupils. "Because I know you were about to." I close my eyes and nod.

Angela hurries over to us and claims it. She returns to Vance and wraps Quinn's arm herself. Quinn's veins rise under the pressure. "Hold his arm steady, dear."

"Sure thing...da," she returns. He huffs a laugh and trains the needle on the largest vein. He injects the blood into Quinn's pale arm.

He removes the emptied syringe, tosses it over his shoulder absently, and dives back into his bag. He retrieves a small bottle with a clear liquid inside. "This..." He says, forcing the second syringes needle into the cork top. "...is a concoction I created myself...both anesthetic and antibiotic in one." He fills the syringe and then holds it up. He taps it until the bubbles float to the top. He pushes the plunger up, forcing a bit of the mixture out. "Steady now," he says to Angela, who nods. He places the needle in the same vein he used earlier with a marksman's precision and forces the medicine into Quinn's arm.

He removes the needle and tosses the empty syringe over his shoulder. He sighs as he sits back. "He should be out of the woods." He removes mother's ribbon from Quinn's arm.

"Not exactly a good thing for wolves," Angela jokes, proving why she is my Nathan's best friend.

"In this case, it is," Vance says. "Wrap him up." Two guards place bandages on Quinn's chest and apply gauze. "I couldn't have done it without you, Angel," Vance says and kisses Angela on the forehead. She closes her eyes. I shiver…fearing that my vision may still come true…that Kya will never get to be with her father in that way.

Angela's eyes drift over to us as if she could hear my thoughts. No, she stares at the man we both love in the same way. She sighs and her heartbreaks that much more.

"We have to make funeral arrangements," Nathan says.

"Yes," Christopher replies. "His body is on its way back from Japan…" Nathan trembles, and a warm tear falls onto my collar, followed by another. "…and the elders have been called."

"Yes," Nathan rumbles. "The new Alpha has to be installed."

"Hmm," Christopher returns. "So, will you tell us what happened here now?"

"Let's start," Natavius says from the doorway. "…with this."

Christopher and Vance turn and then gasp. "Rosalind?" Christopher breathes. "That's not possible." I turn to Natavius, holding Rosalind in an arm bar.

"Rosalind?" Corey says. "She told us her name was Rose. You mean she's really…?" He points at Nathan. "Damn it!" he snaps. "We got played hard."

"It seems the time to 'deal with you' has come," Vance says, stepping away from Angela. Vance glares at his younger brother. "Talk. Now!"

"And it better be good," Christopher adds.

Corey recaps recent events, starting with my kidnapping, Mona's murder, and ending with Nathan's rampage.

Christopher covers his face. "That definitely explains the mess."

"I'll say," Angela adds. "Somebody's gonna have to dig that guy out of the drywall." She points her thumb at one of the male wolves, buried in the wall, his pupils whited out, and his mouth open in pure horror.

Christopher sighs and returns to Corey. "Continue."

"Stop," Rosalind snaps, jerking away from Natavius. She sighs and stares at my Nathan and me. I hug him tighter. She shudders with rage.

"You stop," Natavius grumbles. "Where've you been for the last hundred years, Rosie? Nate got pretty bleak for a while…knowing you were alive could've helped with that."

"She's En Quosque," my Nathan says. He stands, slipping free of my embrace. I give him both hands, and he pulls me up. "Get out of here."

"What?" I complain.

"Not you," he returns. "Never you." I nod. He glares at Rosalind. "You get out of here…and never come back…"

"Nathan?"

"Nate," Christopher starts. "Do you think that's…?"

"You heard me," Nathan says, stomping over to her. "Get out of here. Go back to your masters in En Quosque and tell them they'll have my child over MY DEAD BODY!" I clutch his arm. "And as for you, I never want to see your face EVER again! Leave with your life…I owe what we once had that much at least." He turns to me and wraps me in his arms. "This," he purrs. "This is my whole world now."

Rosalind crumbles. She falls to her knees. "I have nothing…I have nothing and no place to go." She emits a stuttering sigh. "En Quosque will kill me for failing to deliver…"

"Tell someone who cares," Nathan says. "My feelings for you died a slow, agonizing death over the last hundred years. I have none left."

"Nathan, you can't mean that…I'm…" She glares at me, while motioning to herself with her clawed hand. "…I'm your wife!"

Nathan tips his head toward the door. "You're his wife." He pats my hand. "This is my wife…her name is Alana…and that is my child she carries…the child you were going to give to En Quosque."

Rosalind scrambles to her feet, runs out the door, and vanishes. He destroyed her. He has been her dream for the last 100 years and now… I stare at him. …that dream is gone. I was only without him for a few weeks…I could not imagine the agony of 100 years.

His honey and emerald eyes drink me in. *I love you.*

I love you more, I reply with two silver jewels. *…and I always will!*

#####

Chapter 32: Aftermath

I sit on the relocated desk. Scowly wolf, Christopher, called some cleaners to come in…wolf cleaners to clear the room. They pulled that one guy out of the wall. They said Nate shattered his spine and crushed his skull. The wandering arm belonged to another guy…they found him behind the door. I groan. Massacre doesn't even touch what happened in this room.

Vance examines Nate. Yeah, because they definitely had any chance of hurting him. Nate looks at me. I shiver and look away. "Hey," he says, right in front of me.

"Hey, yourself."

"Are you afraid of me now?" I look at him and frown as if he's the idiot he sounds like. "I understand…I mean…"

"Nate, Nate…no, dude…" I sigh. "I could NEVER be afraid of you. I mean, I…I…" I feel a knot in my chest and if I had a heartbeat, I know it'd be pounding in my ears right now. I have feelings for Balthazar, I do…but standing here with and staring at Nate…everything else just seems…less. "…I love you…" He looks down. "…man," I add awkwardly and punch him on the arm. "I love you, man. You're my best friend."

He sighs and nods…and does me the huge favor of not pushing it. "Bring it in," I say, slipping my arms under his. He hugs me. I hold my breath. He smells so good that I could actually bite him. He lets go and steps back.

Two of the guards from Midnight come back in with Kyra. They put her in a chair next to Corey. She glares at me…can't say I blame her…especially since delivering that heel kick to the top of her egotistical head felt amazing.

"So," Natavius says. "Nate…still…?" I look up at him with just my eyes. "Even though you…went to see Balthazar."

"Natavius," I whisper. "Is this really the time or place for this conversation?"

"Fine." He evaporates, leaving me reaching for empty air.

"What'd you do to my brother?" Kyra growls.

"We'll be asking the questions here," Christopher says, storming into the room. He holds his phone up to his ear.

"Are you alright?" Vance asks, sitting down next to me on the desk.

"Yeah, da," I breathe and lean my head against his shoulder. He actually kind of reminds me of bio dad. He's warm and fuzzy, while my mom…sire-mom's the bad ass. He always seems to know the right thing to say at the right moment. Not actually, but I'm sure he'd know how to kiss all the boo-boos too…like bio dad did.

"So, it's true," Corey says. "You claim this vampire?"

"Questions. Me," Christopher snaps.

"It's fine," Vance says, and Christopher concedes to his pack brother. "It's about time this came out." He motions to me. "Corey, Kyra…this is Angela Price…she's the sire-daughter of Raven Gregory…my wife."

"You married one of them?" Corey snarls.

I hop down at the same time that Nate takes a step toward Corey. Vance puts a hand on my shoulder. I look at him, and he smiles with all the warm and fuzzies. Yep, just like bio dad. I hop back onto the desk with him.

"Yes," Vance says. "I've been married to Raven…for more than 130 years…we began seeing each other regularly after I…" He looks at Nate. "…we returned our second sire-daughter, Margaret, to her." He puts an arm around me. "I love my wife very much…and her sire were reborn of her blood. I love all four of my sire-children as if they were my children."

"You disgust me," Corey groans.

"Says the guy who was trying to help En Quosque take someone's baby," I carp. He looks at me. "Yeah, that's right. I said it, Uncle Corey."

"Don't call me that."

"Why not? It's true."

"Alright," Christopher says, ending another call. "Quinn is fine. He's under the care of a physician, and he's already healing well."

"I'm glad," Nate says. Alana hugs him and kisses his cheek.

Christopher shakes his phone. "I talked to the Council, and they agreed…begrudgingly…" He looks at Nate. "You can guess who." Nate nods. "…that because Quinn and his pack threatened Alana's life…that…" He points his phone at Nate. "…you won't have to face a tribunal."

"I notice you didn't mention the thing in her womb," Kyra carps.

Nate tries to step away from Alana, but she holds on to him. She holds his face and pulls him in for a kiss. "Ignore her." He nods.

"How would you have felt if someone said that about you while you were preggers, K?" She glowers at me. "I'm not saying that. I'd never say that about a mother but think about someone saying something like that to you…about you while you were carrying your son." She looks away. "Exactly."

"Stop talking to me, vampire."

I hop down again and again Vance catches my shoulder. "I'm okay." He lets go. "K, I am still the exact same person I was…only now…" I count off. "…I have to drink blood to survive…I know some badass ninja moves and…well, that's pretty much it."

"Yeah, but you crave human blood."

"I do, but I've never had any and God willing, I never will. Tiff's cool with me like this, why can't you be?"

"You've seen Tiffany since you…"

I nod. "Have you? Has she met your son? Do you know that she's seeing a new guy?" I bob my head. "…and that to make sure he's not a douche canoe, I used vamp hearing to help her stalk him…a little bit."

"Same old Tiff," Kyra says and laughs. I do, too.

"K, if not for Raven, I could've died. I was attacked by a vampire and that's the only reason she changed me." She looks at me. "If you'd said anything…anything about vampires, I might have known what to look for." She opens her mouth, and I wave my hand. "I'm not blaming you…not in the slightest, but…you hid this huge part of yourself from two people that you said were your best friends. Me? I've always been honest and upfront with you. Even when I became this…or I would've if you hadn't vanished after high school."

"You know why I did."

"Now. For me and Tiff, at first, it just sucked."

"Great another wolf kissing up to a vampire."

"A vampire that saved your life, Uncle Corey. Nate would've torn you a new one too if I hadn't tossed your ass out of here."

"And I'm supposed to say thank you," he barks, jumping to his feet. I hear Vance hop down behind me. One of the Midnight Guards forces Corey back down in his seat.

"No," I answer. "…and I don't expect you to. You don't have to." I motion to Vance. "Whether you like it or not, he's my da…you're my uncle. Even if I knew you'd try to kill me in the next minute, I'd still save you all over again." I look at her. "You too, K."

I look around at every pair of eyes staring at me. "And I'm hogging the conversation." Vance wraps his arms around me and kisses the back of my head. "Geez, you're such a dad."

He laughs. "I've had over 130 years of practice."

"Alright," Christopher says. "Now, for you two, what happened to my cousin? I know that Quinn wouldn't challenge the Alpha without his pack nearby."

"I wasn't there," Kyra says. "I was asked to stay here…because I needed to take care of my son."

"How is he?" Vance says. "I'm sorry. I haven't seen him since I helped you deliver."

"He's good. His father's been…understanding…to say the least." She looks at me. "He's human."

"Is it…?" I gasp, thinking of her high school boyfriend, Calvin. She nods.

"What about you?" Nate asks Corey, who leans away from him. "Were you there?"

"Yes. He said he wanted me to witness that it was a one-on-one fight."

"And was it?" Christopher asks.

"Of course. They fought…they changed into wolves and went at in a forest outside of Nanbu."

"Details," Nate growls.

Corey sighs. "Alpha Quinton was beating Quinn handily. The Alpha…the old Alpha offered him a chance to surrender. Quinn changed back into his human form…and grabbed his gun."

"Sadness," Alana says. "Anger…frustration…" Corey looks at her. "…regret."

"He shot him…twice…" Corey wipes his mouth. "…I asked him if his claim was legal…you know, with him using a gun and all. He shoved me away and said he'd finish him off while he was injured." I shiver. Vance does too and turns his head away. "He…" Corey chokes. "…Alpha Quinton reverted to his human side…he was breathing hard…I could hear the blood in his lungs. He tried to say something…" He looks at Nate. "…about you, but I couldn't hear it."

Christopher crosses his arms, looks at Nate, and then bows his head.

"I asked Quinn to hold up a sec, but he threw the Bark at me…and I fell back." He sighs. "He turned back into a wolf…Alpha Quinton said he loved him…and then it was over."

I wipe the tears away from my cheeks. I can't believe Alpha Quinton's gone…I mean, I'm not even a wolf…and haven't even known him long, but…

Nate shivers and turns away. Alana puts her arms around him, and he rests his head on her shoulder. He cries…like a little kid, and Alana tries to soothe him, but it doesn't work. Christopher sheds tears but doesn't bother hiding them or wiping them away.

"I…" Kyra says with a weak voice. She sniffs and wipes her nose as tears start moving down her face. "…I-I didn't know. I swear." She shakes her head. "I am so out of this pack…"

#####

Chapter 33: Next

I feel so uncomfortable. I haven't dressed like this since my dad died. I tug at my jacket sleeves. It's weird, but this is worse. It's not worse for me personally; God knows that day was hell though. It's worse, because my best friend is dying on his feet, and I can't do anything for him.

I've been staying away from him for the most part. I mean, we're about to put his brother in the ground or whatever wolves do with their dead. The only family he's had for the last hundred years…the only family who still acknowledged him…the only person who has ALWAYS had his back…since the day he was born. I sigh. That should be me now, Nate. I'll be the one who has your back every day until the day I'm a pile of ash. Nice sentiment, idiot. Now you should try saying it to his face. His stupidly gorgeous face.

At least, Quinn's not here yet. Nate gave us a preview of his brother's eulogy… I scoff. …he made everyone cry…wolf and vampire alike. There wasn't a dry eye in the house…except that smug little, turd burglar. He was too busy, telling everybody what it'll be like when he's formally installed as Alpha. No more playing nice between the vampires and wolves. Don't know if that means all-out war or just separation.

Separation might actually be a good thing for me in the short term…since I haven't talked to Natavius since shortly after he kissed me. He kissed me, really kissed me. Not fake out, boyfriend-girlfriend kissed me. Until today, I hadn't seen him since he dragged Rosalind's ass in. He kissed me. What the hell was that about? He's like the *Pretty in Pink* Duckie to my Andie, without the 'clingy, secretly in love with you' vibe. Unless…he really is secretly in love with me. Okay, maybe Duckie's a bad example, because Natavius is ridiculously, over the top gorgeous.

And then there's Bal, who…is holding my hand right now…

"Angel," he whispers.

"Bal, what are you doing here?" I whisper through clenched teeth.

"I had to see you."

"And you had to do it in the one place where the three people on the planet who can detect you would be? And if two of those three sense you, there's going to be trouble." His other hand slips around my waist and pulls me back against him. It also knocks all the air out of me and not because he did it rough.

"You left and didn't leave a note or anything."

"No, that was you."

"I'm sorry. I had…"

"…En Quosque business?" He nods against the back of my head. "I know because after I left your place, I had to pull my best friend out of the Hudson and then rescue his wife from a power-hungry wolf."

"I don't think Anaras left him in the Hudson…" I squeeze his fingers intertwining with mine. "Ow."

"Don't make jokes. Nate could've died. And you guys want to take Alana's baby?"

"Yes."

"Do you know how twisted that is?"

"I do what I must."

"Then so do I." His hand moves away from my waist. He steps around me…and I can see him. Not his glamour, but I see him. "What the…? Bal, are you insane?" I look around quickly. "Someone will see you, are you crazy?"

"Yes." He replies. "That day I spent with you…was the best of my very long life. I was hoping for more days like it." He backs me up against a pillar. "Did you…not enjoy it…?"

"Oh yeah," I breathe at the thought of his hands all over me. "But Bal we're on different sides of this thing…and…"

"…and? I thought you were falling in love with me."

"Maybe."

"Maybe?" He looks away, and his jaw tenses.

"Okay, definitely…but you're asking me to put you on one side of a scale and my entire life on the other. That's not fair."

"If you were truly falling in love with me, that scale would be unbalanced."

"And if you were REALLY in love with me, you wouldn't ask me to put you on the scale." He caresses my cheek. "Bal, I do…okay? I care about you…and that day was amazing…" I move his hand away. "…but it ended with me pulling Nate out of the river…with a shattered arm and a broken jaw, all because you want to steal his daughter." I shake my head. "It's not right."

"What part of our relationship has been?"

"And that's okay? T-to build a relationship on total dysfunction?"

"Balthazar," Natavius says from my left.

"Natavius," I say, stepping closer to him.

"Natiel," Balthazar says.

"Don't call me that. My name is Natavius."

"You are my youngest brother, and I will call you what I always have."

"Guys," I say, putting a hand on both their chests. Hopefully, this ends the pissing contest. "Not here. Not now. Okay?"

"Fine," Balthazar grumbles. He puts his hand on mine. "We should go somewhere and continue our conversation…privately."

Natavius shoves him away. "She's not going anywhere with you."

"We'll see about that."

"Guys, I…" I feel hands on my shoulders, and I don't even have to catch his scent to know exactly who it is. All the same, I feel dizzy just from the warmth of his touch.

"Balthazar, I presume," Nate says with a voice bordering deep, bassy silkiness. Balthazar glares at him. "This is my brother's funeral…and in wolf culture, the burial of an Alpha is marked as a day peace. I have heard of our tribe withdrawing from battles that we could have won easily to put to rest our fallen leader…"

"Nate…?" He pats my shoulders.

"…thus, I will leave you…unmolested today." Nate takes his hand away and holds one finger out to Balthazar. "…but know this, if you continue talking about my best friend as if she were your property and not a living, breathing woman with a mind of her own…" His hand returns. "…I'll break that peace by breaking your spine."

"She does have a right to choose her own path. Which is why I am supremely confident that she'll choose me."

Nate's hands vanish, and he slams Bal against the column, by his throat. "Listen to me," Nate growls, his eyes flashing green and gold. "You…and your people nearly killed me…kidnapped my wife…threatened our child…and now you come to my brother's funeral…" He squeezes, causing Bal to groan. "…adding insult to our injury, which I will gladly repay you tenfold, right now." Nate draws back to punch Bal.

"I was…invited…"

Nate scoffs. He releases Bal, who breaks into a coughing fit, and glares at me. "Don't look at me, dude…I didn't invite him." Nate nods. Bal stares at me, then Nate, and comes back to me.

"I did," Quinn says in stride, walking over. "And I would appreciate it if you didn't harass my guest…at my father's funeral."

"Nathan," Alana says, tugging on Nate's arm. His head bows, and he puts his hand on top of hers.

"I mean," Quinn continues, and I just want to punch him in his smug little face, repeatedly. Turd burglar. "If you can have these…" He glowers at Alana and then me. "…things here, why can't I have my guest."

"Because your guest is trying to bring about the end of the world," Alana warns.

"The end of the…?" Quinn laughs her comment off. "Who would believe such a thing?"

196 | Midnight Princess

"You would," I say. "That's why a turd burglar like you decided to work for him."

"A t-t...?" Quinn stammers over. He trembles he becomes so angry.

"Pardon me," Christopher says. "I hate to break THIS up." He stares at Balthazar. "But I need to speak with you for a moment," he says to Nate.

"Cousin, can't it wa-"

"No." Christopher straightens his tie. "You should come as well, Alana." He steps away.

"Whatever," Nate growls as Alana pulls him after Christopher.

"Shouldn't you say, 'Pardon me, Lord Alpha'?" Quinn mocks.

Nate freezes. He turns back to Quinn. "You've not been sworn in as Alpha yet!"

"Oh, the elders are here, Uncle Nathan. It'll be done by day's end and my first order of business will be dissolving this farce of a marriage of yours...and destroying that thing in the vampire's womb..."

Nate roars, and his eyes faze to green and gold again, but this time black replaces the whites. I move between them. "Go! Your wife wants you elsewhere." His entire mood drops. He turns to Alana. She nods and caresses his cheek. He steps past her as she mouths a silent, 'Thank you' to me. I nod into a sigh.

Balthazar turns to Quinn. "I believe you may have overstepped your bounds," he says. Quinn swallows a lump, as nervous sweat beads move across his forehead. "The child Alana carries is to be cared for above all else."

"Of course," Quinn says. "My apologies...I got too carried away antagonizing my uncle."

"What kind of Alpha are you?" I complain. "What kind of Alpha does what somebody else tells them to? What kind of leadership is that?"

"Oooooooo," Natavius emits in an overexaggerated way, while covering his mouth.

"I'll be the kind of Alpha who will gladly take your he-"

He cuts out when Balthazar glares at him. "Quinn, would you mind giving...Ms. Price and me a moment?"

"Of course." He steps back and then walks away.

"Turd burglar," I whisper with my arms crossed over my stomach. Balthazar steps closer...and so does Natavius. "Natavius, would you..."

"Whatever," he growls and vanishes.

Balthazar watches him with just his eyes. He comes back to me. "So, you have the next Alpha wrapped around your little finger?"

"That's not..."

"Isn't that convenient?" He reaches for me; I block his hand because I REALLY don't want him to touch me right now. "Go away, Bal. I've had enough of this soap opera for today." I turn, and he catches my arm this time. "Bal," I whisper.

"My duties and my heart have taken me in two different directions since the day I met you. You have known that about me."

"But still, you feel like you can ask me to choose one or the other?"

He steps closer and holds both my arms. "My heart is bleeding," he whispers into my hair. "You are the weapon that has injured me the most in my nearly three millennia."

I shiver as tears fall from my eyes. "You don't think I'm in pain, too? You have no idea how much being around you hurts."

"Come to me." He releases me. I turn, and he's gone. "…come to me at dusk…and we'll share in our divine pain."

"That's cheesy," I whisper while wiping my eyes, not mentioning the part where I've already agreed to meet him in my head.

#####

Chapter 34: Legacy

"Christopher," my Nathan says. "Where are we…?"

"Just follow me," Christopher says, opening a pair of wooden double doors. "There's something you have to hear."

We walk into the room decorated in mahogany tones complete with matching large desk, opposite the entryway. Christopher closes the doors behind us and hurries to the antique desk with its floral engravings. He retrieves a tablet from the lower left drawer…and stares at it as if the entirety of the world were inside it.

"Christopher?"

"You have to hear this," Christopher says, then places the tablet on the desk with its stand holding it upright. "You too, Alana." I put my hand on my Nathan's arm…trying to stay close to him…to keep my stomach obscured as I have done all day…for all the good it does me, I am huge.

"I don't have time for this, Chris," Nathan begins trying to contain his anger and pain. It crashes into me over and over again. Kya reflects that emotion. "In case you haven't noticed, I have to go and put my brother to…"

"No!" Christopher snaps. "YOU…have to hear this…first." He taps the device's screen.

"Ahem," Quinton's voice begins. "Nathan, hello…" Nathan swallows, and his trembling eyes swell, filling with tears. He looks at Christopher, who already has tears streaming down his face.

We return to the tablet, and there Quinton is…on the screen sitting at this very desk. He places his hand over his mouth and clears his throat. "…I made up my mind to document this on the day that you were born…and after I became Alpha…I made it into a recording. Then, I remade it with each new technology over the last century." He pauses to laugh. "The things I couldn't say to you…Nathan…" My hand meets Nathan's, and our fingers intertwine.

Quinton seems visibly shaken as well. He collects himself. "…if you're listening to this…then I am no longer Alpha of the A'kani…because I'm dead." Nathan scoffs, and a tear escapes as a fresh wave of pain washes over him. Kya feels it, too. I have to be strong for both of them.

"First of all, let's clear away all deception." Quinton trembles in the recording. "First step along that path…hard to believe, but it's actually become more and more difficult to say this with each recording…" He sighs as his head bows. He lifts his eyes to the camera. "…I am NOT your brother…" Nathan gasps and looks to Christopher, who simply stares at the back of the tablet.

"…as smart as you are you probably sensed it on some level, but there it is…lain out bare. I am not your brother, in as much as, Alpha Nathaniel was

NOT your father." Quinton inhales deeply, looks down at his clenched fists then back to the camera. "He WAS your grandfather…" I look at Christopher, his jaw clenches and more tears escape. My Nathan mirrors his pained expression…and the emotions coming from them…I try to clear some of the tears from my face, but it is no use. "…because I…AM your father…" Nathan twitches as if pricked by a thousand pins. Quinton nibbles his lower lip. "…I was your father," he ends with tears streaming down his face.

"No," Nathan gasps.

Quinton laughs through his tears. He wipes his face on his sleeve. "I've made this stupid recording 15 times and every time…I cry…" He swallows deeply. "…I'm your father and…" His voice cracks, and the tremor that ripples through him reflects in my Nathan…in his son. "…and I never held you once…I have failed you so many times…I failed your mother…I failed myself…but I'm so glad…" He growls. "…that at that one moment…I did not fail you…I couldn't fail you…not then."

He sniffs and wipes under his nose. "Stop the recording…I can't…" It cuts out and returns with a much more collected Quinton. "…hopefully, my failures haven't passed on to the next generation."

Christopher's eyes swell, and he looks to me. "He knew?" he whispers. Nathan pulls me closer, and I step behind him more.

"Oh God," Quinton's recording weeps. "You must have so many questions, but you already know the answer to most of them…if you think back on every conversation that I had with you." Nathan's mind goes back over it all. Every second that his brother and he spent together, rushes back in a flood of memories. The way he ALWAYS protected Nathan, the way he talked about Nathan's mother, the way he taught Nathan so much, even the way that Quinton said everything…it all makes so much sense now. None of it makes more sense than the clarity of his reason for challenging…Alpha Nathaniel.

"I have always said that I would tear apart Heaven and Hell for you, Nathan," Quinton continues. "…and I would, but I couldn't even be honest with you. You are my son…my first…and I love you like no other; always hold on to that.

"You will have time to grieve for me…but more than likely…now is not the time. Your people need you…our people need you…" A new sense of determination surges in Quinton. "…for you are the new Alpha of our tribe and you will have to guide them through whatever turmoil stirs around my death…you will have to…."

Nathan taps the screen. The image freezes on Quinton leaning forward with a fierce scowl. "This is some kind of sick joke, right?" is all my Nathan manages out of sheer shock.

Christopher shakes his head. He puts his mobile up to his ear. "Send them in," he says plainly and ends the call before a response comes. The doors open behind us. We turn just in time to see Christopher's father, Reginald, enter the room. He is followed by Mosif, the Second, and Amelia soon after.

"Why is the Council here?" Nathan asks, returning to Christopher. He takes a seat on the desk and bows his head.

"It is with great sadness," Mosif begins, clutching his cane tighter. "That another First has passed from this world."

"But with the passing of each First from this life," Reginald says, looking at Nathan. "…to the next."

"Another must rise from the ashes to take their place," Amelia ends. She looks to me. "…and prepare a place for…" She swallows deeply. "…the next generation."

"You know?" I ask without being able to dismiss any of my shock.

"You know everything?" my Nathan asks.

Mosif leans forward on his cane. He pushes his glasses further up on his face and smiles. He looks at me, still clinging to my Nathan's side…still trying to keep Kya obscured. "Why do you think I 'miscounted' the number of greats at your wedding?" Mosif explains with a wink. "I know my brother's descendants just as well as I know my own." He steps closer and focuses on my stomach.

"I only found out after my brother's passing," Reginald submits. "Not that it surprised me…considering how much Nathaniel doted on all his pups, but you." He scratches his head. "Not that any of them besides Quinton could hold a candle to you."

"I was told fifty years ago," Amelia says. "…on the first day that I became an elder." She nods and crosses her arms. "We figured out the rest after we watched the video to confirm its validity." She scowls. "Unfortunately, I was outvoted as to what to do with your…" She clears her throat. "…thing growing in the vampire's womb."

"Careful," Christopher growls. "That's your next Alpha you're talking about." I offer a weak smile to Christopher. He nods.

"Besides, Amelia," Reginald picks up for his son. "You know that Alpha Quinton's final wish was that we protect the child Alana carries." Amelia huffs and looks away. "Are YOU willing to deny an Alpha his final wish?" Her head bows.

Christopher bounds off the desk, sighs, and sweeps his hand over his mouth. "As executor of Alpha Quinton Mosi'son's Will…and at the admission of the Council…" He offers a hand to them as if presenting them. Each member nods in turn…including Amelia, though begrudging her acknowledgement. Christopher steps closer. He puts his hands on either side of Nathan's face. "…I, hereby, install you, Nathan Mosi'son…6th First…or Alpha of the A'kani tribe and our new leader…"

Christopher steps back and kneels in front of me. The others kneel as well. "…and," Christopher continues with warmth in his voice. He lifts his hands near my stomach. "…may I?" I gasp and nod. He places both hands on my stomach…on our daughter. "…I name you…" He pauses and looks up at me again.

"Kya Anara," I say.

"After her grandmothers," Christopher laughs. He nods. "…seems fitting…considering what they both did for our people. I name you…," he whispers. "…Kya Anara Mosi'son…destined to be our 7th Alpha…should, regrettably, your father fall. Blessed by the Goddess Anara may you both…may you three be."

"Blessed be," the Council repeats.

Nathan trembles. "I'm the Alpha? I'm…" He shakes his head feverishly. "…I can't…I don't deserve…"

"Nathan," I whisper. He looks to me. "No one is better suited to see your people…" I smile. "…our people through whatever comes next better than you…someone who has gone through the darkest night and come out shining brighter than ever. Someone who has lived apart from your tribe…and has had to find his own place in this world. Someone so…accepting…" I laugh. "…that he fell in love with the Midnight Princess…and made her fall in love with him in return."

"Do you really think I can do this?"

"Yes, but more than that, my Nathan…" I caress his cheek. "…you will do it because your people need you to. Moreover, you will do as you've always done. You'll put everyone's needs above your own."

"Almost everyone's." He holds my stomach…his daughter. "Everyone comes second to her…" He kisses me. "…and you."

"That is not the Alpha…" Amelia starts, but Mosif's hand on her shoulder stops her.

"It is the Alpha's duty to protect the next generation," he says, peering at us over his glasses.

"What is the meaning of this?" Quinn grumbles, throwing the doors open. The Council and Christopher stand. "Why is the Council gathered in here…?" He glares at my Nathan. "…with you?"

Christopher smirks. "In light of the…5th Alpha's passing…" He peers at Nathan and me. "…the Council saw fit to install, the new Alpha."

"HIM?" He growls. "My uncle…? I challenged and defeated my father. I'm the rightful heir…"

"No," my Nathan says. "…brother…you're not."

"What?"

"Christopher," my Nathan says with determination, matching his br-
father's, peppering his voice. "Please show my younger brother the video that
OUR father made." Quinn's jaw falls, and his mouth remains open. "Council
as my first act as Alpha, I'd like to name a fourth member to your number…"
They nod. "…Christopher will be your newest member. All oppose?"

No one says anything, but Mosif smiles.

"Good. Congratulations, Elder Christopher."

"Th-thank you?" Christopher replies as more of a question.

"No," Quinn snarls. "No." He takes out his gun and points it at Nathan.

Nathan takes the weapon from him before he can register what
happened. "Quinn…" He glares at him. "…Brother…Quinton…" Nathan
swallows deeply. "…father didn't fight you to the best of his ability because
he loved you." He shows him his weapon. "He was faster and stronger than
I am…he could've taken this from you and shoved it up your ass…"

"Language," I pant. "Your daughter has ears now."

"Sorry, Anara."

"Kya…shove it up his posterior…"

"Thank you, dear." I nod. "…he would've shoved this up your posterior
and emptied it without breaking a sweat." Quinn swallows a lump. "You,
little brother, are banished."

"WHAT? You can't do that…I challenged my father because it was my
right…"

"That's not why I'm banishing you." He steps closer to his…brother.
"I'm banishing you because you have become and by extension attempted to
make this tribe become slaves of En Quosque. I will not allow that…for the
safety of my child, my wife, and the humans we've sworn to protect since
Anara, my wife's mother, set us free! I will not allow it!"

Quinn lifts his hand. My Nathan puts his free hand on Quinn's chest.
"Are you challenging me, little brother? Because Quinton…father didn't kill
you because he loved you. I, on the other hand, have no such qualms." Quinn
swallows a knot and lowers his hand.

"I thought not. Challenge me on this or anything else if you'd like…" He
pushes Quinn back a step. "…and I, unlike father, will not hesitate to kill you.
Banishment is the utmost of my…benevolence…" He steps back, turns to me,
and caresses my face. "…my charity, considering all that you almost cost
me…including my life."

"Nathan," I purr.

"Right." He tosses the gun to Mosif. He snaps his fingers and points at
his brother. "Quinn, watch the video before you go…and go you must.
Christopher, send me a copy…" He extends a hand to me. "…and

Love…come. I have to revise my eulogy." He sighs and another wave of pain, more intense…deeper than everyone before it…crashes against me. "I have to put my father to rest."

#####

Chapter 35: Pain

"I don't see how he did it," my Nathan complains. "Quinton...my father always made it all seem so...easy. So manageable."

"He trusted a lot of the work to his friends, to his family, to his pack...and to the Council," I reply. He continues rubbing my feet, and I purr. "It is alright. You handle everything required of you as Alpha and still manage to come home to me every night, answer my ever whim of a craving, and sing your daughter to sleep."

"Sh-sh-shhhhhh," he issues with a finger near his mouth. "The guards will hear."

"Oh, we would absolutely not want the guards to hear..." I lean back against the sofa, tilting my head toward the door. "...THAT YOU SING TO YOUR DAUGHTER EVERY NIGHT!" He laughs. I do, too. Moments like this one, I forget my mother's warning...until it comes rushing back with horrible, terrible clarity.

"Are you alright, Love?"

I refresh my smile. "Yes."

He tips his head. "What is that anyway?"

I look down at my bowl. "It is Rocky Road ice cream with bits of streaky bacon..." He hums his approval. "...ox blood..." He makes a face. "...strawberry sauce, and dill pickles." His face twists. "Would you like some?" I offer him a spoonful.

"No, I would not." He lowers my foot and crawls closer. He kisses me on the cheek and hums. "Even after you get home from school..." He kisses me again. "...I still sneak out during the day sometimes..." Another kiss. "...to do some of the financial stuff..." Another. So many tingles rush through my body. Our daughter loves the emotions I get from her father, and I feel because of him. "...and go over all the rules being proposed." He sighs. "Some of our tribe can be so petty with their requests."

"After meeting Amelia and her daughter...I can only imagine."

"Believe it or not, Cassandra's one of the nicer ones," he says and kisses me again.

I take another spoonful and enjoy the sweet ice cream offsetting the savory bacon, mixing with the ox blood, mellowing out the tang of the dill... "Mm!" ...and the strawberry sauce because...well, strawberry sauce is yum.

"What's wrong, Love?" he asks again. Sometimes I fear that he feels my emotions as readily as I feel his. My eyes search his handsome face, so loving...so caring.

I sigh. "I went to Mona's grave with Joseph last night." He takes my hand away from the bowl, leaving it balanced on Kya and kisses the back of it. "He is still so angry and in so much pain." He nods. "Their family name was Walters…" I stare at my spoon. "…Joseph Walters and his mother, Mona Walters. It was there on her headstone…*Ramona Erickson-Walters. Beloved wife and mother.*"

"How are you dealing with…?"

"Your traitorous nephew who turned out to be your traitorous brother who attempted to steal our child and killed her would-be nanny…" I lift my eyes to him. "…superb."

"I was gonna say…" He nods. "…how's school?"

"I have learned to ignore the contemptible sneers and emotions of the faculty and staff…so that's better. Better still, now that I have managed to convince everyone else that while yes, I am pregnant with your child…no, neither of us has been disowned by our parents… no, we will not be putting the child up for adoption… and no, you did not, in fact, drop out of school to get a job to support us." I sigh. "Meredith and Angela have helped curb the rumors tremendously."

"Knocked up by your high school boyfriend…" He faux gasps. "…the scandal."

"I know," I breathe. "Speaking of which…" I bob my head and eat a bit more ice cream. "Have you talked to her?" I ask, before licking the spoon. He wants to ask 'who,' but he already knows.

"Everyday."

"About her…relationship with Balthazar?"

"It's not my place to comment on her boyfriend."

"She is your best friend…one of the people who you trust most in the world." He shakes his head. "You know that it is true…" I point the spoon at him. "…and he is not quality boyfriend material."

"Yeah, well…people said the same about me…" He shows me his ring. "…and now you're stuck with me."

"You were not trying to resurrect a demigod and take over the world…and I am stuck with you by choice…I have to admit, your nice buns won me over." He laughs. "You do not feel it is your place, because she is still in love with you?" His head bows. I swallow a lump and decide to press forward. "We knew we would have to talk about this at some point." His thumb sweeps across his lower lip. "Am I wrong? Is that not the reason?"

"It's not NOT the reason."

"Without the double negative, please."

"It's a part of the reason." He nods. "The other part is that I trust her judgment, but more than that…I trust her to do the right thing."

"You have supreme faith in her?"

"There's only one person I have more faith in…" He points at me. I smile and lean forward, as much as our daughter and my massive belly will allow, to kiss him. He avoids my mouth and kisses me on the cheek. I scoff. "You have ox blood breath…" My mouth falls open. "…not helping…and even worse than the ox blood…" He fans in front of his face. "…dill pickles? Really?"

"You love it!" I whisper, collecting a hand full of his shirt. I pull him to me, and he kisses me…I inhale deeply at the gentle tug he gives my lower lip. I love it when he does that. We part. "You have to go?"

"How did you…?"

"I could sense it…but more than that, the look on your face told me." I steal a quick peck. "Go. Be brilliant and lead our people."

"I'll try," he says, standing.

"You will. I know you will because I have supreme faith in you."

He smiles. "Rachel says she'll stop by later…and Raven's supposed to have something delivered, but I thought it'd be here by now."

"Go, you silly wolf. Knowing you, you are already running late." He checks his watch and laughs. "Bye, my Nathan…Kya says goodbye as well."

"Bye, Love. Good day, Anara." He hurries out the door before I can gather a pillow and throw it at him. The door opens again as my guard detail hurries into the room. I push myself up into more of a seated position.

"Ma'am," the leader of my detail, Jackson, barks. His buzzcut, salt-and-pepper hair belays his age. He's fifteen years younger than I am. Nathan selected him to be the leader of my guard, specifically because he didn't fight in the war. He stands at attention, his hazel-gray eyes focused and ready.

"At ease, squaddie," I pant with a loose salute. He nods and instructs his five fellow wolves to filter to their guard positions throughout the apartment. "If any of you are hungry, I had Nathan stock the fridge with mutton shanks."

"We're not allowed to eat on duty, ma'am. You know that."

"First time for everything, Jackson," I say with a complaint, while trying to stand. Jackson hurries over to me and offers me a hand. I take it, and he pulls me to my feet. "Thank you. Any day now and you will not have to help me up anymore."

"It's not a problem and in fact, my pleasure, ma'am."

I carry my bowl toward the kitchen where the only female in the detail meets me. "Ma'am." She claims my bowl and returns to the kitchen.

I sigh. Being guarded with such diligence is so boring. I suppose I could watch something on the tellie. "What are you in the mood for, Jackson?"

"Ma'am?"

I return to the couch and collect the clicker. "From what I understand there is a wonderful…rom-com…on tonight." I turn on the television. The massive monitor comes to life with a buzz and the smell of ozone from the electricity sparking within it. *"Better Off Dead...*what in Heaven's name? Hmm, Jackson is that a good one?"

"It's one of my favorites, ma'am. It reminds me of a simpler time."

I nod. "Then the work of one John Cusack, it is."

Jackson sniffs and glares at the door.

"What is...?" A finger placed close to his mouth silences me. He moves over to the door. He peers at me and makes a patting downward motion with his hand, pinching his thumb and index fingers on his other hand. I nod and lower the volume on the tellie.

He slips his gun from its holster. I stretch out with my emotions. I sense...something, but it is muffled...like someone trying to distract himself or herself...trying to keep a thought out of their head. "Jackson," I pant. He peers at me. I tap my ear. He nods and returns to the door.

I slip my phone out of my pocket...and find Nathan's number. I tremble and hold my phone, closer to my face. I hear a thud from the guest bedroom and then another from the kitchen. Jackson heard them as well. He turns from the door, but I can feel the conflict in him. He wants to investigate, but he knows something is in the hall.

A fist smashes a hole through the door. "Jackson?" It catches him by his belt and pulls him through the door shattering it. "Anaras," I growl, finally sensing him. I gasp. "BALTHAZAR!"

I feel a pinch at the base of my neck. "Goodnight, Midnight Princess," Balthazar purrs in my ear. He injects something into me. It burns. The world spins...as Anaras enters. "I have her." I am moving...I feel as though I am floating.

"Will the mixture...injure the child?"

"Of course not."

"N-"

"She is conscious."

"Not for long."

Everything goes dark. My mind struggles...I have to stay awake...I have to contact Nathan...protect Kya with...

"...your everything?"

"Mother?" She smiles. "Mother, what is happening?" She looks down...her stomach is smaller than last time. "Mother, please tell me, what is happening." I hear a sound. It is a voice...a man's voice. I do not recognize it. I turn to hear.

"Stay with me," she whispers, claiming my hands. "Stay with me, my clever, beautiful girl..." She shakes her head as tears well in her eyes.

She has visited me so many times over the past few weeks. Her stomach swells and shrinks at random…each visit must coincide with a vision I gave her. Her silver eyes shimmer with tears.

"What do you not want me to see, mother?" A sting of pain rips through my body. I bend. "Ugh…"

"Stay with me, child. Please, stay with me." Tears pour from her eyes, mirroring mine.

"Mother, what is…?" The pain spreads and moves across my abdomen. "Kya," I breathe. I lift silver eyes to mother's matching pair. Her veneer crumbles. "Is it Kya? Are they taking her?"

"Yes, my precious," mother weeps. I fall to my knees because of the pain coming from my stomach and my heart. They are tearing my daughter from me… "Shhhhh," Mother says cradling my head and stroking my hair.

"Sir," a woman says. "I think she's awake."

"It doesn't matter. We have our orders. Keep going."

"Mother," I cry. My vision blurs.

"Stay strong, my dearest Alana." I nod as my flesh separates. I clench my teeth as more tears fall and the stinging burn moves across my midsection. "Be strong." Cool air sweeps into me. "You are so strong, my dear." Something moves within me…my mouth…my throat…I want to scream, but I feel as though I am choking. "…swrasi, vi pone…"

I do not know how, but I know those words. They are not of any language I know or have heard in this world. She said, *Courage, my heart.*"

"AAAAAAAAAAAAAAAAAAAAAAAHHHHHHHHHHHHHHHHH," I scream…blood erupting from my mouth, pouring down my face.

"Almost there," the man says, his hands buried in my stomach. "And…" A baby's cry fills the room. My baby's cry…my daughter's cry. "…here we are." The woman next to him extends a towel, between her arms. The man places Kya in her arms. She carries her away. Pain almost blinds me, but I keep my eyes on my daughter. I reach for her…but my arms are restrained… I hiss. …by silver.

"Nurse, remove the clamps please."

"That won't be necessary," Anaras says. I peer up at him, leaning over me. Tears stream from my eyes, and a shiver moves up my spine as my body goes numb. "As I told your mongrel husband…" I sneer at him. "…a true god…has no parents."

I open my mouth as a silver blade passes under my throat. I turn my head to my daughter again. She cries and her fear echoes in my mind. "…Ky…a…swra…si…vi…" Another bout of tears falls. "…po-"

#####

Chapter 36: Tower

"Sir," the large wolf snaps, holding the door for Nate. He slips out of the limo and tips his head to him, never taking the phone away from his ear.

"Your caramel latte, sir," I say, imitating the wolf. He takes the cup and swallows a lump. "Nate?"

"I've got a bad feeling...an Alana feeling." I nod. "And she's not..." I take his phone. He wipes his mouth and nods. "Thank you."

"Anytime." I end the call. "Besides..." I search through his contacts until I find Raven's name. "We know someone..." I give him his phone. "...a couple of people..." I take out my phone and search for... "...that can go and check on her in an eye blink." ...Natavius and hit the little phone icon. I put the phone to my ear at the same time he does.

"Why are you...you know, not with your boyfriend?"

"Do you really want to do this now, Nate?"

"Wife's orders."

"Only person who should boss an Alpha around." He nods. "Natavius isn't answering." I lower my phone.

"Raven either." He lowers his. "Any of the other Magistrates still in the city?" I shake my head.

We turn toward his cousin's building. "Besides, I've been pulling triple duty lately, mister. How's the feeling?"

"Still there." He searches through his phone again.

"Well, I've been playing daytime bodyguard to Alana, helping you in the afternoons, and still playing vampire rogue roundup at night."

"And still...you and Balthazar..."

I draw my lips into my mouth. "Still, me and Balthazar...in fact, the only reason I had time to get you a coffee was because Bal canceled...on..." We stop walking. "...me."

"He canceled..." Nate points at me with a look of disbelief. "...on you?"

"That son of a bitch," I growl. "His heart...and his duty...always take him in two directions." Nate turns back to the car and marches away, dropping his latte. I follow.

He puts his phone to his ear. "Christopher. Priority Alpha One."

"Understood. I'll have a location ASAP." The phone beeps three times.

"A location?" I ask when we reach the limo.

"Her wedding rings...after Quinn...we thought it best if we installed a tracking device in both her rings." I nod. Nate's phone rings. "Yeah."

"Heading north...fast...like helicopter or small plane...fast." Nate growls and his phone groans under his grip. I reach for it. He turns away. Crap, he blames me... I sigh. ...I blame me, too. I thought it was weird that

Bal...can't think about that now. "Not to worry," Christopher says. "The helicopter's being prepped on the roof."

Nate looks up. "Good man."

"I'll be there in..."

"And me and the chopper will be gone already by then." He crushes his phone.

"Nate...?"

"Did you know?" I freeze. He turns to me with green and gold eyes. "Did you know?"

"Of course not, Nate..." I step into him. "...Nate, I love you guys too much for that...and you know that." He wipes his mouth, tears roll down his cheeks, and he nods. He walks toward the building. "Nate?"

"You comin' or not?" he growls, peering at me. I run after him. We cross the lobby, then hit a full sprint up the stairs and reach the roof in no time. There are four wolves in riot gear waiting for us. "Benjamin," he says to the tallest one. I remember him. He was in the lobby of Nate's building when we got back from Paris.

"Sir." He looks at me. "Are you sure about the...?"

"She's coming. End of story." Benjamin nods and climbs on the black helicopter. The others follow. "Do you have?"

I nod and lift my jacket. "Never leave home without it." He reaches around me and taps the knife. God sometimes I swear he knows what he does to me still...even with Balthazar being all...distracting and whatnot.

"Good." He motions to the copter, and I climb aboard.

He takes the seat beside me as Benjamin offers me a pair of headphones. I put them on. "Trust me," he says over the little microphone attached to his. "The noise would be so much worse without these." I nod.

As the helicopter lifts off, my phone vibrates. I take it out and read the text message:

Scowly Wolf:

Why isn't Nathan answering his phone? Never mind.

Followed the tracker's signal to a building in upstate NY.

Coordinates in next message.

I tap Benjamin in the front seat and then pass him my phone. "What are you...?" The phone buzzes, and he checks the display. He takes the phone and holds it out to the pilot, who nods. The copter tilts to the right and speeds up.

I look at Nate, who looks like he could rip the head off...pretty much anything standing between him and his wife and child. I grab his hand, before common sense gets the better of me. He doesn't flinch, there's never any reaction from him for how cold my hands are. Even Balthazar flinches sometimes. Nate never does. I love that about him.

"We'll find them," I whisper. "We'll find them and when we do…I'll put my foot up Bal's ass."

He sighs and bows his head. "I know you will." I hook his arm with mine and put my head on his shoulder.

"Sir," Benjamin says. "Our target's dead ahead."

"They know we're coming," I say.

"How's that possible?" the wolf next to me grumbles.

"They have a psychic on their team…minus the crystal ball. He's the real deal."

"So, we could be walking into a trap?" my neighbor asks. I nod.

"Either way," Benjamin says, pointing down.

The helicopter swings around near a dark gray, stone tower, sitting in the middle of clearing surrounded by trees on all sides. A small rural road leads away from the tower's main entrance. "That thing's huge," I mutter, realizing it's almost as wide as Scowly Wolf's building and about half the height.

There's a bunch of people outside in gray sweat suits and other similar workout gear. A woman in black signals for everyone to head inside.

"Ange?" I look at Nate. "How does it look?"

"Right," I say as my eyes switch over. "She's here…but…" I close my eyes and try to shake the feeling of all the little flickering lights, each one representing a supernatural being, moving up the tower making it look like a friggin' Christmas tree.

"They're all hunters, aren't they?"

"I think so."

The helicopter touches down and Nate and I file off. The soldiers follow. "You," Nate says to the pilot. "Stay put. If we need to make a speedy evac, I want this thing ready to go." He nods and gives a 'thumbs up'. "Ben, I need you and one of the others to stay here. I want my ride to be here and intact when we come back." Benjamin nods.

"You two with me and Ange…you're support only though." They nod and ready their assault rifles. Nate and I turn to the building.

"Sir," Benjamin snaps. "Don't you need a weapon?" Nate lifts his clawed hand, and his pupils faze green and gold. Benjamin nods. Nate storms off with the other two soldiers on his heels. "Ma'am," Benjamin says.

"It's Ange."

"Ange," he repeats, offering me a pistol, handle first. "It couldn't hurt."

I take it, cock it, and slip it under my jacket behind my knife. "It'll hurt whoever I use it on." He nods. I hurry to catch up to Nate and the others.

212 | Midnight Princess

"You, um…"

"Kendall, sir," the guy says.

"Kendall, you and…"

"…Ward, sir," the girl says.

"…Ward…you'll cover us…stay near the nearest exit…leap frog each other…and if you see anything that doesn't look like my wife or a baby…shoot it first and we'll sort through it later."

"Sir," they bark at the same time.

"Nate," I say as we reach the glass double doors with a big, Egyptian-looking eye on them. "These are humans…we're going up against. You're asking your wolves to kill humans."

Nate scowls. He turns to Ward and Kendall. "Do either of you have a problem with that?" They frown. "I won't use the Alpha's bark on you if you do."

Ward checks the sight on her rifle. "No, sir…to protect the Alpha bloodline…" She lifts her eyes to Nate. "…I don't have a problem with that at all, sir." Kendall nods.

"Thank you both." He looks at me. "There you go." Nate pulls the door on the right open.

I shrug. "If you like it, I love it." I follow with Kendall and Ward behind us. It's a long narrow hallway leading toward what looks like the center of the building. We reach a large circular opening. Across from us are four elevators with silver doors. There's a stairwell to the right that goes up and around…and up…and around…and up…and around…

"Holy crap," Kendall says. "Do those stairs go all the way up?"

"Looks like," I say.

"Footsteps," Nate says, staring up the tower. He takes a deep breath and his eyes drift closed. He moves to the center of the circle without opening them. "She's here…and she's panicking…" His eyes faze again. "…I can smell her blood," he says through clenched teeth.

All four elevators ding at the same time. Kendall and Ward aim at them. Ropes fall all along the walls lining the stairs. The elevator doors slide open, and ten men pour out of each with assault rifles of their own. About three men and women…oops, there're women in the mix, too…slide down each of the ropes with weapons trained on us. Footsteps echo in the hallway behind us too. All of them dressed in black riot gear from head to toe, complete with masks covering their goggled faces. Kendall and Ward don't know where to aim first. I motion to them to lower their weapons…not to antagonize these guys with silver bullets filling their guns. They do begrudgingly.

I look around the room and sigh. "Crap." I walk over to Nate.

The men fan out more, surrounding us. Nate just keeps staring up the tower. They raise their guns and take aim. "You there, wolf," an older male voice growls. "Step away from the vampire so that we can deal with her." I gasp and glance around the room quickly…and notice all the little red dots are on me.

I come back. Nate still hasn't moved…but I know that look on his face…he's thinking…calculating…figuring out a way to do what he always does. He's finding a way to do what everyone else would say is impossible…like…I look around again at the men surrounding us…hopefully figuring out how to get us out of this mess without being filled with silver bullets…so that we can…

"Save her," he snarls. I look at him.

"I beg your pardon," the older voice complains. He lowers his gun and steps forward from the elevator crew.

"I have to go save my wife."

"Fine," the soldier snarls. "Go. Save your wife. We'll deal with the vampire."

"You won't deal with anyone," Nate barks at the man from right in front of his face. All the little red dots land on him. "That is my wife's niece…"

"Not anymore. She's a…"

"I'm talking," Nate snaps in a soft but deadly tone. "She is my wife's sire-niece…"

"That means…"

"Talking. My wife is a vampire…and I am going to save her and I'm taking her niece with me…and you will either get out of my way, help me, or force me to kill all of you."

"We…"

"TALKING!" The hunter's spine goes rigid, and his heart skips a beat or two…he might want to check his drawers, too. "My wife is a vampire…unlike any that you have ever seen before…EVER…" Nate wipes his mouth quickly.

"What makes her so different?"

"Easy." Nate looks up again. "The fact is that she is so kind…so tender hearted…so…noble, that she would sacrifice her life…give her life to save all of you, knowing that you'd all try to kill her for her trouble…"

"And you…?"

Nate glares at him. "…I would kill every single one of you in this room to save her…" The head soldier lifts his goggles and then pulls down his mask, revealing a weathered, old, tan, leathery face. "…without hesitation or regret."

The old man seems lost. "But you're a wolf."

"Yes."

"And she's a vampire."

"Absolutely."

"And we're human."

"True."

"And you'd kill all of us…for her?"

"Now, you're getting it…" Nate nods. "…all of you…in a heartbeat and with no remorse…at all."

The man swallows deeply. "They're scent-bonded," I squeak. The old man looks at me like something that shouldn't be. I stand still…I have to be as strong as Nate is. "If anything happens to her…it would be bad…" I point at Nate without looking at him. "…HE would be very bad. Help us…please!"

"Why is the vampire speaking to me, wolf?" the old man snaps, pointing at me.

"Because," I start, stepping forward…dots back on me. I point at myself. "This vampire…" I point at the man. "…is trying to stop you…" My arm swings wide. "…and all your men from being killed by…" I point at Nate. "…this wolf."

The man frowns. "In case you don't know, wolves are VERY particular about the people they have scent bonds with. This wolf in particular gets very angry very quickly when his wife's life is in danger…so are you going to help us save her or not…because if he goes off…I can promise you, guns or not…none of US…and I do mean NONE of US…will make it out of here alive."

The old man sighs and stares at Nathan…whose eyes have already switched over to green and gold…and they're starting to turn dark around the borders. "NATE," I snap. His head jerks around to see me quickly…scary quickly. "I need you to stay you…Alana needs smart, problem solving Nate, not angry, destroys everything around him Nate." He sighs and nods. He turns his back on the old gray hair.

"Who exactly is this wolf, vampire?"

"Who am I?" Nate snarls, still with his back to the old leader. "My name is Nathan Jerome Dumont…" He walks toward the old soldier. "…I am the son of Quinton Dumont and Kya Wolfspaw…the grandson of Nathaniel Mosi'son…great-great grandson of Mosi the First. I am the Sixth Alpha of the A'kani tribe, husband to Alana Isis Gregory-Dumont, father to Kya Anara Dumont the next Alpha of our tribe…" He stops in front of him. "…and I WILL save my wife and my child. Is that understood?" The old soldier swallows a lump and nods.

"Let's go," Nate says and heads toward the stairs.

"Sir," a younger voice barks. "Are we just going to…?"

"Of course not," another snarls. I look around. Some of the hunters have lowered their guns while others…keep their aims on me.

"SIR?" another voice calls.

"Open fire," the old gray-hair says…and then gurgles erupt from his throat. The old man falls, as one of his hunters…a woman steps forward.

She removes her mask and goggles in one clean snatch, revealing…

"Raven?" The red dots land on her.

"Well, t'at blew muh cover, didn't it? GO!" she barks. "We'll handle t'em."

"We?" Several of the hunters fall with blood pouring from their sides.

"We," Natavius says, tossing a mask to the side and wearing matching black, hunter riot gear. "Go. Save Alana." Nate grabs my hand…and pulls so hard that my feet come off the floor. We move up the stairs faster than I've ever moved. I didn't know Nate could move this fast, especially carrying someone. He slows down on…sign blurs by…the 22nd floor. I put my feet down and start moving them to keep up. He let's go of my hand as a hail of gunfire comes up from the first floor.

"What about Kendall and Ward?"

He looks up and keeps running. "Natavius and Raven are down there…do you think anyone will be paying any attention to two slow movers like Kendall and Ward while trying to survive Natavius and Raven?"

"Right. I don't know what I was…" I gasp.

"What?"

"Balthazar…" I stare at the door to my right. "…Balthazar's behind this door." Nate scowls. "He's the only person fast enough and…stealthy enough to get the drop on Raven and Natavius…and I bet he's just waiting on us to pass by to go after them."

"Do you sense Anaras, Alana's grandfather?"

I look up. "I can still sense Alana…and…that being that feels like her is next to her…wait…" I frown and look at Nate. "…Alana…doesn't have that swirl of you in her anymore."

"They've taken the baby," he growls.

"Go. I'll deal with Bal."

"Are you sure? I mean, he's…your…"

I nod. He grabs the back of my head and kisses me on the center of my forehead. My eyes drift closed, and I inhale his scent.

"I'm sorry you have to do this," he whispers.

"Me too. Go."

Nate vanishes.

#####

Chapter 37: Unbearable

I pull the door open and march into the hallway. I sense him…see his trail moving right, and I follow it. I take my knife out and move it to my left hand. I take Benjamin's gun and keep it ready in my right. Bal's faster than me…but I'm as physically strong as he is and hopefully, being invisible most of his life has dulled his fighting sense.

"Angel," he says from a doorway to my right. I aim at him. He sighs. "Oddly enough, not the rudest way you've ever greeted me." I shiver. I've stared at his stupidly gorgeous face more times than I can remember over the past few weeks. He's my boyfriend…and I love him…but…

"My heart and my duties take me in two different directions," I whisper, cocking the hammer.

"As do mine," he whispers. "Do it."

"You want me to shoot you?"

"I wasn't talking to you."

"Crap…"

"Adflictio." I groan. It feels like something's peeling my skin off and lighting it on fire. I drop the gun and the knife and fall to my knees. It hurts so bad that whatever scream I might've gotten out won't escape…I'm stuck in this weird soundless yell while wave after wave of torment washes over me. Every muscle in my body tenses at the same time, and it feels like I'm being torn apart.

Two hands move to either side of my head from behind. "Now…" I recognize this girl's voice. "…the real fun starts." The pain feels like it's moving inside…like it's burning through to my bones…every part of me feels like it's on fire. I shiver…still not able to scream.

"Get this over with," Balthazar says.

"Oh, don't want to see your pretty little girlfriend suffer?" Bethany says behind me in that nasally whine of hers…if I didn't already feel like nails on a chalkboard all over my body, her voice would definitely hurt more.

"Jealousy is not a pretty color on you, Bethany Triste."

"Then don't say and do things to make me jealous," she grumbles back. Wait, does that mean…?

I lower my head…until I see Balthazar looking down at me. Didn't even realize my head was thrown so far back. I twitch all over…feeling like the fire is moving back out from my bones. "…y-you…pl-played…me…?"

"Like a cheap violin," Bethany chimes. "And you fell for it, you dumb whore."

"Bethany, get to work. You know what we need. Do you have the spell?"

"Yes," Bethany says, sounding remorseful. "I have it memorized."

Balthazar looks at me…tears start pouring from my eyes…well, more tears…the pain's bad…heartache always sucks…but both, at the same time…unbearable. "S-s…" I sniff as another wave of pain rolls over me. "…s-son…of…a…"

He cups my chin. "Don't," he begins in a whisper, his eyes darting back and forth between mine. "…ever think that my feelings for you weren't genuine…" He nods. "…every moment spent…I will treasure for the rest of my days…but my duty…"

"…a-a-and h-h-heart…" Another bout of tears. He nods again.

"Amoris purissimi," Bethany starts, and my spine stiffens again, throwing my head back. "…profundissimum desiderium…" Weird…I just thought about Nate and me…dancing in Paris. His hand was so warm on the small of my back.

"…qualis existo devotionis…" My hands are on his cheeks…I'm trying to convince him to talk to Alana. He was so stubborn, but I pushed him toward her because I knew she was his happiness.

"…indissolubili vinculo copulatae cohaerentiae." Every time I leaned my head on his shoulder, or he kissed me on the forehead…every hug…every time I was scared, and he held my hand…every conversation about random whatevers sprung into our heads that made us laugh with, at, and even of each other…everything…everything…everything…that makes me love him so much.

"Discretor." He lets go of my hand…moves away…breaks the hug…don't let go, Nate…please…

"Sectis." I push Alana into his apartment…into his arms…the door closes behind me. I can't breathe.

"Discinderet." I walk away from Nate at his brother's…at his father's funeral…to go see that lying bastard, Bal. He looked so sad that it broke my heart all over again.

"Aufero!" The image of Nate in my head…smiling…happy becomes hazy…and I…I…

I inhale deeply and lunge forward. I barely get my hands up to stop myself from faceplanting. I pant like a wild dog, tears pour from my eyes, and even though the physical pain has stopped…my body feels like a raw nerve…worn…beaten…pulsing with recent injury.

"Did it work? Did you get it?" Balthazar asks.

"Yeah," Bethany answers, sounding as exhausted as I feel. "That spell…took everything out of me."

"The prize was worth it. Go. Use the hellgate…take it to the haven."

"Love you," she purrs, walking away.

"Love you, too," he replies.

218 | Midnight Princess

I swallow a lump, and my stomach turns. "What?" I snarl, between clenched teeth. "What the hell did you do to me?"

"We needed a component from you, for Eden's resurrection spell," he says, casually. "We needed the purest love of a daywalking vampire." I glare at him. "I know you're confused, but…" He kneels. "…a vampire's love…because it is so…" He makes a chopping motion. "…singularly focused…and enduring, given their lifespans…that energy provides longevity, which Eden's new body will need. The love of a daywalking vampire in particular because it is the purest…strongest form of a vampire…with the purest, strongest love."

"You played me…for that…?"

He nods. "Yes, my Angel."

"Don't call me that," I sob.

He takes a deep breath. "I am sorry, but as I said my feelings for you were genuine…" He looks away. "…that was unexpected…in fact, you being our target in and of itself was unexpected. We approached Renee Savoy first."

"Duchess…?"

"Indeed…the Duchess…she had no…focus for her love. We…" His eyes come back to me. "…convinced her to find us a new target." I twitch. She pointed them at me. She sent them after me. "She had you undergo the ritual to that end…and she led us to you. It was my goal to make you love me."

He shakes his head. "Unforeseen side effect…you made me love you in return…" He takes a deep breath and moves the hair away from my forehead. "…but love you or not…my duty to Eden, I could never turn my back on that." He grabs my knife and stands. I look up at him. "So, you see…I had to steal your love for me…" I gasp. "…and now, I'll do you the kindness of putting you out of your misery…which will last through the rest of your days otherwise, believe me."

He lifts the knife above his head with both hands…he's aiming for my skull. He brings the knife down. I grab the gun and jump at him. I put my left arm around him, and the gun on his stomach. I squeeze the trigger…and squeeze…and squeeze and squeeze. He loses a breath with each round fired into his gut. His arms flop to his sides.

"H-how?" he groans, blood dribbling from the corners of his mouth. "Your feelings for me…the feeling of uncertainty surrounding me…" He groans. "…should've left you…unable…to move…against…me…"

I tremble as the rage of what he REALLY stole from me rushes through my mind. I squeeze the trigger again, and he jerks away, but I hold him close. He drops the knife, and his chin rests on my right shoulder as his entire body slumps.

"Don't you get it, Bal?" I snarl between clenched teeth. "I still love you…" My tears dribble onto his shoulder. "…I'm still IN love with you."

"Wh-what? How?"

"You didn't steal my love for YOU…" I sniff as more fresh tears roll down my cheeks. "…you stole my love for HIM…you stole my love for Nate…she took my feelings for HIM away." I squeeze the trigger two more times. "If you had waited…another month…another week…hell, maybe even another day…it might've been you." I lower him to the floor, laying him on his back. I sit up. His eyes find me. "But you couldn't, could you? Your duty…made you move faster…"

Tears stream down his face, toward his ears. He mouths something, but it's lost in blood.

"What…?"

He swallows deeply. "You…never…loved me…?"

"I did…I just loved him more…"

"…but…married…you pushed him…to-ward her…"

I nod. "Self-sacrifice…true mark of loving someone." I smile. "He taught me that…putting someone else's happiness…their needs ahead of your own…doing what's best for them, in spite of it tearing you up inside."

"No wonder…so…noble…"

"Yeah," I say with a nod. "…so, you ended up stealing how I felt for Nate, not you." I scoff and wipe my nose. "It's always been Nate…always was…and you took that from me…I know that it was only going to cause me pain and misery, but it was mine…and you stole it…" I stand. "…and for that, despite loving you," I weep. I sniff as a fresh wave of tears washes over my cheeks. "…despite being in love with you, I'll never forgive you. Goodbye, Bal." I aim at his face…look away…and squeeze…and squeeze and squeeze…and click…and click…and click…

"Stop it, dear," Raven whispers, putting her hand on top of the gun. She takes it from me and tosses it away. I crumble, falling to my knees. "I know, love…I know…" She wraps her arms around me and holds me…as I sob like a three-year-old. I've lost two loves in one day…I didn't think this kind of pain was even possible. I feel empty…broken and hollow and like screams are just filling a big black space in the center of my chest…and my mind just keeps telling me to run…run…run…but all I can do is cry…

#####

Chapter 38: Parenthood

"Mother?"

"Princess?" I turn to my Nathan as the white space dims and grass springs from the ground. Trees come into view and the sweet smells of wildflowers, honeysuckle, and jasmine fill the air.

"Nathan? What are you doing here? How did you…?" I swallow a knot. "We're in your head again, aren't we? Because I'm dying."

"Probably," he says, wrapping his arms around me.

"No. This is different. The last time, I saw myself through your eyes…and Jeremiah was there…I healed because of his blood. This time…" I nearly gag on the warm sensation in the back of my throat. "What? What is that?"

"I'll do anything for you, Princess," my Nathan says in a pleading voice. "You know that, right?" I nod. "But I need you to come back to me."

"Come back to you…?"

"I can't do it," he weeps. "I can't raise that little girl without you. Please, come back to me."

I inhale deeply and nod. I smell it a moment later. The scent of the night air in summertime…the smell that made me fall in love with him. I close my eyes and feel as though I'm falling or floating. "Come on, my angel…come on…please, please, please, please."

I open my eyes…I try to close my mouth, but my Nathan's forearm is in my mouth. "Nathan," I mumble.

"Lana!" He removes his arm and moves beside me on the slab. "You're alright?"

I nod, feeling completely healed even if a little stiff and sore. "You fed me YOUR blood?"

"I was desperate. I'm half-skinwalker…a higher order daemon…" He nods. "…Angela drank Devon's blood, and it healed her wounds…" He holds his forehead to mine. "…I took a shot."

"And as always, you hit your mark, my love." I kiss him. We part. "Help me sit up." He does.

"Oh," I breathe, taking in the blood-soaked remains of my uniform. It fits me rather awkwardly, since…my body healed to its normal shape and size before pregnancy. I check my belly and there's a small, nearly invisible, crescent-shaped scar below my bellybutton. I issue a stuttering sigh and lower my blood-soaked shirt. "I'm a mess."

"Can you still sense Kya?"

"Oh," I purr. "You called her, Kya!"

"Lana, focus…we have to go rescue her." I nod. My Nathan moves away. I turn and throw my legs over the side of the slab. I tighten my belt and force the prong to create a new hole, securing my skirt. I toss my necktie away. I slip my cardigan off and toss it aside as well.

I look around this faux hospital room at all the unconscious hunters, including the doctor and his nurses. They breathe still but suffer injuries of varying degrees. My Nathan exhibited amazing restraint…considering. My eyes flash silver. Which is more than I will be capable of when I track down our daughter.

Nathan returns with a small tactical vest and a pair of boots. I take the vest from him and slip my arms into it. He kneels and places the boots on my bare feet. I secure the vest over my loose-fitting blouse. He ties the boots as I check the vest's pockets…I find a few magazines for the assault rifles, a flash bang, and a taser to go along with the silver-bladed combat knife, pointed upward over my left collarbone.

"Ready?" he says. I nod, and he steps back. I hop down. He marches toward a pair of shredded white doors, bowing inward from his pummeling outside. "I think they used one of those scent masking grenades on the higher floors." He kneels and collects a blade from one of the downed hunters and then another. "I'll need you to guide us to her."

"Indeed," I say, kneeling to collect one of the assault rifles. I eject the magazine, check it, and reinsert it. I do the same with a second. I stand with one in each hand. "Our daughter is moving up towards the roof."

"Helicopter."

"Undoubtedly," I say. "And Nathan…" He turns to me. "…she is upset. I can feel her crying in the back of my mind. She needs us." His eyes flash honey and emerald, and he hurries out. I follow.

In the hall, three hunters jump out at him. He runs them over like a freight train. "Pardon," I issue, rushing past them. We reach the stairs, and the air becomes electric…in front of me and then around me. We run up the additional 20 floors in no time.

We reach a door marked, *Helipad Access.* My Nathan stops at this door. "What? Why are you…?"

He holds one finger up in front of his mouth. I take a deep breath. "Remember the vow," he says. I nod. "I hear about thirty heartbeats on the other side of this door."

"And I hear our daughter crying."

He nods…silver reflects off honey and emerald. "I'll take point…you cover me." I nod. "I love you."

"Love you." He kisses me and turns towards the door. "Go," I snap.

My Nathan kicks the door off its hinges, sending it crashing into three hunters. He rushes forward, through a hail of gunfire. I lift both guns and return fire on everything within my eye line. I hit vests at times...I hit legs...arms...chests...even a neck...I do not care. My daughter is in danger. I march through the door.

Nathan runs towards a group, standing between him and Anaras... Anaras, cradling our swaddled child in his arm. Nathan leaps half a meter off the ground. I gasp as the blades move around him as if independent of his body...he's doing his father's attack...the Dance of Death. No. It isn't the technique he showed me. This one is less destructive. He only wounds, not kills. He slices through them quickly...they fall in all directions around him...as he stands amid where they once were.

"Did you not learn your lesson the first time, mongrel?" Anaras snarls. "I have...this time, I'll be sure to choke the life out of you with my bare hands."

My Nathan moves to him in a blur and slices at him with his left dagger...Anaras moves Kya into the blades path. Nathan checks his swing. Anaras swipes at him with his free hand and Nathan evades the attack. Nathan brings the right dagger down across Anara's outstretched arm...his sleeve shreds, but the blade shatters against his arm. Nathan leaps back gaining some distance.

Anaras shakes his arm and checks his tattered sleeve. "Your strength is impressive, mongrel. I actually felt that." He examines the slash over his forearm. "Mind you, it felt like a gentle tickle against my skin, but I felt it all the same. You can't beat me."

Nathan marches forward. "You know, while I was sinking...thinking that I was about to die..." My Nathan drops the dagger and the remains of the other. "...I realized something." His exposed skin darkens. "You're tougher than me...there's no doubt about that. Your skin feels like it's made of diamond..." Anaras nods. "...but you're not stronger than me..." My Nathan's muscle-mass nearly doubles.

My eyes swell. How did he...? I sense it before I can ask. I sense his wolf and his skinwalker...working in concert...his skinwalker half, drawing power from the wolf within him. A noise to my right, I fire without looking. A bullet rends flesh, and I continue marching toward our daughter behind my husband.

"...you're not faster than me either," my Nathan adds in a voice emphasizing the duality of his current state. "I will claim our daughter...and then we'll retreat...and if you or Balthazar or any of the rest of you comes anywhere near her again..." He clenches his clawed fingers into fists. "...I'll keep pounding on you, until you break," his voice thuds like rolling thunder.

The Alpha Bloodline | 223

Anaras steps closer to the edge, as the sound of an approaching helicopter grows louder. He smirks. "You will not escape," I warn, dropping one weapon in favor of focused aim with the other.

"Escape is not my thought...Alana," Anaras says. "We have been planning Eden's great resurrection for well over two thousand years. We have considered every factor, every eventuality, and ever happenstance..." He looks at Kya, nestled into the bend in his arm. "...and while this child was important to our plans, she is not the end all, be all of them. There are ways to resurrect Eden without a host body...though having a powerful vessel such as this one, would deter betrayal in the future."

He takes another step back. "What are you...?" I pant, lowering the weapon.

"Don't you understand? The child is not required, but she could become a force to challenge Eden in the future, so..." He lifts Kya, holding her in one hand... My still heart trembles. ...over the edge of the building. "...if En Quosque can't have her, then no one will."

My Nathan roars at him. "That is madness," I pant. "She is your great-granddaughter...your blood..."

"And you are my granddaughter, but I did not pause when slitting your throat."

"Do it, and you're dead," Nathan growls. Anaras smirks. "NO!" Nathan yells as Anaras rolls his hand. Our daughter begins to fall, and the world slows.

"NO!" I scream, running after Nathan.

Nathan leaps up...what is his plan...? Our daughter is... He jumps at Anaras, planting both feet in his chest. He springs off and moves towards Kya. Nathan, Kya, and Anaras move over the side of the building. My Nathan twists, and his honey and emerald eyes meet mine.

Remember the vow.

I drop the weapon as Nathan gets a hand underneath her...he tosses her toward me. I cradle my arms and slide on my knees. She falls gently into my waiting arms. I gasp and hold my breath for a second that seems to stretch into infinity.

"Kya?" I whisper. She opens her eyes after clenching them shut so tight. She sees me and coos. I smile. "My daughter..." I lift my eyes. "...my husband?" I run to the edge and peer over. "Noooo," I weep...my vision has come true...I have my daughter, but I've lost...

"LANA!"

"NATHAN!" I shift Kya to my right arm and lean further over the edge. My Nathan landed on the back of a stone gargoyle. The pain of his landing is apparent on his face. "Are you alright?"

"Superb. I'm just sitting on a gargoyle about a quarter mile off the ground."

"It's not nearly that far, you silly wolf." He laughs and breaks off into a groan of pain. "Anaras?" He tips his thumb toward the ground. I nod. "Give me a moment, I will find something to pull you up."

"Come in, Order Command," a voice comes in. "This is Thunder Stick, over." I look around, finding no one conscious that could have said it.

"This is Order Command, over," comes from the radio on my vest.

"Command, it's just as we feared…the tower seems to have fallen, over."

"What about the asset, Thunder Stick? Over."

"We do not have visual…but the target is on the roof, and she has the package." I look at the helicopter in the distance, fast approaching from the west. "Should we engage? Over."

"Negative, the package is still viable. Return to base. Over." I sigh in relief.

"Command, we have a visual on target 2…should we engage? Over."

"Is the package near target 2? Over."

"We feel confident that we can engage without endangering the package. Over."

I gasp. "Permission granted. Over." Anaras was the asset…and clearly, Kya is the package. If I am the target, then that means… The helicopter turns to the side, and the door slides open. A hunter readies a rail gun.

"NATHAN!"

"Go! I'll be fine."

I turn. "No, you will not, you silly wolf." I look around. "Our daughter is safe…I am safe…which makes you the current priority." I collect an assault rifle from one of the downed soldiers. He groans a complaint, while reaching for it. "Sorry, I need to borrow this to save my husband…" I hit him with the butt of the weapon, knocking him unconscious. "…you understand, I am sure."

I look down at Kya nestled in my arm. "Dear, hitting is wrong…please know that. Do as mummy says, and not as mummy does." Kya coos and stares up at me. "Good girl. Now, bear with me…things are going to get a bit loud."

I stand and return to the edge as the rail gun opens fire. I return fire…ignoring the man and the weapon. I hit the helicopter's tail propeller.

"Command? Target one just took out our rear propeller…we have to break off. Over."

"Acknowledged. Get that bird down safely. Over."

"Roger." The helicopter veers hard to the right and moves down.

I drop the weapon and look over the edge again. "NATHAN!" I gasp, realizing that the gargoyle he was lying on…is now gone…broken from its pedestal. "NATHAN!" I shriek, causing Kya to cry. A black blur moves upward past me. My Nathan lands behind us and kneels.

He stands and turns to face me…with a bullet wound on his lower left abdomen. "What?" he whines. "Is this what being married to you is going to be like, Princess? Nag, nag, nag. *Do not fall off the building, Nathan.*" He imitates my accent. "*Do not land on gargoyles, Nathan. Do not get shot by helicopter fire, Nathan.*"

I run over to him and wrap my arm around him. "Yes, you silly wolf, that is exactly what being married to me is going to be like."

He shrugs. "Alright, as long as I know what I'm getting myself into." I smile and kiss him on the cheek. "How is she?"

Kya inhales, coos, and her eyes open wide. "Scent-bonded," I sigh. "She recognizes her mum and dad." She yawns, closes her big, beautiful, amber-colored eyes, and her tiny fist moves up to her face.

"She's so beautiful," my Nathan whispers.

"Yes," I weep. "She is."

#####

Chapter 39: Promise

"Alana," Raven whines. "Let someone else hold her."

I cradle Kya in my lap. "Not on your or anyone else's life," I return, staring at my beautiful angel. Her perfect almond skin tone…full lips…hm, there is a slight imperfection on her lower lip…but that just makes her even more perfect. She is perfectly imperfect. "Hello, my angel," I sing. She sighs and falls deeper into her sleep.

"Thank goodness. She looks more like you, than Nate," Natavius says over my shoulder.

"You think so?"

"I know so," Vance says, leaning over her. "About the only thing she got from Nathan was…hmm…" He examines her. "…skin tone, maybe?"

I giggle. I look between Natavius and Raven's smiling faces. "I still do not understand how the two of you were already in the Order's Tower before they brought me there."

"We just got lucky that they happened to bring you to the same tower where we were," Natavius says.

"Aye," Raven agrees. "We took it upon ourselves to track down t'e nearest branch…we found it was t'at base for the group t'at took t'e manor." Raven nods. "My plan was to kill every single one of 'em, one by one."

"Honey," Vance says.

"Aye, aye, not very Christian of me, but t'ey took it upon t'emselves ta try ta kill me entire coven…includin' your sire-daughter." Vance nods.

"I talked her down from mass murder," Natavius says. "We decided to observe and see what their next move would be."

"But how did you remain hidden from them? They have enhanced senses like the rest of us, so they should have been able to detect that neither of you was human."

"We found the grenade packing room on our first day," Natavius says. "We smeared that scent neutralizing mixture all over ourselves and then stole random items from peoples' chests."

"Before ya knew it, we smelled human enough ta pass inspection," Raven says. "Plus…" She nods. "…I visited Renee, before we snuck in…" She sighs. "…t'at's why I missed Quinton's funeral…it took me a bit longer ta recover t'an Angela."

"So?" I begin. "Sister, you can…?"

"Aye," she purrs. "Muh first day back, muh husband took me on a stroll t'rough t'e park…and indulged me as I lay in the sun all day."

"I still can't believe what Renee did to her sister," Vance says, looking away.

"Aye, I gave her a good scoldin', dear. If she comes back States' side…I promised I'd give her a bit more t'an t'at."

I still find it difficult to believe that Duchess turned En Quosque's focus towards Angela. She has endured so much in the short time since her transition. First almost dying before the end of her first year, on multiple occasions, falling in love… I sigh. …with my husband, only to have that love stolen by En Quosque's dark witch. "…and she killed Balthazar," I whisper.

Kya stirs and begins to cry. "Oh, I am so, so sorry, my angel," I hum. "I let my emotions slip free. Yes, I did." She hums as I lighten my mood. She comes down to a sigh, sniffs…and drifts off again.

"Amazing," Vance says.

"No," Raven starts. "Alana was t'e same way when she was born. She could sense emotions as clearly as she can today." She looks at me. "So, you'll have ta be on your guard."

"I will have to do that anyway. If Anaras is as tough as Nathan thinks he is."

"I doubt any of us could survive a fall from that height," Vance says. "Do you really think it's possible?"

"A silver blade shattered against his skin," I explain. "…not broke…it shattered like glass, and he said it tickled. He is as tough as Nathan says." Kya wakes and coos. "I know, my angel-face, I sense him, too."

"You sense…?" Natavius begins.

"Ugh," Nathan complains behind his pack brother. He rubs his forehead and then moves his hand back over his head. "That was annoying."

"I'll say," Maggie purrs behind him.

"So, how'd it go?" Raven asks.

"The Order seems to be in chaos," Christopher says, entering the suite. "How do you find your new digs, Chief Magistrate?"

Raven scoffs. "I still can't believe ya just gave us a buildin'."

"The Chief Magistrate's younger sister is married to our 6th Alpha. Whether factions within our tribe or the vampire magistrates like it or not, we're all family now."

Nathan walks over and sits beside me. He looks Kya over and smiles…no, it is a smirk…it is his roguish smile. His secondary implement for stealing my heart when we first met. Kya coos louder. "And now you are using it to steal her heart?"

"What can I say?" he hums. "I'm adorable, and I can't help it." He leans forward. "Isn't that right, Anara?" Kya giggles…she actually giggles.

"Angel-face, your name is Kya. Ky - ah." Her nose scrunches up, and her tongue parts her adorable lips. I gasp as Nathan erupts with laughter.

"Toldja." Kya smiles along with him.

I growl. "Very well," I concede. "You are my beautiful angel, Anara." She smiles. "Now…" I lift her. "…would you not like to be held by your father?"

"Of course, she would," he says, taking her from me.

"An' I just asked ta hold her," Raven complains.

"Yes, but he jumped off a building to save her." I stand. "Christopher, Margaret, would you mind continuing with the report…on how negotiations with the Order went?"

"We met with Sera Markovic," Christopher says. "She's one of the Order's top trainers and leading the effort that did not like the orders handed down from command."

"Aye," Maggie continues. "Basically, tha Order's breakin' inta two factions…fightin' against each other…those loyal to Ezekiel… and those loyal to the mission that he originally set them on. Anyone who abides by the old rules is the Order…anyone who does nae and just follows orders from Command are consider Ezekielites."

"It's insanity," Nathan says, holding Anara up to his face and allowing her to gnaw and dribble on his nose.

"Do not do that," I groan. "If she does it to you, she will think it is alright to do it to me." He laughs.

"It went a long way in our negotiations," Christopher starts. "…that even though most of the Chief Magistrate's coven was wiped out by their proclaimed rogue element, there were no casualties in the tower." I think back on the hunter that I shot in the neck. How did he survive that?

"Almost no casualties," Nathan says. Did he survive it?

"Yes, but as you know, cousin, they didn't consider a two-millennia-old daemon a causality."

"Angela does," I say in Nathan's place. Raven sighs, and Vance puts his hands on her shoulders. "She has not spoken in days."

Maggie throws her fist into her waiting, left palm. "Aye, and if I ever get muh hands on our lovin' sister…"

I turn to my Nathan. "You should go and talk to her."

Nathan shakes his head. "Every time…" Kya…Anara whines. "…every time…" She begins to cry. "…she can't stand the sight of me," Nathan blurts out causing Anara to bawl. "Mummy," he says. "I think she's calling you."

I sigh and go over to him. I collect our daughter, cradling her head, and begin to bounce her. I focus on keeping my mood light, despite what needs to be said. She calms and coos. "Margaret," I say. "Would you go and get her some more warm blood…?" Maggie nods and hurries out. "Pig…not sheep. She prefers pig."

I return to Nathan. "Angela made herself a promise, Nathan." I bob Anara up and down. "When Quinton passed…she…" I laugh humorlessly. "…she doesn't even have my empathic abilities, but she knew exactly how you felt. She was worried that you felt that the last person…who really and truly 'had your back'…who would crawl through the mud and muck right alongside you…was gone." He looks away as tears fill his eyes.

"She felt that Quinton's death created a void in you. She vowed to help you fill that void again." He looks at me. "She promised to be the person that always has your back regardless of the pain that it caused her…and I know you know how conflicted she felt around you." He nods. "She truly loved you, my Nathan. The only two people who could have loved you more…dare I say it, are right here. Although, I would wager her love was…braver than ours." He frowns. "Because it was not returned…not in the way she hoped for, at least."

He walks over to us. He trembles. "She still loves you…" He looks at me. "…just not in the same way… never again in the same way."

He sighs. "I have to go see her, don't I?"

I nod this time. "Go. She needs you to tell her what's next. She needs you to tell her that…it will be hard…but it will be all right…that the way she feels right now, won't last forever. And you know that because you've been there before." He looks down and draws his lower lip into his mouth. "Make me proud."

"I always try."

"You have yet to fail."

"Princess." He kisses me and then… "Princess." …kisses Anara on the forehead. He peers at Christopher with that roguish smile of his. "Tell my guards…" Christopher frowns. "…catch me if you can." He vanishes, causing Anara's face to become a wrinkly little knot.

"No," I whisper. "No, no, no, no, please do not do that. He will return soon. I promise."

"Okay," Christopher says. "I can help with this one." He leans over her. "Boop," he says and touches her nose. She sniffs. "Boop," he repeats and touches her again. And again, she sniffs. "Boop."

"What are you doing?" I frown. "And why is it working?"

"Honestly, don't know," he replies. "Boop. I just know that it worked for Christian and Rashon when Rachel went back to work."

"Thank you."

He looks at me. "Don't mention it…cousin." I nod and smile.

"Here ya are," Maggie hums, offering me a bottle.

"Thank you." I take it and return to Raven's relocated office couch. Maggie nods. I look around the room. It is odd. Everyone's emotions are…jubilant. Happy. I look down at Anara, who looks up at me. "Are…you doing this?"

"I think she is," Vance says. "I noticed it earlier, but I thought it was just normal baby behavior." He sighs. "I hate to say it, but I'd go as far as to say that we're in her thrall."

"Vance, I…"

"It's alright," Raven says. "When you were a babe…you had entire towns linin' up outside our castle wit' baby gifts…and none of 'em could even tell us why."

"Raven," I gasp, staring at my daughter, staring at me from behind her bottle. "…but did…I ever do…this?" Raven leans in and stares into Anara's eyes… that have a gold border and glow with alternating silver and emerald streaks moving toward her iris.

"No," she says. "You weren't able to use your silver eyes until you were six."

"Do you think something is wrong? I mean, I do not sense anything from her, but…"

"I can examine her," Vance says. "After she's had her bottle and will likely be less fussy. Unless Uncle Christopher wants to stick around and boop her nose more," he adds in a baby-ish voice. Christopher, Maggie, and Raven laugh.

Which reminds me that someone's laughter is missing. I search the room. "Where is Natavius?"

"He took off," Vance says. "Right around the time that you and Nathan started talking about Angela."

"Oh no."

Raven looks at me. "What?"

"He probably went to see Angela…and I sent Nathan to see Angela."

She sighs. "I'll go check on them." She rushes off in a blur.

"What's going on?" Christopher asks.

"I suppose you are the last to know," I say. "Well, it would seem that your pack…has a preference…at least, at a rate of 3 out of 4…"

"Natavius is scent-bonded to Angela," Vance says.

"Oh, that…" Christopher shakes his head. "…I realized he was heading that way back at Nathan's apartment after Paris." I frown. "Natavius couldn't take his eyes off her."

"Why would ya be worried about 'em fightin', Auntie Lana?" Maggie asks.

I sigh and shake my head… because I do not want them to know that the same thing that I feel from Angela now is the same thing that I felt from Nathan every time anyone brought up Rosalind before her untimely return.

He had one constant passion moving along the back of his mind…and Angela now shares that passion…

#####

Chapter 40: Run

I'm not hungry…I haven't fed in days, but I'm still not. I'm a vampire repulsed by the sight of blood. Every time I think about feeding, I see Bal's face or what was left of it, after I murdered him.

"So," Natavius says. "Your mom thought you might like some deer." He extends the thermos. "It's a little different but…" I shudder and turn away. "Okay, so not hungry."

He puts the thermos down on my dresser. He swallows a lump and sits on the bed with me. I sigh. "Ange, look…I know how you feel…" I glare at him. "…I've lost people I care about, too." Yes, but you've never shot any of them…repeatedly…for…I tremble…and sniff… "Awwww, don't do that." Tears roll down my cheeks. How can I help it? I killed Bal, who I was falling in love with because he…and that witch…stole it from me… It caused me nothing but misery…a constant headache and a nauseating, twisting feeling in my gut…but it was mine… More tears fall. …even if he wasn't.

"Ange," Natavius says taking my hands. I snatch them out of his and move away from him. I pick up Mr. Beasley and squeeze him against my chest. "So, you, Kyra, and Tiff together again, huh?" I look at him. "I was the…constantly absent older brother when you and Tiff used to come visit." I look away. I never thought about that. Kyra and her brother…Tybalt of all names…Natavius adopted and raised them after their birth parents died. He treated them like siblings, not his kids. She used to tell me all the time how grateful she was for her older brother.

"Have you met her son, yet?" I shake my head. "I'll get her to bring him around sometime…and her very stupid human boyfriend." I frown. "He…had a lot of trouble accepting all of this. Tybalt still doesn't trust him, but he's not threatening to kill him anymore so that's progress."

I sigh. Tybalt's a year older than Kyra…back when we were in high school, he used to be the typical jock, bully guy. He used to have the biggest crush on me…the feeling was not mutual. I liked brave, selfless types…not arrogant asses. Okay, so a little cockiness, but still.

"Nice bear," Nate says from my bedroom door. I gasp and that tremble moves up my spine…and then the pain in my chest…and…I can't breathe. I start to… "Hey, hey, hey…" He says from right in front of me. Natavius climbs off the bed in a bit of a huff. "…it's okay." I shake my head. "It will be…I promise." I stare into his eyes. He pulls at my heart still…but it's not the same. I love him…but he's just not the same…not to me.

"I know that right now, you feel like someone…" He makes a claw of his hand and then clenches it into a fist. "…just punched a hole right into the center of your being and ripped out everything that you had inside…." I nod.

"…and that hole, just feels…" He clenches his teeth…and pants. He does know…he knows how I feel.

"…like a black hole?" I sigh. Natavius gasps.

"Did she just talk?" Raven asks from the door. I guess Natavius nods, because I don't hear a response, I can't take my eyes away from Nate.

"Yes. Like a black hole…and it just sucks in everything else in your life…your good feelings, your bad ones…your hunger, your pain…your joy…even light…" More tears pour from my eyes, because that's exactly how I've felt over the last few days. "…it takes away…everything, until even the light at the end of the tunnel, seems to go away.

"It's there though," he says. "I promise you, it…is there." His eyes flash green and gold. "What do you want to do?" I shake my head. He grabs my hands and holds them in front of his heart. "Ange, be honest with me…be honest with yourself. What…do you want to do?"

"I wanna run." I shake my head and more stupid, stinging tears come out. "I don't know why or where I wanna run to, but I just…I feel like I have to go."

He nods. "Then go."

"WHAT?" Natavius and Raven snap at the same time.

Nate kisses my hands and nods. "Then go…because you need to…" I nod and stand up. Nate moves with me. "We'll all be here, when you come back."

"No," Raven says, shoving Nate out of the way. She wraps her arms around me. "Please don't go…I just got ya…I don't…"

"You're being selfish," Nate says.

"So, what if I am…" She steps back and caresses my face. "She's muh daughter, and I love her."

"Then let her go."

"Let me go," I whisper. "Please…" I try to swallow down more tears. "…because being here…seeing you…seeing ALL of you…" My eyes dart to Nate and back. "…it just hurts too much." I step back, and her hands fall away. "I'm going…I have to." I step around her, and she's already at the door.

"NO! I refuse!"

Nate wraps his arms around her and pulls her from the door. "GO! NOW!" he barks. I hurry out the door and down the hall.

Mom…bio-mom…meets me in the living room. "Here," she says, offering me a bag. "I have about three outfits in here, fresh from the dryer…there's a thermos of blood, because I know you're starving, even if you don't…and your knife's in there too, so be careful going through metal detectors. Oh, and there's also money for cabs and bus fares and stuff."

"You heard…?"

"Jamie Baggett taught me a spell that amplifies sounds." She nods, kisses me on the cheek and gives me a hug. "Now, go...Nate can't hold sire-mom forever."

I nod and rush to the door. "Bye, mom...I love you...and I'll call you."

"I know. Go." I open the door and move downstairs in a blur. I hit the security door and...

...Natavius is standing on the sidewalk. "Don't go. Please."

"I have to...even looking at you...hurts."

"Why?"

"He was your brother...and I killed him in cold blood."

"He knew what he was getting into..." I shake my head. "...don't worry about that," he says as I walk down the stairs. "Ange..." He swallows a lump. "...if for no other reason, stay for me. I need you!"

"You need me?"

He nods. "I'm scent-bonded to you...and even before that...I felt it..." He shakes his head. "...the first time I looked at you...REALLY looked at you...I felt something..." He taps his chest. "...and ever since this stupid thing's been whispering it back to me. Now, it's shouting at me. It's saying, 'You love her, you big idiot! Don't let her leave!'"

"Natavius, I have to...I'm sorry."

He wraps his arms around me. He feels warm and safe and...a little like the light at the end of the tunnel...but the black hole sweeps it away again. "Ange," he whispers and kisses me. A little peck, at first, then his lips move around my lower lip and then it's deeper. His hand moves up into my hair and his other down to the small of my back. I drop my bag and fall into the kiss... He's such a good kisser...but... I push him away. "Ange?"

"I can't...I can't use you to get out of my own feelings...I can't...and I won't. It's not fair."

"Let me decide what's fair for me, Ange." I grab my bag. "No."

"Let go," I say as his hand catches mine. He does. "I can't do that to you." He stares at me. I put my hand on his cheek and kiss him. We part, and my thumb strokes his lower lip...his gorgeous lower lip. "Bye, fake-boyfriend..." I turn and run...at a normal human pace at first. I look back and Natavius hasn't moved. He still stares at the stoop leading up to mom's apartment. The air feels electric around me...and I hear Nate's voice in my head. "Run."

I pull the bag onto my back with both straps. "Run." I move one foot forward. "RUN!" ...and I book it...I run toward the setting sun, and I don't stop...I keep running...where will I go? What will I do? Will I ever come back? I don't know...I just know...that for right now...

"I just wanna run," I say aloud as Brooklyn becomes a memory behind me.

#####

Epilogue

Bethany Triste sits alone at a marble-top table. Tears pour from her sapphire-colored eyes as she glares at her clenched fists on top. Her long ebony hair hangs down in sleek, straight strands, framing her face. She sniffles before releasing a stuttering sigh.

Daphne Baggett walks up to the chair opposite her. She leans on the backrest, causing her ebony, wavy strands to dangle over her shoulders. She stares at her would be sister-in-arms with sorrow. "I'm sorry for your loss," she says with sincerity.

"I didn't lose him," Bethany snarls. She lifts furious eyes to Daphne. "That blond bitch stole him from me."

"Stole him from us all," Anaras says, moving up to the table. He takes the chair to Daphne's left.

Daphne falls into her chair. "I thought you'd be more broken up about this. I mean, he was your 'brother' for what? Almost three thousand years?"

"Balthazar will continue to be my brother for the rest of eternity."

Bethany sits up. "And you're sure you don't sense her anymore?" Daphne sighs and crosses her arms. "Are you sure? Or are you just protecting your friend's daughter like you protect your own?"

"I would crush you like the bug you are, but I have a rule about not attacking people who've had their hearts broken." Bethany glares at Daphne. "If you want, you can perform the tracking spell yourself...I mean her emotion, her love...if that is what you extracted...is definitely a good catalyst for the spell."

"I trust you," a young voice says. A young Chinese boy steps up to the table, wearing black sunglasses. His youthful appearance betrays his nearly 800 years of life. He tosses his long braid back behind his head and folds his arms behind his back. He sits in a chair to Bethany's right. "You have my deepest condolences."

"It's as if the entirety of the supernatural world has learned of us and turned against us all at once," a singsong voice chimes. A tiny green light appears over the chair to Bethany's left.

"You can reveal yourself," Anaras says. "You're among friends here."

"I don't think so," the fairy replies. "Something's going on here. We have a being with perfect future sight on our side and somehow we've still come up short over and over again."

"How do you mean?" Daphne asks. "We lost the crystal, but we got it back."

"Yes," the fairy snarls. "But your daughter should've never been given the opportunity to take it. Moreover, it took four of you to go down to our master's resting place to retrieve it. Maybe Balthazar was right, and we should've taken the younger McCabe witch."

"BAGGETT WITCH!" Daphne roars, rising from her chair. "And if any of you goes after my daughter…"

"No one is threatening your daughter, Daphne," Anaras says. "Please sit down." Daphne falls back into her chair. He takes a deep breath. "I hate to agree with you, but you have a point. For centuries, Ezekiel's visions have allowed us to shape the world to our ends while remaining in the shadows… but lately…not only does the supernatural world seem to know of our existence, but they've also been actively trying-"

"-and succeeding," the fairy interjects.

"…yes, and succeeding at thwarting us."

"Brother," a voice calls that rings with almost as much authority as Anaras's says. An old man with gray hair and sagging, weathered pale skin steps into the light wearing a simple tweed suit. He removes his fedora and holds it in his two wrinkled hands, before tossing it on the table. He lifts eyes of white on white to Anaras. "Have you begun to doubt my visions?"

"Is there reason to doubt?" Anaras returns. "You foresaw that Natiel would return to us once he regained his memories…and it never came to pass. You foresaw that I would kill the half-breed dog and my granddaughter and claim their offspring. That too failed. You foresaw that killing the 5th Alpha would break the wolves' spirit and remove them as a threat to our plans. If anything, they've grown bolder in his absence and formed an alliance with the vampires as well as the rogue half of your hunters."

"You foresaw," Bethany sobs. "…that Balthazar would claim the love of that bloodsucking whore and kill her…but that was a lie."

Anaras looks on her with tender eyes. "Indeed," he agrees.

"You all seem to be missing a common factor here," the youthful Chinese vampire says. "This girl…this blond vampire…Raven's sire…she is the common factor in all of these instances. She managed to kill Balthazar when she was supposed to be immobilized after the extraction of her emotion. By her own admission, she pulled the wolf hybrid out of the river. Your wolf…Natiel's affections for her were probably the determining factor in his allegiance since he was willing to challenge Balthazar for her. Her…companionship with the wolf-hybrid is what renewed his spirits and allowed him to lead the wolves…she even guided him through the tower in time to find his mate, thus allowing them to rescue their child."

"Come on," Daphne says. "Look, I'm not one to down vampires…aside from the whole parasitic nature of your lives…but any vampire…even one from a bloodline as strong as Maria's is…"

"She can use magic," Bethany growls. "You know that…you've seen it."

"As have I," Anaras says. He sighs. "It's as if she has been purposefully placed close to Alana and Nathan...but it can't be the work of this one little vampire."

"It must be," Ezekiel says. He rubs the scruff of his chin. "She's something of blind spot for me. I never saw her undergo the ritual...Duchess recommending her was a surprise to me...I never even saw her turn into a vampire..." He bows his head and removes his gold-wire framed sunglasses. "...do you think she's immune to all of our abilities?"

"How do you mean?" Daphne asks.

"It's possible," Anaras returns. "It would be maddening if it were true, but it would explain several things."

"How so?" the vampire asks.

"Think about it," Anaras states. "She was able to match Bethany magic for magic... she could sense Balthazar even behind his glamour...she's been a constant blind spot in Ezekiel's visions...and she's immune to my eyes."

"Impossible," Bethany snarls. "That whore can't get everything she wants."

"Clearly, she's not getting everything she wants," Daphne says. "The aim was to make her fall in love with Balthazar and steal that love away from her, but...that didn't work. So, her affection for whom did we steal?"

"Probably, the wolf hybrid," the vampire says. "From what my spies told me, she caused a bit of a rift between the Midnight Princess and him."

"Speaking of which," Daphne says. "Xiao, how's your relationship with the Chief Magistrate? Is she still suspicious of you?"

"Unfortunately," Xiao groans. "Thanks to Quinn Mosi'son's flippant mouth and the actions of that rogue vampire hunter in Japan...she's frozen me out of most talks. She only confers with Michael, Florencia, and the B'ashas now. She's already made her choice for the new magistrate, but she hasn't even given me that information." He shakes his head. "In short, overing 'our' tracks in Japan seems to have blown my cover." He glares at the fairy.

"I had to keep the kitsune siblings and that elf off you," the fairy chimes. "If I hadn't...not only would you be exposed, but we would've lost our chance to get the artifact, and you might be dead."

"And where is the artifact?" Xiao poses. "That's right...the kitsune still have it!" The fairy floats around feverishly before darting toward Xiao.

"ENOUGH!" Anaras bellows with his right hand raised, palm facing out. He sighs and half turns to Ezekiel. "How do we proceed, brother?"

"So, you still put your faith in me, brother?"

"In absence of our other brothers...it has no other home."

"Ah," Ezekiel hums. He replaces his glasses and leans forward. "Things will only get worse from here…" He looks to Daphne. "Now that your daughter has chosen one of the fae-daemon brothers…she'll be more focused than ever on stopping you. Moreover, with her father and her half-sister at her side, she'll be more of a threat than ever, especially considering that her father plans to give her the only existing translation of Medea's grimoire."

Daphne crosses her arms and looks down. "He's going to break her binding rings, isn't he?"

Ezekiel nods. He turns his focus to the fairy. "Your mother has chosen…you know that…whether you actually know it or not. Twelana the 107th will be named her heir."

The fairy flies back and forth, seeming to pace in air.

"What you may not know is that even by naming her successor aloud, she has already begun the process of transferring power. Twelana's abilities will magnify instantly. She will not be the easy target you hoped her to be."

His head turns to Xiao. "Raven's choice for her latest magistrate will stir things up…some, including you, will attempt to turn against the rule of the magistrates." He shakes his head. "It's a fool's errand…and thus, I advise you to let the fool play his part. He will distract from your activities, if only a little."

Xiao places his hand under his chin and ponders Ezekiel's words.

He looks at Bethany. "Your enemies…how curious that they're cousins…" She clenches her teeth. "…they will only grow stronger."

"WHAT?" Bethany gasps.

"The vampire-witch will train her body to a near perfect killing machine…focusing the entirety of her existence to that end. She will only be lacking in magic training, which she will seek out as well." Bethany's clenched fists clutch together. "The elf-witch…being a direct descend of Evangeline of Light and Medea will study magic with the Baggett Witch. She'll become a tempest to be reckoned with as well. Furthermore…"

"There's more?" Bethany whines.

"The strange aura'd kitsunes…having liberated themselves from the oppressive ways of their clan…will attempt to become all that race of fae could be…and they will attain it."

"My enemies only grow in strength," Bethany snarls. "That's fine…my vengeance grows deeper with each step they take forward…" She smiles the smile of a schemer with evil machinations burning behind her sapphire eyes. "…I will crush them all…in Eden's name."

"Indeed," Ezekiel says as an afterthought. He looks across the table at Anaras. "The Chief Magistrate will use her relationship with a witch to gain access to knowledge of spirit magic." Anaras frowns. "Though it is a natural talent for Aldiens, Alana's vampire bloodline makes her the perfect weapon to wield it to a degree that could rival you, brother, with training." Anaras drives his fist through the table. "Moreover, her mate...if she masters spirit magic...she will aid him in focusing his rage."

"What?" Daphne says. "If that's true, he would be..."

"Unstoppable. Indeed."

"How do we proceed with this information, Anaras?" Xiao asks.

"As we always have. Cautiously." Anaras stands upright and pulls his fist from the marble table. "We defeat our enemies through any means available and continue upon our glorious path. Eden will be revived...Eden must be revived...the world needs our master..." He sighs with a nod. "...and we will act accordingly. Understood?"

"Aye," Ezekiel says with nods from the remainder of En Quosque.

"Dismissed."

#####

THE CLAIMED SAGA